The Sweet Trade

The Sweet Trade

a Peg-Leg Production

Printed in the United States of America

Disclaimer

This is a work of fiction, a product of the author's imagination. A few of the characters, locales, and events portrayed in this novel were taken from actual history, yet were used fictitiously. Any resemblance or similarity to any actual events or persons, living or dead, after the 17th Century, is purely coincidental. Although the author has made every effort to ensure there are no errors, inaccuracies, omissions, or inconsistencies herein, any slights to people, places, or organizations are unintentional.

Credits

Cover photos courtesy Can Stock Photo

Editing and cover design by Harvey Stanbrough
harveystanbrough.com

Formatting by Debora Lewis
arenapublishing.org

ISBN-13: 978-1517644529
ISBN-10: 1517644526

The Sweet Trade

Debrah Strait

This book is for Aline Thompson,

without whom it would not exist.

Contents

Isle of Bentyn, Caribbean Sea, 1653

Dirk van Cortlandt heard another great boom, like thunder. He climbed faster up the hill from the cove. The grey, pre-dawn sky was clear and no wind had rustled the fronds on palm trees lining the beach. He was only eleven, but he knew the scent of rain in the air and there wasn't any. Something was wrong.

He topped the volcanic ridge that divided the island and stopped, panting, to scan the shoreline below. Two ships crowded the entrance to the tiny harbor. Dirk's stomach grew queasy. Trading vessels didn't announce their arrivals with cannon blasts. He rubbed his belly. His fingers found the newest rip in his cotton tunic and picked at it.

Behind him, the four other boys scrambled up the trail, crackling through brush and knocking stones loose. And still bickering about bones they'd found amongst broken sea shells and coconut husks in a midden heap at the cove.

The twins' voices, shrill and insistent, drifted up to him. "Were too people bones! Cannibals...."

Then Mic, oldest of the group at twelve, who always knew the most, said, "Pig knuckles, you dunderheads."

Dirk pushed a thick lock of wavy brown hair out of his eyes and stared at the ships below. He couldn't see any men aboard, but sails were being furled. Then the ships' cannon puffed smoke. A moment later he heard the shots and the waterfront warehouse exploded, lighting the sky. Mud bricks, shattered timbers, and chunks of red dyewood flew into the air amidst billowing smoke. The Dutch West India Company had stored powder and shot alongside their market goods, and now a series of explosions tore the building apart.

Little Baldric crested the hill and ran to Dirk's side. Then the other three arrived.

"Oh, look!" Jan said, dimples pitting his fat cheeks. He jabbed an elbow at his twin brother. "The pirates came back."

Joost returned the jab and added a light kick. "Papa said they landed at the cove to take on water, but they must've been spying, too, 'cause here they are." His grin showed white teeth still big for his ten year old face.

Dirk breathed faster now. "Pirates don't blow up things they came to steal."

Both ships in the harbor fired their cannon at once. A blade on the settlement's windmill broke away, along with a chunk of the tower. The west corner of the Company's office and that of the director's residence above collapsed. The stink of burnt powder wafted up the hill. Dirk's nostrils contracted. Baldric's black eyes widened. He edged closer to Dirk. The little one's body heat and fear were palpable.

Mic hunched narrow shoulders inside a worn shirt with sleeves that dangled below his fingers. He pushed the sleeves up his arms. "We're still at war with the English." His statement held a question; smoke hid the ships' flags.

"Spanish." Dirk's voice rose. "Might be the Spanish."

A boat edged around the stern of the closer ship, headed for shore.

"They're landing!" Dirk whirled toward the sunrise, shoving the twins ahead of him. "Run home!"

Jan ducked aside and gazed at the flaming settlement and smoke-filled harbor. Mic and Baldric ran past. Dirk raced after them, looking back for the twins. He saw Joost tug at Jan's arm, and finally they both ran, jostling each other in their hurry to catch up.

Dirk pounded along the rough surface of the ridge top, frantic that some of the raiders might already have landed somewhere. Bentyn's Isle had no treasure, just stands of dyewood being felled and shipped east to Curaçao. And now even the tree stumps were disappearing into salt pans and cornfields.

No, there was nothing worth stealing on Bentyn's Isle, but it was an island to conquer and cleanse of those who dared try to live here, who dared raise food to support the Dutch empire, or sell it to pirates who raided the Spanish Main.

Up ahead, Baldric left the trail. Dirk cut away to follow him. Baldric's house stood closest to the harbor and his parents could sound an alarm across the island. If his father had already risen and found Baldric gone, however, the man would probably give him a strapping first and listen later. He might listen to Dirk right away, though.

The nine year old was hard to see in the murky light with his black hair, sun-darkened face, stained tunic and dark linen knee-breeches. But Dirk knew the way among stumps of dyewood trees. He leapt over some and swerved around others smoldering with an internal fire that would clear the land for crops.

He caught up with Baldric as the younger boy slipped into the cornfield behind his home. Then, as they neared the house, Baldric fell. Dirk reached down for him. Baldric ignored the proffered hand and stared between cornstalks. His black eyes were enormous. His mouth hung open. Dirk parted the green leaves blocking his view of the house.

The two-room, raised cabin was a smoking mass of charred timber, as were the tool shed, slave shack, and corn crib. Baldric's parents, little sister, and the baby brother just learning to walk were sprawled, broken and still, in a heap by the coastal road. Slaughtered animals and slaves lay scattered in bloody lumps about the garden and barnyard. Dirk's chest tightened.

Baldric crawled toward the road. "Mama!"

Dirk tugged him deeper into the field. "Maybe they're still here. Can't let'm get us, too."

With one arm up to hold off the corn leaves, he dragged Baldric back to the ridge. Then Dirk fled east, a sobbing Baldric on his heels.

Where the ridge narrowed and the trail dipped off the top, the twins came stumbling out of the brush.

"Our house!" Jan cried. "We ran... Everybody's dead!" Blond curls, come loose from a leather tie and wet with tears, stuck to his face. He gasped for breath, then gagged on hair as he wept.

Dirk grabbed Joost's arm and shook him. "The raiders—English or Spanish? Did you see?"

"I saw Grandmother burning on the stoop!" Joost wailed. "She's got no hair and her arm's black and her nightshift was on fire! She just looked at us..."

Dirk pushed the twins onto the trail and ran. "Follow me!"

His father's plantation was the farthest from the Company's office. Maybe the raiders hadn't reached it yet.

The trail rose again to the ridge top. Mic stood there, white-faced and stiff against a pale dawn, staring down the hill at his home. He worked his jaw from side to side, clicking his teeth. Dirk swallowed hard and turned to look.

Thick black smoke rolled out of Mic's house. Flames spread into the field his father had planted with sugar cane, a new crop from Brazil. Over a salt breeze full of smoke came the squeal of hogs as their pen burned around them. Dirk thought of Mic's beautiful sister, sixteen and engaged to a planter from Aruba. And the older brother, just returned from schooling in Holland.

"To my house!" Dirk cried, and led the way, his breath coming in short spurts. If they didn't reach his home in time to give warning, he would be an orphan, too. The raiders would kill or enslave everyone on the island. The Spanish had done that on Hispaniola and St. Martin, and the English were just as cruel. Even now his home might be aflame, his family dead, he and his friends the only Dutch left on Bentyn's Isle.

At the back of the van Cortlandt plantation, Dirk scrambled down a faint path and plunged into a cornfield, the other boys right behind. Leaves crackled and cut at Dirk's arms and face. The smoke of burning timbers and the sound of foreign voices wafted up to him. *Words like music,* he thought. *Spanish.*

He stumbled to a halt just before breaking out of the field. The others huddled around him.

Screams, shouts, musket shots, and the clang of swords rent the air. Three musket-toting Spaniards herded Cook and the two field hands to the road. Abram, who tended the animals, ran toward the sea, but managed only a few yards before a soldier shot him.

Silver-crested helmets flashed in the yellow-orange light of flames from the slaves' shanty. Men set the small barn afire. Inside, the only horse on the island shrieked. A bearded soldier, scabbard bouncing against his ankle, chased a squealing piglet across the kitchen garden.

Dirk lunged toward the house where his father was fighting on the rear stoop, but Mic dragged him back among the cornstalks. The younger boys crowded close, quivering. Dirk shook, too, as the all-powerful master of his world fought the raiders. But the big

Dutchman was a farmer battling soldiers, and while he held off one, three crashed into the two-story house.

His mother's voice rose in a scream that ended abruptly. Dirk forgot to breathe. When his father collapsed under slashing steel, Dirk grabbed at cornstalks to stay upright.

His sister Anneke slipped out the front door and ran screaming across the long porch. Her pale yellow nightshift billowed as she jumped off the end, plump little legs buckling at the two-foot drop. Hopping up, she raced straight toward the cornfield, as if she knew her big brother awaited her there.

A musket fired. Anneke's narrow chest thrust forward and her head snapped back. She stumbled, then rolled almost to the edge of the field. Blood soaked the top of her gown.

Dirk blinked at her. "But you're only five and too little."

Men ran out of the house just ahead of smoke and threw torches into the cornfield. Dirk stared at Anneke's body, the ruins of his home. It was all gone. And there was nothing he could do.

"We have to leave!" Mic said, his voice high and tight. He shook Dirk's arm hard enough to pull him off balance.

Finally Dirk remembered to breathe. He choked on tears and smoke.

"To the ridge," he said, coughing, then fled from it all.

Mic, long-legged and fine-boned, raced ahead through the corn rows. The twins crashed along beside him. Baldric—

Dirk tripped, caught himself, then bent over to gasp and hold his side. He peered back through the smoking cornfield. He couldn't go back there. He had to.

Tears burned his eyes and cheeks as he ran toward smoke and the roar of burning corn. The stench of burning flesh nearly overpowered the smell of charred wood. He wanted to vomit and each breath he gulped smelled as if he just had.

He found Baldric still gaping at the flames. Dirk grabbed his arm and yanked him almost off his feet.

"Come on, dammit!"

Baldric ran a few yards, then fell. Whirling to retrieve him, Dirk swung into the edge of a corn leaf. It sliced his forehead, down across his left eye and into the middle of his cheek. With a howl, he jerked Baldric up and clouted him on the head. "Let's go!"

Crying, Baldric ran on his own.

Minutes later, Dirk pounded up the side of the ridge, stumbling the last few feet to where Mic and the twins waited. Baldric collapsed to the ground, his silent tears puddling in the dust. The twins clawed at each other's sleeves and wailed. Mic's shoulders rose and fell with great, ragged breaths. Dirk looked around. Huge plumes of smoke rose from his home. Away to the southwest, smoke filled the air, and the faint boom of cannon fire resounded over the island.

Jan's voice cracked into a sob. "What do we do now?"

Dirk turned to find his friends looking at him. Baldric stared up through tears. Mic's teeth were clamped tight on his lips. The twins sniffed and licked snot off their upper lips. *Do they expect me to know what to do? I'm only a boy, too. I just want to climb onto Mama's lap and cry.* Tears burned inside his nose and throat.

Finally Dirk wiped at the sticky blood on his face and swallowed hard. "Maybe that canoe we found tonight will float. We can go to Curaçao."

Mic nodded. "It's not so far. And I found a paddle in the mud. There might be more."

"Let's go." Dirk spun on a heel and ran west, the panting sobs and thumping feet of the others right behind. He ran away from the loss of almost everything he knew, toward the devastation in the harbor. Surely now the Company's office and the half-dozen workers' houses were destroyed. Everyone he knew there must be dead, too.

He glanced toward the harbor once more. Sunlight gleamed on helmets and weapons moving through heavy vegetation toward the ridge.

"They're coming up the hill," Dirk said. "Run faster!"

He raced on, lungs burning as he gasped for air. Finally, there was the path down to the little cove where just hours before they'd been digging for pirates' treasure. He tumbled down the hill, the others noisy behind him. He sped past the old midden heaps, splashed across a shallow creek, and tore brush off a dugout canoe.

Mic scrabbled in the muck, pulling out paddles, most rotted or split, but half a dozen useable.

Remnants of a short mast wobbled and caught on bushes as the boys wrestled the dugout into the creek. The canoe had been burned out unevenly and the bottom not sanded at all, but it floated. Mic knelt straight-backed in the bow. The younger boys scrambled in behind the mast, and Dirk pushed the canoe into deeper water before he crawled aboard. They paddled thirty feet to the sea, helped by a slow current.

The murky, blue-green creek nudged them into the surf, then onto a clear blue sea with the morning's out-going tide. Dirk heard shouts in Spanish, looked back to the shore. Metal flashed among the palm trees. "Paddle faster!" he cried.

They did. Dirk stabbed his paddle into the water, over and over, faster and faster, and thought he heard a musket firing. The Spaniards in Bentyn's harbor couldn't weigh anchor and sail a ship after them any time soon, but they might have a masted launch or a swift pinnace that could easily catch five boys in a canoe.

The Dutch island of Curaçao lay east, a day's sail in a ship. He didn't know whether they could paddle that far, and he'd have to trust Mic to set their direction. To the south, Spanish Venezuela lay much closer, but they dared not land there. Dirk pushed the lump in his throat down to his chest where it grew and cut off his breath.

Was it only last night they had sneaked out of their beds and run to the cove to hunt pirates' treasure? They'd been certain pirates had anchored a ship there the week before to bury their plunder, and the boys were going to find it.

That was so few hours ago, and now he was at sea with no home but this lumpy canoe, and with no family but these four friends. The twins bickered constantly and often were the dunderheads Mic called them. They, in turn, called Baldric "chicken liver" and "bangbroek," and that was true, too. Baldric was a scaredy-pants. It made him good at sneaking around, a skill Dirk had found useful when his gang played pranks. Now, though, Baldric's fears made him an extra burden. Mic was sensible and smart, but not even all his book learning could save them if they didn't reach Curaçao soon.

By mid-morning Dirk's arms were tired. The air was hot. There'd been no sign of Spanish ships in pursuit, but there was nothing else on the horizon, either.

The heat worsened by afternoon, despite a freshening breeze. The sea rose, splashing water into the canoe. The boys took turns bailing with their shoes. The slash on Dirk's face dried, and the skin grew taut, pulling the wound's fragile edges farther apart. He patted water on it, despite the salt sting, and used the fat end of a paddle to keep the sun off.

In late afternoon, Jan said he was hungry.

"We don't have any food," Dirk said. "Nothing to drink either."

"Where's Curaçao?" Joost asked. "I'm thirsty."

Dirk's face felt hot and swollen. "It isn't so far anymore. We'll be there tomorrow."

"I think so, too." Baldric curled into Dirk's shadow. "Tomorrow or the day after we'll have lots to eat."

Mic looked over his shoulder with cold, blue eyes.

Dirk shrugged.

Mic resumed paddling, his back rigid.

Sunset brought relief from the heat, and the three younger boys lay tumbled together, whimpering in their sleep. Cool air on his sunburn made Dirk shiver as he stroked, determined to keep the canoe moving.

At moonrise, Mic stopped paddling and turned sideways in the bow. His head drooped, and his dark hair fell over his face.

"I can follow the stars east, Dirk, but I don't know where we are anymore." Mic took a deep breath, pushed his shirt sleeves back up his arms. "My brother told me about a sea current that flows northwest, then east. If we drift too far west, we might land in New Spain. If that current carries us far enough, we might land on Cuba or Jamaica."

Dirk's stomach felt heavy, as if he were swallowing stones. He'd always counted on Mic to know facts and details. A year older and much better schooled, Mic seemed to remember everything. But Dirk didn't want to know all the dangers they faced.

"Those big islands are Spanish held," he said. "We have to head east. If we miss Curaçao... Well, Bonaire and Aruba are Dutch, too."

"And if we miss them all?"

"We'll have to go farther east to the lesser isles."

"Some of those are Spanish," Mic said. "Or Caribe cannibals live on them."

Dirk saw no help in the black starry sky, the nearly full moon, nor on the endless swells.

"We can't go any other direction."

"I know." Mic spoke in a soft, quavering voice. "We must go east, and pray we don't miss the islands and paddle out into the Atlantic Ocean."

Before long, Mic, too, fell asleep, slumped against the stubby mast. Dirk paddled on, not knowing where he was, or even who he was anymore. He wasn't a farmer's heir, nor a dependent of the Dutch West India Company. He'd never again be a son, or a brother. He could never be an uncle, for Anneke would not grow up to bear children. She'd never be any older than she was last night, waiting for him on the front porch when he crept out of the house....

Her whisper had sounded as loud as the dinner bell. "Where you going?"

"To the necessary house."

"Liar. It's out back and you're all dressed. You're going out to play with the other boys in the dark."

His own whisper grew hoarse and loud. "No, I'm not. Go back to bed."

"I'm coming too."

"Oh, no, you're not. You're only five. You're too little."

She stamped her foot. Brown curls, a shade lighter than Dirk's own, tumbled out of her nightcap.

"You let me come or I'll go wake Papa."

Dirk smacked her cheek and she gasped. He clapped a hand over her mouth.

"I'll do worse if you say a word to Papa. Promise not to wake him?"

Anneke, brown eyes wide and tearful, nodded. When Dirk released her, she opened her mouth as if to say something, but he raised a fist and she scampered inside the house. She must have gone straight to bed, for he'd seen no lamplight appear in the windows as he escaped across fields and pastures....

She'd gone back to her cot and now she was dead. If only he had let her come along to the cove.

The moon rose higher and lit the wave crests. The sea grew emptier; the canoe seemed to shrink. Once, Dirk thought he saw a ship's lantern but didn't know whether to be glad or afraid. A ship could mean rescue or death. He feared they would all die, and soon. Yet he thrust his paddle into the sea over and over, stroking the canoe a few more feet eastward.

The next morning was hotter. Baldric's face darkened, but the others' skin burned in sunshine reflected off water. Already the twins' faces were bright red under their tangles of golden curls. Mic's face was red, too, and Dirk's felt puffy and stiff. The cut across his eye and cheek hurt. Pus oozed from the broken scab. Worse, his tongue was thickening. He was so thirsty.

He paddled on, slowly.

By afternoon, all but Dirk slumbered under the blazing sun. Then he dropped his paddle, saw it bob off on the waves just before he, too, fell asleep. In dreams he hid in the cornfield, saw his father fall, heard his mother scream, watched Anneke die.

Toward evening, a rippling sea rocked the canoe and sprayed water over the side. Dirk lay cramped and tangled with the other boys in the bottom. He shifted his head out of rising water, blinked salt-swollen eyelids against the constant spray, and then drifted away into his nightmares.

Over and over Anneke ran toward him, hair streaming out behind, face glowing with confidence in the safety of her big brother's arms. He tried to run out to her, to shield her, to take the musket ball himself. Yet she died every time, blood spreading over her chest, just beyond his reach.

Dirk's lumpy bed rocked, but his clothes were dry. Sails snapped and rigging clicked. Deep voices rumbled. He lay under torn canvas draped over three barrels and tied at one corner to a ship's side rail. Water seeped from between swollen barrel slats, cooling the musty air. He blinked, wide awake, remembering a struggle against strange hands lifting him out of the canoe. Mic and Baldric slept on either side of him. The twins were curled together at the back of the tent. Dirk rolled over to look out.

Crusty, bare feet and hairy legs in short breeches passed by in the mid-morning sun. Over a dozen men were wandering about, giving off the tangy odor of salt-dried sweat. Others were sleeping, sprawled on crates or propped against the chests and barrels that lined the narrow deck. Five men were tossing dice and bones, cheering, groaning, and slapping each other's shoulders. They weren't speaking Dutch, but their language didn't sound like Spanish, either.

Dirk looked around for crucifixes or red and gold pennants flying from the masts. He found none, nor was anybody dressed in a black doublet. The men wore colorful, though stained and torn, cotton tunics, brocade surcoats, linen blouses with billowy sleeves, and muslin jerkins without overshirts. Instead of the round, silver-trimmed helms the raiders on Bentyn had worn, these men wore only bright head scarves and a few moldy caps. *Not Spaniards, then.*

He took a deep breath of relief and scooted back under the tent. He poked Mic in the ribs.

"What?" Mic didn't open his eyes.

"Look out there. I think those are pirates."

"French ones."

"Can you understand them?"

"A little."

Dirk rolled onto his back, almost on top of Baldric.

"Move off," Dirk said.

Baldric sniffed. "I just wanted to be close."

"You are close... too close."

Baldric scooted a few inches away. "Are those really pirates? Will they hurt us?"

"They only attack the Spanish."

"Where are we going?"

"I don't know. Go back to sleep and don't lay on top of me anymore."

Baldric obeyed and fell asleep. Then his hand inched out to rest against Dirk's arm.

Dirk rearranged his bed of canvas bits, closed his eyes and smiled. *Adults.* He didn't have to worry about paddling or bailing or where they were headed. *And pirates.* Notorious enemies of Spain, pirates would die to protect their ship from capture. He was safe again. He slept.

In the afternoon heat, Dirk rolled over, opened his eyes and saw Mic. Then remembered where he was: not in his little room under the eaves of his house. His throat tightened. He was on a ship of strangers, at sea. *Where are we going?* Baldric's question echoed in his mind and he had no answer.

Someone shoved a little cup of brandy and a platter of boucan-cured beef just inside the makeshift tent. Dirk roused the others to share it. Sucking on a chunk of the hard, red meat, he stuck his head outside. The other boys crowded around behind and beside him.

A lot of men, maybe thirty-five of them, had encircled the mainmast. There was a hiss, a crack, and a scream. Dirk scrambled outside, the others right behind. They climbed onto crates and barrels to see. A swell rolled under the ship, pitching Jan off his barrel. He climbed onto a bigger one with Joost. Dirk grabbed the edge of his crate.

A man had been stripped to the waist and tied to the mast for a flogging. He twisted against the ropes with the next blow and threw his head back to scream.

A huge pirate with meaty arms and shoulders called out, "Three!"

Dirk stared, caught his breath. Once, when he was seven years old, he'd taken a whip to a slave lad. His father had snatched the whip away and laid two stripes across Dirk's back, ripping his shirt. Remembering the fierce burn of welts that remained tender for days, Dirk winced with each hiss and closed his eyes for every crack.

"Sixteen!"

"Seventeen!"

"Eighteen!"

Crouched beside Dirk, Baldric choked back sobs. The twins, slack-jawed, knelt shoulder to shoulder, heads inclined toward each other.

The screams became moans. Blood splattered the deck and dripped from the shirt hanging about the man's hips. His pantaloons were red almost to his ankles.

"Twenty-nine!"

"Thirty!"

The moans stopped. The man hung as if dead in his bonds, though he jerked from the force of each blow. Some of the pirates grinned. None showed a trace of sympathy. Dirk shivered.

At stroke fifty, the whipping finally stopped. Pirates scattered about the ship. Someone threw a bucket of seawater over the man, who moaned once and collapsed again. The man who'd done the whipping cleaned the bloody lash on his own shirt and glared at the boys.

Queasy, Dirk climbed off the crate and walked toward their tent among the water barrels. Baldric and the twins scurried ahead, crawled all the way to the back of the tent and sat like wide-eyed dolls against the side of the ship. As far as Dirk knew, the twins had never been punished for anything. Only once had he seen their father go after them with a switch, and they had run to their grandmother. She'd tousled their curls, kissed their dimpled cheeks, and told her son-in-law to practice a bit more Christian forbearance. But she wasn't here to protect them from the pirates.

Mic joined them a few minutes later.

"Did you hear why that man was whipped?" Dirk asked.

"I heard talk about smoking below deck."

"Anything else?"

Mic shook his head. "I can't understand much. But that scary fellow doing the whipping, his name's Lucien and he's some sort of officer."

A loud quarrel broke out near the tent, then moved astern. Mic crawled out and crouched against a barrel. After a few minutes, he sank back into the murky light, clicking his teeth.

"What is it?" Dirk asked.

"That Lucien doesn't like us eating their food 'cause we can't fight. But the other one, the big one with all that black beard and the one eyebrow over his nose—"

"The one that called the strokes?"

Mic nodded. "His name's Alencar. He said we couldn't eat much, and he's the captain."

"That's good."

"But he said if the food or water ran low he'd toss us overboard."

Dirk felt as if he were swallowing rocks again.

For the rest of the day Dirk wouldn't let any of the others go outside of their tent, and not even the twins argued with him. Instead they all watched the pirates through holes in the canvas. At eventide an argument over dice grew into a fistfight, with most of the crew jumping into the fray. The few spectators climbed into the lower reaches of the rigging to avoid more than twenty large bodies hurtling back and forth across the deck.

The fight quickly shrank to just two men who fought with a lot of groin kicking and eye gouging. One got a bloody nose; the other lost a tooth. The pirates laughed, shouted encouragement, and bet on the outcome. No one tried to stop the fight until the combatants fell and crushed a cask of rum. Then Alencar waded through the crowd, grabbed them by the collars and crashed their foreheads together. He left them sprawled on the deck.

That night, Dirk's nightmare about Anneke returned. He woke in the morning with an aching chest and a sick fear that he would never again know how to be safe.

A metal wedge held by the waist tie of his pantaloons poked at Dirk's belly, but he squeezed himself even tighter against the mast anyway. The wood was slick with salt spray and he curled his toes around the horizontal parts of the shrouds. "Ratlines," Mic had called them. Dirk didn't care what they were called as long as they didn't break under him. He climbed higher into the rigging and at last handed off the cleat to a pirate making repairs at the top yard of the foremast. Now he had to feel his way down.

The *Arras Revenge*, named for the town in France where most of the pirates had been born, was just eight of Dirk's strides from side to side and nineteen from bow to stern. But it looked even smaller from aloft. He slid down to the second yard. With his feet secure on the smooth, round wood, he hugged the mast and took several deep breaths. The mast swayed above the water and it felt as if the ship would tip over. The deck was so far away, and not even underneath him anymore. Dirk tightened his grip against sudden dizziness and closed his eyes.

When he opened them again, the sea lay out before him, rolling and rolling in shades of blue and green. He felt as if he were floating. *This must be how the birds feel.* He wanted to fly away home and thought for a moment he could hear his mother's voice in the wind, crooning to baby Anneke as they rolled back and forth in the rocker Dirk's father had built for them. His chest ached with longing and he searched the horizon in all directions for a glimpse of Bentyn's Isle. There was nothing but sea and sky.

"Where are we going?" he whispered to the foremast, and turned a little to look down at the pirates on the deck. *How can people go on doing things when I feel so numb?*

His foot slipped. He swung out into the air, his right foot sliding along the yard before it dropped. With one hand on the shroud, Dirk curled a leg around a line running from the mast until he could grasp the shroud with both hands. Gulping a breath into his too-tight chest, he groped his way down to the deck, a task harder and scarier than climbing had been.

He stumbled to the mainmast, flung an arm around it and for a few minutes watched the other boys mop water over the deck. Baldric looked up at him with red-rimmed eyes.

Jan stopped working and in a surly voice asked, "Why we gotta do this?"

Mic raised his mop as if to strike Jan. Joost stopped working and stalked close to his brother. Dirk hurried over.

"Stop it," he said in a low voice. "Don't fight. Do you want to be whipped? Do you want them to throw us overboard?"

"But why we gotta do this?" Joost asked.

"So the boards won't shrink apart," Mic said.

"I told you," Dirk said. "We have to make the pirates think we're useful. Worth the food they give us." He looked hard at the twins and balled his hands into fists. "Do you want to go hungry?"

The twins sniffed and screwed their mouths back and forth.

"You're a big, fat bully," Joost said.

Baldric shuffled closer to Dirk and sucked in his breath. Dirk looked around, saw Lucien coming their way. With straggly, sand-colored hair and beard flying in the breeze, the man stalked toward the bow. He swung his coiled whip close to the boys as he passed. Baldric sobbed.

"Keep swabbing," Mic said.

All four boys bent to their work. Dirk scurried away from Lucien, toward the stern. There, Alencar was taking a turn at the wheel. Usually the huge man ignored Dirk, but today he might have some chore for him. Anything to appear busy and avoid Lucien's ire.

Alencar did not acknowledge Dirk's presence until he reached back, bumped him, then cuffed him hard. Dirk slammed belly first onto the deck. Winded, he lay for a few minutes, expecting to be beaten at the very least. But Alencar never looked at him, merely reached out a hand thick with black hair for the cup of brandy sitting on a crate behind him. When Dirk regained his breath, he staggered off.

He made his way to Jacques who sat by the rail amid ship mending sails with an awl. The man didn't have many teeth, but his eyes twinkled with humor and Dirk felt safest in his company.

The man winked. "Stood between the man and his brandy, did you, boy?"

"Never again," Dirk vowed in his slow, clumsy French.

Jacques laughed and tossed him a pile of sail scraps. "Sort those. Some won't be good enough to hold a stitch. Can't use them aloft." The man added hand gestures.

Dirk was grateful to have something to do and tried hard to concentrate while Jacques taught him a few more French phrases. Mic's French had improved rapidly, but Dirk had known only a few words when they'd been brought aboard. Learning to speak the language of the pirates made him feel less afraid. Just as protecting the other boys made him feel less sad.

That night after a meager supper of hardened meat and even harder biscuits, the twins clowned and begged to join the endless dice games. The pirates grinned and taught them all how to throw the dice and bones, even giving them coins for bets. They let the boys have turns at a bottle of brandy and the twins' drunken antics became that evening's entertainment.

As the moon rose, Jan vomited and Joost began to snore, still sitting but slumped over. Dirk and Mic dragged them into the tent for the night. Baldric crawled to the very back and was soon whimpering in nightmares. Mic fell into an exhausted sleep. He had spent the day, as he did every day, going from one pirate to another, learning what he could of working sails and charting a course, and generally making himself useful. So Dirk lay awake on his lumpy bed of sails, lonely in the dark, listening to curses and harsh laughter, and wondering how long he and his friends would be safe among these pirates.

During the boys' third week aboard the ship, a black squall hit. It darkened the sky and spun the ship from wave crest to trough and back up again. Men crowded under the two overturned boats lashed to the deck. The boys' tent cover blew overboard; the barrels tipped with each roll. Dirk and Mic pushed Baldric and the twins down into the hold, then dropped in after them.

Dirk hated the hold. It was dark and musty; rats scratched and scurried about. Hammocks swayed from the beams overhead, all full now with smelly pirates. Rum casks and bundles of dried beef strips, plus piles of rope, muskets and carpentry tools filled the spaces between. Crates tipped and slid with the waves hitting the ship. Being in the hold was only a little safer than being on deck during a storm.

Jan poked his brother. "Let's look for treasure."

"There is no treasure," Mic said. He had crawled all through the hold soon after they came aboard, and reported to Dirk there was little below beyond supplies and the boys' canoe. Dirk looked at it now, stashed in the stern with grappling hooks embedded in the wood. *Maybe if they throw us overboard they'll toss the canoe over, too.*

Half an hour later, the sea calmed. Dirk and his friends followed pirates up the ladder into sunshine. The crew, quiet for once, brought the deck back into a haphazard sort of order, then gathered into a loose circle to eat and pass around brandy. The boys wriggled to the circle's inner edge and Dirk caught an onion bottle full of brandy as it passed in front of him. He cradled the bulbous clay vessel in his lap, one hand around the stalk-like neck, until he was sure that none of the men noticed it. Then he took short swallows of the burning stuff and passed it to Mic, who took little sips and made a face. Baldric coughed every time he tried to swallow any, but the twins drank until Dirk took the bottle away.

"A story!" someone shouted.

Others took up the cry. A gnome-like fellow missing one eye and covered with scars cleared his throat.

"Give us back the bottle," Jan said to Dirk.

Mic elbowed him. "Be quiet. Bonar's gonna tell a story."

The twins settled down, but only after Joost jabbed a finger into Jan's thigh and Jan kicked his ankle for it.

"It were a hundred year ago that Pierre Le Grand won his name," Bonar said. "He was the Caribbean's first great pirate, for he captured a Spanish treasure galleon with just twenty-eight men. And from a piragua they did it, a mere cypress dug-out with a single sail."

Dirk forgot the brandy in his lap as Bonar described the galleon's cargo of Philippine gold, bars of Inca silver, bales of East India silk, and fist-sized rubies, emeralds, and yellow topaz. The vast treasure had been amassed in the royal warehouses of Panama on the Pacific coast, carried by slaves to Porto Bello on the Caribbean, then loaded aboard a galleon for transport to Spain.

But the ship never reached Spain, for Pierre and his men closed in on it near Providence Island in the southwestern Caribbean. There, Pierre chopped a hole in the bottom of the piragua, forcing his men to win the galleon or die. They took the ship, threw all the Spaniards overboard, and sailed off to France to live the rest of their lives in luxury. The pirates laughed, hooted and clapped each other's shoulders.

Dirk and Mic looked at each other.

"So much wealth on a single ship," Mic said. "So much for only twenty-nine men to share."

"So easy," Dirk said. "From a piragua with so few men." *What humiliation for the Spaniards! And what revenge such a capture would be for that raid on Bentyn's Isle! Oh, to capture giant ships and sack wealthy cities! Maybe even Panama!* Someday he would be a pirate. He would kill a lot of Spaniards, and make the rest homeless and hungry as they had done to him. *Oh, yes, that's what I will be. A pirate captain.*

Dirk looked at his friends. He already had four men.

"How come we have to stay here? It's hot." Jan stuck out his lower lip.

Joost crawled half out of their rebuilt tent. "I'm hot too."

Dirk hauled him back inside by the ankle. "Jacques said to stay here while the men are drinking."

"They always drink," Jan said.

"But this is important drinking," Mic said. "They're going to raid Trinidad over there." He pointed out the tent opening to an island off the larboard side.

Dirk peeked out. It was late afternoon already and the men didn't look dangerous. But Jacques had said they would get that way.

Dirk didn't want a drunken pirate to hurt any of the boys. They were his only family now and he was determined to keep them safe.

"Jacques is an ugly old clinchpoop," Jan said with a pout.

"A fat-wit," Joost said.

"A... a... poop-noddy," Jan said with great force, and they both giggled.

"Be quiet," Dirk said. "I can't hear what the men are saying. I want to know how they're gonna attack."

But the pirates didn't talk about strategy, just about the treasure they would win and how they'd spend their loot. Alencar urged them to drink more.

"We'll have an easy time of it, lads," he said. "Those papists never fight for the king's treasure." He whipped his cutlass through the air. "Show them some steel, and they'll cower like the dogs they are."

Men raised their swords in a cheer. A few blades clanged together and five men hopped up to fight. The swordplay ranged up and down the deck for a while, and then the men fell to drinking again. Their voices grew louder and sounded angry. They shoved each other and tripped those who stood to piss over the side. The pirates grew so rowdy even the twins stopped complaining about staying in the tent.

At dusk, the men eased the *Arras Revenge* close to the island, anchored, and rowed boats ashore over and over until only a few men remained aboard. When he heard the anchor chain rattling up again, Dirk scrambled out of the tent and raced the other boys to the bow to watch. The last of the raiding party stumbled and cursed and clattered their swords together as they disappeared into a forest. Their noise continued long after the vegetation had swallowed them and grown still.

Baldric edged closer. "The Spaniards... will they kill us?"

Jan laughed. "You dunderhead. Don't you know pirates always win?"

Joost giggled. "What a poop-noddy."

Dirk bounced his fists on the rail as the ship, with half the sails furled, eased around a sand bar and tacked toward a single pier at the end of a small harbor. Ashore, wood shattered, muskets fired, and men roared. If only he could be there, too, killing Spaniards and stealing treasure.

Baldric caught Dirk's sleeve. "Oh, look at that!"

Pirates were stumbling toward the harbor, chased by villagers firing muskets and pistols. A few pirates staggered with heavy canvas bags, but most were empty handed. The ship slammed against the pier. Dirk fell onto the rail, pinching his left thumb. He shook his hand and grabbed the rail again as the ship rolled, then slipped toward the rocky shore.

The pirates clambered aboard, leaping over the space between dock and ship. Bonar, bleeding from a wound, fell into the water and was lost. Other pirates ran along the shore, waded into the water and grabbed the ropes mates threw them.

"Come on!" Dirk yelled. "Faster!"

This was wrong. Pirates weren't cowards who ran from villagers. In all the stories they were superior fighters and vigorous looters. They always won the treasure. These men had sounded so brave before the raid, were so ferocious with the boys and each other. They couldn't be running from Spanish villagers.

The twins hooted and cheered as each pirate came aboard. Baldric coughed on a sob, then stood biting the side of his lower lip. Two pirates on shore dropped the small chests they carried, filled their pockets with silver cobs, then staggered into the surf. They dove under an in-coming wave. Breathing heavily, Dirk leaned over the rail to watch them resurface. They didn't.

Pirates swarmed into the rigging to make sail. The *Arras Revenge* creaked, rolled. Sails caught the wind, the ship heeled to larboard and made way for the open sea.

The crew gathered in the ship's waist and tossed their meager plunder in a pile on the deck. They cursed as they sprawled beside the booty and shouted for rum. The boys brought a dozen bottles up from the hold. Then, with Baldric on his heels, Dirk hustled the twins toward their tent. Mic circled the men, then ran to join Dirk.

"Eight, they say." Mic frowned. "Eight altogether didn't come back."

"Are they dead?" Baldric's voice was soft and quivering.

"I don't know," Dirk said. "But I don't think we'll ever see them again."

That night he fell asleep imagining himself a great pirate captain who punished those Spanish people for what they'd done. He would kill them and steal their gold and never lose so many men.

For several days afterward the pirates shuffled and stomped about the deck or muttered in small groups. Few spoke to Alencar or Lucien. On the fourth day, the men held a general council. There was talk of Captain Alencar's poor tactical leadership. And as quartermaster, Lucien should have chosen better things to steal than heavy and abundant silver. The crew voted the two men out of office.

The mood aboard ship lightened for a week, until the new captain and quartermaster led an unsuccessful raid. Another man died. The next raid also failed and three men were lost. Fights grew frequent and vicious, and the boys spent most of every day hiding from one spot of trouble or another. After a third failed raid, the men voted Alencar and Lucien back into office. Still, the *Arras Revenge* sailed through the Windward Islands without capturing a single ship or town.

With a fair wind, they slipped through the Mona Passage between the islands of San Juan de Puerto Rico and Hispaniola, and sailed to Tortuga, off the northern coast of Hispaniola. From a distance, the smaller island looked like the tortoise it was named after. Up close, Dirk saw a great pile of hills littered with boulders. Huge trees stood anchored by roots grown over the rocks. Guinea grass and wild cane covered the shoreline.

They entered a small harbor alongside another vessel. Cheering and laughing, the crew of the other ship held aloft jewel chests and tossed coin bags into the air. The men aboard the *Arras Revenge* stood about the deck glowering.

That evening all the crew stayed aboard. From the bow, Dirk, Baldric, and the twins watched the little harbor settlement come alive.

Mic came to stand on the other side of Baldric. "Jacques says it's the biggest town on the island."

"It's just shacks," Dirk said. "I don't see any streets."

Lights flickered as people lurched in and out of doorways. Laughter and squeals of anger mingled with shouts of triumph and cries of dismay. The smell of vegetation and cooking fires floated out across the water. Dirk's feet tapped the deck in time to fiddle music and drum beats. Beside him, the twins hopped up and down.

"Why don't we go ashore?" Joost asked.

"Why do we have to stay here?" Jan asked.

Baldric drew closer to Dirk. "What will they do with us? Can we live in that town?"

"Cayona. It's called Cayona," Mic said. "And see the stockade on that hillside? That's Fort Rocher."

Dirk looked over his shoulder at Alencar, Lucien, and a few others sitting, heads together, near the stern.

"I don't know wha—"

A woman screamed, and Dirk turned back toward shore as a quarrel graduated from shouts to a sword fight near a beach hut. When the swordplay ended with both men down, panting in the sand, Dirk dragged himself away from Cayona's spectacles and wandered aft. Maybe one of the men knew what would happen to him and the other boys.

As Dirk neared the pirates, Alencar turned, smiled, and handed him a full bottle of brandy. Grinning, Dirk ran back to the bow. The boys sat on the deck passing the bottle around until it was empty. Long before then, the liquor had ceased burning Dirk's throat, and he had ceased worrying about tomorrow.

The next morning, he struggled to waken as men lifted him over the side of the ship and dropped him to pirates in a small boat. His head throbbed and the sunrise was too bright. The boat rocked as the other boys tumbled down beside him. Mic looked as if he were sick, but he had brought all their shoes.

As the men rowed the boat to shore, Joost scrambled to a seat in the bow. "Oooo, look at all the men sleeping on the beach."

Baldric held his head and shut his eyes tight. Tears squeezed out anyway. Jan retched over the side.

"Look at that woman," Joost said. "Her blouse isn't tied an' I can see her bubbies hanging out."

Mic groaned. "If he doesn't shut his maw, I'll whack him."

Dirk couldn't laugh. The shoreline wavered and his stomach was just as bad. He shut his eyes and concentrated on sitting upright. When the hull scraped sand, men lifted him over the side into ankle-deep water. He took a few steps, swayed. The sand rolled as badly as the waves.

He stumbled into Cayona behind the men, with Baldric lurching between him and Mic. Joost dragged Jan along, stopping every thirty feet so Jan could bend over for dry heaves.

The town didn't look exciting in the daylight. Snoring men in filthy rags littered the narrow dirt streets.

"Look at that." Joost pointed to a drunk passed out on his knees, face in the sand, buttocks in the air. Then he laughed—screeched—at a woman sprawled with her skirts above her hips.

Dirk twisted his left ankle on a large, jagged piece of an onion bottle before noticing all the shards of bottles shattered against walls. Watching where he put his feet made him dizzy, and the sour stink of old beer, vomit, and drying rum made his stomach heave. If only Joost would quit jabbering. If only there was a quiet, dark corner to curl into and sleep. *If I have to die to escape this misery, I don't think I'd mind.*

The pirates nudged them up a hillside to Fort Rocher, a rectangle of uneven stone and timber walls. Once inside, Dirk collapsed in the shade of a wall. At least the air was fresher here, whatever they were doing in the fort.

"Sold!"

The auctioneer thrust his pudgy fist into the air. Then he adjusted a faded brocade waistcoat over his bulging stomach while an assistant pushed another naked African man onto the raised wooden sale block. The auctioneer resumed cajoling prospective buyers, his French too rapid for Dirk to follow.

He sat with Mic, Baldric and the twins in the shade of Fort Rocher's only tree. Dirk glanced at Alencar and Lucien, who were leaning against the trunk. Fifteen well-formed slaves had been sold already, and the pirates hadn't bid on a single one.

Dirk squinted through biting sunlight at the forty or fifty men crowded into the little stone fort. There were men of every race. Most were dressed in scraps of clothing, although a few wore velvet coats and hats with feathers. Three men in wide, plumed hats, long pantaloons and blue coats with worn, dirty white braid leaned on muskets near the gate. Dirk considered wandering about, but his head still hurt. There wasn't much to see anyway, only the sale block and a reed shack built into a corner.

Nearby, Joost drew a boat in the dirt. Then he and Jan quarreled over it. Dirk tried to quiet them, but they started hitting and kicking each other, and the boat disappeared into a little cloud of dust. Dirk jumped in to separate them. He choked on dust and a knee rammed his chin.

Alencar hauled him out of the skirmish and shoved him aside before going after Jan. Lucien grabbed Joost and slapped him on the head. Dirk brushed himself off, but the dust turned muddy in his sweaty hands. He wiped them on his breeches, then realized every eye in the fort was focused on their little patch of shade.

The auctioneer smiled and pushed away the slave about to be sold. His hand cupped, the man beckoned to Dirk. Puzzled, Dirk looked at Alencar. The big man nodded once before he and Lucien pushed the boys to the auction block. At the bottom step, Dirk swung around to find Mic and Baldric staring at him, their eyes wide. Dirk's early morning nausea returned.

Slavery was common enough. Dirk had seen the great slave market on Curaçao when he and his father visited there once. And everyone in Dirk's world served somebody or an entity like the East India Company. But never in his life had he imagined he would be sold and forced to serve without any say in the matter. He glanced around. The fort was full of men, and the gate so far away. He looked back at Mic and Baldric, and shook his head. There was no help for it. They would be sold, like animals.

With his teeth clenched and a steady push from Alencar, Dirk climbed the five steps. The others followed, the twins still jabbing elbows at each other. The auctioneer jostled them into a line and straightened the feather in his beret.

"Listen well, brethren," he said. "Here's your chance to win a good helper and strike a blow against Spain at the same time. Look and see for yourself that these are strong, healthy boys. Good for cabin boys, valets, and apprentices. They were orphaned by the filthy Spanish during a raid on Bentyn's Isle."

Muttering curses, the crowd surged closer to the platform.

"Sadly enough, these unfortunate boys had no money for safe passage from Bentyn. So in exchange for promised servitude of seven years, the men of the *Arras Revenge* brought them here. Where they can grow up among free men."

The auctioneer's voice rose over cheers. "And someday repay the Spanish bastards for their terrible deed!"

Dirk glared across the fort grounds at Alencar and Lucien, who lounged against the tree once more. There had been no request for, nor promise of, payment for passage. The lie was only to hide the pirates' failures. Jacques had told him that in six months at sea they hadn't captured anything bigger than the boys' canoe.

Then Dirk's neck grew hot as he was tugged out of Baldric's grasp to stand at the front of the platform. The sun burned down and he flushed even hotter. When Lucien smirked and Alencar gave a short salute, Dirk's muscles tightened until he shook with fury. He barely heard the calls for bids.

Only when the bidding ended and the auctioneer pushed him toward the stairs, did Dirk think of something worse than being sold. He was going to a new life alone. His stomach felt as if he were swallowing stones again. All the fear and sorrow he'd held off by trying to protect his friends returned worse than ever, for now he had no one.

He turned back, slipping from the sale block onto the first step. Joost's mouth hung open. Jan clasped his brother's arm with both hands. The wrath in Mic's face matched Dirk's own. Mic managed half a smile, though, and Dirk felt a little better.

"Seven years!" he called out in Dutch. "We meet here in seven years!"

Mic nodded.

"Jan, Joost! Baldric! Do you understand?"

While the twins bobbed their heads, Baldric stood rigidly, his eyes clouded. The way he'd stood in the cornfield on Bentyn. Swallowing hard, Dirk stepped up toward Baldric, but heavy hands yanked him off the three-foot-high platform. He landed hard on the ground.

"Mic, help me. Make Baldric understand."

"I'll try." Mic waved. "Seven years."

Fingers dug into Dirk's arms as a short, barrel-shaped man tugged him through the crowd.

"My name's Gilbert," the man said in French. "I'm your master, boy."

Gilbert pushed Dirk into the corner shack, where a clerk shuffled papers across a rough wooden table. Dirk couldn't follow the two men's rapid conversation, but caught "*boucanier*," the French word for buccaneer, when it was used to address his master.

Dirk studied the man, as the buccaneer hunters of Hispaniola were legendary in the Caribbean. They provisioned pirate ships with beef smoked and dried over a boucan grill, and were known to commit piracy on occasion. Maybe his master would take him to sea as a pirate and he could begin to make the Spaniards pay for the great stabbing pain of loss he felt.

Gilbert set his six-foot-long musket against the table and pushed up the sleeves of his filthy tunic to sign an "X" on the papers. Dirk could hardly see the sandy arm hair and freckles through all the dirt. Under his thigh-length tunic, the man wore ragged knee breeches. Leather thongs bound leggings to his calves. From a wide leather belt hung three pouches, a big knife, and a shortsword. Even indoors, a small-visored cap stayed on his head.

Finding neither a long blade suitable for piracy, nor white traces of spindrift that bespoke a seafaring man, Dirk stomped to the shack's only window to watch the sale of his friends.

Seven years. A bond slave 'til he was eighteen and almost an old man. Seven years before he could become a pirate. Seven years without Mic and the others. And all this because those pirates weren't good enough to take prizes. Dirk kicked the wall below the window. *If I were a man, no one would dare sell me or my friends.*

Dirk's new master led him to the shore where they boarded a twenty-foot, deckless freebooters' launch. When Dirk asked where they were going, Gilbert said only, "Hispaniola."

One of the freebooters added, "A mere hour's sail to the south, lad."

Dirk nodded his thanks to the man and eased past cargo and passengers to the bow. There he stood, elbows on the railing, chin resting in cupped hands, as the bigger island loomed in the southern sky. High green mountains snatched at clouds scuttling by. Near the peaks lay patches of brown, as if forests had been scorched by lightning storm fires.

The western horizon turned red and gold. Shadows mottled the Hispaniola mountains a dark green, and the valleys, murky with evening mists, blackened. The island almost filled the sky now, and looked poised to swallow him.

The freebooters furled the single sail and anchored just off a narrow beach where four men dressed like Gilbert waited. A last bit of daylight glowed on large bundles of cured beef, hides, and the rolled palm fronds leaking tallow on the sand at their feet. The freebooters hurried to unload their cargo of musket balls, powder, and open crates of onion bottles. They just as quickly took aboard the buccaneers' bundles, unfurled the sail and were gone.

The four men picked up boxes and disappeared into a thick stand of palm trees. Gilbert hefted three large bundles and gestured for Dirk to fetch the five little ones remaining. He picked up the parcels and, struggling with the awkward load, trudged after the man.

Seagulls squawked over smidgens of meat left by the freebooters. Surf crashed in the evening tide. As the last bits of purple sky disappeared behind the horizon, Dirk followed his master into the dark.

A short distance from the beach lay a campsite with three palm-thatch huts. Eight men lounged around the fire. If four of them had been on the beach earlier, Dirk couldn't recognize them. Six boys of various sizes and ages scurried about, tending the fire and keeping the men supplied with food and brandy. An uncountable number of huge dogs roamed the camp.

The men quieted and gazed at Dirk and Gilbert. A little man with the longest, sharpest-pointed nose Dirk had ever seen raised a hand in greeting. "Yo, Gilbert," he said, and pointed to the row of huts.

The men resumed their French talk, and Gilbert hustled Dirk off to the smallest hut. Exhausted and still wobbly from his hangover, Dirk curled into a corner. But he was too scared and lonely for Mic and the others to sleep well and, despite the smudge pots burning outside, mosquitos whined in his ear all night.

By morning, Dirk was covered with bites, even under his clothes. He crawled outside to stretch and scratch in the sunlight. Before he finished, a large, black-haired youth marched over. Looking up and down Dirk's stocky frame, the fellow sneered, spoke rapid French, then waved a fist under Dirk's nose before stalking off. Dumbfounded, Dirk stared after him 'til he felt a tug at his sleeve. He looked down into a mop of faded, brown hair, a sun-burned face, and a shy smile.

A boy of perhaps six years stuck a thumb in his own chest. "Henry." Then pointed to the bully. "Edoardo."

"Oh." Dirk tapped his own chest. "Dirk."

Henry smiled again, and led Dirk to the center of the camp where hunters had gathered to break their fast. Though appearing black the night before, the men's clothes were unbleached cotton stained a deep, uneven brown. Shaggy beards, full of knots and twigs, covered hard, lined faces.

Pointing to each man, Henry gave Dirk everyone's name. Matt, the long-nosed fellow who'd greeted Gilbert the night before, smiled and nodded.

A tall man, so thin his bones appeared to be held together by skin only, stood and came to shake Dirk's hand. "Fenton," he said.

"Dirk van Cortlandt."

"Dirk." Fenton shook his head. "No van Cortlandt."

Dirk nodded. Henry hadn't mentioned anybody's last name either.

Fenton gave him a cassava flour biscuit. Dirk nibbled on it as he followed Henry about the campsite. The little boy talked on, his narrow chest thrust forward in pride, but Dirk understood only that Henry, Matt and Fenton might all be English. William was African; Carlino appeared to be part African, part Indian. As near as Dirk could tell, the rest of the men were French. By the time Henry introduced him to all the other boys, names and faces had blurred to the point Dirk saw only that the boys were somewhat cleaner than their masters.

Finally, he sat down at the edge of camp to finish his breakfast while Henry disappeared into the swirling mass of men, boys and dogs. He wondered how he could live in this new home for seven years. Amidst the turmoil, he felt alone.

Half an hour later Dirk was put into service helping dismantle the camp. Tents came down and belongings rolled into sleeping bags. Gilbert draped a rolled tent and sleeping bag over his own shoulders. Blades and ammunition pouches hung from his belt. With his musket in its leather case in one hand and three net bags of onion bottles full of brandy in the other, the man marched into the forest. Dirk followed, loaded down with cooking utensils, boxes of musket balls and powder, and a crude leather sleeping bag given him by Fenton.

The buccaneers followed a narrow, rocky trail uphill all day. Dirk had to trot most of the way and by sunset, when they halted in a clearing near a stream, his arms ached and his legs trembled. But he wasn't allowed to rest. While the men built hut frames of bamboo, the boys stripped thatch from palm trees and wove it into sheets tight enough to keep out the rain. They pitched tents inside the huts then filled the smudge pots with tobacco that would smoke all night. After a supper of cured beef and hard cassava biscuits, the men began drinking. Dirk collapsed with the other boys.

Morning came much too soon. Dirk pushed away Gilbert's demanding boot and cursed in Dutch. Gilbert picked up a corner of Dirk's sleeping bag and dumped him onto the banana leaf mattress beneath. Groggy, Dirk stumbled outside. The eastern sky had just turned pink, but the camp was alive. After a drink from the nearby stream, Dirk hurried through a breakfast identical to last night's supper.

Then everyone trotted off toward the faint barking of dogs sent out hours before, according to Henry. In a wide savannah, the dogs had brought to bay a herd of feral cattle. Growling and nipping at the beasts' short legs, the dogs separated ten from the larger herd and ran them to exhaustion. Then the men moved in with their knives.

Dirk helped his master drag a bull's scrawny carcass almost to the edge of the campsite. There, Gilbert slit the animal's gut and scooped out steaming entrails. He held them up to Dirk, and pointed to the green-stick, hooded grills set over fires in the center of the campsite. Dirk looked around for a dish or bucket, or even a big leaf to carry the mess on, but at a growl from Gilbert, took them in his hands.

The entrails were hot and slippery. Dirk's stomach churned. He dumped the steaming things beside the closest boucan grill and ran to the stream to wash his hands. When he returned to the butchering, Gilbert tossed shins, hooves and globs of fat at him.

The bloody parts went into the flames. Gilbert cut meat off the bull in long strips, which Dirk gathered, then took over to the fires. Edoardo laid the strips flat across the boucan shelves.

For the next hour Dirk ran between carcass and boucan. After placing the last strip across the grill, he collapsed near a fire and wiped sticky hands on his bloody shirt. Nearby, dogs fought over the bull's bones.

The other men returned to camp, dragging carcasses. By nightfall all the meat was roasting over smoking boucans and the hides were stretched in wooden frames hung between the huts. While hunters drank, boys ran between the fires and the brandy supply.

The smoke slowly turned the meat strips into hard, brittle sticks as red as ham. Working near the boucans, Dirk's eyes watered constantly. He often did not hear, or could not understand, the men when they demanded food or brandy. For that, Edoardo cuffed his ear.

Finally, William sent the boys to bed. Snug in his patched sleeping bag, with a layer of tallow smeared on his skin, Dirk closed his burning eyes and was asleep.

Sometime in the night the side of the hut crashed onto the tent over his head. Outside, men shouted, muskets fired, and boys hollered. A smudge pot tipped over. Smoking tobacco spilled into the hut.

Gilbert crawled out of the tent, knife in one hand, musket in the other. In growing panic, Dirk fought his sleeping bag, then the pile of banana leaves under it. There was no light. The tent sagged onto his head. Just as he found a way out, the fat tail of a giant cayman slammed through the side of the collapsing hut. With a cry, Dirk rolled out into the night, his sleeping bag caught on one foot.

Untangling himself, he scrambled to his feet. Little Henry sped by and climbed the nearest tree. Men fired muskets into the mêlée between Gilbert's hut and the next one. The alligator, with a fresh cowhide stuck on long rows of teeth, thrashed its tail and snapped mammoth jaws at anyone and anything close. Heart thumping in his chest, Dirk climbed a tree near Henry.

Under an onslaught of thick clubs and flaming torches, the monster finally retreated. When the camp settled for the night again, Dirk wedged himself tighter between the limbs of his sanctuary and tried to sleep.

He awoke in the morning to stiff muscles, a multitude of welts from insect bites, and the stench of rotten meat. His clothes had hardened with dried blood. Dirk slid out of the tree to go wash in the stream. Halfway there, Gilbert caught him by the arm and shoved him toward the fires. The man gestured at the flames and wood stacked nearby, then stalked off to a hut.

Hungry, thirsty, and for the first time in his life truly wanting a bath, Dirk threw wood and pieces of blood-encrusted entrails onto the coals. He muttered all the Dutch curses he knew and was starting on those he'd learned from the French pirates when Fenton joined him. With much bone creaking, Fenton sat beside the fire, grinned, handed Dirk a roasted platano, and pointed at the stream. Dirk smiled his thanks and scurried off, gobbling the platano.

At the stream, he looked about for the giant cayman, drank deeply, then scrubbed his hands and face. He threw shirt, then breeches, then himself into the chilly, blue-green water. He splashed and scrubbed away the grime of three months, then tried to scrape the dried blood out of his shirt.

The men stayed away from water, washing their hands with spit and wiping them on filthy tunics. Dirk remembered the warm, soapy baths his mother had forced him to take every few weeks and wondered why he had resisted. Not that he would ever like bathing, but suffering a bath was better than smelling like a rotted cow carcass.

At an angry shout, he looked up to see Gilbert pacing the stream bank. Dirk gathered up his clothes and waded ashore. He hurriedly dressed under Gilbert's glaring eye and half-screeched lecture, catching only the words "wash" and "protection." He had no trouble understanding the rain of fists on his head and shoulders, however. Dirk bit his lip to keep from crying out. *He will* not *see me cry.*

Gilbert dragged him to the campsite and flung him toward the fire where Fenton still sat. Dirk rolled almost into the boucan, stopping against Fenton's stretched-out leg. Dirk lay stunned. His father, though strict, had never struck him for no reason, and never with a fist.

While Fenton argued with Gilbert, Dirk escaped into the woods. He ran, one hand on his swelling jaw, until he stumbled against a dwarf-apple tree. Its sap raised blisters on his arm. He looked for an aloe-wood tree that might give him some relief from the fierce burn but couldn't find one. The pain worsened. His eyes teared.

Certain no one would ever know, he crawled under a tangle of fat leaves and cried for Bentyn's Isle and his two-story home amidst green fields. For the scent of hot bread and butter cookies wafting in from the kitchen shack. For his down mattress swaying on cord supports in the big wooden frame.

He cried for his parents, their laughter that filled the house, and for Anneke, that squeaky-voiced tattletale. He longed for the feel of his mother's hands, always busy yet managing to pat his cheek whenever it was within reach. More than anything, he wanted to go home.

When he was exhausted from crying, he curled into a ball and dreamed of being a big man, a pirate captain who always found rich prizes for his men. He would kill Spaniards, and those French pirates, too, if he could find them. He would never own a slave, and after he killed Gilbert, he would never, ever, allow anyone to have so much power over him again.

The next blow broke his nose. After the crack, hot blood ran down the inside of Dirk's nose. He licked it off his upper lip. Both eyes watered. He shook his head to clear them, ducked and covered his face. Edoardo pounded his left ear. Dirk fell away and staggered to the edge of the firelight before collapsing.

Men cursed, hooted, and called to each other.

"Pay up."

"Hand over my three cobs."

"Hah, Carlino, that's ten more you owe me."

"You best teach that boy how to fight, Gilbert."

Somebody stomped close.

"I don't know what to do with you, boy," Gilbert said. "You learned our talk well enough, but you're slow to learn our ways and you can't even fight. I lost a lot of money on you tonight." He pushed a booted foot against Dirk's rump. "I bought you 'cause you looked strong and smart. I was wrong." Gilbert booted him again and stalked away.

Pain replaced numbness in Dirk's nose, but it was overpowered by a stabbing throb in his ear. Exhausted and queasy, he lay still until all the fights ended and bets were settled, then crawled off to his sleeping bag.

In the morning he fished a hunk of cassava bread out of the communal hamper, and walked stiff-legged to a nearby creek, then upstream out of sight of the camp. The fierce pain in his ear worsened when he leaned over to splash water on his face. Straightening up took all his strength. Nauseated, he sat against a breadfruit tree to take stock of Edoardo's handiwork.

Except for the nose and ear, Dirk felt no worse than he did after a beating from Gilbert. He had bruises everywhere and at least a dozen cuts, including a long gash over the knuckles of his right hand.

That one would leave a scar, he thought, right next to the jagged white line he'd earned fighting a month ago.

Dirk touched his nose. What did it look like? And the rest of his face? Maybe he'd changed so much in the past nineteen months his friends wouldn't know him when they reunited. Would he recognize them?

He was taller; his breeches no longer reached his knees. They hung loose around his waist, though. He'd lost his chunkiness to constant hard work. And despite Gilbert's taunt, Dirk knew he was strong. He just wasn't a good fighter.

Someone stomped through the woods, and Dirk opened one eye. Matt walked up and held out an onion bottle. Dirk took it and drank, grateful for the brandy's warmth and promise of dulling his pain.

Matt cocked his head and said something.

"Can't hear you." Dirk touched the ear Edoardo had pounded so hard.

The little man moved to Dirk's right side. "Can't do a thing for your ear, but let me see that nose." He wriggled his own over-long nose and reached for Dirk's.

"Ow! Don't touch it!" Dirk jerked away. The sudden movement brought on the stabbing pain again.

Matt chuckled. "When the swelling goes down, we'll consult Ansel."

Dirk took another swig of brandy and sighed. "I always lose."

"Eh?" Matt settled cross-legged on the ground beside Dirk.

"I'm not weak 'n' I'm not slow. But I always lose these fights."

"You know what you are. Do you know what you're fighting?"

"Edoardo... it's always Edoardo."

"That's the boy's name. Do you know anything else?"

"He always wins."

"Think, boy. A fellow shows his soul fighting. Know his soul and win the fight."

"I need more than that."

Matt nodded. "The one on top, the big one, never learns about the smaller ones below, and that's his biggest weakness." He sniffed, then slid a finger under that long, pointed nose.

"I never fight anybody littler than me," Dirk said.

"Now, take the Spanish." Matt stretched out his legs and leaned back on his elbows. "We know 'em. How they think, what they want, what their religion says they should do. We even learn their language, so we can spy on 'em when they come across from Santo Domingo to raid our camps. But they never learn ours, not even the French most of us talk.

"They have horses and big guns and fleets of ships. The might of the Spanish Empire covers the world, but they'll never kill us off, because they don't bother to know us."

Dirk swallowed more brandy and bounced the bottle against his knee.

"What do Spaniards have to do with me beating Edoardo?" He lifted the bottle for another drink.

Matt sat up, took the bottle away and wagged its neck at him. "If you want to be a good hunter, you need to do more than lose fights to Edoardo."

"I don't want to be a hunter at all," Dirk said. "Nor a freebooter, either. I'm not gonna sail back and forth between here and Tortuga day after day."

He reached for the brandy. Matt hesitated, then let him have it.

Dirk coughed on a long swallow. "And I'm not gonna be a habitan. No farming or keeping a store on Tortuga for me."

"Then how will you live?"

"I'm gonna be a pirate."

"Most of us in the Confederacy of the Brethren of the Coast play at piracy now and then."

"Now and then isn't enough."

Matt rose, pulling a small hatchet from his belt. "I'm off to tap some wine palms." He nodded toward the creek. "Don't let Gilbert catch you bathing. You know he's afraid you'll wash off all your protection and become sickly."

"Better sickly than stinking the way he does."

"Boys all feel that way when they're new to the hunt." Matt smiled. "They outgrow the practice soon enough."

Dirk glared at him. "I haven't."

"Is it worth a beating just to be clean?"

"Sometimes."

"Have you thought of how prideful Gilbert is, too? And that he owns you?" Matt grunted. "You're nearly thirteen years old, Dirk. You look to be a large and powerful man someday. But you'll never live to reach your full growth, much less become a pirate, if you don't start to think."

Matt left, taking the brandy with him. Dirk sat back against the tree and fumed. He hurt too much everywhere to think. Brandy was much better than thinking.

Yet two weeks later Dirk approached Matt as the man broke his fast by a fire. "Teach me Spanish."

Matt patted the ground beside him. "Sit down. Let's get Ansel over here."

He summoned the wiry, black-haired Frenchman, and Ansel felt Dirk's nose, turning his head this way and that. Dirk gritted his teeth. The nose had quit hurting just yesterday.

"No good," Ansel said.

"Don't I look right?"

"Merde. Looks don't matter. You breathe through your mouth."

That was the most Dirk had ever heard Ansel say at one time. He didn't have a valet of his own and rarely said anything to the other boys.

Matt leaned closer. "From the swelling?"

"No, healing bad. Cause trouble rest of his life."

"Can you fix it?" Matt said.

Ansel lifted his chin in half a nod. "Hold him."

Matt knocked Dirk backward and pressed his shoulders to the ground. Ansel straddled his chest, one hand on his forehead, grasped his nose and twisted.

At the piercing snap, Dirk howled. "Let me up, you scabby lizards!"

The men obliged, grinning.

Dirk's nose filled with blood. "You broke it again!"

Ansel half nodded. "Good break this time. Use bandage, heal right."

"God. Oh, God!" Dirk moaned as Ansel walked off. "It hurts worse this time! Why didn't you warn me?"

Matt shrugged. "I didn't know. Let's find a bandage and teach you some Spanish."

Dirk moaned again.

The lilting tones of Spanish came out of Dirk in guttural chunks. Understanding Matt when he spoke it was even more difficult. Still, Dirk practiced hard, promising himself he'd use it against Spaniards someday.

With Matt, he tried to speak only Spanish. When he learned that many pirates spoke English, he practiced that language with Fenton and Henry. The rest of the time Dirk spoke French, as did everyone else in camp. At first he often mixed languages in his sentences. When excited or in a hurry, he broke into Dutch, which nobody understood.

Gilbert tolerated only French from Dirk. When his tongue slipped, the man cuffed him.

"No boy needs to know more than the language of his master!" he'd shout.

Despite Gilbert, Dirk did not stop practicing. He merely avoided Gilbert whenever he could. While sober, the man could be pleasant, teasing and joking with coarse humor, but when drunk, nothing Dirk did could please. So he offered to help Fenton or Matt whenever they foraged in the woods. He cheerfully dug cassava roots for making veycou liquor, or for grinding into bread flour. He collected the yellow, melon-sized fruit of the abelcoses tree, and always watched out for Arawak shagg, a weed the men smoked in their pipes.

Yet not even Matt and Fenton's rough affection was enough to suppress Dirk's anger and frustration over the boys' nightly fisticuffs. He tried to follow Matt's advice and observe Edoardo instead of charging blindly into a fight. But Edoardo's viciousness at the end of a fight, when he'd clearly vanquished the other boy, often undid the best of Dirk's intentions.

Early one morning Gilbert and five of the brethren carried heavy bundles of cured beef and hides north out of camp. As soon as they were out of sight, Dirk snatched a hunk of meat off a boucan and trotted south. Following a nearby stream, he found the spring that fed it.

He bathed, then washed his clothes in the chilly water. His mother had sewn them of heavy linen, but after nearly two years of constant wear the material had worn thin and was stained beyond cleaning. But at least the odors would be gone. He spread the shirt and breeches on a rock and sat in the hot sunshine to dry.

Any other day, Henry would be with him. The little boy and his shy fears reminded Dirk of Baldric, although Henry was more talkative. Dirk enjoyed having someone follow him around again, and more than once had stepped between Henry and a beating from Edoardo. Today, however, Henry was going to the coast with his master Carlino and the other hunters.

They'd trot all the way to the sea to sell their beef to freebooters or pirates who'd pay three pieces of eight for each hundred pounds. With that money the buccaneers would replenish brandy and ammunition supplies. Even by running all the way back, the men could not return before sunset.

So the day belonged to Dirk alone. The glorious day, with warm sunshine and a light breeze ruffling the pale yellow blooms on a nearby cotton tree. White clouds scudded across the sky, now and then disappearing behind green mountaintops.

Dry and warm at last, he dressed in garments still damp at the seams and twisted his shoes on. They were too tight to buckle, even without the thick hose long since worn to shreds, but he couldn't worry about them now. He'd heard voices in the night. He wakened Gilbert, who said there was nobody. He told Dirk to shut his mouth and go back to sleep.

But Gilbert must have been wrong. Months ago, when Edoardo hit him so hard, Dirk lost the hearing in his left ear for three weeks. Since that time, the ear had grown sensitive and sometimes he heard things others didn't. He had heard people last night, and today he would find them.

Setting off southeast, he walked until mid-day. There were no signs of people, nor any noises except those of birds, the ever-present insects, and small animals rustling in the underbrush. He pressed on westward.

Circling the camp, he found a narrow trail and a knife glinting in the dirt. He picked it up. Hunters favored this kind of broad-bladed knife that stabbed, chopped, and skinned so well. This one might be coated with dried blood, but the blade looked sharp and the hilt was sound. Why had a buccaneer discarded it?

A drone came from farther up the trail. Dirk followed the sound. At the edge of a large clearing he stepped behind a bush. Parting the leaves, he found the source of the knife: a buccaneer campsite.

The huts and tents were heaps of grey ashes. Smudge pots, though knocked flat on the ground, still spewed their foul smoke. Yet despite the smudge, flies hovered in black clouds over corpses.

Dirk swallowed. Seven hunters and four boys. Two men lay across broken boucans, their flesh charred grey-black. One little boy, eyes open wide, sat pinned against a tree by a lance through his neck. A shadow winged across the camp. A vulture landed on a buccaneer's chest and pecked at his eyes.

The droning grew louder, filling Dirk's head. Dizzy with the stench of death and the pain of memories, he backed away. The leaves he'd been holding aside snapped back into place as he whirled to run.

And faced a Spanish soldier on horseback.

The Spaniard sat motionless astride a huge grey stallion. Sunlight glinted off the silver trim of the saddle and a saber dangled from the man's belt. A narrow, ruff collar drooped onto his black doublet, and his pointed face, set without emotion, beaded with sweat under a stiff cap. He held reins in one hand, a pistol in the other. Slowly, he leveled the pistol at Dirk.

Throat dry and chest tight, Dirk fought to make his voice work. *"Buenos días."* The greeting ended in a squeak.

The man's eyes widened and his brows pushed together. He turned the pistol a few inches to one side. Dirk dove into the bush he'd just left, rolling as he hit the ground, nicking himself with the knife he still carried. The pistol's charge rattled the branches above him. His left ear rang.

He scrambled out of the bush and ran straight across the campsite, startling the vulture from its meal. Behind him, the horse crashed through underbrush into the clearing. Dirk plunged into bushes on the other side. The horse pounded into the forest close behind, snorting amidst the swish and crackle of a sword slashing through foliage.

Darting around trees, Dirk tripped over roots, fell into thorny shrubs. He had to find the trail back to camp to warn the others. This time he'd be quick enough. The Spanish were not going to destroy this home, too, bad as it was. Breaking out of the underbrush onto a trail, Dirk raced along it until hooves were thudding behind him. Then he fled into the forest again.

When sounds of pursuit faded away, Dirk slumped against a cedar tree to catch his breath. One ear pounded with his heartbeat, and the other still rang from the pistol shot. His breathing finally slowed, then quickened again. He must not run to the buccaneer camp for help. A single soldier couldn't have killed seven hunters in that other camp. There must have been more soldiers with him and they might be close enough to have heard the pistol fire. At this moment they might be riding to investigate, and Dirk would lead them all to his own camp. With most of the men gone to the coast, there'd be a slaughter. Instead of going back to camp, he'd have to hide until the soldier quit looking for him. But where?

The silence in the forest was unnatural. How long had he rested? He should have been running all this time. A twig snapped on his right. Inside a thicket something moved and Dirk thought he heard a dull thud, like a footstep. He backed away. The huge bush moved again. He turned to run.

And there was the Spaniard, right in front of him, sword dangling from his fingertips. He kicked the horse forward. The sword rose.

"*¡Dios mío!*" Dirk fled.

The stallion leapt almost upon him, snorting in his ear. Foam from the horse's mouth splattered his ankle. He ducked away, but too late. The man caught him by the neck of his shirt, lifted him off the ground. Dirk slammed into the wet, heaving belly of the horse.

"*¿Quién eres*?" The man's voice was harsh, almost a growl. "*¿Qué haces aquí*?"

Dirk kicked and twisted. The horse skittered on the trail. Unable to reach the soldier's arm, Dirk plunged his knife into the stallion's shoulder. The animal shrieked and reared, forelegs pawing the air. Dirk's shirt ripped. He fell into the dirt and rolled away, just escaping the horse's hooves as they landed. The man roared. Dirk ran.

He ran until his lungs burned and his legs shook, 'til the horse's screams grew faint, and he no longer heard the man's angry shouts. Then Dirk crawled inside a hollow log, pulling leaves and dead branches after him. Something rustled away from his head. Torn between fear of the Spaniard and fear of the scorpions or centipedes or deadly snakes that might be sharing his hide-out, he almost cried.

During the next hour, Dirk watched the Spaniard go by twice on foot. The third time he led his limping horse and there were other soldiers with him, talking. Dirk listened hard, but caught only the word "Tortuga."

Finally, near dusk, he crawled out of the log and hurried to find the trail back to camp. He had to reach it before Gilbert returned from the coast. On top of all the cuts and bruises of the day, he didn't need another beating from his master.

It was dark by the time Dirk found the buccaneer camp, and the place was in an uproar. Cursing men were stomping around the single fire. Boys ran about with food and brandy, stopping only to yell at each other. By the fire, Gilbert jerked his arms in the air and shouted something about the Spanish and Tortuga. He didn't appear to notice that Dirk had just arrived.

Henry raced by, saying, "Isn't it awful? What will we do?"

At the edge of the firelight, Ansel sat alone, drinking and sharpening his knife. Fenton was arguing with Matt, and Dirk sidled over to them.

"Where you been, boy?" Fenton asked. "You 'bout missed the excitement."

"This noise. The Spanish will hear and attack."

Fenton nodded. "They already did."

"One chased me. I forgot my Spanish."

"Make sense, boy," Fenton said.

Matt pulled Dirk toward the fire. "You took a bath?"

"Yes."

"But you're filthy. This blood on your arm?"

"I fell on the knife."

"What knife?" Fenton moved closer. "Where is it?"

"I left it in his horse."

Matt shook his head. "Tell us from the beginning."

He did.

Fenton lit a candlewood torch and the three of them went to inspect the other buccaneer camp. Dirk fidgeted in the dark while the men poked through the remnants. Then Matt told Dirk to look for campfires. He shinnied up the nearest tree, strained for the sight of a fire, but didn't find any.

He waited there for the men, fighting down panic, hating the constant warfare between Spanish soldier and buccaneer.

Eight months earlier, the hunting group had come across a small Spanish patrol. After a short, fierce battle, the buccaneers had stripped the five dead Spaniards and staked the two still alive over anthills. That night the hunters' angry, drunken voices almost drowned out the soldiers' dying screams. Dirk lay awake a long time, torn between gloating and guilt.

By morning, there was little left of the soldiers but bone and cartilage. Dirk inspected the anthills, his skin tingling as he imagined white ants devouring his own flesh. It could happen if the Spaniards ever caught him.

Matt joined him and sniffed. "Horrid custom, isn't it."

"Why do it?"

"The Spaniards started it, 'bout fifty years ago. They captured two English vessels near the Bahamas and claimed all the crew were pirates. So they cut the nose, ears, hands and feet off every man. Then tied 'em to trees and smeared 'em with honey to attract ants and flies."

"So this is revenge."

"It is."

Dirk pondered that for a while, then said, "We hunt the cattle. The soldiers hunt us because we sell beef to pirates. The pirates steal gold from the Spaniards, who stole it from the Indians. So we die, the Spaniards die, the Indians die, over stolen gold."

"These cattle we hunt are the wild get of some the Spanish brought here a century ago," Matt said. "So they call us thieves. But there's also land and trade, and wars in Europe and religion and other things involved. Don't fret over it. 'Tis life, and life is a single, long fight, with nothing but stolen pleasures to ease it."

Dirk had made no sense of the violence eight months ago, and still couldn't. But Spaniards had murdered his family and were trying to kill him now, so he hated them.

On the way back to camp, Dirk said, "Will the Spanish come for us, too, do you think?"

"Probably not for a while," Matt said. "They attacked Tortuga three days ago. Most of the brethren escaped and landed here on Hispaniola today."

Dirk's breath caught in his chest. The Spanish were everywhere, closing in on him.

"But what of Tortuga? The Confederacy?"

"The Confederacy will last," Fenton said. "But it looks like the brethren lost Tortuga."

Two months later, Dirk awoke to the sound of a strange voice in camp. Eyes still closed, he rubbed tallow that had slid into his elbow creases. Strangers were common. Buccaneers often hunted alone, joining a group when convenient. After a time, they'd leave as suddenly. A stranger's appearance created excitement at first, but soon the new hunter became just another man for the boys to serve.

"Name's Guy," the strange voice said. "Took it from the first man I ever killed. He didn't need it anymore."

Dirk heard Fenton's soft voice, then Guy's rough French again.

"Had to kill him. He was mean to a good huntin' dog."

Several men chuckled.

"This here's my boy. Smartest fellow you'd ever meet. Greet these men proper, Mic. In French, not that Dutch you talk."

Dirk's eyes popped open. *Dutch? Mic?* He wriggled out of the pigskin bag, shook insects out of his shoes and jammed feet into them as he raced from the tent. Worn leather and buckles flapping at his ankles, he ran toward the fire, then stopped short of the little group breakfasting in the pre-dawn light.

The stranger was a tall, thick-chested man with a round face, a dull-witted grin, and a belly-length, sand-colored beard. Behind him stood a youth, aloof and dignified. He was almost the same. Taller. Must be fourteen now. Thinner. But with the same pale, blue eyes.

"Mic!"

Mic turned. A smile crossed his face and the glint in his eyes softened. Dirk ran across the camp, wanting to tackle him, but choosing instead to punch Mic's upper arm and grin for a long time. Finally Dirk nodded toward Guy and spoke in Dutch.

"Does he beat you often?"

"Never. And he's easy to outwit. I do as I please most of the time. He feeds me well and buys me things. Look."

From behind Guy, Mic retrieved a six-foot, tooled leather pouch and pulled a long-barreled, broad-butted musket from it. Dirk whistled in admiration. It bore the mark of Galin of Nantes, who, with Brachere of Dieppe, made the only two kinds of muskets buccaneers used.

"It's taller than you are," Dirk said. "How can you hit anything with it?"

"I can hardly ever use it. The kick knocks me down every time."

Dirk snickered.

Mic glared at him, then laughed, too. "You should have seen Guy teaching me how to fire it. I'd fall down every time and he'd run over to pick me up. And every time he'd say, 'Put more weight behind it. Lean into it more.' Once he got the idea to give me the thing, he never thought I might be too small for it."

Dirk laughed, then sighed. Muskets were often a farewell gift at the end of a boy's servitude. Rarely did a boy receive one before that time. Dirk doubted he'd ever get one, since Gilbert refused to buy him even necessary things like shoes.

"Where've you been all this time?" he asked.

Mic wrinkled his nose. "Hunting pigs on Jamaica."

Dirk grinned. Pig-chasing chasseurs were the butt of many jokes around the campfire. Gilbert might be a brute, but at least he wasn't a chasseur.

Mic set the musket aside. "We went to Tortuga just before the Spanish took it."

"Did you fight when they attacked?"

"Naw, we ran off the back of the island with everybody else. And it's just as well. The English attacked Jamaica, so most of the Spaniards went there to fight 'em. Only a few stayed on Tortuga so we retook it. It wasn't much of a battle."

"Did they burn everything?"

"Nothing. They added guns to Fort Rocher. And some to those cliffs that flank the harbor. Remember them?"

Dirk nodded.

"They put a watch tower on the highest peak and tore up that little trail to the fort. Now we can't get in there except by ladder. But they left us plenty of shot and powder for their new guns."

Mic laughed. "When those fools couldn't save Jamaica from the English, they tried to capture Tortuga again last month. But they couldn't."

Dirk gazed at his friend. *To have a generous, manageable master, to own such a musket, and to be in the midst of a fight against the Spanish... how wonderful it must be.* But Dirk felt no envy. To have Mic beside him again was better than anything else.

Over the next few months, Dirk found it hard not to be jealous of Mic's friendship with Guy. The man joked about his own dim wits and called on Mic for important details. Guy also let Mic make a lot of decisions and routinely asked for the boy's advice. Mic humored the man, easily double-talking him out of anger or foolish acts.

In contrast, Dirk's relationship with Gilbert grew more strained. Dirk had learned to display the outward signs of respect, even while considering the man a swaggering fool. Yet the degree of misery inflicted by Gilbert still depended more on his mood than on Dirk's behavior.

One day, six months after Mic's arrival, Guy and Gilbert made a selling trip to the coast. Against orders to stay in camp, Dirk and Mic sneaked off to explore the surrounding hills. They climbed until mid-morning, stopping to rest on a bluff over-looking a small valley. Patches of mist floated from hill to hill, brushing the summits and darkening, in phases, the lush valley floor. Bright specks of yellow, pink, orange and purple dotted the green. On the far side, a waterfall splashed into a pool.

"Let's go there," Dirk said.

They raced a dizzying course down to where the green enveloped them. Every spot of color seen from the hilltop was a flower: red here, yellow nearby, white overhead, a delicate purple just beyond the next bush. While Mic ran on ahead, Dirk stopped and reveled in the profusion of scents.

Mic called out, "I found it!"

Dirk followed Mic's voice through a tunnel of greenery. Ten feet high, the falls roared into a clear, blue-green pool surrounded by bushes and large rocks. Schools of minnows darted across the sandy bottom.

Dirk stripped, dove into the water, then floated on his back. Mic took off his shoes to wade in. He howled and scampered onto a rock.

"Why didn't you tell me it was so cold?"

Laughing, Dirk knocked him off the rock. Mic rolled into the water, thrashed a bit, and came leaping out. They wrestled, water splashing high amidst their laughter.

Later, the boys wandered the valley, eating fruit and the nutty kernels of prickly-palms. In late afternoon, they started back to camp.

"Look." Dirk pointed to a faint trail leading up a foothill. "Let's follow it."

"It's late. If Gilbert gets back before we do, he'll beat you."

"He beats me for nothing. I may as well do something."

Dirk started up the hill. Mic followed, grumbling.

The trail led to a cave with a low entrance nearly hidden by thick brush. Dirk pushed the brush aside and cautiously stepped inside. As he stopped to let his eyes adjust, Mic joined him.

A flat-topped pile of stones leaned against the cave's rear wall. Dirk walked closer. On the platform sat two wooden carvings of elongated human faces over a foot tall. Their eyes followed him as he walked from one side of the cave to the other.

"What do you suppose this is?"

"Looks like an altar." Mic stepped farther into the cave. "Maybe the Arawaks come here to worship."

"I thought all the Indians were dead."

"Matt says some still live in this part of the island."

Dirk bent to study the carvings. "Slaves."

"What?"

"Slaves." Dirk straightened. "One of the slaves at home had things like these, only littler. He kept them in the shanty 'til Papa found them. He burned them as heathen things, but I think they made more and hid them better."

"Then these must have been made by runaways from plantations at Santo Domingo," Mic said. "I wonder how many of them live in these hills."

Dirk backed away from the altar. "This is a sacred cave. Let's leave."

"Now!"

They ran out of the cave and along the path that led toward their camp. Once in the hills beyond the valley, they slowed to a walk to catch their breath.

"We're going to be late," Mic said.

"I don't care. I'm tired of being scared of Gilbert all the time." Dirk kicked at a clump of dirt. "I wonder why that cave felt so strange."

"It was just a heathen place. It wasn't really sacred."

"Of course not."

They walked awhile in the lengthening shadows. Then Dirk spoke. "Do you ever think about religious things? Now that we don't go to services anymore, or even pray at mealtimes?"

"Not much. Guy says I shouldn't even think about it. That the brethren are all lost souls. A long time ago he had the Roman faith. Now he lives as he pleases and hopes to find a priest before he dies."

"We're no papists." Dirk pulled a thin branch off a bush and stripped the leaves as he walked. "A priest at our deathbed won't do us any good."

"Papa told me our fates were determined at birth. That we might be destined for Hell from the very first."

"Then why did they always tell us to be good?" Dirk swished the branch through the air like a sword. "If we're already lost, then what did it matter if we were bad?"

"I think it's because we don't know if we're lost. And if we're not, why do something bad that'll make us fall from God's grace?"

They trudged on, both quiet.

"I wish we could know if we're already lost," Mic said finally.

Dirk snorted. "*I* know." He whacked a short palm tree with the stick, which broke. He tossed it aside.

"You can't know."

"I do. Look at us. We're orphans. I have a terrible, mean master, and the Spanish are everywhere, trying to kill us. I am certainly damned. I think I knew it the day we were sold."

Much later, as they neared camp, Mic spoke again. "If we are truly damned and there is no help for us, what do we do now?"

"Anything we want. We can be as bad as the devil. It doesn't matter. I'm not going to worry about my soul anymore."

When the boys finally reached camp, glow worms flitted about in the dark. Crickets filled the air with their crisp night calls. And at the edge of the firelight, Gilbert waited, switch in hand.

Hispaniola, 1658

Dirk stretched, kicked sand, flexed his arms. He paced the edge of the surf in shoes, Gilbert's last gift, that were already too snug. Dirk's gaze flitted back and forth between an approaching freebooters' launch and Tortuga, that speckled brown hump on the northern horizon.

Ruled nominally by France, in reality by the Confederacy of the Brethren of the Coast, Tortuga controlled the shipping lanes through the Windward Passage. The island served as the market for French pirates' booty, as well as a prison colony of sorts for wayward women. Transportation of fallen women not only cleared the Paris streets of prostitutes, but stabilized Tortuga society by providing wives for the Brethren. Or a wealthy planter, if the woman was pretty enough.

Mic had dubbed the island the Great Tortoise of Plenty, for the exotic foods, merchandise beyond imagining, wanton wenches, and all the ale, mead, rum, brandy, grog, wine, beer, and whiskey available. Brethren with fresh money in their pockets celebrated raiding the Main, or hunting for another year under the noses of Spanish patrols. For men united by hatred of Spain, the struggle for survival, and a quest for mind-numbing pleasure, Tortuga was a reason to live.

It was for Dirk, too. A whole year he'd been waiting for this single week. A whole year of tedious hunting and tending fires and serving Gilbert. Only fights with other boys and practice with a wooden sword had relieved the boredom.

The launch arrived at last. The freebooters lowered the main sail as the bow slid onto the sand. Men unloaded supplies, then tossed hides and cured beef aboard. Freebooters haggled with buccaneers over rates of exchange, then everyone sailing to Tortuga boarded. As the launch bobbed out to sea, Dirk settled next to Mic on a pile of hides.

"Hey, Dirk," called one of the freebooters in Dutch. "Are you going to fight again this year?"

"Certainly."

"What'll you do with all that money you win?" The freebooter adjusted the tiller and ducked as the boom came about. "Buy a woman?"

"Naw. A musket."

"Good idea." Another freebooter edged astern between men and cargo. He grinned at Dirk. "You'll mess up your face fighting and then no woman'll want you. Not even with a fistful of doubloons." He touched the scar that ran over Dirk's left eye and down into his cheek. "Sword?"

Dirk laughed. "Corn stalk."

The man slapped Dirk's shoulder and guffawed. Then Gilbert sat next to Dirk, cutting off the conversation. With a smile, Dirk turned to watch Tortuga grow larger on the horizon. Nothing could ruin his mood today, not even Gilbert.

During last year's trip to Cayona, Guy had given Mic a small part of his share in profits from the hunt. With that stake, the boys had roamed the streets, picking likely opponents for Dirk to fight. Mic handled the wagers and collected the winnings afterward. Rarely had Dirk lost a fight and the money provided the boys with liquor, fancy foods, and clothes for Dirk, as Gilbert refused to buy them.

By the end of this coming week, Dirk was certain, he'd own a musket. And maybe after he purchased powder and balls, too, there'd be enough money left to buy time with a woman.

Two years before, when he was fourteen, Dirk had finally beaten Edoardo in a fistfight. Gilbert, always forced by pride to bet on Dirk against long odds, had won a small fortune. So when next in Cayona, he bought Dirk a pair of much-too-large shoes and took him to a doxy.

Long past midnight they traipsed out along the beach to a row of palm-thatch huts. The woman Gilbert chose was homely and old for her trade. She welcomed them with a smile of few teeth and the sour stink of dirty flesh.

"This kind of woman is good," Gilbert told Dirk. "They're cheap and got no airs."

Gilbert paid her, saying, "This boy's from a fancy home. He takes baths and everything. Teach him what the brethren do."

The doxy, whose name Dirk never learned, stroked his smooth cheeks.

"A bit new at the game? But not to worry. Even animals learn how it is." She reached between his legs and fondled him, chuckling. "It's going to be a while before you're a man."

Gilbert snickered.

Having spent over three years in the hills with men and other boys, Dirk knew his genitals were not small for his age and size. But his cheeks still flushed hot at her laughter. Worse, Gilbert might stay there to watch. Dirk almost ran out of the shack. Yet he wanted so much to try a woman.

Then the doxy pulled him onto her smelly, reed-mat bed, and before he could decide whether to stay or run, it was over.

After they left the shack, Dirk asked Gilbert, "Why didn't you buy a pretty woman? There are lots around."

The man hawked and spat. "A waste of money. Women all feel the same when the candle's blown out."

Dirk thought Gilbert must be wrong about that. The woman's skin had felt loose and dry, with no cushion of flesh under it at all. Her sharp bones had poked him, and surely the plump and pretty women on the island wouldn't feel quite the same.

A year later, Dirk approached a doxy on his own. In the midst of asking her price, his voice broke into a high squeak. The woman giggled and, hot with embarrassment, Dirk ran off.

He was sixteen now, though, and his voice had not broken in months. He slid a hand across his cheeks. If only his beard would grow.

"This is the last one," Mic said. "If you win, we'll have more than enough for your musket."

"Hmm." Dirk had already chosen a musket with a leather case. His mind, though, was on his opponent, a twenty year old named Baldessaire.

The man stood taller than Dirk by several inches and looked strong, like all of his opponents. Mic insisted on the difference in size, for it raised the odds against Dirk and small wagers paid off handsomely.

"You ready?" Mic asked.

"Fine. I'm fine." Dirk spoke without taking his eyes off Baldessaire.

In truth, he hurt. He'd been fighting at least three times a day for the past four days. There were bruises and cuts all over his face and hands. He had to win this fight so he could buy the musket and rest.

A large crowd had gathered where Cayona's main thorough-fare widened into the wharf. Many men shuffling about kicked up dust from the sunbaked dirt street. Matt, Fenton and Henry stood close, repeating advice and slapping his back. Mic lightly punched his arm, then strolled through the crowd, negotiating odds and accepting bets.

Baldessaire stood with his fists at his waist, looked Dirk up and down, laughed and turned his back. As the spectators' jeers and shouts increased, he rolled his heavy shoulders and strutted about on thick-muscled legs.

Dirk shut out the crowd's noise, listening instead to his own heart beat. He caught Baldessaire's eye and grinned. *Come get me*, the grin said.

Baldessaire charged.

Dirk ducked aside. Baldessaire's smirk disappeared. He growled and charged again, this time hooking a foot behind Dirk's left leg. Dirk fell where he wanted and let Baldessaire dive at him before rolling safely away. Baldessaire landed hard, raising a small cloud of dust. He lay still a moment, then clambered to his feet. Dirk let him rise just far enough to make a good target, then swooped down and, with all the power in his legs, came up with a fist under Baldessaire's chin. The man toppled onto his back.

The spectators roared. Baldessaire looked around, reddened, then rolled to his feet. He began a series of showy moves and punches that elicited cheers but were easy to ward off. Dirk used quick jabs here, glancing blows there, watching the man's eyes and hands, the slight shoulder movement that announced Baldessaire's next swing.

When Baldessaire finally slowed, Dirk moved in. He punched the man's gut until he leaned heavily into Dirk's moving arms for support. Dirk lowered him to the dirt, then laughed as Matt, Fenton and Henry rushed up, clapping him on the shoulders. Dirk smiled, even as they struck old bruises.

"The musket," Henry said. "It's yours now."

Matt nodded. "A good fight. A smart fight."

Mic flashed Dirk a satisfied grin, then worked his way through the crowd, collecting on wagers.

Dirk bought a musket crafted by Brachere of Dieppe, France. Longer than he was tall, it had a carved stock and smooth bored barrel. He propped the musket over his shoulder and left the shop grinning. The weapon meant power, the ability to hunt, feed and defend himself. Still stiff with bruises, he limped down the center of the narrow street and felt he was a man.

Later that night, Dirk stepped into the Chez Madame Céline tavern and paused to survey the room. Mic walked in behind him, muttering.

"You'd better find a woman in here. This is the fifth place we've been to and— Holy Jesus! This place looks expensive!"

Dirk laughed. "Isn't it grand?"

The place was quiet, compared to other taverns in Cayona. Along the rear wall, stairs rose behind a heavy counter. Flowers, perfumes and scented tobacco sweetened the air. Finely woven mosquito netting, a rare luxury, covered the windows.

The well-dressed patrons were somewhat clean, and their garments sported few rips or stains. Some of the men wore dark, wavy wigs. Elaborately coifed women strolled from table to table rather than call to men from across the room.

Dirk patted the pouch at his belt. There were seventy-five pieces of eight in there, more than enough to buy a doxy's services for an hour or two. He stepped down from the doorway and walked among the tables.

"Listen to me, friend," Mic said at his shoulder. "Even if you do find one who suits you, you won't be able to afford her. Not in this kind of place."

Dirk stopped suddenly; Mic bumped into him.

"There she is," Dirk said.

"Where?"

"In the corner."

"Oh, no."

Dirk gazed at black hair, clear green eyes, the creamy skin of a high, rounded bosom. Plump, well-proportioned, and dressed in green silk, the woman sat apart, surveying the room. A smile played on her plush lips as she listened to a man sitting beside her.

"No, Dirk, not that one. She'll cost too much. Wouldn't you like money left over to buy shoes or something?"

"I want her."

"But you could have two women for the price of her."

"I don't care."

"Well, you're not getting any of my money."

Dirk grinned. "I didn't ask."

With a grumbling Mic close behind, Dirk made his way to the counter where a spindly man with an eye patch issued the liquor. Dirk asked him about the black-haired woman.

"She's expensive," the man said. The gaze of his remaining eye roamed up and down Dirk's plain buccaneer garb.

"I have enough."

The man shrugged and called to a thin fellow with a nose like a vulture's beak. The man slithered over, never once jouncing a single ruffle of the lace that tumbled out of every opening in his brocade frock coat. His garters held up a spray of the dirty white stuff, too.

"Pierre," the counterman said, "these fellows asked about Marina."

Pierre looked at Dirk, opened a tiny box, sniffed at the contents, then sneezed violently into his handkerchief. The force of the sneeze knocked some dust from his wig. For a few moments a tiny cloud swirled around Pierre's shoulders.

"Buccaneer, Mademoiselle Marina is not for the likes of you."

Dirk slapped his money pouch. "I have coins."

"But certainly not enough."

"How much does she cost?"

The vulture's beak rose. "One hundred and fifty pieces of eight."

"One hundred and fifty? For an hour?"

Pierre sniffed. "Mademoiselle entertains but one man a night. She is not a street doxy who takes all comers."

"But a hundred and fifty pieces of eight... I could buy a slave for less."

"Perhaps you should." Pierre turned away, dismissing them with a wave of his lacy handkerchief.

Dirk stared after him, cheeks blowing in and out. Mic tugged on his arm. With a last despairing look at the lovely Marina, Dirk followed his friend outside.

In the street, Mic said, "Let's go to Chez 'Ti-Noir. There are lots of pretty girls there."

"No, I'm going to bed."

"Just because you can't have that fancy woman is no reason not to have any at all. A cheaper one will do just as well."

"Oh, I'll have her. I'll fight tomorrow until I win enough money. So now I need to rest."

Mic groaned. "You're a fool."

Dirk shrugged.

"Well, I'm not going to wait another night."

"Enjoy yourself."

Mic waved and strode off toward the Chez 'Ti-Noir. Dirk walked to La Taverne Rouge, where their hunting group had taken a room for the week, and went to bed alone.

In three fights the next day, Dirk won fresh cuts, more bruises and another hundred pieces of eight. After a brief nap and a scrub in the surf, he entered Chez Madame Céline and marched straight for the lovely Marina.

Pierre intercepted him halfway across the room.

"Why have you returned?" Pierre sniffed. "I told you Mademoiselle Marina is not for you."

Dirk stretched himself taller. "I have enough money."

At the counter Pierre bent over Dirk's elbow as he counted out pieces of eight.

"Exactly one hundred fifty," Dirk said, handing them to Pierre. Then swept the remaining coins back into the pouch, away from the fop's glittering eyes. He started for Marina. Pierre caught his arm.

"There is an extra charge for Marina's nakedness."

Dirk paused. It was customary for a woman to charge extra for taking off her clothes. But burrowing into the silky folds and flounces of Marina's dress might be fun.

"She can stay dressed."

The vulture's beak went up. "Marina would never allow her gown to be ruined that way."

"Well, then, how much extra?"

"Twenty-five pieces of eight."

"Twenty-five?"

Pierre rolled his eyes, twisted a finger in one of his wig curls, then, with a deep sigh, held out the 150 coins. Dirk counted out twenty-five more from his pouch.

"Wait here." Pierre walked over to Marina.

Dirk shifted from one foot to the other. Those last twenty-five pieces of eight had been meant for the cobbler. It would be a year before he had another chance to buy new shoes. But she was so lovely, and his current pair hurt only a little. Maybe he wouldn't grow much this next year.

"Well?" Marina said as Pierre approached her table.

"You have a customer, *chère*."

"How much did you get from him?"

"One hundred, plus fifteen for your luscious nakedness."

"So much. And he looks so poor."

Pierre smirked. "He bought you until daybreak."

"My God, he is too young. He will last all night and I'll be miserably sore tomorrow. Oh, no, I'll not have him."

Pierre squeezed her arm.

"Listen to me, bitch. This is the first man willing to pay your price in four nights. Our account at this tavern is too high and the owner wants payment tomorrow. Do not act so particular. You are a whore, and it is time for you to work."

He smiled then, and nodded to someone across the room while he pinched the underside of her arm.

"All right," Marina said, her eyes watering. "But at least give me a bottle of wine to make him drowsy. Perhaps he'll sleep most of the night."

Pierre stroked her arm. "Naturally, *chère amie*. I shall even add something to the bottle to help the cause."

Dirk held his breath until Marina nodded. Pierre took a lit candle and a wine bottle from the counter and beckoned. Dirk followed him up the stairs and into a small room. A large bed dominated the longest wall. A cane-and-linen screen cut off one corner from view, making the place feel cramped.

Pierre set the bottle on a table near the bed and lit the candle stub in the only wall sconce.

"Mademoiselle Marina will soon be here," he said. "You will remember that she is delicate, not one of those cows you buccaneers favor during your hunts."

"Cows? No, I ne— "

Pierre held up a hand. "Until daybreak, and not a moment later."

His left eyebrow shot up and stayed in the middle of his forehead until Dirk nodded. Then Pierre left.

Dirk was standing at the end of the bed, imagining the delights he would soon find there, when he heard the rustle of skirts on the stairs.

For a second time, the tension in Dirk exploded, flooding in waves throughout his body. He sighed with pleasure as he slackened onto Marina.

After a moment, she pushed against his shoulders.

"I can't... breathe."

"Oh. I'm sorry." Dirk eased off her body to lie on his side. Drying sweat cooled him.

"You are so heavy." She took a deep breath. "I never expected it in one so young. Are you even full grown yet?"

He chuckled. "I hope not."

Marina closed her green eyes and patted his upper thigh. "You're so big already."

Dirk's smile faded. The compliment had slid out of her mouth as if it were something she said to all men. Rolling onto his back, he stared into dark shadows among the roof timbers. Two years ago, a woman laughed and told him he was small. This time, a woman sighed and told him he was big. Both had lied, but it didn't matter. He was getting what he wanted. And it was so very good. Grinning, he tried to think of anything better, but could not.

That he'd purchased Marina's willingness filled him with a sense of power, for he could always fight again to win more silver. And she was his until daybreak, to take again and again, as often as his body could manage it. Soon, he'd be ready for a third time.

Rising onto an elbow, Dirk laid a hand on Marina's breast.

She frowned. "Not now. I need some time to rest." She slid away, left the bed, and ducked behind the tattered screen.

Dirk took a long swallow from the wine bottle on the bedstand and lay back down. Water splashed in a basin. His body grew heavy; he drank more wine. The fat candle in the wall sconce sputtered out, leaving only the bit of moonlight coming through a small window. Marina peeked over the screen at him, or maybe not. She was taking so long and he felt so sleepy. He would rest his eyes for just a moment.

When he opened them again, the room was grey with pre-dawn light. Dirk moaned as he sat up. He'd wasted the whole night.

Beside him, Marina slept naked, black hair splayed over the pillow. Just a few hours ago her breasts had pressed against his chest with a softness he hadn't known existed. Now, pale and velvety in the growing light, they rose and fell with her breath. Legs, long and smooth and firm around his back last night, lay tangled in the sheets, closing off that hot, damp place between.

Almost on its own, his thumb brushed the puff of breast spilling over the edge of her ribs. She twitched. He withdrew his hand for a moment, then stroked across the nipple. It hardened and rose. Her other nipple did the same when touched.

His caress wandered between her breasts, down over the slight belly mound, then beyond. As he shifted to a position near her hip, Marina stirred and opened her eyes. Dirk froze, fingers caught in silky black curls. When she arched an eyebrow and cocked her head, he managed half a grin that felt more than sheepish. She rolled her eyes, closed them and her cheeks billowed slightly, hinting at a smile. With a low chuckle, Dirk went exploring.

He turned her this way and that, and firm, but yielding flesh rose to meet his hand. Light pressure down her back and buttocks elicited a muffled sigh. As he feathered the softest skin from inner knee to groin, her thighs quivered and parted. Then, as he flicked his tongue up her ribs, she giggled in a little girl's voice.

"How old are you?" he asked between licks.

"Seventeen."

"Oh, my."

He'd thought her much older, the doyenne granting favors. But only seventeen, that made her a playmate. Cheerful now, he went back to work.

Finally he rested, head pillowed on Marina's buttock, a finger swirling the fine hairs at the nape of her neck. The night before, he'd been in awe of this woman while feeling competent at the same time. What little he'd known about romps and tumbles was so good it had seemed quite enough.

Now, however... There was an art to knowing when to hold or stroke or kiss or lick or push or slide or tug. When to use a fingertip, an arm, a handful, a knee. Developing these skills would require much practice. He grinned at the timbers overhead. Oh, happy ignorance.

Full daylight arrived, yet Marina didn't protest when he eased her onto her back and pressed a knee between her thighs. As he slid onto her, his other knee slipping in beside the first, her legs parted to make room for him. He bent to kiss her, a thing she'd refused him the night before. Now she used her lips and tongue against his.

Too quickly, and not fast enough, the inundation of sensations ended with a violent shudder. He rolled over, pulling her with him. She wasn't heavy on his chest, and to rest inside her extended the pleasure. For a moment, her flesh around him tightened and quivered, but then they both lay still.

Then both jerked at a bang on the bolted door.

"Marina!" Pierre shouted. "Is that boy still with you?"

Marina's eyes darkened with a shadow of fear.

Dirk answered. "Yes, I'm still here. And your woman is quite safe."

Pierre hit the door harder. "Open up! And if you've had her again this morning, you have to pay extra!"

Dirk looked up at Marina. "I don't have any more money. I had only the hundred and seventy-five."

"One hundred and seventy-five?" She sneered at the door, then ran her tongue over Dirk's upper lip. "Don't frown so. I won't tell."

When Dirk carried his musket into the hunting camp on Hispaniola, Gilbert exploded.

"You are too young for that," he said, even while Dirk demonstrated his ability to withstand the weapon's tremendous kick.

"Hear me, boy, you'll not be using that thing. You'll be a danger to everyone. So I'll keep it for a couple of years."

Dirk backed away. "No. I earned it. I won't give it up."

"I'm your master, boy, and God damn you, you'll do as I say." Gilbert held out his hand. "Give it to me."

"No." Dirk held the musket tight against his chest. He was still bruised from the fights in Cayona and covered with scabs. He would not be without his musket for a day, much less the two years until he was free.

He glanced around the silent campsite. Mic stood ten feet away, his lower jaw working back and forth. The other boys watched with wide eyes, while the men continued drinking, sharpening their knives or braiding narrow vines into rope. Dirk knew that none would take his side in this, for despite the men's frequent jibes at Gilbert behind his back, they would never risk undermining the master-slave relationship.

"I said to give me that thing! Now! Or I'll take it and destroy it!"

Dirk shouted in Dutch, "You whoreson will never lay hands on this musket!" Then he spat toward Gilbert's boot.

With a roar, Gilbert charged.

Dirk sidestepped him and swung toward Mic. "Catch," he called in Dutch, and sent the musket flying.

Mic caught it and scurried away to sit beside Guy. Dirk turned back to Gilbert.

Red washed up the man's neck, covered his rage-distorted face. He grabbed Dirk's shirt, jerked him close, then set upon him with both fists. Dirk twisted and ducked. He ached to land a fist in the man's face, a foot in his groin, but a slave who struck his master courted death by any means the master devised. Even if Gilbert didn't kill him, he could brand or mutilate him, maybe cut off his right hand.

So Dirk accepted the beating, quiet at first, but soon low moans escaped. He tasted blood on his teeth and white lights flashed across his left eye. After a hard blow just under his ribs, he gasped for each breath. When he doubled over, fists pounded his shoulders and back. Knees smashed up into his face. Hard boots slammed against his legs.

A kick landed on the side of his right knee and Dirk collapsed. On the ground, he rolled to avoid more blows, but could not escape. He curled into a ball and tried to faint.

At last, it stopped. Dirk looked up at Gilbert's red face and heaving chest, then shut his eyes. Colored lights played against the inside of his left eyelid. Blood and dirt caked his lips, gritted between his teeth. Any movement shot pain everywhere.

Gilbert shouted for Mic to hand over the musket. Dirk rolled over, moaning, and opened his right eye. Gilbert stood in front of Mic and Guy, waving his arms.

Mic shook his head. "It's my musket."

"That firing piece belongs to my slave and therefore to me." Gilbert's voice rose. His hands balled into fists.

"I lent it to Dirk."

"You lie! Give it to me!"

"No."

Mic placed a hand on the musket lying between himself and Guy. Gilbert leaned over to take it, but Guy clapped a huge paw on his arm.

"You don't take my boy's things."

Gilbert snorted. "That's not his. He's lying and you know it."

"My Mic never lies. Now you leave him alone or I'll do to you what you did to that boy over there."

Cursing, Gilbert retreated to a hut. Tension in the camp eased. Hunters called for brandy and their boys raced to fetch it. Muted conversations resumed, and Mic stood up. Guy caught him by the arm.

"It is your weapon, boy, isn't it? I can't fight a brother for a lie."

"Of course it's mine."

Guy nodded, then chewed his lower lip. "But I already gave you one. Why do you need two?"

"Well, Dirk doesn't have one. I thought I could lend it to him."

Guy pondered that for a moment. Then, grinning, he cuffed Mic on the shoulder.

"That's the spirit of true brethren. I'm proud of you, boy."

Dirk started to laugh, but that brought on waves of pain. Then Mic's hands were on him, strong and gentle. Dirk closed his eyes and let his friend minister to him.

Dirk shifted the musket to his left shoulder and limped up a faint trail. It felt familiar, but he couldn't remember where it led. Behind him on the valley floor a small waterfall crashed. Hot and tired, he'd swim after he climbed this hill and looked around.

The day after Gilbert had beaten Dirk so badly Ansel checked him for broken bones. Yet even without fractures, Dirk needed more than two weeks to recover. During that time, Gilbert daily berated him and demanded he do chores. The other men shunned Gilbert, and finally Matt and Fenton took him aside to convince him to let Dirk rest longer.

He could walk well enough now, three months later, except for the knee that hurt a little all the time. So when Spanish soldiers increased their raids in the area, the men sent Dirk out as a scout. With his sensitive ear and knowledge of Spanish, they said, it was a logical task for him.

Each morning, Dirk borrowed his musket from Mic, who kept it safe at night and filled the ammunition pouch. Then, with a knife at his belt, Dirk limped off into the forest, glad to spend the day alone and out of Gilbert's sight. Anger over the beating still festered. Masters had a right to punish disobedience, but what justified such ferocity against somebody who dared not defend himself?

He worked his way up a steep rise in the trail and remembered where he was—at the sacred cave he and Mic had found a few years ago. He pushed aside the brush cover and stepped in. The little altar still leaned against the far wall. Dirk walked over to pick up one of the dusty, wooden statues.

He'd first seen such carvings when he was a child, with no thought beyond his next adventure and what Cook would serve for supper. He wondered for a moment what kind of man that child might have grown to be if not for the raid on Bentyn's Isle and the slave auction on Tortuga. There was no way to imagine, for the child was lost. Dirk could not change himself back. He replaced the statue and left the cave.

After a quick swim under the waterfall, Dirk started back to camp. He'd neither seen nor heard any signs of Spanish patrols. The buccaneers were safe for tonight.

Less than half a league from the campsite, he met Ansel in a small clearing. The man raised his chin in greeting.

"Master's after you. Lathered 'bout something."

Dirk heaved a sigh before nodding. Ansel moved on, and Gilbert soon appeared, carrying a heavy stick.

Gilbert swung the stick at Dirk's head. "You run off when there's work to do!"

Side-stepping, Dirk said, "You sent me off to find Spaniards."

"And you wasted time bathing."

Dirk glared, and realized that his eyes were almost level with Gilbert's. Dirk had grown, even in the last three months.

Gilbert must have realized it, too, for his grey eyes widened, then narrowed. He raised the stick. "You lazy, irresponsible slave."

Dirk braced himself to take the blow on his shoulder. Pain shot down his arm and across his chest. He tried to set his mind on other things, then saw the stick poised to strike again.

Tossing his musket aside, Dirk caught the stick as it swung down, the sting on his palm feeding his anger. He snatched the stick out of Gilbert's grasp and broke it over his own knee.

"No more!" he said, flinging the pieces at Gilbert's feet. "Never again!"

"You dare be so insolent?" Gilbert's voice rose. "Bond-slave, you must respect your superiors!"

"I *do* respect my superiors!"

Gilbert gasped, roared, and leapt at Dirk.

For a moment, Dirk was prepared to accept the assault, but somehow his fist came up and punched the man hard. Gilbert stumbled backward, lips bloody. The satisfying thunk of knuckles on flesh, the blood, and the years of beatings fed Dirk's rising heat and dimmed his vision. He charged.

The next thing he knew, Gilbert was lying in a heap of blood and dirt. Hands were tightening around the man's neck. The hated face grew red, then purple. Swollen veins striped the low forehead. At last Dirk recognized those clenched hands as his own. They flew off Gilbert's neck, tingling as if burned, and he jumped to his feet. Gilbert lay still, struggling for breath. Finally, he moaned.

Dirk backed away. French pirate curses weren't bad enough for this. No words were. He could die for it.

With a last look at the crumpled Gilbert, Dirk snatched up his musket and ran toward the buccaneer campsite. His one chance to survive was to flee into the mountains before Gilbert returned to camp.

Ansel was close enough to the clearing to hear Gilbert shouting. He walked back to watch. He wouldn't interfere, though. No need to change the natural order of things.

Still, he smiled when it was over. Tugging a dry leaf out of his hair, Ansel thought about a master in France, last seen curled in a bloody pile at his own feet. Just before he fled to the New World.

He watched a while longer. Gilbert rolled to his knees, then stood, legs wobbling and torso swaying in an uneven circle. He rubbed his throat and looked around. Ansel dodged behind a tree. Gilbert staggered away. Still smiling, Ansel sauntered off to find shagg to smoke that night.

Dirk raced to the tent he shared with Gilbert. He checked the other two tents within the sheltering hut, found them empty, and was throwing cooking utensils into his sleeping bag when Mic appeared at the tent flap.

"What are you doing? You ran past me and didn't say a word."

Dirk added flint, musket balls, and firing powder to the pigskin bag. "I had a fight with Gilbert. I'm leaving."

"So he beat you again. You can't run off just for that. They'll find you and you'll get worse than a beating."

"He didn't beat me. We fought and I won."

Dirk glanced up and even in the shadows of the hut could see his friend grow pale.

Mic's teeth clicked. "They will kill you for this."

"I have to leave now. Gilbert can't be far behind me."

Mic turned to go. "I'll get my things. Maybe some bread and brandy, too."

"No."

"If you run, I run."

"Then you'll be hunted, too, and punished just as bad if they catch us. I better go alone."

Dirk shook the bag, sending the contents to the bottom. Laying it flat, he began to roll it.

"I am your matelot," Mic said. "Your hunting brother and even more. I go with you."

They wouldn't be parted again. Dirk was ashamed of the relief he felt, as Mic might die for his loyalty. Dirk nodded and ducked out of the tent. Still inside the hut, he slung the bag over his shoulder, then attached a knife and a pouch of powder and balls to his belt. He picked up his musket. "I'll wait for you. A league to the west at that giant ycao tree by the river."

"I know the one." Mic slipped out of the hut.

A moment later, Dirk eased out between two of the hut's rear panels and strode into the forest. A short distance from camp he broke into an awkward, limping run.

He was free, but he felt no joy. Gilbert and the Spaniards would hunt him for the rest of his life. Capture by Gilbert meant at least a flogging, or a foot chopped off. Spaniards might stake him over anthills, or stab oil-soaked barbs into his flesh and set them afire. Even worse, for a few minutes, his mind had stopped, and during that time he'd almost killed a man. He had blindly done something that changed his life forever.

Beside the river, the ycao tree sprawled like a mushroom, its branches touching the ground. Dirk parted them and crawled inside. There was enough space underneath to pitch a tent. He dropped the sleeping bag to the ground and settled onto it. He loaded his musket, laid it across his knees and waited.

Mic finally appeared an hour later, bursting through the branches empty-handed and grinning.

"You can come back."

Dirk rose. *What a relief. Damn.* "Did they find Gilbert? Is he dead?"

"Nobody saw the fight?"

"I don't think so. Why?"

"Then nobody but Gilbert can accuse you." Mic chortled. "He stumbled into camp just as I was leaving." He punched Dirk's shoulder. "Oh, he's a mess. You did a fine job."

Dirk caught his arm. "What happened?"

Mic sank onto Dirk's bag. "I need to rest. I ran all the way."

"Mic!"

"I'm coming to it." He panted through a grin. "Gilbert almost fell into the fire. Everybody can see he's covered with dirt and blood and they run up to ask what happened."

"What did he say?"

"At first I thought he was going to tell about you. His face turned all red and he started cussing. Then he looked at everybody and grew real calm, and tells them he ran into a bull."

"A what?"

"A bull. He says, 'I espied a monster of a bull.'" Mic imitated Gilbert's whine. "'I managed to cut one hock, but he swung on me so fast, I couldn't reach the other. He caught me on his horns and threw me twenty feet at least.'" Mic laughed. "Can you imagine him telling a lie that way?"

Dirk snorted. "Oh, yes. He'd tell that kind of story."

"Then he talked on and on, boring everybody. Carlino finally told him to save his bragging for the whores in Cayona. Gilbert's not going to tell them about you and he can't do anything really bad to you for it unless they know why. So you're safe."

Dirk grinned. Gilbert would never admit Dirk had beaten him in a fight. He picked up his musket. "Let's go."

Still chuckling, Mic dragged the sleeping bag out through the ycao's drooping branches.

In the following weeks, Dirk and Gilbert did not speak except for the man's orders, screeched in a voice higher pitched and louder than before. Dirk obeyed, but he did not hurry.

Only once, at a kill site after all the others had left, did Gilbert threaten to beat him for working slowly.

Dirk raised an eyebrow. "You'll beat me?"

Gilbert raised a hand. "Strike me and you die."

"But not before I've broken you in front of the others."

With a curse, Gilbert stalked off. Dirk whistled as he hauled the last carcass back to camp.

On the buccaneers' next trip to meet freebooters, Gilbert ordered Dirk to help transport the cured beef to the coast. Dirk sighed. A day in Gilbert's company wouldn't make a heavy bundle of beef any easier to carry. Nevertheless, Dirk picked up his share without grumbling and trotted down the trail after four of the men. He'd left his musket with Mic and felt almost naked without it.

Ansel lit his clay pipe and perched on a piece of driftwood while Fenton haggled with Cor, the freebooter captain, over the price of supplies. Gilbert stalked back and forth near the surf. Bad mood again. Not that he'd ever been pleasant. But since the lad whipped him, Gilbert was down-right evil-tempered.

The lad stood quietly, watching freebooters unload their launch. Gilbert complained about the slow unloading, then slapped Dirk on the head.

"Go help. Hurry things a little."

Dirk smiled slightly at Gilbert. The fool reddened, took a step back. *Must a seen how the lad was looking down at him,* Ansel thought, then coughed on a chuckle. *Should be some action now*. But Dirk finally did go.

Hands fisted, Gilbert watched Dirk and the freebooters for a while, then stomped over to Cor, a large man with a square face that looked even broader with that curly brown beard. Gilbert must have asked why there were only three freebooters this trip instead of the usual four or five.

"Oh, Karel, you mean?" Cor's voice boomed. "That old one died. We haven't found anyone to replace him yet."

Now might be a good time to wander closer, Ansel thought. *Wash m'pipe out in the sea.* Ansel bent into the surf, and listened.

"Would you like to have my boy?"

"That big one over there?" Cor pondered a moment. "He's Dutch, yes?"

At Gilbert's nod, the freebooter said, "I will talk to Theo."

He called to his mate, an older man with a belly paunch. They stood aside, talking rapidly, pointing at Gilbert, then at Dirk. Gilbert fidgeted. Ansel scrubbed his pipe. At last the freebooter returned.

"We'll take him," he said. "How much and for how long?"

"Two hundred pieces of eight. His term of service runs four more years."

Cor frowned and went back to confer with Theo. Ansel straightened and, shaking his pipe, sauntered over to Gilbert. Ansel gestured toward Dirk with the foot-long pipe stem. “Don’t mind the lie about his years of servitude, but you ask that much for a boy who beats his master?”

Gilbert’s mouth opened, but nothing came out.

“Just wondering.” Ansel raised his chin and stepped back a foot or two.

Cor returned, shaking his head. Gilbert glanced at Ansel before answering.

“Well, then, how about ninety pieces of eight for fifteen months?”

“Fifty pieces.”

As Gilbert hesitated, Ansel said, “Worthless lad. Sell him at any price.”

Gilbert hunched his shoulders. “Take him.”

The freebooter shook Gilbert’s hand and counted silver cobs from the pouch at his belt. Ansel raised his chin and drifted on down the beach.

When the buccaneers started their journey back into the hills, Dirk hefted a large box of supplies onto his shoulder. Gilbert ordered him to stay.

One of the freebooters called out in Dutch, “You’re with us now, boy.”

Dirk turned on Gilbert. “You *sold* me?”

“And good riddance.”

Dirk set the box down. He whooped with joy and danced in the sand. He was free of Gilbert forever. No more beatings, nasty glares or slaps on the head. No more insults and humiliating chores. Dirk danced around the buccaneers, shouting good-byes. No more hunting. No more bloody entrails to toss on a smoky boucan. No more endless hours of turning meat and fetching brandy for ungrateful hunters.

Ah, to spend the last fifteen months of his servitude with men who spoke Dutch, to be in the fresh sea air all day. To spend each night in the gentle harbor of Cayona, and maybe the taverns. To live without Gilbert and his viciousness. Without Guy and his stupidity. Without Ansel and his cruel silence.

Dirk's dancing slowed. He'd also have to live without Matt and Fenton and their kindliness. Without tag-along Henry. Without Mic.

Dirk stood silent and still in the sand as the buccaneers disappeared into the forest.

"Oh, Mic, I didn't even bid you farewell."

Cayona's Harbor, 1659

Dirk gulped air into his lungs and dove again, a line clenched in his teeth this time. He went down two fathoms through clear water to the *Annemie*'s anchor. Its chain had snarled around a rock and caught on one of the anchor's arms. Every attempt to raise it had levered the other arm deeper into the sandy bottom.

He slipped the line through a link of the chain, fashioned a knot and gave the line two yanks. It grew taut, then lifted the heavy chain far enough for him to work the links beneath it off the anchor's fluke. Lungs burning, he kicked for the surface. His head broke out into bright sunshine. He gasped for air.

Over on the *Annemie,* Cor shouted, "Is it clear?"

"Ready to raise."

Aboard, Rijk and Theo turned the capstan, walking 'round and 'round it. Tackle creaked, lines strained, and the anchor finally surfaced. The heavy chain dragged in the water as lines hoisted the anchor to the cat-head. It hung there off the larboard bow, dripping water and seaweed, ready to drop at their next anchorage.

Dirk swam over to the bobbing launch and climbed a rope ladder up the side. Cor ordered the mainsail raised, and they sailed out of Cayona's harbor on yet another voyage to Hispaniola. Along with a small fleet of other launches, Dirk's freebooter masters transported supplies to the many groups of buccaneers on Hispaniola. They returned to Tortuga with the hunters' products. It was their third trip today.

Dirk sighed, from boredom rather than unhappiness. The *Annemie* was large for a freebooters' vessel, but still a small area in which to spend most of his waking hours. It had just a single mast, with two triangular sails, the smaller one fixed foreward. There was a deck, with a cargo hold below too small for the four of them to shelter in during bad weather. And the deck was always crowded with boxes, barrels, water casks, plus boucan beef, palm leaf bundles of tallow, and piles of hides, or bottles of brandy and rum, bags of salt, powder and balls for muskets.

The *Annemie*'s three owners were not soft masters, but had been patient while teaching Dirk his new chores. Cor's reasonable commands were delivered in a firm, deep voice so different from Gilbert's angry screeches that Dirk never resented obeying. As soon as he could do his full share of the work, the men bought him breeches and a tunic that fit. And although he went bare-footed most of the time, the men gave him high boots made of leather so soft he could fold the wide tops down according to fashion. They also gave him a few coins each month and allowed him to spend one evening a week on his own in Cayona.

At first Dirk tried to make friends with Rijk, youngest of the three freebooters. The stringy fellow had dirty, yellow hair and smiled often, but never had much to say. He often drank brandy from an onion bottle. Because of Rijk's mild, but daily intoxication, all tasks requiring agility and quick reactions fell to Dirk. He was the one to scramble up and down the mast to untangle halyards or jump into the water to loosen fouled lines.

Cor was friendly enough, but always busy. Theo, on the other hand, required only a simple question from Dirk to launch into elaborate tales. Wiry and strong, Theo was nearly forty, old for a seaman, and his stories reminded Dirk of those he used to hear from sailors at the harbor on Bentyn's Isle.

Born in the Netherlands, Theo had watched the rise of the Dutch East India Company, and once sailed to the Orient on a run to the Spice Islands. He talked of slave trading on the West African coast, and of seeing one of India's kings on his gem-studded throne. He'd spent a short part of his life at the Hague, which housed the States General, and bragged of how the Dutch dared live without a king or queen to rule them.

Theo also talked about a Dutch West India Company settlement far north of the Caribbean. Nieuw Amsterdam, he called it. The name pricked at Dirk's memory until he recalled his father mentioning an older brother or two living there.

Dirk preferred hearing about the clash of empires fought in the Caribbean. He tried to understand why Spaniards would raid Bentyn's Isle and murder everyone they found. Was it only because a hundred years earlier a pope in Rome divided the non-Christian world between Spain and Portugal? Was it because English sea dogs like John Hawkins and Francis Drake weakened Spain's hold on the New World? Was it because the Dutch fought eighty years to win independence from Spain and built an empire of their own? Nothing Theo told Dirk seemed a good enough reason to kill a five year old girl on a small island in the Caribbean Sea.

Thus day after day the freebooters sailed between Tortuga and Hispaniola, while Dirk grew taller, stronger, and impatient to be free. By day he practiced, under Theo's tutelage, with a wooden sword on the launch's moving deck. At night he dreamed of reuniting with Mic and the others, of going on the account as a pirate and finally taking revenge on the Spanish.

Now he sighed again, looking astern at the island of Tortuga growing smaller on the horizon. He'd spent an hour with Marina early this morning, unbeknownst to Pierre, who always slept until midday. She'd met Dirk outside of Cayona, dressed only in a cotton shift and shoes. Her black hair flowed loose to her waist. He chased her along a narrow rocky path, helping her over boulders and trying to kiss her on their way to the east coast of the island.

She let him catch her at a place where the low tide left a strip of sand just eight feet wide and a tidal pool of clear water. Dirk leaped down into the tiny cove, then reached up for Marina, letting her body slide down his to the sand. Laughing, and still panting from their run, they tore off shoes and boots, then tunic and shift and breeches. They came together quickly, surrounded by rocks that sheltered them from people, hot morning sun, and even the roar of the surf.

They finished much too soon, then sat on their crumpled clothes with their feet in the little pool and talked. There was nothing in life better than tumbling, Dirk thought, but he enjoyed her stories, too.

"My parents put me into service at the manor house beyond the next village," she said. "I was lucky they took me at seven. But then the old master died, and the new young one gambled everything away in just two years. I was thirteen by then, and there were other ways to earn more than I ever could in service.

"So Father took me to Nantes and hired me to Pierre. He was supposed to send my earnings to my parents. I think he did for a while, but then he brought me here. He probably doesn't send my money to France anymore."

"Do you miss your family?"

"I miss the manor house more. I got enough to eat and slept on a pallet near the kitchen fire. And nobody beat me much."

"Do you ever dream of something else?"

"Of something other than being a doxy on a rocky island on the back side of the world?" She laughed. "Peasant girls from starving families don't dream of anything but food and a dry place to sleep."

Dirk thought about that. Only once had he been truly hungry, and always he'd had a future to plan.

"When I'm a pirate, I'll win a fortune and come for you. I'll fight Pierre for you."

She grinned at him, and patted his cheek. The gesture made him feel like a child.

"But I'm not so miserable here," she said. "At least Pierre feeds me. And the chances of finding a husband are better here than even in Paris."

Dirk lay back on their clothes and pulled her down on top of him. He kissed her and stroked her buttocks.

"Will your husband let me do this?"

Her laughter was hot and soft on his neck. "Certainly not. So make it good now."

Afterward, he'd given her what coins he had. There weren't many, but at least she didn't have to share them with Pierre.

Hours later, on the *Annemie*, he decided yet again that his time with Marina wasn't enough. He ached with desire and almost groaned. Then he turned foreward, looking out over the bow at Hispaniola looming on the southern horizon. He wondered what Mic was doing, and how the hunting group fared. For weeks after he was sold to the freebooters, Dirk had awakened full of things to tell Mic. But in eleven months of landing on the beach at Hispaniola at least three times a day, Dirk hadn't seen Mic or any others from their group.

"Dirk!"

He turned just as Theo tossed a wooden sword at his feet. Dirk grinned. The freebooters possessed but one saber among them, and Cor had fashioned a wooden one for Dirk. It was heavy, rough, and left splinters in his palm, but he welcomed the chance to practice this vital skill for his future pirating. And despite the heat he wanted something to break the tedium of the trip.

Dirk hopped up, sword in hand, for another lesson in handystrokes. Theo pursued him across the tiny deck, over lines, around water casks. Dirk leaped onto a crate, and for a few moments enjoyed the advantage of height. Then Cor jerked the tiller over, which surprised Dirk as there was a fine, steady northeasterly wind. Before he reacted, the boom came about and swept him off the crate. He caught the boom with one arm and worked a leg over it, howling as he swung out over the waves. The men laughed, and as Cor brought the boat in line with the sail, Dirk swung back. Theo knocked the wooden sword out of his hand and overboard.

When the boom passed over the boat again, Dirk dropped onto the deck, angry and puzzled. His masters had never played tricks on him before. Then, as all three men stood grinning at him, Rijk tossed him a long, hide-covered bundle. The sails filled again, the boat heeled, and Dirk unrolled the hide cover to find a saber.

It was old, the blade nicked and even bent a little near the point. The hand guard was cracked. But it was steel, and it flashed in the sunshine as Dirk whooped and thrust it skyward. It felt like a feather in his hand. He looked at the men again. They grinned, and he didn't know what to say.

"A crew of four men needs more than one blade," Theo said. He leaped at Dirk with the crew's other saber. "And you need practice, lad, or the first time you try to imitate a pirate, you'll lose your head. Look alive!"

Dirk laughed, parried Theo's saber aside with a satisfying crack of steel on steel, and the lesson resumed. They jumped on and off crates, danced around the mast and anchor capstan, hopped over lines, ducked behind water barrels. The saber felt glorious in Dirk's hand, less a weapon than an extension of his arm.

When Theo finally called a halt to the handystrokes, Dirk collapsed against a rail, wondering yet again how such an old man like Theo could be so nimble and have so much stamina. The fellow was barely breathing hard, while Dirk's chest heaved for air. He bled a little, too, from the nicks and scratches where Theo's blade had caught him.

When he stopped panting, Dirk gazed foreward, startled to see they had reached Hispaniola already. It was time to lower the sail and drop anchor in shallow water. Then Dirk swam a line ashore and tied the boat to a palm tree. After unloading most of the cargo, he lifted an empty water cask onto his shoulder and trotted off to a freshwater stream a short way from the beach. There he washed out his clothes before scrubbing himself clean of the dried sweat and seawater that felt so heavy on his skin.

Dressed again, he carried the filled cask back to the beach. And there, among the freebooters and buccaneers haggling over prices, stood Mic.

"Mic!"

At Dirk's shout, Mic turned and ran to him. Dirk set the cask down and punched his matelot on the shoulder.

"You're bigger," Mic said. "And is that a beard?"

Dirk rubbed his hand across sparse whiskers. "Yes, finally. And where's yours?"

Mic just grinned.

"Tell me. How's the hunt this year?"

"The same," Mic said. "Guy is still stupid, Ansel still quiet. Matt and Fenton are skinny as ever. You can see for yourself."

Dirk glanced over the sand at the two men. They returned his wave.

"How's Henry?"

Mic hesitated. "He's dead. A Spanish patrol raided the camp about a month ago."

Dirk shut his eyes and took a deep breath. "The Spanish have so much to pay for."

"They killed Gilbert, too."

"I'm not sorry for that."

"Nobody was. He made such a pest of himself the last few months. Always bragging, but never doing much. And after Gilbert died, Ansel told everyone about you beating him bloody. We all laughed about his story of the bull attack."

"Good."

Mic nodded toward Cor and Rijk who were loading boucan and hides into the boat.

"Do the freebooters work you hard?

"The work hardens my muscles, but I don't ache all the time. There's not much to do but load and unload cargo. And I'd better start doing it now."

Mic helped Dirk tote loads of beef and tallow through the surf to the boat.

"Have you seen the others?" Mic asked. "Anything of the twins? Baldric?"

"Nothing of Baldric, but I saw the twins for a few minutes a couple of months ago." Dirk chuckled. "I found them in a grog shop. Just as they were telling me about a beautiful woman and all her charms, the door banged open and a big man stomped in. Jan and Joost jumped up, shouted, 'That's him! The husband!' and ran out the back door. The man ran after them, and I never did learn who bought them or where they lived."

Mic laughed. "The twins haven't changed."

"Naw, they're just bigger." Dirk grinned. "Four more months, and we'll be meeting at the fort in Cayona."

"It's hard to believe seven years are almost over." Mic said quietly, then smiled. "I'll bring your musket."

In the last hour of daylight, the *Annemie* sailed for Tortuga. The men were quiet. Dirk lounged against a pile of hides, his hand resting on the crew's new saber.

Four months and he'd be free. Four months and he'd be his own master. He would find a pirate ship at once, and finally make the Spanish suffer for what they'd done to his family.

The boat crested a wave and Dirk saw a few lanterns from Cayona. He recalled the first time he and his friends approached the harbor with no idea of what lay ahead. Now, after so many years, they all would be together again. If they returned to the fort in a few months as they promised. If they were all still alive by then.

The twins had always been lucky, and at least were together, but Baldric....

Baldric's buccaneer master was a quiet loner. He never gave his name, nor did he ever use Baldric's. The man took him to Hispaniola the day of the auction, loaded him down with bundles, then strode off toward the hills. Baldric stumbled along as fast as he could. When he tripped over a stone and fell, the man jerked him to his feet and waved the indenture papers in his face. When his eyes filled with tears, the man slapped him, then resumed walking. Baldric ran to keep up with him.

Baldric was too frightened to run away, even when he found chances during the next few months. He didn't know how to live in the forest by himself and he didn't know where anybody else was. He sobbed for his parents in the night and day-dreamed of being with Dirk again. Most of his hair fell out and his clothes sagged. He saw his reflection in a pool once. Deep, purple-black shadows encircled his eyes and he looked like a tiny, old man. The master cursed him for his ill health.

Finally, Baldric could not bear to think of his family anymore, nor to dream of a reunion with the other boys. So he stopped thinking, and concentrated on whatever task the master gave him. He avoided beatings that way, and his pain dwindled to an ache that dulled with time.

After eight months of fresh air, ample food and exercise, his hair grew in blacker than before. His body filled out; muscles rounded off the sharp bones. But the dark circles around his eyes remained and no matter how many different pools he stared into, he never lost the visage of an old man.

At the end of the first year, the master took him to Tortuga. Baldric hoped to see one of his friends, but when he didn't, refused to feel any disappointment. Back on Hispaniola, he stopped longing for the company of others. The master avoided other buccaneer groups, so the two wandered by themselves over the mountains, hunting both cattle and wild pigs. Most of the money earned was used for supplies.

They spent evenings around the boucan, silently feeding entrails and hooves into the blaze. Baldric mended clothes and whittled, while the master stared at the fire or out into the darkness, listening for danger. Sometimes he'd signal to Baldric and they'd fade into the forest, leaving everything but their weapons for nighttime raiders.

One night soon after their second yearly trip to Tortuga, the man signaled and they slipped into the woods. Baldric crouched behind a bush, waiting for raiders to appear. He didn't hear anything, but his ears weren't as well trained as the master's.

A hand clamped on his shoulder. Baldric turned, knife in hand. It was the master, but with an odd expression on his face. The man never touched him except to cuff his ears or teach a skill. What had he done to deserve a beating this time?

The master took the knife away, ran his hands over Baldric once and shoved him face down over a fallen tree. He struggled to breathe; he tried to get up. The master clouted him on the side of the head and Baldric fell over, dizzy. The master jerked his breeches down. Pain ripped through him, tearing him apart. A hand filthy with dried muck and blood stifled his scream. He couldn't breathe and the tree bark tore at his bare legs and belly and he burned and bled and knew the pain would go on forever.

The master walked back to the fire. Baldric lay on the ground, biting off sobs.

In the morning he limped around the campsite doing his chores. The master's gaze followed him, and he shivered. For three days, Baldric vomited whenever he thought about the assault. Then it too faded into numbness. Although the master assaulted him every week or two, Baldric refused to let it touch him.

During their next trip to Tortuga, the master once more spent just a day there buying supplies. Baldric followed him through the busy town, seeing men all over Cayona tumble doxies on the beach, in alleyways, even propped against walls or trees. Why had the master chosen a boy when women were so easy to find?

Although Baldric didn't grow tall, his body developed quickly and proportionately, without the usual clumsiness of rapid growth. At age twelve, in his fourth year of servitude, his voice dropped, and the master did not touch him again.

Then the master bought him a musket. It was smaller than the usual buccaneer models, but it had come from Nantes. When Baldric picked it up the first time, his stomach tightened and he found it hard to breathe. He felt something—pride, joy, or something—but he fought the sensation. After all, the master could take the musket away from him, and he would have to suffer the pain of loss once more.

Even so, the musket became the center of Baldric's life. He practiced with it until he could shoot a twig off a faraway branch and kill charging bulls with a single shot. He polished it every night, taking it apart and reassembling it, often fixing it in the dark. He became quicker than the master at loading the weapon. He did not count the years remaining in his indenture, or think of Dirk and the other boys. There were only his chores, the hunting, and his musket.

One bright morning, they came across a lone sow in a large meadow. The master shot her and quickly set about the butchering. Baldric sat on a boulder nearby to keep watch. Across his knee lay the musket, primed for firing.

A boar squealed from the edge of the clearing, its nostrils flared and sharp tusks weaving from side to side. The master raised an arm and shouted, but instead of running off, the hog merely snorted. The man reached for his musket and powder bag. The boar squealed and charged. The master dropped everything and ran.

Baldric already had his musket to his shoulder, aimed at the path his master would run. The man swerved, fleeing across the clearing, leaving Baldric an open shot. He sighted down the barrel, following the charging boar. The master cried out, shouting for him to fire. Baldric shifted his aim, held his breath, and fired.

The master crumpled as the shot mangled his hip. The boar dove into him, tusks ripping through flesh. Screams filled the beautiful, still morning. Baldric reloaded his musket. When the man stopped screaming and the boar raised his bloodied snout in triumph, Baldric fired again. The boar dropped.

Baldric sat on the boulder a long time. He gazed at the deep greens of the forest. The air smelled sweet. The rock beneath him grew hot in the sun. Flies buzzed around the bodies of man and hogs. Baldric felt no sorrow for his deed, nor any relief from his anger.

That night he cured fresh pork over a boucan and fed the master's body into the flames along with pig entrails.

For the next year Baldric hunted alone, avoiding buccaneers who might question the master's whereabouts. He sold his beef and pork to freebooters and bought from them all the supplies he needed.

On a grey overcast morning in his fourteenth year, Baldric found a destroyed buccaneer camp. Silence hung over the place. Bodies of brethren lay scattered about, one across the boucan, three in a jumble with broken lances. The hunting mastiffs had been slaughtered as well.

Baldric slipped into the clearing, alert for sounds of raiders who might still be nearby. He heard only the drone of hundreds of flies and insects. Coals under the boucan were cold. Working his way around the campsite, he looked for anything he could use.

As he knelt to search a buccaneer's belt pouch, something brushed his leg. He jumped, fell on his rump, and kicked at the small brown and black beast that had startled him. With a yip and a squeaky growl, it bit his leg.

It was a puppy. He shook his leg. The puppy held on, either stubborn or caught by the teeth in his leggings. Cursing, Baldric took a piece of dried meat out of his pouch and bribed her loose. He doubted she could eat it with her milk-teeth, but at least he was free to finish his search.

There was nothing. The Spaniards had taken their own dead as well as everything of value. Baldric kicked dirt at the boucan and strode away from the camp. He had not expected to be lucky.

A little way down the path he felt the presence of something alive behind him. He turned and leaped to the side of the trail, musket ready to fire. Here came the puppy, stubby legs almost a blur as she ran along the path after him, the meat still in her mouth. He stuck out a foot. She shied away and sat down.

When Baldric walked, she followed. He turned back once more, picked up a stick and swung at her. She rolled onto her back, waving her paws.

"Oh, hell." He threw the stick down and walked on.

The puppy trailed him all day. That night he tossed her a piece of fresh meat. When he went to sleep she lay on the opposite side of the fire. In the morning he found her curled up between his ear and shoulder. He nudged her awake. She stretched and yawned, then licked his nose. He raised a hand, she jumped at it, and he laughed.

He cut off the strange noise. He hadn't laughed in five years. He tried it again. And again. He and the puppy wrestled, yips and giggles filling the air.

One night a few weeks later, he let himself remember his family and all he'd lost on Bentyn's Isle. He cried into the puppy's fur. She trembled with his sobs, but never moved away. Two months after that, he let himself think of being with Dirk again, of the adventures they might have with Jan and Joost and Mic. He would see them in less than a year.

On the first day of what he believed to be his official freedom, Baldric sailed by freebooters' launch to Tortuga. He carried his weapons, indenture papers, and all the coins he and the master had saved. That night he tried to have a drink in every grog shop and tavern in Cayona.

When the sun rose, he lay collapsed against the rear steps of a punch house. The dog sat beside him, probably the only reason no one had robbed him during the night. He'd made his way through only eight of Cayona's taverns. Still determined to visit every one, he spent the better part of a week doing it.

Then he decided to do the same with all the doxies. His first experience was over before he knew what was happening. So was the second. The third time that night took longer and afterwards he sat beneath a palm tree and discussed it with his dog. He'd had enough, and could live without women quite nicely. It was a sad business, the way men spent great amounts of money, won with such risk to their lives, on an experience of so little consequence.

The next night, after a bit of brandy, Baldric changed his mind. By the time the money ran out two weeks later, he'd bedded twenty-three doxies.

He hired on as helper in a leather shop near the fort, and convinced an old pirate to give him lessons with a sword. Every moment possible, Baldric watched the fort for one of the others from Bentyn's Isle.

Tortuga, 1660

Bright tones from a flute and harp danced in the air over the mellow notes of a guitar. On the tavern's center table, a copper-skinned serving wench swirled her multi-colored skirts in time to the music. Loud talk and laughter, punctuated by angry shouts, filled La Cave au Diable.

Dirk sat at a rough table toward the back of the room eating roasted beef off his knife. Ale drunk from pewter tankards gave his body a warm glow and softened the din in his ears. Baldric, with a hunting mastiff at his feet, lounged beside him; across from them the twins each held a woman on his knee.

As of two days ago, Dirk was a free man, eighteen years old with health and strength intact, a beard on his chin, and coins chinking in a pouch at his belt. Last week he'd found Baldric working in a small leather shop near Fort Rocher, and just this evening the twins had arrived at the fort. They waited a short while for Mic, but at dusk the taverns called. Dirk tacked a note for Mic on a tree below the fort's entrance before following the others to La Cave au Diable

Dirk reached for more of the soft wheaten bread heaped in a basket on the table. Life was good at the moment, but not complete. Marina had recently married a wealthy planter from Trinidad. Dirk was glad she had settled so well, but he missed his friend and playmate. And Mic had not yet arrived. There was the possibility that he never would. Many things could have happened to him in the past four months since Dirk had seen him last. Dirk would not feel himself completely free of the world of buccaneers until Mic, too, was free of it.

But at least the other three were with him again. The twins hadn't changed much, except for their size. Their bright blond hair had darkened a little, and Jan looked a bit more boyish, perhaps because Joost's face appeared slightly longer and he'd lost one of his dimples. Both were still handsome devils who, at the moment, were well on their way to charming the wenches out of their clothes.

"Where have you been all these years?" Baldric asked them. "Who bought you?"

Baldric's lined, swarthy skin and purple under-eye smudges implied a long, troubled life, but his voice still sounded like the sixteen year old he was. Dirk twitched at the contrast.

"A couple of chasseurs," Jan said.

Dirk laughed. "You chased pigs for seven years?"

Joost looked up from nibbling his companion's bare shoulder. "Pigs. And women. Lots of women."

"You had two masters?" Baldric asked. "Did they beat you often?"

"Naw," Jan said. "They used to brag about owning twins. And most of the time, if one of us got caught at something, we could convince 'em to blame the other."

Joost laughed. "Only one time we confused 'em so much they beat us both. But mostly they thrashed us only for fighting."

Joost punched Jan's shoulder. Jan toppled over slowly, taking the wench on his lap with him to the dirt floor. She squealed as he wrestled her down and drew a finger across her throat. Men at nearby tables laughed.

"We were great pig hunters," Jan said. "But nothing tastes as good as a woman."

The woman giggled and squirmed as he buried his face in her bosom.

No, the twins hadn't changed much at all. Baldric, on the other hand, had changed a lot. Dirk watched his friend drop a hunk of meat onto the dirt floor for the dog. Though still smaller than the twins, Baldric's shoulders had rounded with muscles and his arms looked hard and strong. Yet there was something more, and it occurred to Dirk a few minutes later that Baldric had no fear. He sat quietly and gazed about as if nothing in the world could frighten him. Dirk turned to ask what had happened to make him that way, and caught sight of Mic in the doorway.

A musket case in each hand, Mic stood surveying the tavern. At Dirk's wave, he hurled one of the muskets across the small room. Dirk rose, caught it, and Mic squeezed through the crowd to the table.

Dirk gave Mic a punch on the upper arm, received one in return. As he sat down the last of his concerns faded away, to be replaced by the glow of contentment. He'd soon be raiding the Spanish Main and making Spaniards miserable. With friends, his musket, and the new cutlass Theo, Rijk, and Cor had given him as a parting gift, life was grand. And especially good tonight.

Grinning, Dirk tugged a passing woman onto his lap. She struggled, but laughed as she did so. And then he didn't know which was better: his hands on her, or hers on him.

The notice nailed to a tree near Fort Rocher had been issued by the Council of Jamaica. It proclaimed, in French, English, Spanish and Dutch:

The Island of Jamaica will grant to Privateers Letters of Marque against the Spanish for the following reasons:

Privateers make many commodities available to the people at low prices.

The poorer plantations survive by supplying the privateer ships.

Privateering keeps many artisans busy at high wages.

The tax revenue from the sale of booty, sent to the king, is large.

Privateering increases the slave trade and thereby enriches the plantations.

Privateering replenishes the island's supply of coin, bullion, cocoa and indigo, and brings New Englanders and their products for trade.

Support of privateering is the only way to keep the buccaneers and pirates from becoming the enemy of Port Royal and sacking the colony.

Dirk read the notice twice, then turned to Mic and Baldric. "Maybe we should go there. I haven't seen a pirate ship here in the harbor all week."

"Our money's about gone." Mic hooked his left thumb in his belt and splayed his fingers over the coin pouch hanging from it.

"Fenton used to say no true buccaneer ever went on the account with a single coin in his pocket," Dirk said.

"We're not spending all of this." Mic's fingers tapped the coin pouch. "So we have to do something soon, unless you want to freeboot trade between islands."

"I don't."

"Or go back to hunting on Hispaniola."

"Not even as a free man." Dirk looked at Baldric. "Jamaica's an English colony now. Do you want to learn another language?"

Baldric shrugged. "Wherever you plan to go. I can learn English."

"Let's find the twins and see if they agree." Dirk headed downhill.

Baldric laughed. "Don't ask them to decide. Just promise them liquor and women."

The freebooters' launch sailed by a small stone fort on the tip of Port Royal's cay.

"Good Lord Almighty," Mic said. "There must be two dozen guns on those walls. All aimed at us."

The freebooter working the tiller chuckled. "There are fifteen or so guard ships around here, too, somewhere. Nobody gets into that harbor without the governor's permission."

"I've heard it's the wickedest city in the world," Dirk said.

"And the richest." Mic leaned out over the bow to see better.

"'Tis both," the freebooter said. "You've not been here before?"

When they shook their heads, he grinned. "You'll never see another city like it. The soil is barren and there's no sweet water. If it weren't for the privateers and contraband traders, Port Royal wouldn't even exist. Except as a fort, maybe. But it's the richest city in the Americas, all right, with trade from everywhere. Mostly stolen, so profits are high.

He thought a moment and continued. "And I suppose it's the wickedest, too. Folks say so, anyway, and we do have prisons. Even one for women. But we have churches, too. A lot of 'em. Though I don't suppose that'll help much. The religious men say Port Royal is going to be destroyed by the hand of God someday soon."

"Not today, I hope," Dirk said.

"Don't think so. Not today."

The launch slipped into a harbor almost closed off from the sea. Over a hundred ships rode at anchor in the deep water and shark fins were circling everywhere. Two forts built on high ground trained polished ordnance onto the bay. Dirk smiled. He would sleep soundly in this colony.

As the launch maneuvered past ships, the city came into view. At the water's edge, shacks had been built atop pilings driven into the sand. Other houses on the hillside stood four stories high, and every inch of space in between was filled with shops or people or animals.

When the launch bumped against the wharf, the freebooter said, "Out, and be quick. Damned wharfage rates are so high we can't afford to be here long."

"Where do you anchor?" Dirk swung over the side after the others.

"North side of the harbor." The man tied up his boat and hustled to unload the cargo.

Mic elbowed Dirk and pointed. "That's why the sharks are here."

Three fishmongers tossed bloody scraps into water churning with black and grey bodies. Dirk shivered, then stepped off the wharf into the mêlée of Port Royal. For a moment he stood still in the blazing afternoon sun, unsure of where to go. Then passersby nudged and bumped him into moving on.

For a while the five Dutchmen stayed near the wharf, fascinated by the energetic commerce. Shingles, flour, and dried and pickled meats from New England were traded for rum, sugar, molasses, spices, indigo, and mahogany. Large ships from England unloaded their cargoes of cloth, tools, glass and paper into single-sail boats. A one-legged, one-eared fellow perched on a barrel told them those small boats were bound for night-time visits to towns on the Spanish Main.

Mic lingered near traders, listening to them dicker and discuss profits, while Jan and Joost edged into the city. Rather than let the group separate, Dirk pulled Mic along after the twins. Baldric and his dog followed.

They wandered through narrow streets and crowded lanes where Spanish coins circulated freely. Housewives and servants jostled them in the rank fish, meat and vegetable markets. Children of all shades from beige to copper to ebony roamed everywhere, running, playing, and picking pockets. Booth merchants sold silks from the Orient, laces from Europe, and gold and silver ornaments that carried the seal of the king of Spain. Buyers competed for pearls, emeralds, brocades, and chalices from Spanish churches. People conducted their quarrels, gossip and haggling in more languages than Dirk could count. Patrols of militiamen marched through the streets arresting loud drunks and men who were fighting.

In a quieter area, they found St. Paul's Church of England, and agreed it was the largest and most impressive building in the city, although the royal Customs House was nearly as big. They also found a Jewish Synagogue, a Presbyterian Church, a Quaker Meeting House, and a Catholic Chapel tucked away in various neighborhoods.

The wealth of Port Royal included high prices, however. Slaves cost 100 pieces of eight or more. The price of a doxy was even higher, sometimes 500 pieces of eight for a night. The English Crown had a monopoly on brandy, and the Dutchmen were forced to drink rum and ale. Mic refused to part with any more coins than necessary for a light supper in a grog shop.

At nightfall, shops closed and booths emptied. For a short time the streets were quiet. Then scarred, well-armed men in ragged, briney clothes wandered into town, rubbing the sleep out of their eyes. The lanes grew ever more crowded. It seemed to Dirk that half the city's buildings were taverns, grog shops or punch houses, and by full dark every one of them was filled with seafarers. Music from the taverns grew loud, and quarrels both playful and deadly spilled out into the streets.

Jan and Joost charged into one punch house and grog shop after another, claiming each time to have found the best in Port Royal. Dirk, Mic, and Baldric followed, hauling the twins out of trouble before it started. Sometime after midnight they all left the rowdiness to sleep under a shoreside house, just out of reach of the tide.

The next morning, in search of a pirate crew to join, they followed the shoreline of the harbor, wandering among the hundreds of men who slumbered in hammocks strung between palms. Dirk found several crews that would welcome him and the others. One captain noted their unbleached tunics and short breeches.

"We always take on buccaneers," he said. "You're near always healthy and strong. Loyal, too." He grinned. "And we could sure use your skill with muskets and blades."

Though flattered, Dirk was unable to choose among the various crews. So at midday, the five trooped back into town for lunch.

On Lime Street, they found a taphouse owned by a stout Dutchman named Willem. Bustling with cheerful efficiency, the place boasted a plank floor worn smooth by frequent scrubbings, and clean linens on the beds upstairs. Seated with the others at a wooden table near the front door, Dirk watched the busyness of Port Royal while gobbling roasted pork basted in pimento sauce, baked maize drizzled with honey, and fresh wheat bread. It was all served with ale and beer far superior to the veycou buccaneers drank when they ran out of brandy, or the banana liquor not even Ansel would drink undiluted.

Comfortable amidst Dutch speakers and feeling safe from the Spanish, Dirk relaxed. This city, and perhaps this very taphouse, would be their new home. All he had to do was find a pirate crew for them to join.

That afternoon, Dirk trudged the water's edge alone and found what he was looking for: a sleek schooner with a large, experienced crew. He stood a long time gazing at the ship anchored twenty yards from shore. This was a vessel fit for raiding the Spanish Main.

Mic had gone off, also seeking a ship, but Dirk dragged the three others out of Willem's taphouse and down the beach for a look at the schooner. He was describing the crew when Mic ran up.

"I found our ship," Dirk said.

Mic gave the schooner a quick glance. "I found something better." He tugged at Dirk's arm. "You have to see this."

Grumbling, Dirk and the others followed Mic along the shore to where a piragua had been beached. Seven men sat nearby throwing dice.

"There."

Dirk stared at a canoe hollowed out of the trunk of a huge cedar tree. A tattered sail hung limp on the single, wobbly mast. He looked at Mic. "This?"

"Yes." Mic grinned.

Jan snickered. "I remember sailing in a canoe before. We didn't get rich in it."

Joost elbowed him. "Be quiet. Mic's serious."

They laughed.

"Now listen," Mic said. "Those men own this piragua, but don't have money to provision it. So they offered to sell us half the vessel, and only for what we have left in our reserve."

"I don't want to own half a canoe," Baldric said.

"Dirk, you know that after a raid the prize is divided into shares and every man gets one. The officers get extra." Mic's voice rose. "And the owners of the vessel get forty!"

Dirk frowned.

"Don't you see? If we own half the ship—"

"It's only a canoe," Jan said between giggles.

Mic turned his back on the twins. "If we own half the ship we'll get half the owners' shares. That's twenty. Four for each of us. With our share for fighting, too, that means we get five shares for each raid. Even the captain only gets two."

Dirk understood the mathematics of it, but shook his head.

"There are five of us and seven of them," he said. "What can we win with just twelve men? What good are five shares of nothing?"

Mic waved a hand at the dice players. "They said they used to win a lot with just fourteen men."

"Fourteen? What happened to the rest of the crew?"

"Oh, they died in a raid."

Dirk raised his eyebrows. *Half the crew died in a raid? Do I want to sail with these men?*

"They said we'll take on more men when we have a ship."

"And how do they plan to get this ship?" Dirk asked.

"They said the Spanish will give us one."

"What?"

Mic grinned. "We'll steal a ship."

Dirk pondered this for a while, staring at the ground, then looked up. Mic was rocking from one foot to the other. Baldric scratched his dog's head. The twins were watching a girl walk along the path into town. Finally Mic stopped fidgeting and put his fists on his hips.

"You'll have more freedom in a smaller crew, Dirk. And as an owner, you'll have more say in what we do."

Dirk turned to gaze once more at the schooner. *Such a beautiful ship*. Then he looked at the dugout, and saw freedom and power. He nodded. "We'll buy into the piragua."

The Spaniards gave them a ship.

After fifteen miserable days cramped in the piragua, eating turtles, drinking putrid water, and learning the names, quirks, and stink of his new crewmates, Dirk was tempted to resume buccaneering. But finally, along the western coast of Puerto Rico, they spied lugsails on the horizon.

They followed, and within a day had drawn near enough to see the ship. It rode low in the water, suggesting a heavy cargo, and in the light wind it could not outrun the piragua. For two days they trailed in the ship's wake, just out of range of the lone swivel gun mounted on the stern.

During the third night, the wind died and the piragua closed in with oars. By morning it was riding safely beneath the stern gun's line of fire. With grappling hooks and boarding pikes, the pirates climbed the lugger's stern and broke into the single cabin. Three of the merchant crew died in the short, hard fight. The other eleven were tossed overboard near land. Tying the piragua to the stern, the pirates set sail for Port Royal.

Thanks to Mic's foresight, Dirk was now part-owner of a fine, three-masted vessel. It was flush-decked for action at sea, and narrow enough to navigate small rivers where a Spanish Man of War could not follow. With its four-cornered, boomless lugsails, the ship was swift, easily maneuvered, and his crew mates said it could out-sail almost any other vessel afloat.

Even better, the hold was nearly full of useable ropes, nails, candles, pots, wine, sails, and wood for the cook's stove. The rest of the cargo—bales of linen and cotton, a few silks and brocades, a heavy necklace of gem-encrusted silver, gold dust, and even a pouch of silver reales— would be sold. All the way home Dirk sat in the bow, grinning.

Back in Port Royal, the crew renamed the ship the *Avenger* and divided the booty. There wasn't much for each man beyond the items needed for the next voyage. Dirk used part of his small share for a brace of pistols to carry in his belt. He threw away the brimless cap he'd worn as a buccaneer and bought a yellow silk scarf to wind over his head. Then, because the older men swore it would improve his eyesight, Dirk had Baldric pierce his left ear for a slender gold hoop.

The *Avenger*'s twelve owners drew up Articles of Regulation outlining rules for life aboard and for dividing future spoils. They swore to the Articles on a Bible, then recruited more pirates. When the crew totaled thirty, they elected a captain. Though neither big nor loud, Addison was twenty-five, experienced, spoke Spanish, and had shown confidence and common sense during the fight for the lugger. Dirk found him easy to like and respect.

The crew also elected as quartermaster a swarthy, average-sized man with quick dark eyes and a manner that implied he'd always be ready for anything. Then a navigator, sailmaster, gunner, boatswain, and carpenter were chosen on the strength of demonstrated skills. Zeke, a former slave missing half his right foot, offered to be cook. At the last moment, a blustery man named Ogden, who claimed to have medical knowledge, signed the Articles and was elected surgeon.

Perry, the new quartermaster, took five men into Port Royal's markets for supplies. When they returned two hours later, Addison held a conference. Halsey, a scrawny little man with dirty brown hair and a quick grin too wide for his face, knew of a town on the east coast of Santo Domingo that would make a good prize.

"There's a tiny pearl fishery in the harbor," he said. "Few know of it, but it yields a good amount of pearls."

"Aren't they sold immediately?" Mic asked.

"Naw. They're hoarded for a year or two, and then shipped to Spain." Halsey's grin spread almost to his ears. "For the king's pleasure."

Dunstan laughed, his drink-reddened face growing even darker. A great, paunchy man with a voice to match, he drowned out all conversation. "It's bound to be an easy prize, then." He waved his arms as he spoke, popping stitches in the back and shoulder seams of his velvet surcoat. "Those Spanish never fight hard for the king's property."

Addison sat with one hand on his stomach, rubbed his chin with the other. "Where are the pearls kept?"

"In the alcalde's house," Halsey said.

"How do you know this?" Dirk asked.

A shadow crossed Halsey's narrow face. "I was a slave in that house. Just escaped a few months ago."

Mutters and curses rose from the crew. The target had been chosen.

Three days later Dirk sat cross-legged with the others in a loose circle on the deck, passing bottles of brandy hand to hand. The liquor warmed his muscles, and he felt the same hot excitement he'd felt as a child when he and his gang were in the middle of an escapade.

"The treasure there will make us all rich." Addison's voice carried over the rowdy conversations. "The Spanish don't deserve to keep what the sea provides. They'll put those pearls on graven images. And remember what they did to our brother Halsey, here. They took a free Englishman and made him a slave."

The pirates roared. Dirk hefted his cutlass. Perhaps he would finally kill a Spaniard tonight.

Close by, Baldric scratched a spot behind the ear of his dog, long since rescued from Willem's younger son, Arvie. The six year old had cared for the dog at the taphouse while Baldric, silent and morose, sailed on the piragua.

Mic also appeared unmoved by the growing rowdiness of the crew. Yet Dirk recognized the flicker of anticipation in his pale eyes. Behind Mic, the twins bickered over how much brandy Jan should risk drinking. This raid felt so much like their childhood pranks, those adventures might have been practice for this night.

Addison restricted the flow of brandy. The rowdiness subsided, though Dirk could sense the men's eagerness to attack. Their anger and greed were suppressed only deep enough to build into frenzy.

Shortly after dark, the *Avenger* entered an inlet and that frenzy exploded. Dirk had no time for doubts or fear as he scrambled over the side and landed hard on the end of a short, wooden dock lined with fishing boats. He ran with the others down a narrow dirt street into the village plaza, the pirates' collective energy pumping through his own muscles. War cries from many homelands filled the air. It was time to wreck havoc in Spanish lives.

Pirates scattered in all directions, torches lighting the way. Dunstan led three men toward the little, mud brick church and, after a moment's hesitation, Mic followed.

"This way," Dirk called to Baldric and the twins. They joined those running after Halsey.

At the entrance to the largest house on the plaza, tall, dark-skinned Talbot engaged a solitary guard while the rest battered in the door with clubs and kicks. Swept along by the crowd pouring inside, Dirk lost track of the twins. Baldric remained at his elbow as they followed Addison, Perry and Halsey across a patio.

"That's the room!" Halsey pointed toward a carved wooden door. "That's where the alcalde sleeps, the bastard!"

Dirk burst through the door; pirates fanned out beside him. The room was lit by two wall lanterns. The elderly alcalde, dressed in a night shirt and clutching a saber, stood by a massive mahogany bed. In the next chamber a woman screamed. The alcalde waved his blade. With a flash of cutlass, Addison knocked the saber into a corner. Halsey scurried over to hold a knife at the alcalde's throat.

"Remember me, you papist scum?" he asked in Spanish.

The gentleman nodded, his long, white hair spilling out of a linen night cap.

"Didn't I warn you about enslaving good Englishmen?"

"*Sí.*" The man coughed, his gaze riveted to the door of the adjoining room where the woman was still screaming.

Perry jabbed his knife at the alcalde. "We want the pearls!" he said, also in Spanish, "or we'll have your ears."

The elderly man protested weakly until the knife pricked his earlobe. He gestured toward the bed. "There."

Halsey dove under the bed. "Nothing."

Perry sliced the alcalde's earlobe. Between moans came, "The bedpost."

"Pull those posts out," Addison said. "If they don't come easy, find an axe."

Halsey and Baldric worked at the posts. Addison tested the latch on the door to the next room. The alcalde cried out and lunged feebly toward Addison. Dirk shoved him back.

Addison held out his hand. "The key."

"My wife, if you harm my wife—"

Perry slapped his forehead. "Pay attention. The key."

Glaring at Addison, the alcalde tugged a thin gold chain around his neck. Perry snapped the chain and tossed the key to Addison. Certain that Perry, Halsey and Baldric needed no help, Dirk followed Addison into the other room.

The alcalde's wife was young, and pretty, too, with hair that shone red in the lamplight. Dirk kicked the door shut.

She stopped screaming and panted as she looked from Addison to Dirk and back again. Then she beseeched God for a quick death before the inevitable rape. She also demanded that God let her live long enough to see the pirates drawn and quartered for the deed.

Dirk bit his lip on a smile and leaned against the door as Addison walked to the bed, raising his cutlass. The woman shrank into her pillows. With the blade's tip, Addison whisked the bedcovers out of her hands. She snatched at them, but the cutlass point touched her throat. She raised her chin, blinking rapidly.

Grinning, Addison worked the blade tip into the neckline of her shift and slit the thin material to her waist. He flicked the tattered edges, exposing her breasts.

"Señora," he said in Spanish, "do you possess any jewels other than these?"

Never taking her eyes off Addison, she pointed to a small chest on a dressing table. Dirk set the chest on the floor and broke the fragile lock with his heel. It was full of gemstones and filigreed gold jewelry. Tucking the chest under his arm, he edged toward the door.

Addison smiled at the woman, said "Gracias" and left. The alcalde's wife sat motionless on the bed, her mouth forming a soundless *Oh*.

Chuckling, Dirk slipped back into the alcalde's chamber where Baldric axed one of the bedposts. He felled it onto the bed and Halsey retrieved eight bags of pearls from the hollow core. Baldric tapped the other posts with the axe handle. Each sounded solid.

"I think this is all of 'em," Halsey said. "It's a small fishery."

Addison nodded toward the patio. "Let's go see what the others have won."

Pirates, all toting booty from the alcalde's home, gathered on the patio. Jan and Joost were dragging a serving girl between them. Even though she didn't look unhappy about it, Dirk made them release her. She scampered back into the house.

Outside in the dirt plaza doors banged open and shut. People screamed. A few blades clashed. A musket fired now and then. Torches cast flickering light against trees and houses as Dirk trotted across the plaza, the jewel chest tight under his arm.

"To the ship!" Addison shouted.

Men carrying bundles of loot ran for the lugger where the navigator, sailmaker, and a few others held the ship against the dock with ropes. Dirk climbed the net ladder one-handed. Pirates helped him up, others tumbled on board, then poled away from the dock. At the last moment, Talbot lumbered along the quay, tossed a canvas bag aboard and leaped across the water. He caught the rail and Dunstan hauled him over. As the sails caught wind, half-dressed Spaniards raced onto the dock, firing muskets. The pirates returned fire until the *Avenger* escaped the harbor.

Dirk's cutlass whirled high, flashing in bright sunlight. His happy shout drew laughter from the other pirates. He laughed, too, as he caught the blade, then with the tip, lifted a leather pouch full of coins and jewels off the sand.

For a moment Dirk contemplated the riches on the end of his cutlass. It was more than he'd ever possessed and winning it had been so easy, so quick. Much more fun than running down cows and infinitely more profitable.

Neither Dirk nor his friends had been injured and now, after the share-out on the beach near Port Royal, they were rich. With a flick of his wrist he flipped the heavy pouch into his left hand, then grinned at them. "Let's go play."

Food appeared at the toss of a coin. No need anymore to traipse into the forest and climb a tree to pick it, or dig for it with the ever-present danger of caymans or snakes. The dishes came ready to eat and Dirk relished every bite, especially the meat. He didn't have to track, chase, slaughter, butcher, or cure it. The beef appeared well-roasted and tasted all the better for it.

He tested his skill at dice and cards and knuckle-bones, laughing when he won and shrugging when he lost. The money had been easily won. Why worry about its loss?

The tavern wenches were all beautiful, with soft mounds of flesh that filled his hands. They flirted, caressed, and enticed Dirk to leave the gaming tables for a tumble. He couldn't get enough of them.

Through it all gushed now-affordable brandy. Each night Dirk drank until his body grew hot and sluggish and the world swayed delightfully. A week passed, then two, before he faced a morning sober. The money was gone. Taverns, doxies, and dice games had taken it all.

Only Mic had any coins left, and Port Royal grew unfriendly. The merchants were rude, the women haggard and too busy for pirates without coins. Noisy celebrations grated on Dirk's ears. Despondent, he and his friends left the city, trudging along the shore to the *Avenger's* anchorage. At least they would have a place to sleep out of the weather.

The rest of the owners were already there. By the time the sun went down, they had provisioned the ship and recruited a full crew, nearly all the same men who sailed with them the first time. They elected the same officers and on the next morning's tide set sail for Cuba.

The *Avenger* cruised to the western end of the island. There, another village fell to the pirates. With no soldiers to defend them, the villagers ran into the forest. The pirates spent two days sacking the town.

After three more easy raids, they held another share-out on the beach near Port Royal. The prize money was just as quickly spent. And so it was back to sea once more, where raid followed spending spree followed raid. Port Royal merchants, doxies, and tavern owners grew rich.

Dirk was happy enough, though, for there were always more towns to sack, more Spanish wealth to plunder, and always more men to replace those lost in the fighting. And at the start of each voyage, nearly every pirate spoke of taking a ship or city so grand he could leave the sweet trade with his share, and live out his days in the pursuit of pleasure.

Dirk thought it a splendid way to live.

The Florida Straits, 1661

"Fire!"

Ship's gunner Dunstan farted as he whacked a tin pan with a ham bone.

Dirk laid a burning match against the touchhole of a gun, then covered his left ear. All three of the *Avenger's* five-pound starboard guns thundered in a broadside, rattling gunports and spewing black smoke over everybody nearby.

Dunstan strutted across the deck, shoulders straining the silver and blue brocade surcoat he'd acquired in their last raid. The coat was too small to be worn over a shirt, much less buttoned. "Fire!" He whacked the pan, his hairy pot belly jiggled, and the *Avenger's* three larboard guns boomed. Now smoke drifted over the whole deck. He ended the drill. "Good enough."

"Thank the heavens," Baldric said, and snapped his fingers. His big dog ran from her hiding place behind a bale of linen. She squirmed as Baldric scratched around her ears. "I know," he said. "It's loud for me, too."

Dirk drew a bucket of water up over the side and rinsed soot off his face and neck. Then he looked around the ship for something to do. The *Avenger* had been becalmed for two days now, with boredom the worst enemy. He'd cross blades with Dunstan, but they had practiced twice already today. Late afternoon was too hot for such exercise anyway.

Mic joined a card game on the deck. In the bow sailmaster Farley settled on his workpile and began to patch the right knee of his green pantaloons with a scrap of plaid wool. Perry resumed circling the deck, his dark eyes looking everywhere. Grimbald, the boatswain, walked by, Halsey at his elbow.

"Jest a sip," Halsey said. "'Tis for me joints. You know they need a touch'a the brandy now and again."

"You've had your share for the day." Grimbald tossed his grimy, blond hair out of his eyes. "It's no one's fault but your own if you drink it all before noon." He walked off.

Halsey glared after him. "Feckin' clinch-poop."

Grimbald waved over his shoulder.

Jan and Joost settled against one of the ship's two boats with several other men to tell stories of their wife.

"She's English, you know," Joost said. "That's how we can speak that tongue so well."

"Bedchamber talk, that's all you know, laddie," Dunstan said, sauntering by.

Jan shrugged. "What else do I need?"

The men laughed.

"Tell us." A listener poked Joost's leg. "Tell us what she does."

Dirk turned away. He'd heard enough of Vinna, the tavern wench the twins had discovered in Boston on the *Avenger*'s voyage north last fall. Her hair and eyes were dull, from hard living, no doubt, and her plump figure threatened to become fat after any big meal. She also rubbed her bosom against any man who looked at her twice.

Jan and Joost, however, had pursued no other women since Vinna accepted their offer to sail south. And for all their bickering over everything else in their lives, neither twin demanded she choose between them. They were matelot, as well as brothers, and did the traditional buccaneer thing. They threw dice. Jan won the toss and officially married her. Then all three of them settled into a room over the vegetable market in Port Royal.

A fight broke out among card players by the foremast. Perry jumped into the middle of it and shoved the combatants toward opposite ends of the ship.

"Be done." He snapped a length of knotted rope. "We'll have us a shooting contest now. Farley!" He called to the sailmaster in the bow. "Give us some canvas."

Farley stood, stretched his small, wiry body, and pulled a piece of sail, not a foot square, out of his workpile. "This'll do."

He tossed it to Perry, who hung it from a yardarm. Men ran for their muskets. Dirk retrieved his hammock from the hold. He practiced often enough to keep his aim true, and besides, there was little pleasure in a competition that Baldric nearly always won. A nap would be better.

Dirk hung the hammock from unused boat davits on the stern. With a rope around his waist for safety, he climbed down and settled in, swaying below the swivel gun. A wave splashed high on the hull, cooling him with spray.

Mic's face appeared over the taffrail.

"Dirk," he said in Dutch. "Farley looked at the sky and decided we'd have a wind tonight."

"That's good news."

"There's talk of sailing to Puerto Rico."

"We can't take any towns there. That island has the most soldiers in the Antilles. And they actually receive their pay."

"Addison says that lots of soldiers make people feel safe and they won't bother so much with defenses." Mic grinned. "He says they'll run to the hills when they see us."

"Humph. We run into a town and expect to walk out with all the booty. We have no lookouts checking for traps, nor any guard for a retreat, either."

"You say that every time, but we're still alive. And sometimes rich." Mic laughed at Dirk's frown. "Are you coming back on board for the discussion and vote?"

"They never listen to me."

"Oh, you don't like the plans because Addison thought them up and gives the orders."

Dirk glared at him. Chuckling, Mic disappeared. Dirk closed his eyes and fumed.

Addison often demonstrated great courage and skillful control of the men, yet had only one battle plan: use noise and surprise to frighten their prey into a quick surrender. If the Spaniards didn't succumb at once, the fighting grew hard and dangerous. Addison's lack of imagination cost the crew dearly in wasted lives and lost prizes.

Until today, whenever Addison planned a raid, Dirk developed his own plan, including provisions for problems that might occur in the midst of a battle. A few times he made suggestions. The older man listened, then grinned and clapped Dirk on the shoulder. "This old way works and everybody knows what to do," he'd say. "Now you go off and grow some more."

For a year and a half, Dirk had done just that. While he fretted daily over Addison's refusal to plan for surprise defenses, Dirk's shoulders broadened, his chest deepened, and his muscles bulged larger with every passing month. Proud of his size and strength, he was also grateful for them. Along with improved battle skills, they gave him an added advantage in fights.

He loved the feel of a cutlass in his hand, and found swordplay invigorating. Yet he resented long and bloody fights. He wanted treasure and his life left to enjoy it. If, on rare occasion, defenders got the best of the pirates, Dirk had no qualms about retreating. Neither pride nor honor ever bought anything in Port Royal.

Still, it wasn't just poorly planned raids that frustrated him. He hated taking orders from the officers. He'd had his fill of commands from Gilbert, and he didn't want to spend the rest of his life obeying others.

He knew that as a sea rover he was freer than most men. The pirates voted on officers, targets and length of voyage, even punishments doled out to miscreants. The vessel's single cabin, while nominally belonging to captain and quartermaster, was not private. Any man could enter at any time, and share the captain's table without an invitation.

Even so, Perry strode the deck breaking up fights and flogging trouble-makers. Farley bellowed orders for trimming the lugger's sails. And there was Dunstan, exercising everyone in use of the big guns three times a day. Grimbald, the boatswain, who appeared mild-mannered, had a stubborn will. He ordered needed repairs on the vessel, and doled out the food and brandy with ruthless efficiency.

No one could leave the crew until after the final share-out of a voyage. If a man secured the crew's permission to leave before that time, he lost his share. If he left without permission and took any booty along, he'd be hunted down and executed as a deserter.

For eighteen months Dirk had sailed where the *Avenger* took him, eaten what the boatswain allotted, practiced on the guns, and fought in ill-conceived battles that needlessly endangered him. So now, instead of attending the battle conference, he swayed in his hammock, pondering how to entice older, more experienced men into electing him captain.

As Addison predicted, the first Puerto Rican village they raided was unprepared to defend itself. Most of the people fled into the hills. A few managed a feeble resistance. After a short fight, Addison offered quarter. With that promise not to hurt anyone or destroy property, the villagers stopped fighting. The crew plundered at leisure. Then with the booty lashed aboard, the men decided to stay near Puerto Rico. The town of San Felipe, a day's sail away, was chosen as the next target.

They sailed into San Felipe's little harbor at dusk. Three small fishing boats rocked gently against a short, stone quay. The *Avenger* tied up at the end of the quay and the crew poured over the ship's side. Addison raised his cutlass, fired a pistol and led the charge into the village. Dirk ran between Mic and Baldric, shouting for gold and revenge, and in sheer exhilaration of a promised fight.

At the plaza, a now-familiar Spanish-style square, Addison raced across flowers and grass toward the church. A few citizens ran screaming into their homes. Doors slammed and bars dropped. Dirk chuckled. He'd soon put a foot or shoulder to those doors and break them in. Behind him, window shutters banged open. He'd investigate them later. He was already at the church steps.

Muskets roared. Hot pain seared across Dirk's chest. Beside him, Mic faltered. Blood spread over his thigh. Baldric crouched, musket ready. Pirates cried for help or shouted curses. Dirk glanced around the plaza. Shutters on every house hung open. Smoking muskets withdrew from windows. Others appeared.

"To the ship!" Addison cried. "Up, lads, and follow me!"

He stooped to hoist Talbot off the dirt, then dropped him. Talbot's face was gone.

"Let's go!" Addison rushed across the plaza toward the harbor.

Dirk fired his pistol into the nearest window, then looked for the twins. Joost half-carried Jan, although Jan appeared to have only a slight wound on his upper arm. Dirk pressed his tunic against his own wound and ran for the ship. Mic limped beside him. The

Spaniards fired another volley. A ball whistled past Dirk's ear. Howling pirates dropped around him.

"Come, mates!" Addison shouted above the noise. "Just a short way to go!"

They struggled on toward the *Avenger*.

"Damn you, Addison!" Dirk yelled, then glanced at Mic. "This was bound to happen."

"Just run."

They ran, then skidded to a stop as soldiers filled the street ahead of them. Dirk whirled to escape another way. Soldiers blocked all the streets leading from the plaza, trapping the pirates in a crossfire.

Waving his cutlass in the failing light, Addison led them headlong into the soldiers blocking their path to the *Avenger*. He cut down three before he died.

Surrounded, leaderless, the pirates shoved each other and stumbled over feet and weapons trying to squeeze together. Dirk fought down fury and panic as he caught Mic's arm to hold him upright. Baldric elbowed men aside to reload his musket.

The soldiers charged.

Soldiers crashed into them from all sides. Dirk fought with every skill and bit of strength he could muster. But whenever he cut down a soldier, two others appeared. Over and over—thrust, slash, parry, hack, stab and repeat. His arm grew heavy. He stopped once to take a deep breath and steel whipped along his ribs. He battled on.

Mic fought at his side, grim-faced, silent, methodical as usual. But every so often he stumbled into Dirk. Joost lay on the ground nearby. Jan stood over him, a grin on his face and a hard glitter in his eyes. He chopped a saber at two Spaniards. Baldric scrambled over to help. A third Spaniard joined that fight. Dunstan lumbered into the space Baldric had left. He carried a club in one hand, a cutlass in the other. His latest coat had torn open down the back and hung from the collar. The panels flapped around his legs.

Dirk fought, though certain they were all lost. They needed an escort from God to reach the ship. And God would never stoop to aid a small, miserable band of pirates.

But maybe a Spaniard would help. "The biggest house?" Dirk shouted to Mic.

After a moment, Mic said, "Behind us. To the left."

"Dunstan?"

"Heard you!" Dunstan feinted with his blade and cracked his club on a soldier's skull. He edged closer to Dirk, still fighting.

The three hacked past soldiers toward an ornate villa facing the plaza. When they finally broke through the line of blades, Dirk slammed into the villa's door. On the second try, he crashed through. Dunstan guarded the doorway. Mic followed Dirk inside, then trotted through the entry hall and out through open doors to an enclosed patio. Dirk ran from room to room through adjoining doors. He found no one. He was about to go up through a trapdoor into a storeroom under the eaves when Mic called.

Dirk followed Mic's voice out the back of the house, across the patio to a cellar entrance. Pale light filtered through cracks in the wooden door. Together they kicked it in, then descended five steps into cool silence, into the scent of wines and vegetables and moist earth.

Barely visible in light from a single candle, four women huddled in a corner behind a portly man with thick grey hair. Jewels on the knuckle bow of his saber glittered as he waved the blade, his dressing gown sleeves flowing after.

Dirk lunged. The man swerved to counter and Mic leapt in. The saber thudded on the dirt floor as Mic's cutlass slid under the man's chin. The women moaned and sobbed.

Clad only in a nightshift, a pale girl of perhaps twelve years stepped out of the group and leveled a pistol at Mic. "Release him," she said, voice and pistol both shaking.

Dirk knocked the pistol from her hands with the flat of his cutlass. She gasped. He caught her about the waist, retrieved the pistol and shoved it in his belt.

The Spanish gentleman moaned. *"Hija."*

Dirk grunted. This was a welcome stroke of luck. She was the man's daughter. "Bring him along, Mic." He hauled the girl up the stairs, across the patio, through the house, and pushed her out the front door. The two soldiers fighting Dunstan saw the girl and drew back. Mic shoved the man out beside her.

The soldiers cursed. One said, *"Alcalde."*

"Stand back!" Dirk shouted in Spanish, hoping the soldiers in this village liked their alcalde well enough to obey.

The alcalde looked at his daughter and shook his head.

"Lo siento, mi hija," he said. "Forgive me." Then, turning to his soldiers scattered about the plaza, he cried, "Kill them all!"

Cursing, Dirk tightened his arm around the girl's waist, and raised his cutlass as if to strike off her father's head. Her scream cut through the noise of battle. Fighting slackened, then stopped.

Dirk half-carried, half-dragged the girl toward the pirates huddled in the plaza. Mic limped after them, keeping his cutlass under the alcalde's chin. Dunstan trailed, snaking his blade at the soldiers who followed closely.

In a slow-moving clump, the pirates retreated to the *Avenger*. Soldiers gave way, stepping just out of sword reach. The alcalde ignored Mic's cutlass and kept his eyes on his daughter. She quaked in Dirk's arm, stumbled along at his hip, then fell against him. He held her up, and when she didn't walk, shook her. He needed live hostages. He shook her harder. She walked again.

At the water, Dirk groaned. A Spanish pinnace was tacking across the harbor entrance, trapping them in the small bay.

The pirates climbed aboard the *Avenger* and pulled the captives up through the gangway. Dirk climbed the rope ladder after them.

"Hold those two over the sides," he said as his feet landed on the deck. "Hold a lantern over them."

With the alcalde dangling from the starboard side and his daughter from larboard, Farley ordered the sails raised. A night wind pushed the *Avenger* out toward the pinnace. Through a spy glass, Dirk watched the Spanish captain order the pinnace's ordnance loaded. Then a sailor ran up, gesturing wildly toward the lugger. The captain put his own glass to his eye once, again, then a third time.

Dirk chuckled as the man pulled a plumed helmet off his head and slammed it to the deck.

The ordnance on the pinnace never fired. The *Avenger* eased by safely and, once out of range of the pinnace's two guns, the pirates dropped their hostages into the water. While the pinnace sped to rescue them, the *Avenger* slipped off into the darkness.

They sailed into a shallow river. When the sails shook, the men poled the lugger farther upstream. They tied up between large trees and took stock of the evening's work. Addison was dead and eleven others of the thirty-seven man crew missing. Whether they were dead or captured, no one knew. Nor did it matter. Execution or slavery was the expected fate of captured pirates.

All who'd gone ashore were wounded. Ogden, the surgeon, pursed his fleshy lips and, with stubby fingers he'd doused in sea water, tended those most severely hurt. Dirk tied a cloth around his ribs, then bandaged the slash in Baldric's upper arm. The twins took care of each other, then bickered over a bottle of brandy.

Mic pressed on his still-bleeding thigh. He smiled weakly at Dirk.

"Quick thinking, my friend."

Dirk shrugged. "I didn't want to die there. Nobody to speak Dutch over our graves."

Mic laughed, then accepted the onion bottle Baldric offered him. The three settled against the bulwark in silence. They drank brandy, then rum, and finally wine.

Dirk's pain and fatigue faded away. The world swayed delightfully as he joined the crew's celebration. Those old stories of Dunstan's were much funnier than the last time he'd told them. Dirk sang louder than ever before, and danced. Had he ever been so graceful? The stars had never shone so brightly. And why did he need the danger of a raid and fear of a painful death to feel so gloriously alive?

Sometime during the night Dunstan raised a toast to Dirk for the plan that led to their escape. The pirates cheered, and in the hearty babble that followed, Halsey suggested Dirk be their new captain. They held an election right then.

By the time dawn streaked the eastern sky pink and Dirk finally drifted into sleep, he was captain of the *Avenger*.

Late afternoon sun pierced Dirk's eyes. The rigging's gentle clicks crashed in his ears. He shifted his head on the coil of rope he'd used as a pillow. He was too tired to move further. Men snored all around him, but a few old hands near the mizzenmast stirred.

"God damn." Grimbald moaned as he fell from a sitting position onto the deck. "Remember what we did?"

"We got out of a Spanish town with just our skins," Dunstan said, scooting into a bit of shade behind a gun. He burped and farted at the same time. "Ahh..." His face lost its frown.

"No, after," Grimbald said.

Squat, surly Normand hawked and spat over the side, not quite missing the rail. "We made that boy captain."

"Without him, we'd be dead." Halsey curled his body tighter around the mast. "He's got good ideas."

"He's too damn young." Kirby sat up and reached for brandy. His broad, pushed-in face was paler than usual against his dark hair. "We'd be better off with Arnaud, here. At least he's got experience as captain."

Arnaud. Dirk swore softly. An excellent swordsman, Arnaud had announced his intention to be the *Avenger's* captain soon after he joined the crew a year ago. At the time, the men were satisfied with Addison and would not make the change. Since then, Arnaud had worked at charming the crew. He shared his liquor, lost often at dice and bones. In any quarrel, Kirby stepped in to do the fighting or bullying for him.

Kirby tilted the clay bottle against his mouth.

"Feckit." He threw the empty bottle over the side. It shattered against a tree. "I say we depose the boy."

Farley rolled onto his back with a yawn. "Ye canna vote him out."

"And why not?" Kirby worked his mouth furiously, as if his cheeks had dried to his teeth.

"The lad must first prove he canna do the job," Farley said. "That be the way things are done. Least-wise on a ship of the brethren."

"That's true," Grimbald said.

Kirby glanced at Arnaud, who shrugged.

"He will lead us to slaughter," Normand said.

Dunstan snorted, flipped the tails of his coat over his back. "If he does, he'll be the first to die, like Addison. Captain's always in the front of a fight."

Farley said, "Whether or no he dies, I'll be catching the wind with me sails, and Crofton'll be navigating. Perry be still alive to keep the books and divide the prizes."

"That's right," Dunstan said. "If the young one gets foolish and dies in a fight, it's not like we'd lose anybody important, like Crofton or the carpenter."

"Then any fool could be captain," Normand said.

Dirk bit his lip. He'd never liked Normand. He was a sly, dirty fighter. Mic called him Arnaud's "bootlicker with pretensions of equality."

"So why not Dirk?" Halsey asked. "He's certainly the biggest fellow on board. Big enough for you to hide behind in a fight, Normand."

He laughed as Normand kicked at his head.

"And he's a match for me with a blade," Dunstan said.

"Oh, leave be." Farley popped joints as he stood and stretched. "There not be a thing ye can do for now and mayhaps he'll be good."

Kirby blew his nose into his hand. "I doubt it."

Dirk closed his eyes. The election had been nearly unanimous. How many others, when sobered, would also regret their votes? His fingers curled into fists. He would be a good captain. He would lead them to rich prizes. This ship would never have another captain, and they'd all want it that way.

Dirk took deep breaths, eased his grip on the cutlass and looked around once more. Through the dense Yucatan jungle, he could see only Mic and Perry, who crouched on either side of him. Before them lay a village of nearly fifty houses, a dozen shops, stables, warehouses, and a little church. Baldric had gone to spy the night before and found no walls or other defenses against an attack from the jungle. Most of the houses didn't look worth sacking, he'd said, but Dirk was certain the church would be full of plate, statues and chalices.

Twenty pirates had come ashore in late afternoon and now waited in the dark for the *Avenger's* signal. At this moment, the lugger was to be sailing into the village's tiny harbor. When the ship's guns fired on any boats there, or at the town itself, Dirk and his men would attack.

After the church was taken and the town accepted quarter, they'd raid the houses, starting with the biggest. They would withdraw to the harbor. If that route was blocked, they could retreat along the trail they now crouched upon, with Baldric and two other marksmen covering their escape. The ship would meet them at a beach to the west.

The other officers had added their considerable influence to Dirk's arguments for this plan. Still, if it went poorly, the men might replace him as captain. He reminded himself to breathe.

Finally, a gun from the *Avenger* boomed. Dirk stood. "Light the torches," he said.

Perry lit seven torches from the coal he carried in a little tin bucket. The torches bobbed through the underbrush, passed by men hidden in a line to either side of Dirk. The *Avenger's* second shot fired.

"Now!" Dirk shouted.

Thick greenery crackled all around him. Cutlass high, he bounded toward the open space around the village. Pirates shouted and whooped as they raced past him. Dirk entered a back street, turned off it to head for the plaza and the church. The *Avenger's* guns fired again, spewing acrid smoke. Spanish screams and cries of warning filled the air.

At the plaza's fountain, Dirk halted.

Dunstan stumbled into him from behind. "Move your arse, leadfoot."

Dirk stayed where he was, staring at a two-story house next to the church. Eight half-dressed Spaniards stood across the front door.

At the command of a short, round fellow, they raised muskets and took aim at the pirates.

"Scatter!" Dirk yelled. "Down!"

Pirates fanned out across the plaza. Dirk heard the Spanish order to fire and dropped to the crushed shell street. Muskets roared; pirates howled and cursed. Dirk jumped up.

"Surround them before they reload!"

He led a charge into the haze of gunpowder. A lookout fired a two-shot warning from the west edge of town. Dirk glanced around. Spaniards hid in the shadows of two corners of the plaza. "To the harbor!"

The pirates ran, firing pistols at Spaniards as they went. At the water's edge, they squatted behind a long row of wooden barrels to reload while the *Avenger* tacked across the harbor.

"Curse them to hell." Dunstan spat on a barrel. "Every town we come to anymore wants to use the same defense."

Kirby sniffed. "It was a terrible plan anyway."

"No better than Addison's," Normand said.

With Perry holding a torch for him, Dirk picked up a pebble and sketched the town's lay-out in the dirt. Maybe if he looked busy, the men wouldn't bother him while he was trying to think.

Five minutes later, he sent four men to the east of the village. Four more slipped around to the west. Dirk gave them enough time to reach a position behind the Spaniards who waited in the plaza's corners, then led another charge.

They entered the plaza at a dead run. At the fountain, they split into two groups and raced for the shadows where the Spaniards hid. Muskets and pistols fired, but none of the men around Dirk cried out, nor did he see any stumble. His eight pirates must have reached the Spaniards' backs.

Defenders at the big house had their weapons primed, but the muskets were aimed at their fellow villagers as well as the pirates. They didn't fire. Caught between pirates, the Spaniards around the plaza soon fell. A few pirates slipped off to circle again, coming alongside the big house behind the defenders. Cutlass whirling, Dirk charged.

The Spaniards fired. A musket ball burned into Dirk's upper left arm. He cursed and kept running. Three Spaniards stood to fight with swords. They soon died. The rest scurried to their homes. The round fellow who'd given the orders limped on a bloody thigh into the big house.

Dirk whooped and laughed. About half the pirates were wounded, but none seriously. Although they did not control the town entirely, they'd proven their superiority. Now was the time to offer quarter. His men could plunder in safety. His first raid as captain was a success.

He heard musket and pistol shots from houses here and there, so he ordered the men back to the harbor. They could dress wounds and plan for sacking the town.

At the waterfront, men aboard the *Avenger* cheered as it sailed close. Farley tossed overboard twenty big sacks he'd sewn from old sails.

"Throw us some brandy, too," Jan called.

The sailmaker obliged. The twins waded out to retrieve onion bottles as they plopped into the water.

Halsey looked at Dirk and flashed a wider-than-usual grin. "What now, oh, great captain?"

"We offer them quarter, of course."

Perry nodded. "They'll accept it."

"Good. We've already done enough work tonight." Joost gulped brandy. "We shouldn't have to fight any more."

Men nearby laughed.

"I'll go now," Dirk said. "I know where one of their leaders is."

"Wait, you're bleeding." Ogden finished tying a bandage on Kirby's head and walked over.

Dirk shrugged. "Not much."

"Let me see."

Ogden pulled him around to get better light from the nearly full moon. He ran a rough hand over Dirk's arm. Dirk gasped and pulled away.

"That ball has to come out," Ogden said.

"Later. I have to offer quarter."

"Let somebody else do it," Mic said. "If that ball stays in your arm too long it could fester."

"Listen to Mic." Ogden tugged Dirk to a rock at the water's edge. "Sit."

"I've done quarter before," Halsey said. "I know the words."

Dirk hesitated, then nodded. "The man you want is in the big house just to the left of the church."

"I remember the one."

Halsey pulled off his brimless cap, ran fingers through long, tangled hair, and replaced the cap. He waved at Dirk and sauntered off to the plaza.

Kirby followed. "I'd better go along and help that little fool."

Sighing, Dirk accepted the brandy Mic offered, drank some and set his jaw. Then winced as Ogden felt through his skin for the musket ball.

"It's not so deep," Ogden said. "Ready?"

Dirk swallowed more brandy and nodded. Ogden's knife sliced his flesh, then probed deep to find and flip out the ball. Dirk sucked in a breath. Mic eased the onion bottle out of his tight grip.

The ordeal over, Dirk was about to thank Ogden when the surgeon splashed water on him. Salt burned into his wound. He jumped away and waved his arm. "You muck-wit! Why did you do that?"

Ogden shrugged. "Seems to make things heal better."

"Water?"

"Sea water. I don't know why."

"Well, don't do it to me again until you learn why." Dirk blew on the wound.

Mic snickered. Dirk glared at him and snatched back the brandy. He drained it while Ogden bandaged his arm. Tossing the bottle aside, Dirk fired pistol shots to call in the lookouts.

Fifteen minutes passed. Halsey and Kirby did not return.

"Maybe the Spanish don't want quarter," Jan said.

Dunstan snorted. "They always accept. They know we'll start fightin' again if they don't. And they know we'll win."

Another five minutes passed. The men grew rowdier.

"By damn," Normand said, "let's go in and fire the place."

A few men shouted agreement.

Dirk called out to the *Avenger* for more liquor. It might pacify the men, if they didn't become too drunk to honor quarter. Farley threw half a dozen bottles toward shore. Dirk waded knee-deep into the water to gather them.

"Hey, Dirk," Mic said. "There's something strange happening."

Dirk joined Mic and the others at the line of barrels. Near the plaza entrance, two men held a big dog that growled and twisted, snapping at a dark object on its back. A third man brought a torch out of the closest house and set fire to something near the dog's rump. They released the animal. It howled and raced for the water, dragging the fire along.

"It's a bomb on his back!" Grimbald shouted.

The pirates scattered. The dog fled past them and into the water. The fire sizzled out. Dirk, Perry and Dunstan raced over to detach the bomb.

"Look at this," Perry said, holding the dog's tail. "They tied rags to him."

Dirk reached for the bomb and touched the blood-matted hair of a man's head. His hand recoiled. He swallowed hard.

"Dear God in heaven," Dunstan said. "That's Halsey."

Dirk turned aside and bent to wash off his hands. Pressure built in his head; his ears grew hot. The excited babble of voices around him faded. He grew faint, then had to fight down a heaving stomach.

When the queasiness eased, he straightened to face the men. They gaped in silence at the head Dunstan held aloft. One by one they turned to Dirk. Yet he could not drag his eyes away from Halsey's blotched and broken face.

"Oh, Halsey," Dirk said. "To die this way... I should have gone... I should have been the one."

"Treacherous bastards!" Dunstan lowered Halsey's head. "Where's Kirby?"

Dirk raised a fist at the village and shouted, “You do this to a man who promises you your homes and your lives?” He spat. “Always and forever the cursed Spaniards. I shall never understand them. I shall never forgive them.”

He clamped his jaws, drew deeper and deeper breaths until his chest heaved. And with each breath came a blow from his past. His father’s murder. His mother’s scream. Anneke dead in a blood-covered nightshift. A little boy pinned to a tree by a lance. Henry. And now Halsey. Like the blaze that had consumed his home, fury raged white hot in him. Dirk took a breath so deep his lungs hurt. His roar filled the night. “HALSEEEE...!”

He tore the cutlass out of his belt, whirled it over his head. Men scattered, then fell in behind as he charged the village. When they caught sight of Kirby’s head on a pike in the plaza, their shouts sounded like thunder.

A musket ball scorched Dirk’s right ear. Blood ran down his jaw. He raced on to the big house by the church, crashed through the door, knocked a blade from the man he’d sent Halsey to see, and plunged his cutlass into the Spaniard’s soft, round belly. As the man sank to the floor, pirates raced by, snatching at furnishings.

“Fire this place!” Dirk ordered.

The Spaniard writhed and gurgled in death throes. Baldric smashed a burning lantern into wall hangings, then dragged the flaming tapestries from room to room. Smoke filled the house. Flames crackled. Men shouted. Women cried out and children wailed. The *Avenger’s* guns boomed.

Dirk ran outside. Mic helped him shatter the church’s side door. Men poured in around them, carrying torches. Some pitched silver and gold candlesticks, chalices, and plates into canvas bags. Others hacked pearls and polished agates out of the wooden altar. Two pirates ran along the walls, snatching statues from niches.

After carting a heavy bag of treasure to the lugger, Dirk plunged back into the village. Fires ate away homes and shops. Families threw their possessions out windows. Pirates donned some of the clothes, took valuable items to the ship, and tossed everything else back into the flames.

Fires now shot to the treetops, brightening the sky with a yellow-orange glow as strong as sunshine. Spanish steel crashed on pirates' blades. Smoking muskets fired lead that pierced and scored. Unarmed villagers ran screaming across the plaza, some in obvious panic, others chased by pirates. Dirk sought out the biggest, strongest-looking Spaniards to fight. He grew light-headed. His right arm weakened. Then Ogden died in front of him. A sword cut across Jan's chest.

Cutlass in his left hand, Dirk fought on. It was not enough to disarm or wound a man and shout for his submission. The Spaniards must die. It was not enough to break into a house and steal a family's treasure. Everything else down to clay platters and children's straw toys must be destroyed, and the house itself set ablaze.

The village was a firestorm. A woman clutching a bundle against her chest jumped off a second-story balcony. She lay broken and silent in the dirt street, a baby squalling against her hip, as pirates rummaged through her garments.

Corpses littered the streets and alleyways. The stench of burning flesh and timbers clogged the air. An elderly man, long hair and bed gown afire, stumbled toward the plaza fountain. He died against the stone foundation, his hand in the water.

With most of the village destroyed and its treasures aboard the *Avenger*, Dirk roared at the lack of prey. Then Gustave, with thick head and thicker shoulders, battered down the door of a root cellar, dove inside and dragged a woman out. He slammed her against a stone wall, shoved a heavy forearm across her throat, ripped her gown apart and rammed his knees between her thighs. Her scream broke and gurgled in her crushed throat.

Ah, yes, that was one thing more they'd promised not to do if the Spaniards had accepted quarter. Dirk grabbed for a young woman racing past him. She yelped, jumped out of his reach, and ran away from the village. He caught her at the edge of the jungle.

The flames of the village bathed her face in a golden light. She was young, not quite a woman. Younger, perhaps, than Anneke should have been by now. But Anneke would forever be five years old, a child with blood soaking her chest as she crumpled in the grass just out of his reach.

Dirk threw the girl down and fell on her. She beat small fists against his chest and face, scraped fingernails down his neck. Her mouth opened, but he heard no scream. He had killed and plundered and burned. Now he would punish this Spaniard for being alive while Anneke was dead. She would suffer the way his mother had suffered. For what those raiders had done to him on Bentyn's Isle, he would ravage this Spanish body.

He caught the girl's arms, pinned them with one hand to the ground above her head, tore at her thin, cotton nightshift. Then he shuddered.

Blood soaked the girl's bodice. Had it come from the girl or one of his own wounds? So much blood spreading across a narrow chest. The mark of a dying child. Dirk swayed, dizzy. For what men had done ten years ago, he would rip into this child's body, as if she were not human but only a mode of vengeance. As if raping a girl in Yucatan could hurt the men who had raided Bentyn's Isle.

He looked down and saw dark eyes blank with terror. She was so young, so small. He eased off the girl, covering her with shreds of clothes he didn't remember tearing. As she scrambled away and disappeared into the forest, her scream burned through his ears.

The world had at last become tranquil and cool. The *Avenger* sailed once more, laden with treasure and snoring men. Crofton and Farley held the ship to an easterly route.

They were going home. The lugger could hold no more treasure and the men demanded a share-out. That night's orgy of killing and looting could be followed properly only by weeks of free spending on brandy, women, and dice games.

Grateful to the darkness for hiding his shame from the boisterous, gleeful men, Dirk had gone to sit on a chest of silks in the bow. There he remained, silent and unapproachable, until all but those needed to sail the ship had fallen into a drunken sleep.

Dirk could not sleep. He felt as if he'd been punched hard in the gut and not yet recovered his breath. Try as he might, he could not forget the terror on that girl's face, nor her blank stare.

Twice now. Twice he'd possessed a rage so great he stopped thinking. And he did things... Gilbert had deserved a beating, but Dirk could have died for it. And now the girl. She certainly didn't deserve to be raped.

Rape... Such an ugly word. He forced it out of his mind. In its place came the girl's golden, firelit face, so small, so young, so scared.

The salt breeze cooled Dirk's face and stung the wounds she'd torn in his neck. In the moonlight he watched waves break on the lugger's prow. Behind him, sprawled on the deck, men snorted or growled, as if reliving the battle in their dreams. Now and then, a man crawled to the rail to vomit over the side. Others didn't make it as far as the rail. Mic approached. Dirk waved him away.

The moon set, faint streaks of dawn appeared, and still Dirk saw himself on top of that girl. Baldric's dog walked up beside him, snuffling and yawning. She nuzzled his hand and he absently scratched behind her ears. "I thought I was a man," Dirk said, "because I do what men do, and better than most. I am bigger and stronger and smarter than most men. But that isn't enough. It only means I am lucky."

The dog licked his hand and Dirk managed a wry smile. He gently clasped her jaw and shook it. "Lucky you are to be animal and not suffer the pangs of a conscience."

Baldric moaned in his sleep. The dog trotted off to lie beside him. Dirk gazed at his crew, then turned back to the dark, rolling water. He felt very young, and for the first time in many years longed to speak with his father.

The *Avenger's* bow pitched into a deep trough, and the loud, roiling mass of pirates lurched foreward on the cedar-wood deck. Amidst the cursing, toe-smashing, elbow-gouging throng, Dirk landed a solid left in Arnaud's belly. It staggered the man. Almost three dozen spectators jostled closer, cheering and shouting half-drunken advice in a cacophony of languages. Dirk roared his frustration as Dunstan and Baldric dragged him off Arnaud.

"One more!" Dirk said, twisting and ducking to get away.

One more blow to punish the Frenchman for his insults about Dirk's courage. For the incessant campaign to be elected captain in Dirk's place. For the rape.

"Let go, damn you."

Dirk tried to shake Baldric off his right arm, but the small man hung on, a solid weight. Not that it mattered. Despite having swallowed debilitating mercury yesterday for yet another dose of the pox, Dunstan could subdue Dirk single-handed.

"Whelp of a Dutch whore!" Arnaud struggled against his own friends. "You'll pay for the stripes on my back!"

Dirk's voice boomed over the noise of the crowd. "You will honor quarter!"

A swell rolled under the keel, throwing Baldric off balance. Dunstan's grasp weakened, too, and Dirk dragged them both a few feet across the deck toward Arnaud.

Mic, black hair streaming, dropped out of the rigging. His bare feet landed with a light thud onto the deck between Dirk and Arnaud. Mic rammed a shoulder into Dirk's chest and drove him backwards.

"Stop this!" he said in Dutch. "The coxcomb isn't worth a flogging!"

Dirk snorted and struggled on. He just wanted to give Arnaud the drubbing of his life.

Someone called for handystrokes to first blood. Others took up the cry. Perry pushed his way through the pirates. Dark eyes squinting in the morning haze, he slapped a coiled, knotted rope against his skinny thigh. He glared at Dirk, then Arnaud. Then he pointed at a low island half a league north. "Farley! To the isle just beyond that leeward spit."

Eager for the show, men swarmed up the rigging to obey Farley's orders. Yet because of choppy seas and erratic winds left from that morning's squall, it was nearly an hour before they hove to and anchored off the tiny island of scrub palms. The ship's two boats were lowered, smacking onto rough water. Dirk hustled down a net ladder into one boat as Arnaud swung down a line into the other. After them piled enough men to nearly swamp both vessels.

As the boats rode through breakers toward shore, Dirk thought of all the names he should have called Arnaud. And all the openings for punches that he'd missed.

Jan, on Dirk's right, gave him a bleary grin through blond mustache and beard. "How fast will you blood the bilge rat, d'ya think?"

Joost leaned over the side to shout across the water at Arnaud. "Dirk'll blood the codless scut in less than a minute!"

Joost drew back, laughing as Arnaud lunged from his seat, nearly capsizing the other boat. Normand clamped a stubby fist onto the back of Arnaud's dirty cotton shirt and hauled him back down.

Dirk laughed with the others until he felt a stare from cold blue eyes. Mic had settled on the foreward trestle and taken up one of the six oars. He frowned over his shoulder.

"This is serious, Dirk." He spoke in Dutch. "Can't you control your temper?"

"The damnedable Frenchy never stops goading me!"

"Just words. Couldn't you find a suitable reply in any of those four languages you claim to speak?"

"The French ones worked well enough."

"On you, fool."

Dirk shrugged. "If it's not him, it's Normand. And if they're not insulting me to my face, they're working on the others to depose me. He hasn't left me in peace since the flogging."

A week ago they had raided a Cuban village. When the pirates gained control, Dirk offered quarter. Soon after the Spanish laid down their weapons, however, he'd caught Arnaud raping a woman. The granting of quarter was a century-old tradition in the Caribbean. The system worked to the advantage of both pirates and Spanish colonists, and that rogue Arnaud deserved a flogging for damaging it.

"So the man was spoiling for a fight. Did it have to be now? Your position with the crew is shaky enough."

Mic's oar tangled with that of the man in front of him. There were immediate curses, growled in English. Mic quickly turned aft and matched the other rowers' strokes.

"Better now than during a raid," Dirk said to Mic's back. "Or after, when I'm tired or wounded."

Mic rowed for a few minutes, then said, "He's the best bladesman in the crew. Have you considered what happens if you lose?"

Dirk knew a loss to Arnaud this morning would leave him vulnerable to other challenges. Enough like this one, or any at all during a raid, and Dirk would be finished as captain.

"I won't lose."

Mic's loud sigh was half a moan.

The boat scraped sand and men scrambled out. Dirk and Baldric splashed ashore while Mic and the twins helped turn the boat for its return to the ship. More boatloads of the crew would come ashore before the fight could begin. Perry ordered the combatants to opposite ends of the tiny island. Dirk marched off, surrounded by friends.

"Remember," Mic said, "you only have to draw blood."

"Oh, you'll see his blood today."

"If you're certain, I'll go earn us some profit on your folly."

Mic's coin bag hung from a cord around his neck. He pulled it out of his tunic, over his head. Tossing it lightly from hand to hand, he crossed the island toward Arnaud's contingent.

"Where the hell's your thong?" Baldric jerked a thumb toward the back of his own neck, where the black hair was cut short to his collar. "You can't fight with hair in your eyes."

"It's on board," Dirk said, thinking of the old yellow silk scarf he used to tie over his head. It always kept both hair and sweat out of his eyes.

"Jan," Baldric said. "Give Dirk your cord."

"What?" Jan grinned at them.

Joost, standing right behind Jan, snatched leather and some hair from him.

"Here." Joost tossed the cord to Dirk, then hopped, laughing, away from Jan's fist.

"Thanks." Dirk tied back his hair.

Baldric walked around blousing Dirk's tunic out from his wide belt. "Maybe Arnaud won't find you inside all this cotton."

"Thanks."

Dirk left them to pace over the grassy dunes on his end of the island. He shut out voices and battled the prickling of uncertainty. Arnaud was the best swordsman he'd ever met, barring one or two Spaniards he'd crossed blades with on raids. The Frenchman was fast, clever, and at twenty-six, in his prime. Dirk, while taller and broader, had never bested him at swordplay.

Switching the cutlass to his left hand, Dirk shook the right one. He'd been gripping the hilt too tightly, the surest way to have it knocked out of his hand. He glanced up. The sky was clearing. He'd soon have a blazing, mid-day sun to contend with, too.

Since Addison's death, Arnaud had stepped up his campaign to be captain. He berated Dirk's plans for raids, and constantly reminded the crew of his youth.

"I shall win," Dirk said, taking the cutlass in his right hand again, shaking the left. "I shall never be just a member of the crew again. I shall win."

He stood still on a small dune, rubbing his left earlobe. Arnaud had torn the gold loop almost out of it. Dirk picked at flakes of dried blood while across the sand and scrub brush, Arnaud strutted among his friends, laughing, pounding their backs.

Dirk took a deep breath. "I've worked too long and too hard to be captain. I'll not let you or anyone else take it away now."

The boats returned full of pirates. Men surged toward the widest part of the little beach. Dirk met Arnaud there.

Perry stood between them on the damp, firm sand near the water. "The first to draw blood wins and the fighting stops at once." He raised a bushy, dark eyebrow at Dirk, then Arnaud. "You both agree?"

Dirk nodded, hefting his cutlass, watching Arnaud. The man sneered as he pushed billowing sleeves off his wrists, but he nodded also.

"Then begin." Perry jumped out of the way.

Arnaud's saber flashed in the sun. His cuts and thrusts whistled through the air. The saber was lighter, quicker, and longer than Dirk's cutlass, and reduced his advantage of greater height and longer reach.

"Spawn of a pig's offal!" Arnaud sliced the air under Dirk's nose. "You presume to order any man whipped?"

Dirk leapt backward to avoid another slice. "The crew voted those stripes for you."

"On your say so."

Arnaud feinted to his left, one of his better-known moves.

Dirk parried the following thrust, catching the saber with the inner edge of the cutlass. He thought, hoped, for a moment that he'd disarmed the man.

Arnaud regained control of the saber. "Merde. It was only a bit of Spanish quim."

Dirk caught the saber with his cutlass again, but this time Arnaud recovered even more quickly. Dirk hopped backward, out of the saber's reach.

"If we don't honor quarter," he said, "every Spanish town will fight to the death."

"And what difference to us, Dutchman?" Arnaud circled, waving his sword at Dirk's chest. "We kill many on every raid."

Dirk turned, blinking against the reflection of sunlight on water. He ducked away from the glare for an instant. The saber ripped through his sleeve. His arm burned and he cursed. It was over, so quickly. And he'd lost so much.

"First blood!" Normand rushed toward Arnaud.

Someone large yanked Normand back into the crowd. Perry caught Dirk's left arm and shoved the tunic sleeve up to expose a welt, but no blood. Dirk took deep breaths. He still had a chance.

Pirates cheered and set new odds for their bets. Perry jumped out of the way, and the fight continued. The loose circle of spectators stumbled along, splashed in the shallows, as the handystrokes ranged up and down the beach.

"Why do you care how many Spanish dogs die?" Arnaud cut at Dirk's legs.

Dirk hopped to one side; his boots slipped on soft sand. He scrambled back onto damp, harder sand.

"We'd die with them," he said. "We want to live. Enjoy the prizes we win."

Again Arnaud slashed at Dirk's legs, where a severe wound

might cripple him.

Dirk's stomach tightened. There was more to be lost in this fight than his pride and position.

"What better prize than a plump *señorita*?" Arnaud cut and thrust faster. "A good rut and vengeance at the same time."

Dirk parried and blocked and twisted out of reach.

Arnaud smiled, weaving the saber tip face high. "Think of your mother, Dutchman. Surely you would enjoy it most of all."

Dirk knew he shouldn't talk. Every word took breath needed for fighting. Even so, he filled his lungs and roared, "I will be obeyed in battle!"

The spectators fell silent. Dirk tightened his grip on the cutlass. He attacked with heavier blows, wider slashes, and hacked empty air or caught only steel. The pirates' hubbub resumed. Then the saber struck the cutlass hard enough to sting Dirk's palm and send a shudder all the way up to his shoulder. Before he recovered, the saber connected again. The cutlass flew out of his hand. Pirates howled, tripped and shoved each other dodging the falling blade.

Dirk rolled to escape the slashing, chopping saber, scrambled for his cutlass across hot, loose sand. He caught it in his left hand, struggled to rise against heavy blows. His left-handed skills, more than adequate against Spanish villagers, were no match for Arnaud's expertise. Dirk managed only clumsy, defensive moves.

Arnaud laughed. "Young you were when elected, *mon capitaine*, and young you will be when you die."

Dirk's left arm felt heavy and slow. He knew he would probably lose the fight. And lose the captaincy, too. Fortunes rose and fell rapidly in the sweet trade. *But die? Not this way. Not today.*

Sudden fury destroyed all caution. Dirk lunged at Arnaud, only in the last moment remembering to duck under the saber's deadly arc. He was close now. So close the stench of Arnaud's rotting tooth made Dirk hold his breath. So close the saber point was useless.

Grabbing Arnaud's tunic, Dirk jerked him even closer. As the tip of his short, dark beard brushed Arnaud's face, the Frenchman leaned backward and Dirk let go. Arnaud fell away, his arms wide to keep his balance. Dirk slashed a crimson gorge down the man's chest, from left collarbone to last rib on the right.

"First blood," Perry said over the cheers and groans of the crew. "Stand back."

He pushed Dirk aside as Curtis, the ship's latest surgeon, and Normand rushed in. Dirk obeyed, breathing heavily and swirling his cutlass in circles over the sand. After a few moments, he marched off to join his friends. They pounded his back and shoulders, crowed about the fight. Mic walked among the men, gathering his winnings.

Dirk wanted to dance, to laugh and jeer in Arnaud's face, but instead, rinsed his cutlass in the surf. After drying it on the bottom of his cotton tunic, he handed blade, boots, and leather belt to Baldric. Then he waded into a now-calm sea and swam toward the *Avenger*, laughing until he swallowed a mouthful of seawater.

Few of the crew could swim. They'd wait on shore for the lugger's boats. In the meantime, Dirk knew from previous experience, they'd settle their wagers, squabbling over wins and losses. A fight or two might break out. Perry would settle them with first blood contests, and the betting would start anew.

At the ship, men threw Dirk a rope and hoisted him over the side. They gathered close, asking about the fight.

Farley slapped Dirk's wet shoulder. "'Twas not long to settle that one. I see nary a saber's kiss on ye."

Dirk brushed curling strands of wet hair out of his eyes while mentally switching to English, the crew's common language. He smiled, pulled up his left sleeve and held out his arm.

"Here's one, but it gave up no blood."

Farley grinned. "The luck was with ye, then."

"No luck. I used what you taught me."

Farley slapped his own pantalooned thigh. "Liar." He ambled off, looking pleased.

Dirk recounted the fight to the rest of the men aboard, then went below to his cabin. He stripped, then wrung out the sopping breeches and tunic, and laid them across a stool to dry. Stretched out on his narrow bunk under the slope of the hull, he vowed to keep a tighter rein on his temper when dealing with disgruntled crewmates. He might not be as lucky the next time.

Avoiding fights aboard should not be so difficult. Perry, as quartermaster, commanded the ship when not in battle. Dirk could therefore stay out of most day-to-day business aboard. As captain, he would hold custody over hostages, but they'd never taken any. So planning and leading raids were his only responsibility.

He shifted on the thin straw mattress. There was more than a flogging and Arnaud's ambitions behind today's fight. The man's taunts about Dirk's courage were daily reminders of Halsey and Kirby, and the way they died. Arnaud never let the crew forget that Dirk had sent others to die in his place.

Boats thudded against the lugger's hull, and he heard the chatter of men returning from the beach. He opened one eye as Mic ducked into the cabin and sank onto Perry's bunk. Baldric dropped Dirk's boots, belt and cutlass onto the table bolted to the deck. He sat on a nearby stool and grinned.

"*Mon capitaine*," Mic said, mimicking Arnaud. "The Frenchman is furious. He cursed you, your ancestors and the Low Lands that spawned the whole Dutch race."

"He should have cursed Bentyn's Isle." Dirk sat up. "What do the men say about the fight?"

Baldric said, "Those who bet against you aren't happy, of course. Those who won their wagers..." He shrugged.

"I meant, did you hear anything about the quarrel between Arnaud and me?"

"Well, Normand muttered some threats against you."

"Any others?"

Baldric shook his head. "But some listened while he ranted."

"They don't all trust you yet," Mic said. "Some still want a more experienced man as battle captain. But you've always known that."

Baldric chuckled. "And they certainly were drunk when they elected you."

"That was six months ago! I've led three good raids with plenty of booty. I'm tired of them always testing me." Dirk sighed. They had been at sea nearly a year and he wanted to sail home to Port Royal. But he wanted to solidify his position as captain even more.

"I suppose there's only one remedy for it," he said. "I'll find them another prize."

Dirk spent the rest of the day with Crofton, the *Avenger's* red-faced, sun-wrinkled navigator. A true sea artist, the soft-spoken thirty year old held a detailed map of the Caribbean and all its cities in his head. Together they decided to raid another Cuban village, this one on the northeast shore of the island. The crew voted on the target, accepting Crofton's word it was worth the effort. A few men spoke up for sailing to Port Royal. A couple demanded a share-out; they wanted their reward for the successful raids. They were shouted down by the many who wanted even more treasure.

A ship thirty-six foot on the keel and twelve abeam could provide only so much activity. A bit of sail trimming. Shooting contests that Baldric always won. Gambling, drinking, story-telling. Then fighting over food, shade, and the gambling. Boredom, and everything else, worsened when the rum and brandy supplies ran low.

So when the *Avenger* sailed into the harbor of Villa de Sanchez two mornings later, an excited crew swarmed over the side, some into boats, the rest into chest-high water. The starboard guns fired and the men shouted and cheered. They plunged into the village, only to halt in the central plaza.

On Crofton's assurance the town kept no soldiers, Dirk had ordered a direct attack from the ship. Yet twenty armed Spaniards stood across the front of a mud brick church. He knew most Spanish villages kept their wealth in churches, but they rarely defended a building as small and plain as this one. He considered alternatives to a headlong assault. The Spaniards withdrew into the church.

Baldric raced up. "I found a side door into the church, and another through a lean-to in back."

Dirk nodded, then waved Dunstan and Morris over.

"Take nine to the rear, Dunstan. Morris, nine to the side door with you."

Dunstan clomped toward the church, tapping pirates on the shoulder as he passed them. The leaner, more graceful Morris led his straggling group to the side, but one he chose didn't move.

Morris called, "Normand. With us."

Normand glared at Dirk. "The doorways are too narrow, you stupid Dutchman. One Spaniard alone can hold each door. We'll all be killed."

"Move, damn you!" Dirk raised his voice. "First man through each door wins an extra share!"

Normand looked around for support. "That is a deathtrap!"

The entire crew stopped to watch the quarrel.

Dirk flushed. Without instant compliance to his orders during a raid, he was worthless as a captain, and every moment he argued with Normand gave the Spaniards time to solidify their defense.

"That was a ridiculous order." Normand planted his feet in the dust, pushed his fists into his waist.

"An order, nonetheless." Dirk's breaths grew shallow.

The other pirates shuffled their feet, looked at each other, waited.

"Move," Dirk said, "or die here and now."

Normand thrust out his chin.

Dirk hauled one of the pistols from his belt and shot Normand in the chest. His thick, square body dropped hard.

"Go!" Dirk shouted at the others. "If your backs don't disappear into that church in five seconds, I'll flog the hide off them! Don't let me see any of you again till you come out the front doors!"

The men ran. Smoking pistol in hand, Dirk walked over to Normand, sprawled in the dirt, a look of surprise still on his face. Too angry and confused to feel relieved by his enemy's death, Dirk stared down the man's corpse. Why had he preferred death to obeying an order?

"Dirk!"

He turned at Baldric's shout, saw Arnaud charging at him, Baldric twenty feet behind. With a hand pressed against the seeping bandage on his chest, Arnaud was swinging a saber in broad circles over his head. "Dutchman! You die!"

Dirk stepped aside, flung out his cutlass. He tripped over Normand, wrenching his weak right knee. He rolled away, struggled to his feet. Pain seared through his knee and he could barely stand. Arnaud's saber sliced his forearm.

Baldric slammed his musket butt against Arnaud's head. The Frenchman crumpled in the dirt. Perry ran up, tied Arnaud's hands and feet, and helped Baldric drag him off to the *Avenger*.

Dirk's heart beat rapidly, and he took deep breaths to still it. Then, as he limped toward the church, Dunstan burst out the front door, grinning. Inside, Dirk found captives huddled in a corner. They cowered under Morris's calm gaze and the gently swinging cutlass he dangled by one finger through the knuckle-bow. Other pirates trotted around the church, snatching up statues and silver candlesticks.

Mic waved Dirk over to the wooden altar. "I saw something move behind this."

Dirk nodded. They circled the altar, one on each side, and found a sword-wielding priest. With a short laugh, Dirk raised his cutlass. As the priest swung to meet the attack, Mic disarmed him with a flat-edged blow across his wrist.

"What do you suppose he was protecting?" Dirk shifted weight off his damaged knee and pulled his tunic sleeve tight over the arm wound.

Mic grunted, then nodded to his right. "Maybe this door." Cutlass point on the priest's ear, he said in Spanish, "Be still or I'll split your head on my blade."

Dirk fumbled through the man's robes and found a ring of keys. The fourth key he tried opened the three-inch-thick door. He stepped into a room six feet square. Mic handed the priest off to another pirate and followed Dirk inside.

A barred window high on one wall provided enough light for them to see tall stacks of small, ornate chests. Mic lifted one down and stomped off its lock. He kicked the lid up, then quickly opened two more. Kneeling beside the chests, he reached for the treasure within. "Look at this."

Dirk chuckled. "This is why they defended the church."

The chests were brimming with coins. Gold escudos and doubloons. Silver reales and hundreds of cobs, the squarish pieces of eight struck in New Spain. Easily divided, never needing to be sold before they could be enjoyed, coins were the rarest and most valuable treasure of all.

Pirates crowded the doorway. Word of the coins spread, and a great cheer rose. Grinning, Dirk lifted one of the heavy chests to his shoulder and limped out. Passing through the church, he gave a jaunty salute to the priest, who now sat on the dirt floor, tied to the altar. Dirk's Spanish was good enough to understand the priest as he called down the wrath of God on the pirates, their parents, and all their descendants forever.

By late afternoon, the *Avenger* was at sea again, the hold full of coins, cassava flour, casks of rum, and great coils of new rope. They sailed east to a hidden creek, anchored, and the crew gathered on the deck for a trial. Dirk sat against the bulwark, swollen knee stretched in front of him, bandaged arm cradled over his belly.

Arnaud was accused of trying to murder Dirk. There were four witnesses and Arnaud admitted to the deed.

"That cursed Dutchman killed Normand!" he said.

"Huh!" Dunstan snorted, threw his chest out and popped a button off his embroidered linen surcoat. "Normand disobeyed a battle order."

"A foolish order," Arnaud said. "Many could have died."

"Coward!" André called from the back of the crowd.

A few pirates snickered and Dirk suppressed a grin. Fat little André was the most easily frightened man aboard.

Mic, blue eyes colder than usual, pounded the top of a water barrel.

"A captain has the right to punish anyone during a raid," he said. "Even to kill him."

A murmur of agreement rippled through the crew.

"Disobedience in battle endangers us all," Perry said. "It's worse than a stupid order. And that order did win us all those coins."

Arnaud clamped his jaws shut and stared at the creek bank.

Perry turned to Dirk. "What shall we do with him?"

There were many painful and humiliating things Dirk wanted to do to Arnaud, but he knew what the crew expected to hear. "Make him governor of an island."

The crew's vote to maroon Arnaud was unanimous. Once at sea again, they chose a sandspit out of sight of land. Barely visible at low tide, it would be completely under water at high tide. They left Arnaud a day's supply of water and a pistol with one shot for killing himself if he chose to avoid the agonies of sunstroke and thirst.

Standing at the starboard rail with Mic and Baldric, Dirk kept his eyes on Arnaud until the *Avenger* got under way again. He left the rail, somewhat mollified by Arnaud's fate.

A pistol fired, the ball striking the mast in front of Dirk. He whirled. Arnaud waved his pistol, then threw it after the ship and shook his fist in the air. A string of curses floated across the water.

"Merciful heaven," Baldric said. "Why waste powder and ball like that? Now he'll die so slowly."

"Unless sharks eat him tonight," Mic said.

Dirk stared across the water at an enemy as deadly as any Spaniard.

"Shoot him, Baldric."

Baldric cocked his head in question even as he raised the musket that was never out of his reach. "Everybody voted to maroon him."

"And they expected him to die fast by a shot to the head. Shoot him."

Leaning into the rail, Baldric waited for the *Avenger* to crest a wave. He fired. Arnaud tumbled off the sandspit into the surf.

Behind Dirk, Dunstan said, "He deserved a sorrier death than that, boy."

Farley walked by. "Fine show of compassion. 'Tis good in a leader now and again."

When all but Mic and Baldric had moved away, Mic said, "There's no chance now of Arnaud being rescued by another ship, is there?"

Dirk glanced at him, then back at the empty sandspit. "No," he said, and kept to himself just how relieved he felt about that.

For a day and a night, a storm battered the sea between Cuba and La Florida. High winds tossed the *Avenger* from one crest to another, then dropped her into troughs. Crashing waves threatened to wash men overboard.

Toward the end of the second day, the storm abated. Dirk fought with the wheel, pleased that thunder no longer clapped right in his ears. Each lightning bolt flashed farther away from the *Avenger's* towering mainmast.

Morris, kinky black hair and beard crusted with salt around his narrow, brown face, came to relieve him. Dirk gratefully relinquished the helm. Trying to stay up-right while controlling the rudder had caused terrible pain in both wounded arm and knee. Now, every awkward step across the lurching deck shot fire through his entire leg.

Men in filthy, wet clothes filled the cabin. Too tired even to wrinkle his nose, much less push between men to reach his bunk, Dirk sank onto the deck just inside the door. Eyes closed, body relaxed, he drifted toward sleep.

A tremendous crack jerked him upright. With a shudder, the *Avenger* twisted on her keel. Dirk scrambled outside with the others, reaching the stern just as Morris reported that they'd struck submerged rocks.

"It's the rudder, dammit," Morris said, giving the wheel a spin.

It twirled easily, having no effect on the ship. Dirk looked around and relaxed. Clouds had broken, showing the pink and yellow of an evening sky. The ship lay at the entrance to a cove, an excellent place to shelter and repair the lugger.

"Breakers ahead," Farley called from his perch on the bowsprit.

Between them and the beach, waves broke over a reef. Gusty winds pushed them landward and, without a rudder, the *Avenger* was powerless to avoid the reef. Sick at heart, Dirk joined Crofton at the rail. The sea-artist stared at the line of water frothing over coral, his red face paling as the ship washed closer and closer to destruction.

Carried high by a wave, the *Avenger* crunched onto the reef. Timber shattered. Dirk grabbed the rail as the lugger jerked to a stop and listed to larboard.

"Water in the hold," Dunstan called from below.

Men on deck shouted their dismay. André hopped up and down, his stomach rolls bobbling. "We're going to sink! We're going to sink!"

"Oh, shut your gruel bucket." Crofton had immediately dropped a sounding line over the side. "We're not going to sink in one fathom of water."

The men cheered and laughed. Dirk chuckled as he went to find Sidney, the ship's carpenter. They needed fast repairs. It was dangerous to be stranded so close to Spanish strongholds.

Although the shore lay only 200 feet away, they slept aboard that night. At dawn, the lookout's cry rousted Dirk from his bunk. He pushed his stiff, complaining body up on deck. Perry stood by the rail, looking out to sea.

"Incoming ship." The quartermaster spat over the side and handed Dirk the spyglass.

Dirk put it to his eye and found the sails. "Damn. It's Spanish."

"Do you think they see us?"

"I don't know. Yes, they must. They're headed straight for us. And..." Dirk squinted into the glass and swore again. "Two of them. A schooner and a... yacht."

He bounced the glass against his palm.

"Let's go ashore," he said. "With food, weapons. And Sidney's tools. Maybe if the *Avenger* looks abandoned they'll sail off. We can come aboard later to make repairs."

Perry frowned. "They'll find the coins."

"We can't escape any other way. And we have to hurry."

The men scurried about the ship, rounding up provisions for a landing. Dirk went below to collect his weapons. He heard men drop over the side and start to splash ashore. A shout from Perry brought him back on deck. Spanish soldiers lined the beach. Dirk whirled to look at the approaching ships. Nearly upon the *Avenger*, they had begun to furl their sails. Out-numbered and with storm damaged guns, the pirates could not prevent a boarding.

Shouting men raced across the deck, going nowhere, knocking each other over. Mic and Perry went below, to hide a few coin chests in corners of the hold, they said. Men in the water tried to climb aboard as Spaniards ashore fired muskets at them. Amid the noise, Dirk limped to the cabin for the commission he kept in his personal chest. It was proof they were legal privateers, not pirates.

The *Avenger's* crew muttered and shuffled on the deck as first soldiers, then the captain of the Spanish yacht climbed aboard.

Soldiers encircled the pirates, holding them in a tight clump with primed muskets. Dirk stepped forward and in slow Spanish introduced himself as captain. The Spanish captain acknowledged Dirk with a sneer before inspecting the lugger.

Facing Dirk once again, he said, "The damage is quite extensive. I do not believe it is repairable. We shall bombard the hull to be certain of it."

Dirk clenched his jaws. The *Avenger* would be riddled with shot while helpless upon the reef.

The captain waved a hand at the hatch. "Those chests in the hold. I recognize the seal engraved on them. You are some of the pirates who raided Villa de Sanchez three days ago." He smiled at Dirk. "We hang pirates, and after, we leave their bones to bleach in the sand."

Dirk felt the rope scratching his neck already. Swallowing hard, he handed over the *Avenger's* commission.

The captain scanned it. "So. You are privateers."

"This ship was duly commissioned and you cannot hang us as pirates."

"That is true," the man nodded. "We cannot execute privateers. Except..." He read the commission again. "This letter of marque was issued in Jamaica. It is English. Spain is not at war with England at the moment. This is no longer valid." He smiled. "You are pirates."

The noose tightened around Dirk's throat. He limped aft to the cabin. Fighting down panic, he dug through an oiled-leather box, found a scroll tied with stained blue ribbons, and returned to the deck. He handed it to the Spanish captain.

The captain read the paper. Dirk thought he saw regret in the man's eyes.

"This is Portuguese," the captain said. "Yes, we are at war with Portugal. This letter of marque is valid."

Dirk released the breath he'd been holding.

The captain said, "We take you now as prisoners of war."

Their prison was a square, one-room warehouse built of mud-and-straw bricks. Stripped of weapons and boots, the thirty-seven pirates sat squeezed together on the dirt floor, whispering and glancing at Dirk. Their faces held the same look he'd seen on his friends so often during their childhood. He sighed. In all those months of fighting to be captain, he'd forgotten about the difficult times when those who followed him expected miracles.

He lounged against a wall opposite the door, eyes half-closed, hoping he appeared calm. They were in a village, the Spanish captain had told him, that lay a five-day march from Havana. Farley said they'd be taken there and worked as slaves, beaten and starved, until they died. Escape from the city would be impossible, so Dirk had to find a way out of this village, and soon.

He didn't know what to do. Wrought iron barred the single high window. There was only one door. They might overpower those who came to feed or interrogate them, but, weaponless, they could not simply run to the harbor and take a ship.

Dirk shut his eyes. His knee and arm throbbed with pain. His heart beat rapidly; his breath shortened. The monsters of childhood nightmares, the enemy that stalked him every day of his youth, had caught him at last. This time, his only escape from slavery would be death.

"How long "til we leave this stinking box, do y' think?" Jan's lilting voice was distinct over the other men's grumbles and muttered curses.

"Hard to say." Joost's voice was a little deeper. "If they don't hang us as spies or pirates, we may have to wait 'til Portugal makes peace with Spain."

"Peace with Spain? They've been at war twenty years now. We'll never get away."

"We need a big fleet of brethren right there in the harbor of this pisspot of a town."

Dirk almost smiled. A fleet of pirates would certainly make these villagers quake and plead for mercy. They'd do anything he demanded, maybe even give him a ship and load it with the coins from Villa de Sanchez. If only he could produce a fleet.

By mid-afternoon rank bodies were sweating in the rising heat, and the leaky wooden slop bucket was overflowing. Dirk was breathing through his mouth, and he was relieved when a Spaniard opened the door to call for him and Perry. Six soldiers, bristling with pikes and clubs as well as muskets, pistols and swords, marched them across a dusty plaza bright with flowers. Between the soldiers, Dirk caught glimpses of the harbor.

It appeared clean, deep, and smooth. Five hundred feet out, a brush- and palm-covered island cut off heavy waves and any view of the sea. The schooner and yacht that had captured them that morning rode at anchor in the middle of the bay. The yacht was a beautiful vessel: sleek, two-masted, with leeboards for stability. Fast, easy to handle, and Dutch made, too, if that old freebooter Theo had taught him correctly. The shadow of an idea played in Dirk's mind.

A short sword poked him in the back.

"Faster," a guard said. "The alcalde is waiting."

Dirk climbed brick steps hot under his bare feet, and entered a low, wooden building with a red and yellow flag on its roof.

Perry drew close. "Don't tell them anything," he said softly in English. "Won't do us any good. Just be sent to Havana anyway. Might get a chance to escape along the way."

Dirk nodded. Until he grasped the idea teasing his mind, he'd follow Perry's advice.

Inside, the escort shoved them toward a heavy, carved mahogany table. Behind it sat a soldier, stiff and regal. Although the remnants of his hair were grey and white, his eyes were youthful, alert, and intelligent. All Dirk's fears returned, obscuring the germ of his idea. He shifted from one foot to the other, closing his hands around invisible weapons while the alcalde studied the *Avenger's* commission.

At last the man laid aside the paper. "So you are privateers," he said in slow Spanish, "in the employ of Portugal."

They nodded.

The man shook his head. "I believe you are pirates... simple barbaric thieves. Yet this letter of marque from Portugal appears to be valid. I presume you purchased it in Tortuga?"

Although Mic had won it in a dice game, Dirk nodded.

"You do not look Portuguese. I believe you are English. My captain tells me you attempted to pass off a Jamaican commission that was not valid."

Dirk had no answer. The alcalde appeared undisturbed by the lack of response.

"Jamaica has had designs upon Cuba for many years. I think now you will tell me what is being planned in that devil's stew called Port Royal."

Perry shrugged.

Dirk said, "We don't know of anything."

"We know you did not sail to Cuba alone. The alcalde of Villa de Sanchez reported that four ships attacked his village."

Dirk chewed the inside of his cheek. Of course that alcalde would exaggerate. He wouldn't want to admit he lost so much to so few pirates. The elusive idea danced closer, but Dirk shook his head. "We sailed alone."

The alcalde turned to Perry. "Do you also say you sailed alone?"

"Yes."

The alcalde sighed. "I see that courtesy is not sufficient. We shall have to use other methods of persuasion."

Dirk's scalp prickled. The Spaniards were infamous for their tortures. Pirates adopted some Spanish methods themselves now and again. But nobody was going to wind a wet leather strap around his throat and then tie him in the sun so the strap strangled him as it dried. They weren't going to burn him or cripple his limbs. He was only twenty-one and planned to live, healthy and whole, to at least twenty-five. Maybe even thirty.

If that old Spaniard demanded information, Dirk would tell him exactly what he wanted to hear. Fear disappeared as an idea jumped fully blown into his mind.

"One more time. Did you sail alone?"

Perry nodded.

Dirk said "No" and clamped his jaws against his mate's glare.

The alcalde smiled. "A wise man." He drew parchment across the desk and dipped a quill into a squat inkpot. "Now. You will tell me how many ships are in your fleet."

Dirk counted on his fingers. "Seven ships. Perhaps two days

behind us."

Perry gasped.

"How many men?"

Dirk avoided Perry's glance. "Three hundred or so."

"It is good to speak with a pirate with such excellent recall. However, I doubt that so many men would sail only to Villa de Sanchez. What was your true destination?"

Dirk hesitated a moment. "Havana."

Perry groaned and shook his head. Dirk clamped his teeth down on the insides of both cheeks.

"I suspected that to be your target."

"But now they'll stop here first," Dirk said.

"Here? ¡*Madre de Dios*! Why here?"

"The coins. Privateers don't like to lose enemy stores they've just won."

"They will not know where to find the coins."

"We left a message aboard our ship."

"Satan's crown!" The alcalde slammed a fist on the table. "I told them they should have burned that hulk!" He glared at Dirk. "It is of no consequence. The coins are aboard the yacht which will sail tonight. Your friends will not find them."

"But they won't know that until they land. And then, they'll sack this town so as not to have wasted the trip."

"We shall be prepared for them."

"You don't have enough soldiers to hold off three hundred."

The man frowned.

"If you send to Havana for men," Dirk said, "the governor will assume that our target was the capital. He will demand men from you. What is this place compared to the city?"

The alcalde's jaw tightened.

"You must free us," Dirk said.

Perry rolled his eyes and turned away.

The alcalde exploded out of his chair. "Set you free? In God's Holy Name, why should I do something so foolish?"

"To save your town."

The man sank back into his chair.

Perry stared at the floor, shaking his head.

Dirk took a deep breath. "Our brethren are coming here for the coins and for us." It was hard to keep excitement out of his voice. "They *will* come, even if you take the coins elsewhere. Or transport us elsewhere. They will come unless someone tells them the coins are no longer here."

"You should be that someone?"

Dirk stared at him. "Would they believe you?"

The alcalde scowled.

Dirk softened his tone. "Release us. Our brethren won't attack this place if they know the coins aren't here. Send warning to Havana about the fleet. Win the governor's gratitude and save your town."

The alcalde squinted up at Dirk. "You are being very helpful with your advice."

Dirk shrugged. "You and I can both have what we want if you free us."

The alcalde's face reddened, his brows furrowed. The dark eyes closed. Then his face grew smooth and very still. When opened again, the eyes held a malicious glint. He rose, shouted for his secretary and a captain. He spoke to them in Spanish too rapidly for Dirk to follow. At one point both secretary and captain paled, and glanced at Dirk.

"Pirate," the alcalde finally said, "I will set you free."

Perry's head jerked up. His mouth hung open as the alcalde continued.

"We shall transport you and your men to the island that lies across the mouth of our bay. You can hail your fellow thieves from the seaward shore. There is no water on the island, but you mentioned, did you not, that the fleet would sail by soon?"

He smiled, though his eyes remained cold and hard. Dirk's own smile felt wobbly.

The old man had won. If other pirates did come, Dirk would have to tell them the coins had been taken elsewhere. That Havana had been warned and mustn't be given any more time to prepare a defense. No fleet of pirates would waste time sacking this little place. And if no fleet ever came....

Dirk and his crew would die of thirst waiting for that non-existent fleet.

The *Avenger's* crew stomped up and down their island prison. Few could swim even the short distance to shore, and the schooner and yacht anchored 200 feet away in the center of the bay discouraged attempts. So the pirates shook their fists and cursed the Spaniards. They complained about the lack of food and water, and they bickered over every bit of shade made by spindly palms and thick bushes. They muttered and glared at Dirk.

Dirk sat alone at the western edge of the island, quite aware of the crew's mood. That one last raid to protect his position had lost it all. What good was a fortune in coins if no one lived to spend them? And if by some miracle they escaped this trap, the men would remember that Dirk had talked them out of prison and onto a desert island. They would never keep him as captain. There was but one way off the island. Dirk and a few others must swim tonight. But in which direction? How far would they have to swim before they could go ashore safely? Then they'd have to find a boat, row back for the others....

He rubbed his forehead. A boat could carry only a few men at a time. He needed a ship, perhaps that schooner or yacht still lying between them and the village. There were too many soldiers aboard the schooner, and although the pirates might capture the yacht, they could never sail it out of the harbor past the schooner.

Frustration mixed with fear became an overwhelming weariness. Dirk settled in the sand to sleep.

Much too soon, a kick on his foot woke him. He blinked up through the sunshine at Mic.

"They're moving the yacht."

Dirk sat up. With a lone sail raised, the yacht glided past the schooner, swung close to the island and sailed west out of the bay.

"That's the wrong direction," he said. "Why aren't they taking the coins east? Back to Villa de Sanchez?"

Mic shrugged.

"Sit down and let me think."

While Mic sat cross-legged beside him, Dirk used his finger to draw little circles in the sand.

"We're here. We won the coins here. The *Avenger* lies between."

Dirk brushed away the *A* he'd made for the *Avenger*. It was derelict now and at the moment he had no time to mourn it. He marked Havana to the west and an arrow showing the yacht's direction.

"The alcalde can't keep the coins here. He doesn't want them recaptured by our fleet."

"Dirk, there is no fleet."

"Pretend. And tell me why the yacht isn't taking the coins back to Villa de Sanchez."

Mic rolled his eyes. "Well, if this fleet, that's in your imagination, was with us on the raid and is now moving west, that yacht, eastbound, might sail directly into it."

"True enough. But why sail toward the capital? The ship'll just be lost when the fleet arrives there."

"Maybe it's not going to Havana. Maybe these villagers want to keep all those coins for themselves. Maybe that yacht's going to hide in a cove, or a river for several days. Until your fleet doesn't arrive."

Dirk grinned. "Yes, and how far away do you think that hiding place will be?"

A slow smile crossed Mic's face. "With a pirate fleet out there somewhere, headed for this town? The alcalde wouldn't risk having those coins at sea very long."

Dirk drew an 'X' just west of the village. "I think we'll find that yacht close by."

Toward dusk, the rising tide pushed everyone to the center of the island. Fights over limited space broke out. Dirk ignored them, as well as the pirates' howls for food and water. He huddled with Perry, Farley and Mic on the seaward side of the island.

"Six or eight of us can swim," Dirk said. "We'll head west and go ashore once we're out of sight—"

"And sound," Mic said.

"—and sound of the village. When we find that yacht—"

"Are ye sure ye know where that ship anchors?" Farley sounded worried.

Dirk shook his head. "But we'll take it, then—"

"And what will ye fight with if ye do come upon them Spanish? Ye got no weapons, lad."

"We'll take the ship, don't trouble your mind about that. And then we'll sail it back here and anchor on this side of the island."

"Keep a fair distance, so them on that schooner don't see ye through the palms. And mayhap it be well to swim a rope in for us. That way them papists won't hear any oars of a boat."

Perry glanced at the waves behind him and shuddered. "There are monsters out there. Sharks. Mantas."

"We'll die for certain if we stay here," Mic said.

Farley nodded. "Filling a shark's gut is quicker than dying of yer own empty belly."

"We are not going to die," Dirk said.

The two older men grinned.

Perry patted Dirk's shoulder. "Go for your swim, lad. Maybe you can outsmart the sharks as good as you did the alcalde."

Dirk grimaced, the other three laughed, and the meeting ended. Then while Mic consulted Crofton on the tide and time of moonrise, Dirk spoke quietly with the other pirates who could swim. Several agreed to go, insisting they were eager to escape the island despite the dangers of a nighttime swim in the sea.

At the first hint of moonrise, Dirk, Mic, and seven others slipped one by one into the warm water. They would swim west, just past the breakers, until the moon had fully risen, then go ashore.

Two days had passed since Dirk's last meal. Even in the calm sea, his strength waned quickly. His muscles burned. Little waves broke over his head, most often just as he opened his mouth for a gasp of air. He coughed, spit salty water, and grew thirstier.

He rolled over and saw only half of the moon. He floated awhile to rest. The others swam behind, or maybe beside, him. He was alone between waves, and so tired. Only the vision of dying of thirst in full view of Spaniards kept him from wishing himself back on the island.

Cold flesh scraped under his back. Something hard caught his arm and pulled him face down in the water. He kicked to the surface.

"Shark! To shore!"

He thrashed toward shore with strength he'd thought long gone. His feet hit sand at last, and he slogged through the surf onto a narrow beach. Legs quivering with fatigue, he lurched into the depths of a shrub before collapsing to catch his breath.

Alone, worried, and without a weapon, he sat motionless. Sharks might have torn Mic and the others apart. The moon rose completely, and no one else came ashore within sight. A twig snapped in the forest behind him. A soldier? And that rustling. A deadly night creature?

He concentrated on the sea, searching the waves for the others until his eyelids drooped. The soft whoosh of the surf lulled him almost to sleep, and brought familiar hauntings that always filled him with guilt and despair. Tonight, with no action, no conversation, no planning to occupy his mind, he could not resist them.

Like the ocean's watery breath that slid toward him, then away, his mother's dying scream faded in and out of his hearing, forever blocking from him the sound of her laughter and gentle crooning. A large wave crashed onto the beach, as Gilbert's fist had so often crashed against Dirk's young body, covering his youth with pain the way water now filmed over the sand. From a frothy curl, Baldric's nine year old face gaped at Dirk, who was leaving the younger boy to an unknown fate.

Then there was a girl, her mouth open in a scream that was a barely heard whisper in the leaves rustling around him. And Anneke. Always Anneke, running toward him, arms out, reaching for an older brother who could not save her.

In the morning, feeling light-headed, Dirk picked up a rock and the biggest stick he could find. Guessing his men had come ashore long after he did, he walked west.

He found Gustave, who didn't have enough sense to sit in bushes out of the sun. Although Gustave was neither Mic nor Morris with his calm, dependable ways, he was company, and proof the sharks hadn't eaten everybody.

They found Mic and five others by mid-morning. Roaming the beach and woods, they looked in vain for the last man. Morris, however, found an untended garden full of yams ready to harvest. With the others, Dirk clawed in the dirt for the first food he'd had in three days. The yams were hard and dirt gritted on his teeth, but even a few bites helped. The sweet water in a tiny pond was even better.

Gustave broke into a reed hut, looking for liquor he said. Something inside screeched; Gustave roared. The man hurtled out the door, a tiny, black-gowned figure clamped on his back. On his short, bowed legs, Gustave stumbled around the farm plot, howling and twisting from side to side.

Dirk ran up behind them and yanked the creature off. He shook the woman, then tucked her against his waist. The pirates hooted with laughter.

"Gustave, you fool!" Morris said between snorts. "You can't even best an old woman."

Gustave flushed red. "She's a witch. She put a spell on me and now she's killed me with her poison bite." He drew a blood-covered hand away from his neck. "Look at this."

Mic grinned at Dirk. "Do you think she's worth much ransom?"

"A crushed pearl, maybe." Dirk sat on a tree stump and set the woman on her feet in front of him. She kicked and spat, quieting only when he called her *abuela,* grandmother in Spanish.

"She must farm this sorry little place," Morris said, still on his knees digging.

Dirk held the woman's bony arms and studied her face. The deep wrinkles were rivulets of dirt, but her eyes showed cunning, so he maintained a firm grip.

"What are you going to do with her?" Mic asked.

"I don't know."

"I'll strangle her," Gustave said, "and send her back to her fork-tailed master." He chomped on a yam he'd snatched from Morris.

The old woman cocked her head at Dirk, then gave a cackling smile that almost closed her eyes.

"We can't let her go," Mic said. "She'll raise an alarm."

"This place is a long way from everything," Dirk said.

"We don't know exactly where we are," Morris said.

Dirk pondered the situation. This old woman wasn't much of a threat. He could break her scrawny neck with a light blow, or carry her under one arm for hours, never feeling the weight.

"We'll take her with us."

"She put the enchantment on you, Dirk." Gustave threw his meal to the ground and stomped it flat. "She'll melt us all with her evil eye."

Dirk glanced at the others. Most smirked at Gustave, but two gave the woman furtive looks of horrified curiosity.

"Find me some rope," Dirk said. "And look for weapons."

Mic and two others ducked into the hut, then out again with lengths of rope, a carving knife, a hoe, and a jug of palm liquor. Dirk tied the old woman's hands in front of her, leaving a four foot lead. He told her, in Spanish, to make no sound. The men all stuffed their pockets with yams, returned to the shore and marched west.

At mid-day, they reached the mouth of a river too wide, deep, and fast to cross. Dirk led them inland. Maybe the yacht would be anchored upstream.

Instead, they found a thigh-deep, rocky ford. Dirk hefted his captive under an arm and waded across. Just as he set the woman down on the other side, Morris screamed. Dirk swung back. Men scrambled out of churning water. A cayman, at least twelve feet long, had crushed Morris between huge jaws. The beast swung its snout back and forth, rows of teeth sawing into Morris's back and belly. He was dragged underwater, screams silenced and dark legs kicking in the air as he disappeared.

Dripping pirates panted and cursed. The woman laughed. Gustave stomped over and cuffed her hard.

"That monster was her familiar," he said.

The woman worked her mouth, then spit out a tooth. She grinned up at Dirk, blood smearing her gums and hatred glinting from clear, black eyes.

"Two," Dirk said to Mic. "We've lost two and the only enemy we found is this crone."

With a deep breath, he wound the rope around his hand and moved on. Swift, unexpected deaths were too common to distract the men from their search for the yacht. For his own sorrow, action against Spaniards was always the best cure.

At dusk they found the yacht anchored in a river, bow toward the sea. Dirk tore a sleeve off his tunic, gagged the crone and tied her to a tree. Then he stood in dense foliage counting the enemy and studying the surrounding forest. The Spaniards outnumbered them twelve to seven and had weapons. Yet the prize lay within reach now. He sent Gustave upstream with orders to cross the river, work his way downstream again, and begin collecting rocks.

By nightfall, only two soldiers stood casual guard duty on the yacht's deck. They spoke loudly, words slurred, staggered a bit, and laughed a lot. A rock clipped one on the head. He crumpled.

The other soldier giggled and pointed at the fallen man. "*¡Estás borracho*!"

Dirk stifled a chuckle. They were both drunk.

The Spanish captain who had captured the pirates three days ago strutted across the deck. He shouted at the men, stamped his foot and beat the fallen one with a short whip. The other guard cowered against the bulwark.

The captain crashed to the deck. The rock that had struck him bounced twice on the deck. Silence crept through the ship. Then soldiers shouted, stumbled over each other, demanded to know the source of the danger. When Gustave started a barrage of rocks against the starboard hull, they drew their blades and fired muskets into the dark water.

In the confusion, Dirk boosted Mic, the crone's knife in his teeth, up to the stern gallery. With Dirk lifting and Mic pulling, the rest of the pirates quickly scrambled aboard. By the time Mic threw down a line and Dirk climbed over the taffrail, there were only eight Spaniards left to fight. Three pirates had acquired swords. Another held two soldiers against the foremast with a pistol. Dirk dove into the hand-to-hand fighting.

The next morning, sleepy soldiers aboard the schooner still anchored in the Spanish village's harbor gaped in shock at the island they'd been guarding all night. The pirates were gone. In their place, lying trussed and gagged in the sand, were a dozen soldiers and an old woman dressed in black.

The pirates found food and rum, none of their boots, but many of their weapons and the Villa de Sanchez coins aboard the yacht. They renamed it *Serpent* and sailed through the Windward Passage toward Jamaica, at the center of the Caribbean. Too excited even to quarrel, the men passed the time with stories of how they would spend the great treasure.

The *Serpent* approached Port Royal with half-sails. Two pinnaces, swift in the light wind, sailed out to greet the yacht as it neared the harbor. One of the small ships hove to alongside and across the water came the traditional pirate greeting.

"Whence do you come?"

Perry stood in the bow holding a small chest open so that coins gleamed in the sunlight. He shouted, "From the seas!"

The closer pinnace raised a flag depicting swords crossed under a pile of gold doubloons. The other guard ship hoisted a similar flag and skipped off to precede the *Serpent* into the harbor.

Crofton held the yacht near shore, avoiding shoals south and west of the peninsula that closed much of the harbor off from the sea. A marsh that once had separated the peninsula from Port Royal's cay had been filled in by the English and was used as a graveyard now. As Dirk stood at the starboard rail watching familiar land slide by, Farley came to stand beside him. The older man nodded his dark head at the sun-bleached headstones.

"Do not ponder on the sorry end of us all, lad. Like as not ye'll die afighting soon enough."

"So long as my bones don't rot in a Spanish prison," Dirk replied. "So long as I die a free man."

The little sailmaker laughed, his black eyes dancing. "Think of the living ye'll do tonight, with fresh belly timber and wenches to play with yer cobblers."

Ordnance fired from the harbor's entrance cut off further conversation. The *Serpent* slipped under the fort's thirty guns, and Dirk relaxed as he never could on the open sea. The bay was deep and free of shoals, and big enough to accommodate 500 pirate ships. Port Royal was safe from Spanish raiders who killed and burned in the night. This was one home they could not destroy.

Guns boomed from ships and forts, and in the city, church bells pealed. As Crofton found anchorage away from the wharf, people streamed out of the mass of wood and brick buildings toward the *Serpent*.

The crew quickly unloaded the treasure chests and emptied them onto an old sail spread on the beach. Accompanied by "oohs" and "aahs" from onlookers, Perry began the long task of counting and dividing the coins. The crew ringed the sail, eyes following Perry's every move. They watched each other, too. Dirk chuckled. He'd trust these men with his life, but there was gold and silver on that canvas. Stray coins might disappear into sleeves.

Merchants, doxies and tavern owners pushed as close as the pirates allowed. The governor's long-faced secretary crossed the sand with much fanfare—and two assistants—and elbowed his way to stand on a corner of the sail.

"I am here," he said with a sniff, "to ensure that the Crown of England receives its share of this war contraband." Sniff.

Perry grinned at the bespectacled man. "Many regrets, my dear fellow, but this booty was taken ashore. And under a Portuguese commission. The Crown gets none of it."

The secretary's face grew longer and his shoulders drooped. Many in the crowd snickered. Dirk laughed aloud. Perry scooped a handful of coins into a small pouch and passed it to the secretary.

"For the Governor," he said.

The secretary adjusted his wig of dark ringlets and led his two assistants back to the city.

The newly captured ship belonged to all the crew, so Perry divided the forty ownership shares equally among them.

"Let me have yours, Dirk," Mic said.

"You'll gamble with it."

"No, I'll invest it. Make us a lot of profit."

With an exaggerated sigh, Dirk gave his coins to Mic. He suspected, and approved of, what that investment might be.

Perry counted out the captain's two shares, dropped them into a chest and presented it to Dirk. "Well done."

The men cheered. Dirk gave them an extravagant bow, his left arm sweeping out to the side. Their cheers and praise felt fine, though he knew that when their coins were gone and they were aboard the *Serpent* once more, they'd complain, make demands, and expect miracles. Even so, he would continue the fight to remain captain, for that position gave him the power to protect his freedom and control how he punished the Spanish.

But for a while, at least, he was master of his life. For weeks, he'd have plenty of brandy to ease the persistent ache in his knee. He could sleep away his afternoons in a hammock, swaying in the cool breeze. There'd be dice and card games to enliven his evenings, and endless nights with his arms around soft, beautiful women.

With a grin, he hefted the chest of coins to his shoulder and followed his men into Port Royal.

Port Royal, Jamaica, 1665

In a small attic room over Willem's Tavern, Dirk watched a tiny spider spin a web in Harlan's bushy, dark beard. The long-time member of the *Serpent*'s crew was negotiating the sale of his ownership shares to Dirk and Mic. Harlan thrust out his chin, jostling the spider. It hesitated a moment, then went back to work.

"Not that I want t' sell," Harlan said. "The *Serpent* she's been good t' me 'n all, but I need the money bad."

Mic, sitting behind a wobbly wooden table, nodded, wrote in his ledger. From his perch on a windowsill Dirk breathed through his teeth as Harlan rambled on. The man filled the rented room with the stench of rotten meat, decaying teeth, and stale rum, thus Dirk's choice of a seat in the open window when he had arrived late to the negotiations. Mic drew a small chest from under one of the three beds crowding the room and began to count out some coins.

Harlan went on. "Hungry or no, if Cap'n here..." He nodded at Dirk. "wasn't a part of this, I wouldn't sell. 'Course, if it wasn't for him, I wouldn't never a had a piece t' sell. So I guess it's fitting it comes back t'—"

"Two hundred pieces-of-eight," Mic said. "That's what we agreed upon?"

"Aye."

Mic finished stacking the coins and swept them into a large pouch. Tying it neatly, he passed it to Harlan, then shook the man's grimy paw.

Harlan hurried to the door, then turned back. "Dirk, lad, when'll the *Serpent* sail again?"

"Next week. And we'd be glad to have you aboard, you old gallows bird."

Harlan grinned. He shook the pouch, making the coins chink. "Hope this lasts 'til then. I don't want t' sign on another ship." He left, muttering, "Now for that brandy."

Dirk went to shut the door behind him. As he returned to the window, Mic glanced up from his ledger.

"Been to the barber, I see," he said. "Your neck and chin are very pale."

Dirk ran a hand over his hair. Curls that ended above his collar did feel strange. He'd had the barber shave his beard, as well, leaving only a thick mustache that curved up at the corners of his mouth. "I'm cooler this way."

"And a bath, too." Mic shook his head. "Gilbert's been dead for years and you're still hopping into big buckets of water. And buying new clothes."

Dirk shrugged inside his unbleached cotton tunic. "I'm hoping he can see me from hell."

Mic returned to the ledger, poring over the numbers, a little smile on his face. "A few more good raids, my friend, and we'll be wealthy."

Since they had acquired the *Serpent* three years ago, Mic had used his money and Dirk's to buy up the crew's shares of the *Serpent*. Whenever a crew member ran out of money, became desperate for drink, Mic offered to buy his share. Now every raid put thirty-five extra shares into their cache buried in the floor of Willem's storeroom.

"Good," Dirk said. "I don't ever want to serve another man."

"Or take orders from a stupid one."

Dirk chuckled, remembering Mic's master, a buffoon whom Mic had easily, and regularly, manipulated.

"How many of the crew still have their shares?"

"Only Baldric and the twins," Mic said. "I don't suppose you'll ever let those three get hungry or thirsty enough to sell."

Dirk laughed. "No, I won't." He shifted on the sill to look outside. "There's a fight in the street."

Mic didn't look up from his work. "I can hear it."

Still watching the fighting below, Dirk spoke casually. "We're losing our quartermaster."

"Is Perry sick? That wound he took on Yucatan wasn't serious. Did it fester?"

"No, he says he's tired. He's almost thirty and wants to start a plantation. You should take his place."

"Not I, friend. Not quartermaster."

"With your memory you're the best man for it."

"You know I prefer working the sails."

Dirk turned from the window. "Ready to come down for dinner? The rest are at the table."

"Not quite." Mic dipped the quill in ink and added yet another figure to his ledger. "You go. I'll be down in a few minutes."

Dirk nodded, then left the room plotting how to convince Mic to become the *Serpent*'s quartermaster.

Downstairs in the tavern's main room, Willem climbed up and down a low stool to light lamps that hung from the ceiling beams. His eleven year old son Arvie, with the same stout build and easy smile, carried the stool from lamp to lamp. Settled in a corner, two guitarists tuned their instruments to the tones of the flute player.

Mic came down the stairs. Dirk took two long-stemmed clay pipes from the rack on the wall and tossed one to him. They joined Baldric and the twins at a round table in the center of the room. Dunstan was there, wearing a too-tight brocade surcoat he'd won from the Spanish in Yucatan. Mic packed and lit his pipe, then nodded toward the twins, who were sitting hunched over, staring into tankards of ale.

"Why aren't they home with their wife?" Mic asked.

Dirk clucked his tongue. "Sad story. Vinna's left them."

"When?"

"They sailed to Tortuga early last week and when they came home today, eight people were living in their room."

Baldric grinned. "The landlord told them Vinna ran off with a tobacco planter from Virginia."

A serving maid brought more tankards for the twins. She laid her hands on their shoulders. They ignored her.

"My condolences," Mic said. "A terrible thing for Vinna to run off like that."

"Terrible." Joost moaned. "Terrible."

"I cannot believe she'd do such a thing," Jan said, then added a sob.

They drained their tankards at the same time and plopped them on the table. Dirk signaled for two more.

"I forget," Dirk said, "which one of you was married to her?"

Jan sniffed. "Well, I went through the ceremony."

"Why don't you divorce her? You certainly have just cause."

"That's too much work," Joost said. "Papers to fill out."

"Fees to pay," Jan said.

Two dark-haired serving maids brought them more ale in a clay pitcher. The shorter one brushed her bosom across Jan's ear.

"Poor fellow," she said.

Jan pulled her onto his lap. The second maid slid onto Joost's. He tightened an arm around her.

Mic said, "But if you don't divorce her you'll never be able to marry again."

Jan hung his head. "No matter. Joost can do the ceremony next time."

Joost nodded without looking up. "*If* we ever marry again... it's not likely."

"Oh, Vinna." Jan sighed into his ale. "How could you?"

"We were so good to you." Joost buried his face between the ample breasts of his wench.

She smoothed his hair. "There, there, go ahead and cry. 'Twill do you good. Then later maybe I can help you forget."

"Never," came a muffled reply. "No one can ever replace her."

"No one." Jan leaned against his companion's shoulder and worked at the drawstring of her blouse. A breast popped free and he cupped it with his hand, sighing. "Never."

Dirk winked at Mic and puffed on his pipe to hide a grin.

A small blond woman brought them a plate of beef. As she leaned over the table, her thick curls fell across Dirk's arm. He thanked her for the meat. She flashed him a wide smile and was gone.

"Who's that?" Dirk asked. "I haven't seen her before."

"That's Willem's cousin Frieda," Baldric said, his voice warm. "She's visiting from Nieuw Amsterdam."

"New York," Mic said.

"Visiting?" Dirk watched her walk to the work table in front of the fireplace.

"Careful," Mic said. "Don't let Reba catch you flirting with her."

Dirk glanced at the tall serving wench by the fireplace and snorted. "Don't worry. I can handle Reba."

Reba had been his favorite for nearly six months. By far the prettiest woman at Willem's, she had red-brown hair, a narrow waist, and high, round breasts. And her contagious smile more than made up for her temper.

Dirk sat back in his chair, gazing at Mic, whose mouth curled down.

"What's on your mind, Dirk?"

"I need someone I can trust as quartermaster."

"You want someone to help dominate the crew. I'd rather be sail master or navigator."

"We're not losing our sail master or navigator."

Mic slowly relit his pipe, then took a long swallow of ale from his tankard. "No."

"But, Mic, I—"

Frieda returned with more hot bread for the basket. She set a clay pitcher of ale beside it. Baldric introduced her around the table.

"Van Cortlandt." She sat beside Dirk and smiled up at him. "I've heard the name. Do you have family in the north?"

"In Nieuw Amsterdam, I believe."

"New York," Mic said. "It's New York now."

"Are you sure that little war with England is done?" Baldric asked.

"It didn't last a week, in the fur colonies, at least." Frieda grimaced. "And it wasn't even a war. The Duke of York's men sailed into the river and claimed the colony."

Joost looked up from his companion's wandering hands. "Why didn't the Dutch fight?"

"I think the merchants figured they'd fare better under English rule."

"Do they?" Mic asked.

"I think so. At least their profits don't go to the Dutch West India Company any more."

Frieda laughed. "Director-General Stuyvesant negotiated very good terms for us. Better than any other English colony. And the peace treaty gave us Dutch a spice island in the East Indies."

She turned back to Dirk. "You've never visited your family there?"

"I've never even met any of them." Dirk refilled everyone's tankards. "Maybe we can sail north before the hurricanes start next summer."

"We can't afford to sail north this coming summer," Mic said.

"But if I have family there—"

A loud crack rang out above the taphouse noises. Dirk looked over his shoulder into the back corner where a small barrel, slats grey and loose with age, hung from a ceiling beam. A blindfolded man swung a club at the barrel, a circle of other players laughing at his misses. The club connected again. The cat trapped inside howled.

Dirk snorted in disgust, then he returned to Frieda's tales of Nieuw Amsterdam. A few minutes later Reba elbowed her way between Frieda and Dirk to set another pitcher of ale on the table.

Her back to Dirk, she said, "Frieda, your cousin needs you."

Frieda smiled at the men and left. Reba bent over the table to retrieve the empty pitcher. As she straightened and turned to leave, the pitcher clipped the side of Dirk's head. Pain stabbed behind his eyes. He rubbed his head.

"Oh, I'm so sorry," she said.

He didn't believe her, yet said, "I'm sure it was an accident."

Reba gasped, a hand on her bosom. "Certainly it was." She leaned toward him; the neckline of her blouse fell open. "I've missed you. Let's go up to your room."

"Not now." The sight of her breasts, round and firm as oranges, sorely tempted him, but his ship needed a new quartermaster more.

"But why not? It's been over a week now. You can't be without a woman that long. Not in port, by God."

"I have business to discuss, and I want to finish my supper."

Reba's voice grew shrill. "It's that blond hussy from the north, isn't it? I heard you talking Dutch with her. You're tumbling her, aren't you? That's why you got no time for me anymore."

"Take care. You'll give me ideas."

She whirled to leave. The pitcher would have cracked Dirk on the head again, but he ducked in time. He caught Reba by the waist, pulled her onto his lap, yanked the pitcher out of her hand and banged it on the table.

With a hand tangled in her long, dark hair, he tugged her head back for a kiss. Her arms slid around his neck as he soothed her with kisses on her neck and talk of a gift. When he felt she had relaxed, he set her back on her feet. She was smiling again. Someone at another table called for brandy, and she flounced off to the serving counter. Satisfied, Dirk reached for the platter of roasted beef.

"What did you tell her?" Mic asked.

"That I had a gift for her. That's the easiest way to handle Reba. Kisses and presents."

"You're wasting your money."

"Mic, Mic, sometimes money's more valuable when it's being spent."

"Not likely."

Dirk laughed and took a large hunk of bread out of the basket.

A roar filled the back of the tavern as a short, scrawny man shattered the weathered barrel and a gold tabby wriggled free. Tearing off his blindfold, the man chased the cat as it raced among legs and benches. The game would not be over, nor winnings collected, until the animal was killed.

As the cat scooted past Dirk's chair, the club caught its tail. The cat screeched; the crowd laughed. The man straightened, hefted his club and set off on the chase again. He tripped over Dirk's foot and sprawled head first under a table. Back on his feet in a moment, he cursed and slashed a thin knife through the air. People nearby grew silent and backed away.

"Who did that?" He glared at the crowd. "God damn the bastard who'd pull a trick like that. Speak up, coward, or I'll find y' later and slice yer throat."

Dirk sighed and pushed back his chair.

Fury drained from the other man's face and it took on the pallor of fear. His eyes flicked across Dirk's chest at shoulders twice the breadth of his own.

Dirk took a step, his heavy thigh muscles rippling beneath his short cotton breeches.

"You called for me?" Dirk boomed into the hush. He squinted down at the man.

The fellow dropped his arms to his side. "Why'd y' trip me?"

"Why make a bloody mess on Willem's floor?"

The man shrugged. "It's the game."

"Hmm... I've always played it that the game is over when the cat jumps free."

"Well... I suppose y' could be right."

"If you'd like to discuss it further, we could step outside and let all these people go back to their pleasures."

The man's eyes widened. "Oh, no, that's fine, no harm done. I'll get me money anyhow."

Dirk stared, brows raised, at the other players. When they nodded, he smiled. "Good."

He sat down. For a few moments, he could feel the little man radiating anger behind him. Then Baldric pulled his musket halfway out from under the table and the man finally moved off and rejoined his friends.

The dark-haired wenches did a fine job of restoring the twins' spirits. After the four of them made a quick trip upstairs, the women returned to their chores. Jan called for dice. Frieda brought them, then stayed to chat with Baldric. Dirk smoked his pipe while Mic won some of Jan's money.

Dirk understood why Mic hesitated to become quartermaster. In that position, he'd have more responsibility than Dirk. Besides commanding the *Serpent* whenever she was not in battle, it would be his duty to arbitrate quarrels, impose discipline, keep records of booty taken, and lead every landing party going ashore for water, food or to spy. During a raid, he'd choose what to steal, as different articles brought a wide range of prices in the various markets. He would also have to conduct every share-out.

Mic looked up, narrowed his eyes at Dirk and slowly shook his head. Dirk turned to Frieda, who sat talking with Baldric. She laughed when she heard that Dirk bathed to mock a long-dead master, and bought new clothes just because the old ones were torn and stained. Smiling, she rubbed the white sleeve of his tunic.

"Very pretty. And you're all scrubbed like a babe."

Baldric laughed. "Maybe you'd better check behind his ears."

With a chuckle, Frieda reached for Dirk's ear. Reba swooped down on them and shoved her.

"Because your cousin owns this place you think you can sit and bother the customers?"

Frieda rolled her eyes. "That is not your concern."

With a snarl, Reba grabbed a handful of blond hair and yanked Frieda off the stool. Freida gained her footing and slapped Reba. Red-faced and howling, Reba flung the contents of an ale pitcher at Frieda. Most of it landed on Dirk. His clean hair and new clothes dripped with ale.

Mic burst out laughing. "So you know how to handle Reba."

Dirk wiped ale off his clenched jaw. More of it slid down the inside of his tunic.

Still hollering, Reba tried to scratch Frieda, who swung her face out of reach. Reba's fingernails caught the shoulder of Frieda's blouse, ripping the sleeve to the elbow. Frieda punched the larger woman in the stomach. Reba's screeching rose as she pounced.

With hair, skirts and fists flying, they fell hard onto the plank flooring. The tavern's customers gathered round, cheering them on, wagering on the outcome. Reba pinned Frieda to the floor, sat on her stomach, and swung at her face. Frieda blocked the punches, but couldn't escape. Willem, broom in hand, was trying to reach the fight, but spectators held him back.

"I'll teach you to try and steal my man!" Reba hollered. "He belongs to me and nobody touches him!"

"I don't... want your... scurvy pirate," Frieda got out between blows.

The crowd roared with laughter. Dirk felt his neck and face grow hot. He stood so quickly that his chair crashed to the floor. He stomped over to the women, lifted Reba by the waist and turned her up for three hard whacks on the rump. Then he set her on her feet and shoved her toward the serving counter.

"No earbobs!" he roared.

Reba spat at him and stalked off. Baldric helped Frieda up, his arm around her shoulders. Amid the chuckles and jeers of the tavern's customers, Dirk returned to the table.

Mic's mouth twisted. "So presents are the best way to handle Reba."

Dirk glared at him. Mic grinned and resumed the dice game. Dirk picked up his pipe, cursed, and dropped it on the table. "Too hot." He blew on his fingers and looked around the room for Willem's younger son. "Timmy!"

At his bellow, a wide-eyed boy of five ran up with another of Dirk's pipes and a small pouch of fresh tobacco. Dirk tossed him a coin along with the over-hot pipe. Timmy pocketed the coin and trotted off, holding the pipe by two fingers on the long stem. As Dirk packed the fresh pipe, he leaned back and gazed at Mic. Finally Mic halted the dice game.

"Dirk, we never have enough cargo on board at one time to make a voyage to the northern colonies worth our while. And I won't be your new quartermaster."

"You're the only man for it."

"It's the most difficult and dangerous job aboard ship. And I wouldn't have time for drawing my sea charts."

Dirk nodded, then used his last, and best, argument. "It pays an extra half-share."

"All that hard work and danger for an extra half-share."

Mic looked at the ceiling, the door, the fireplace, staircase, work table, musicians, cat barrel. He looked at everything in the taphouse but Dirk, who struggled to keep his face blank.

Finally, Mic said, "Well, while I'm quartermaster we will *not* be sailing to New York."

New York, 1666

The *Serpent* glided between high, wooded shores brightened by gold, russet and scarlet foliage, then turned into a broad, deep harbor with good winds. The ship rounded an island covered with walnut and chestnut trees, and there, just ahead, lay the island of Manhattan. Hills rose behind the river-front town. Dirk, standing in the *Serpent*'s bow, sighted a windmill and the ramparts of a fort.

He ignored Farley's orders for the sail trimming, and stared at the town as they passed east of it along a wharf. Too many years had passed since he'd walked into a Dutch home, or spent time with people related by blood instead of adversity. His shoulders tightened. Maybe he had no family here. His father had spoken of brothers in Nieuw Amsterdam, but life was hard in the northern colonies, too. Perhaps his relatives had died, or returned to the Netherlands after the English conquest two years ago.

The *Serpent* anchored in the river to the east of town, and Dirk waded ashore through the shallows with Mic and Grimbald. Mic would seek buyers for their cargo, while the boatswain found suitable lodging. Dirk wandered into a bustling town of cobbled streets and hundreds of buildings. Fences guarded neat gardens against scavenging pigs and chickens. Children played everywhere. Some of the newest buildings were English style, but many were thoroughly Dutch: A steep red or black clay roof, gable end of the houses toward the street, benches flanking the divided doors built into façades of narrow yellow bricks.

He left the wharf area, crossed a stone bridge over a canal, and found a broad avenue that led to the fort at one end and a palisade gate at the other. He had no idea where to start looking for his uncles, so he stayed on that street, walking past shops and houses. The shops sold oranges and lemons, fine writing paper, spices, damasks and silks, measuring equipment and almost as many other items as he'd seen in Port Royal after pirates flooded the markets with booty from a rich prize.

He heard as many languages in the street as he'd ever heard in Port Royal, too. When he stopped someone to ask about his uncles, he had to use French. Yet the man nodded and smiled when Dirk gave his name.

"Oh, yes." The man waved his hand toward the wooden palisade. "A van Cortlandt has a tavern on the street just south of the wall."

Dirk followed that street along a palisade of twelve-foot logs, sharpened at the top and sunk deep into a waist-high breastwork. Within sight of the eastern river again, he found a sign depicting a large beer tankard with *'Van Cortlandt Taphuys'* carved below it. He entered the public room of the two-story, timber and plaster taphuys, and in the dim light looked for the proprietor. There were beer kegs and wine casks on a counter, tables, benches, and even a fireplace, but no people.

"Hello?" he called.

A short, round-bodied man in a huge white apron charged out of the back room with a broom in his hands.

"There'll be no scruffy strangers drinking in my taphuys," he said in Dutch. "This is a respectable place and I won't have any naked-limbed people in it."

Scruffy? Naked? Dirk's hand flew to his five-day-old beard as he looked down at himself. His cotton breeches, cut short to mid-thigh, were ragged at the hem, and his tunic had spent weeks at sea without a washing. In contrast, the tavern keeper wore voluminous knee breeches, thick stockings and heavy shoes. His shirt sleeves were rolled up to the elbows, but his collar was tied at the neck. Dirk shifted his bare knees together.

"I seek a van Cortlandt," he said, voice harsher than intended.

The man squinted. "Why?"

"I believe he's my uncle. I am Dirk van Cortlandt."

"Well, my name's Jochem van Cortlandt and I don't know of any Dirk in my family." He raised the broom.

Dirk swallowed an angry retort. "I'm Wynant's boy."

The man blinked, lowered the broom and groped for a bench behind him. He sank onto it and tugged a lock of grey hair.

"Little Wynant has a son as big as you? I thought... We heard the Spanish took Bentyn's Isle a dozen years ago and everybody was dead."

"Four friends escaped the island with me."

The old man popped up and tugged Dirk outside into the sunlight.

"Hmm, you certainly look like the rest of us." Smiling, he patted his own round belly. "Well, except for this. And you are a bit taller than most of us." He stretched to put an arm on Dirk's shoulder and guided him inside to a table. "Sit. Sit. I'll fetch us some beer." Jochem filled two pewter mugs from a keg at the counter. "Tell me how you escaped and what's kept you away from us for so long."

Before Dirk could speak, Jochem said, "There are many of us here now. Your other three uncles settled close-by." He handed Dirk a mug and sat across from him. "They had five or six children each. I had seven. Naturally, they are grown like you. Twenty-some grandchildren I have now. Tell me, lad, what brings you north after all this time?"

Dirk told him about the *Serpent* and its cargo. Jochem slapped the table, chuckling.

"Captain of a ship, you say! Well!" He pursed his lips. "You and some of your mates can stay here. I've several rooms above. For your cargo, 'tis best to see Margaret Filipse. A shrewd trader, but she knows value and will pay well for worthy goods. Use your charm, boy, and she'll be fair.

"As for your family, they live all about, some in New Harleem and some across the river in Brueckelen. A few settled up-river at Fort Orange. I mean Albany. Damnedable English, changing everything. The family will all want to meet you, but not in those clothes. I know a good tailor..."

Back to the wharf they went, where Jochem offered to lodge nearly half the crew. "I'd take them all," he said, "but I've only the four rooms."

After a sigh over his competition gaining so much custom, Jochem went on to negotiate a bribe for the governor so Mic could sell the crew's booty openly. Then he bought the *Serpent's* entire supply of rum and arranged an introduction to the trader Margaret Filipse.

At dusk, after washing off the worst of his sea-grime in the river, Dirk sat down with his crew to a feast. His Aunt Ineke set the tavern's long trestle table with beef, venison, pork, fish and cheeses, as well as koolsla and other vegetables in creamy sauces. She had baked three kinds of bread, plus pastries, and apples in honey.

Dirk had never eaten such rich fare. He filled his plate over and over, accepting everything offered and loosening his belt twice. When at last even one more small cookie looked like too much to swallow, Dirk pushed himself away from the table and went outside.

Most of his men were lounging against trees in the garden beside the taphuys. They belched and moaned about their bellies being too full, but they looked happy about it. Dirk stretched and breathed in the crisp evening air. Jochem appeared at his elbow.

"Would you care for a stroll about the town? We have two hours before the curfew."

"I need to do just that."

They walked along the palisade, with Jochem introducing Dirk to the neighbors. Then they passed through the town gate and meandered a short way into the countryside.

Jochem finally asked, "What happened? To Wynant and your mother and all the others?"

"It was a Spanish raid, just as you heard."

"I knew so little of my brother's life after we parted in the Canary Islands. Tell me, please, all that you remember."

Dirk knew when he planned the voyage north that relating his memories would be the price he'd have to pay for finding family. Still, he hesitated, taking several deep breaths before beginning to speak of his youth and how he came to be a pirate.

That evening and for three evenings more, Dirk walked with his uncle and talked. Jochem clucked in sympathy or whistled in awe at the tales. At times his blue eyes filled with tears, but he never asked Dirk to stop telling the stories.

Most of the pirates kept to their Port Royal schedule of sleeping through the short autumn days and drinking themselves into a stupor at night. Others, hampered by the nine o'clock curfew, began to sleep at night. Some rode a ferry across the eastern river to Brueckelen where many Manhattanites owned farmland. The hunting was rumored to be excellent on the big island, but Dirk refused all invitations to go along. On Hispaniola he'd had enough hunting for a lifetime.

Instead, he helped Jochem build a storage lean-to against the back of the taphuys. Most evenings, he sat on his uncle's front stoop and watched the busyness of New York pass by. He packed his pipe with some of Jochem's spiced tobacco, much preferring the nutmeg flavoring to the dill or lavender. Just at twilight, Jochem would appear quietly with two mugs of coffee. Dirk liked the exotic taste of the newly imported drink, and did find it stimulating, though hardly the wanton elixir that Aunt Ineke called it.

When the lean-to was completed, Dirk persuaded Dunstan to resume their daily round of handystrokes on the commons behind Jochem's taphuys. The first day, other pirates jeered at them for working so hard with no prize in sight, but townspeople gathered to watch. Among the most avid spectators were several young women. The next day Jan and Joost joined the practice, displaying their flashiest bladework.

Every afternoon, as soon as the air began ringing with clashing steel, children appeared. By the end of a week, some of the boys were carrying short wooden swords. After each practice session, they followed the pirates back to the taphuys, the boys strutting, running to keep up, and tripping over their swords.

Late one day in the second week, Dirk borrowed a horse and rode north out of town on the Wickquasgeck Road to visit a van Cortlandt cousin. Two miles beyond the palisade gate, out of curiosity, he turned off the main road onto a path leading to Bouwerie Number One, the largest farm on the island, according to Jochem. Three hundred acres, it was said to encompass, from the center of the island to the eastern river. And it belonged to Peter Stuyvesant, former Director-General of Nieuw Netherlands, Curaçao, Bonaire and Aruba.

Once, when he was very young, Dirk had seen the man striding around Curaçao. Stuyvesant had been the Dutch commander of political and military operations in the Caribbean then, and still had both legs. He lost the right one leading a fight to re-take the isle of St. Martin from the Spanish, and after he recovered he was assigned by the West India Company to rule Nieuw Amsterdam.

Dirk rode past forests and marshy grasslands in the process of being cleared, then stopped near a swampy pond. The orange, white and blue flag of the Dutch United Provinces was flying above the large house to which Stuyvesant had retired when the English captured Nieuw Amsterdam. After a lifetime of adventures, Stuyvesant had become a gentleman farmer. Already a village was growing up around the homestead.

Dirk turned back to the main road, and nudged the horse into a trot.

Pieter van Cortlandt, a handsome, sandy-haired man as big as Dirk, gave him a tour of his bouwerie before supper. In the orchard, Pieter snapped two red apples off a low branch.

"The best on the island," he said with a grin, tossing one to Dirk.

They walked past the barn to fields already harvested. Corn was ripening in the farthest one.

"I'm sorry there's not much to see this time of year," Pieter said as they tramped across barley stubble. "The plantation is beautiful in early summer, with everything green."

"Do you plant a crop for market?"

"Some farmers like tobacco. I prefer wheat and barley." Pieter's sea-blue eyes gleamed. "The barley sometimes grows as high as my elbow."

He stopped walking and gazed about his fields. Hogs were rooting at the edge of the forest.

"The Company chartered this colony to foster the fur trade, but I think the true wealth lies here, in the fields. In this rich soil."

"Do you long for the Company rule?"

Pieter laughed. "Not at all. For years we asked old Peg Leg Stuyvesant for some relief from the corporation's tyranny. A lawyer from just north of this island, Adriaen van der Donck it was, even journeyed to the Hague to request relief. But Stuyvesant called us his subjects and said the Company was the absolute lord and master of this province. No, we're not sorry to see him gone from power."

They turned and walked back toward the house.

"How do you fare under English masters?" Dirk asked.

Pieter's grin broadened. "When we refused to fight off the English, Stuyvesant cursed and stomped about on that wooden peg of his. Then he negotiated Articles of Capitulation that made the English give us everything we'd been demanding of the Company."

Dirk chuckled. "Was he trying to hurt the English?"

Pieter shrugged. "Or maybe he cares about the colony. We don't know. But we kept all our property. We're free to follow our religion, and trade is unrestricted. Even Dutch vessels are welcome. We come and go as we please. Townsfolk choose their own leaders and have a say in laws. We don't even have to house soldiers in our homes anymore."

In a pasture, cows and goats grazed their way toward the barn.

"Cattle on Hispaniola have to be chased," Dirk said. "These just walk to your barn."

Pieter chuckled.

A hog that had recently farrowed nursed her litter in a pen beside the barn. The men tossed their apple cores to her and strolled back toward the story-and-a-half, stone and timber house. Dirk walked slowly, thinking of the demands of crops and animals, the day-to-day routines and seasonal rhythms that were a sharp contrast to his unpredictable life at sea as a pirate. He'd been meant for, and would have lived, such a life on the land, had the Spaniards not raided Bentyn's Isle one night.

The family sat down to a dinner of beef, squash, beans, and garden vegetables, plus clams Pieter's wife Edda said she had purchased from trading Indians. She served it all on elegant porcelain from the Orient.

After the meal, everybody stayed in the big kitchen. Pieter and Dirk smoked sweet tobacco in long-stemmed pipes while Edda knitted. Ten year old Larz sat on a low stool near his father and recited grammar lessons. Then Pieter talked more of the colony under the English, the farm, their problems with weather and the occasional visits from the coppery-skinned Americans.

"They come to trade, or just to sleep in the barn out of the weather," Pieter said. "And the only European language they know is Dutch."

"You've had no trouble with them?" Dirk asked.

Pieter shook his head. "Only a decade ago, when Stuyvesant attacked New Sweden on the mainland. The Swedes' American allies and trade partners retaliated. We lost too many people then, but this country's been peaceful since." He nodded toward his wife. "Edda and the children all know a bit of the Mahican talk, too."

The vigilance Dirk maintained, even in Port Royal, dissipated in the cozy warmth of the evening. Pieter had so much: a comfortable life, a substantial future, and a family. The baby slept in a cradle by the fire. Larz and his younger sister watched Dirk's every move. Another daughter, nearly fifteen, was spending the week up river, at her Aunt Alfreda's home in New Harleem.

Yet Dirk most envied Pieter his wife. While he listened to Pieter's stories, he watched Edda. He'd never seen anyone so lovely. A few blond curls escaped her white cap and framed creamy cheeks glowing with health. Humor sparkled in her soft, blue eyes. When Edda rose to check on the baby, her red and green skirts swayed just above slender ankles encased in embroidered stockings. Dirk's gaze lingered on her as she bent over the cradle to pat the baby back into sleep.

Her hands fascinated him. Clean, broad and strong-looking, they never stopped moving. She put down embroidery to comb and braid her daughter's blond hair. On her way to the fire to fetch them all more tea, she passed close to Pieter and brushed her fingertips against his cheek.

The hands of women in Port Royal always lay open, greedy for coins, or they grasped at a man, to arouse his lust or snatch his coin purse. But Edda was generous, always giving, as his mother had been. And the home Edda had created was so much like the one he lost thirteen years ago that Dirk's chest ached.

That night, asleep in the box bed in the best room, he dreamed of the two kinds of women. He dreamed of his childhood and the home he could have if he possessed a wife like Edda.

In the morning, Dirk said farewell at the kitchen stoop.

"How long will you be staying in New York?" Edda asked.

"Perhaps a few weeks more."

"Then we'll see you again." Her smile warmed him.

"Stay for Kermis," Pieter said.

"Kermis?"

"That's our harvest celebration. We hold it beside Deutel Bay, a small cove a bit northeast of here. There's an old taphuys, and merchants come from all over the colony. It lasts a week." He winked. "I'm sure it won't be as lively as Port Royal, but we do our best to ignore proprieties and enjoy ourselves."

"Pieter!" Edda chided him with a smile.

He grinned. "It's not that much happens, though we do have a lot of new babies nine months later. And not all of them from the right side of the blanket."

"Pieter!" This time Edda had no smile.

The men laughed and, with a wave, Dirk reined his horse onto the road. Restless from his dreams of the night before, he held the horse to a walk. It had been weeks since he'd touched a woman. When at sea, he could suppress his desires, for women were rarely aboard ship to tempt him. But now he was surrounded by so many pretty women and he was afraid to touch any of them. A proposition to a decent woman would insult her, and Dirk might never be welcomed in New York again. Worse, a father or brother might roust him out of bed with a musket and lead him to church for a wedding. Or maybe just shoot him.

There were lesser women available, to be sure. Their first night ashore, the twins had found three. For Dirk to chase a doxy, however, would embarrass his family, and now, after finding Edda, he didn't want to settle for a boughten woman.

He sighed. *Life is complicated in this civilized colony.*

Dirk coiled the fat rope around his forearm and grasped it with both hands. Bare feet planted solidly in the grass, he waited for Uncle Jochem's signal.

"This is the first match for the Kermis championship," Jochem announced to the crowd gathered in a clearing on the north side of Deutel Bay. "Are you men ready?"

Mic, crouching in front of Dirk, said, "Of course."

Dunstan, the first in their line, merely grunted.

Dirk called to Pieter and two other men across a narrow, mud-filled ditch. "Are you farmers ready for a bath?"

They hooted. Pieter waved his end of the rope.

"We buried some treasure at the bottom for you pirates."

The crowd laughed.

Jochem's arm dropped with a snap and Dirk leaned all his weight against the rope. The rough hemp tightened in his hands and he felt it give a little. He took a small step backward. For a minute nothing happened. Dirk's wrists and shoulders strained. The rope gave way again. Mic's sweating back inched closer, and Dirk took another short step to the rear.

Pieter called out, "Heave!"

The rope jerked in Dirk's hands. He leaned more heavily against it, but at the next "Heave!" he stumbled forward to keep his balance. He looked over Mic's shoulder to see what was happening.

"Heave!"

All three farmers took a short hop backward.

"Heave!"

The rope jerked Dirk forward again.

"Pull!" he said. "Now!"

Dirk tugged with all his might, and Mic's back muscles bulged with effort. Yet with each "Heave!" they were dragged another foot toward the pit.

There was a splat, and the rope yanked Dirk so hard he stumbled onto Mic's heels. Then Mic disappeared into the mud. Without time to untangle his wrist from the rope, Dirk followed, roaring in protest. He landed on his backside, with mud oozing into his breeches and under his tunic. He struggled to his feet and someone handed him a towel. He wiped mud splatters off his face, then looked up at Pieter.

"Good trick," Dirk said. "Did you learn that from the goats or the hogs?"

Pieter chuckled and extended a hand. "All that wild Caribbean living, Cousin. It has affected your strength."

Dirk hauled Pieter down into the mud. The crowd laughed, as did Pieter when he scrambled to his feet.

Edda leaned over the edge of the pit. In a jolly voice she said to her husband, "You'll wash those clothes yourself." With a grin at Dirk, she left.

Dirk watched her go, then crawled out of the pit. Dripping mud, he and the others trudged to the river to wash. Dirk took off his tunic and swished it back and forth in the chilly water. When satisfied, he squeezed the water out and laid the tunic across a bush to dry.

Beside him, Mic said, "Race you all to the island!" He pointed to the tip of a long, narrow sand bar in the river.

"Not me," Dunstan said.

But Pieter cried, "Done!" and the two thrashed off across the river.

Dirk whirled in a shallow dive. When he surfaced, he saw the other two were so far ahead he had no chance of winning. He rolled onto his back and let the current carry him downstream, across the mouth of small Deutel Bay. He listened to the sounds of Kermis echoing through the partially cleared woods. Hammers pounded. Musicians tuned fiddles with discordant notes. From somewhere close by, he heard the thud of arrows striking targets. *Men practicing for the archery contest, perhaps.*

Although the early afternoon sun was warm, the water was cold. Dirk swam out of the river current into the bay, then stroked across it to retrieve his tunic. He climbed up the gentle bank to find a woman sitting on the tree stump near his tunic. She was young, and very pretty. A cornflower-blue ribbon that matched her lively eyes held thick blond curls away from her face. Her nose tilted in a familiar way. And when her full lips parted in a smile, showing even white teeth, Dirk's heart turned over.

Her gaze dropped from his face to his naked chest, then to his wet, clinging breeches. Blushing, she turned away. Dirk snatched up his tunic and pulled the cold, damp thing over his head.

The woman peeked at him from the corner of her eyes. Her voice was musical. "Are you Dirk, the pirate captain?"

"Yes. Who are you?"

"Katrina."

"Were you waiting for me?"

She shook her head; her hair gleamed in the sunshine. She waved at Mic and Pieter, who now were lounging on the tip of the sand bar.

"I was waiting for Papa, but I don't think he'll be back soon."

Papa? Pieter? Then this woman—no, this girl—is Edda's daughter. No wonder she looked so familiar.

"Shall I fetch him for you?"

"No, thank you. Momma wanted him to come help with something at Grandmother's, but by the time he gets there it'll be done."

Katrina stood and brushed at her skirt. She was almost as tall as Edda and had nearly the same shape, though she was more slender. Dirk finger-combed wet hair out of his eyes.

"Perhaps I can help."

"That would be wonderful." She blushed. "She—Grandmother Kruger, Momma's mother—lives just half a mile inland."

Dirk reached for his boots, shoved his feet into them. "Lead the way."

They walked a few minutes before Katrina said, "I've wanted to meet you. I'm sorry I was away when you came to dinner."

"I enjoyed the evening, but your presence would have made it better."

She was silent, then, and Dirk didn't know what else to say to a proper young woman. *If I ask her questions, will she feel I'm acting too familiarly? Should I tell her stories? All those I know are about bloody fights. Would they distress her?*

Katrina finally broke the tension. "Everybody talks about you pirates. What an exciting life you must have there in the islands. Is it really summer all the time?"

"It's hot most of the time, that's true."

He told her of the lush green isles, of Hispaniola's dark mountains that raked the heavens, of the uncountable Bahama islets and coves. She asked for details, and by the time they'd reached the Kruger homestead in a meadow surrounded by maple trees, her eyes were aglow.

"Grandmother!" She ran up steps into the kitchen through a split door. "I couldn't find Papa, so Cousin Dirk came to help."

Dirk stopped at the door, resting his hands on the lower half. The scent of freshly baked gingerbread wafted out to him. A slender, white-haired woman stepped lightly across the kitchen to greet him.

"So you are the famous Dirk," she said. "Come in and let me look at you."

He stepped just inside. She looked him up and down quickly, then smiled.

"You and your friends are causing quite a stir, young man. Now I can see why. You're a handsome one. And displaying your limbs that way puts scandalous thoughts into all the ladies' heads. The men can't decide whether to be jealous or run off to sea with you."

"Grandmother!" wailed Katrina. "How can you say that?"

The woman winked at Dirk. "Please do make all the men jealous, my boy, and when you leave perhaps they'll treat their wives a little better."

Dirk laughed. "I'll do my best."

She patted his arm. "Come to the milk house, Dirk. I have a small barrel of wine finally ready to drink and I need a strong man to bring it into the house."

As he followed Mevrouw Kruger outside, Dirk glanced at Katrina. She smiled. He grinned at her a moment too long and stumbled off the bottom step.

Strung by the feet from a small oak tree, the goose squawked and beat its wings. A trader from Albany galloped toward the bird, reached for its heavily greased neck, missed, lost his balance and landed hard on the ground. Spectators laughed as the horse trotted away. Not anxious to stay until a horseman wrenched off the bird's head, Dirk glanced down at Katrina. Her face pale, she chewed on her lower lip.

"Shall we leave?" he asked.

She smiled up at him. “Oh, yes... please.”

He took her arm to lead her through the crowd. They could watch the nine-pin competition or the archery tournament instead. Perhaps they’d see Baldric win yet another prize with his musket.

As they passed a limner’s booth, Dirk said, “I want to take your likeness back to sea with me. Will you pose?”

She ducked her head and blushed, but nodded. The limner posed her on a tree stump, tilting her chin up and a little to one side. As the man began to scratch out a charcoal portrait, Dirk stepped aside for a better view. In a yellow broadcloth dress so nearly the shade of her hair, Katrina looked like a pool of morning sunlight. So kissable. But simply looking at her was fine, too.

When the limner finished, Katrina hopped off the stump to see. She wrinkled her nose, but Dirk thought it a fine likeness. He wrapped it carefully in a piece of paper the limner provided.

“Are you hungry?” Dirk asked.

“No, but I am a little thirsty.”

They strolled across the fading grasses of a small bowling green where Uncle Jochem had set up a keg of beer and a wine cask. He passed them mugs of cool, frothy beer.

Dirk fumbled in his coin pouch for the bead of clamshell among his other coins, the florins, doubloons, stooters, guilders, and schellings all used for currency in this colony. The bead was purple seawan from the eastern shores of the big island and most prized. He’d won it in a game of dice the night before.

Jochem waved off Dirk’s offer of payment. “We’re hosting a party Saturday night. The whole family is here for Kermis and they all want to meet you, though maybe not in those clothes. Perhaps my excellent tailor has a suit half made, and if we go for measuring today, he can have something nice finished by Saturday.”

Laughing, Dirk held up his free hand. Jochem teased him every day about wearing something other than buccaneer garb.

“Enough, Uncle. You win. I’ll go this afternoon.”

Jochem stood on his toes to clap Dirk on the shoulder.

“You do a good thing, my boy.”

A flurry of customers arrived, so Dirk and Katrina moved off to sample Baker Dort’s cinnamon cookies at a nearby booth. Afterwards they stood in the sparse shade of an oak to watch two dark Americans sell a buckskin jerkin and leggings to a trapper.

"Maybe," Dirk said, "I should buy clothes like that. Would Uncle Jochem approve?"

Katrina giggled. "Of course not, but it'd be fun to hear him rant about it."

She tugged him by the hand to Margaret Filipse's booth. "Show me what you brought from the Caribbean."

Her eyes sparkled as he described wresting the silks and filigreed jewelry from Spaniards. Mic joined them. His face a mixture of envy and admiration, he watched Mevrouw Filipse vend goods he'd sold her from the *Serpent's* plunder.

"Look at that," Mic said. "She's selling it for three times what she paid us."

Dirk grinned. "Maybe we should have set up our own booth."

"We'll do that next year."

Dirk chuckled and followed Katrina to a booth selling furs. She told him stories about the fort and settlements up-river. When she admired a blue fox muff from the northern forests, he offered to buy it for her. Katrina shook her head.

"Thank you, but I already have a muff. And...there is something I'd like even more."

"And what could that be?" Perhaps she'd like a more exotic item from the Caribbean.

"I want to see your ship. The inside, I mean."

"You want to go aboard?"

Dirk glanced toward the river where the *Serpent* lay at anchor just south of the bay. The yacht looked sleek and beautiful on the sparkling water, with furled sails white against black masts and yards. He hesitated, though. Up close, the sails were patched and grey. Filth had been ground into the decks, and rats lived below.

"Oh, please." She gave him a pretty smile.

"A short visit."

For a coin, two youths rowed them out to the ship. Dirk helped Katrina aboard, half-carrying her up the net ladder to the gangway. Her lilac scent filled his head.

"You be long, Captain?" one of the youths called up to him.

"No. Wait for us."

Dirk greeted the few men on watch, frowning down their rude stares at Katrina. He led her around the ship, charmed by the dainty way she stepped over coiled ropes and piles of torn, grey canvas.

Her eyes shone. "Oh, I wish I could sail with you."

"That would be nice."

She smiled, as if waiting for more words. When he said nothing, she resumed the tour.

"Where do all the men sleep?"

"Some in hammocks below, the rest here on deck."

"Does the captain sleep up here in the weather, too?"

"I have a cabin." He swept an arm toward the stern. "This way, my lady."

Katrina inspected the cabin while Dirk stowed her portrait in a small trunk. She nodded toward his bunk under the curve of the hull.

"And this is where you sleep? Do you fit in there? You're so big."

"I fit."

She looked at the bunk, then back at him. "Nooo.... I don't believe you. Show me."

Smiling, Dirk stretched out on the bunk, boots touching one end and hair brushing the other.

"It looked so small." She sat down beside him. "It would be wonderful to live on a ship, the waves rocking me to sleep every night."

Dirk rolled onto his side. *She is Pieter's daughter and... she shouldn't be in my bunk.*

"It's time we went ashore." He sat up fast, smacking his head against the hull.

"Oh, did you hurt yourself?" Katrina leaned closer, a hand out.

Dirk caught her wrist. "We should go."

"Why? It's quiet and so pleasant away from the crowds." She eased her hand out of his grasp and laid it on his chest. "Please, can't we stay? Just for a while?" She gazed at him, eyes wide, full lips parted.

Surely she's too young to know the power of her suggestive actions. I must not take advantage of her innocent flirting. "No."

"Please?" She leaned closer, adding the scent of lilacs to her argument.

"Have you ever been kissed?" The huskiness in his voice surprised him.

"Of course. Simon and I... we..." She blushed. "I've been kissed lots of times."

Dirk suppressed a smile. *There can be no danger in humoring a little girl.* He bent to give her a light peck. His lips moved across her sweet mouth, and after a moment his hand rose to her neck, to stroke the delicate whiteness. He felt her pulse beating wildly, and suddenly remembered who it was in his bunk, beneath his mouth. He quickly rolled off the bunk behind her. She blinked rapidly in the gloom.

"Oh. I've heard that pirates ravish women."

Dirk took her hand and drew her to her feet. "Not this pirate." *And certainly not you, woman, child, whatever you are.* "It's time to go."

This time she agreed.

Plump, grey-haired Aunt Marieke laid a gentle hand on Dirk's arm. "Why didn't you come to us sooner? You lived all alone for so many years."

Dirk smiled at the relatives clustered about him. Tonight Jochem's tavern was full of uncles and cousins and their families. Many of them looked like Dirk, in face and body shape, and all accepted him as one of their own.

"I didn't know you were here," he said.

Cousin Michael, secretary and interpreter for the vice governor of the colony, pushed his spectacles back up his nose, then re-balanced a full plate of food against his flat stomach. "But you might have come to be certain we weren't," he said.

A little boy tugged at the broad cuff on Dirk's sleeve.

"Cousin Dirk, how many ships do you sink every year? A hundred?"

"No, no. We take perhaps one or two, and we don't sink them."

Cousin Groot, except for the spectacles a near twin of Michael, even to the same light brown hair and blue eyes, stepped closer.

"Tell me," Groot said, "why don't you privateers take many ships? I thought that's what your commissions were for. Or do you call them letters of marque?"

Dirk grinned. "They both mean a piece of paper from a king that means we can capture ships and towns and won't be hung as pirates if we're caught. But the Spaniards maintain little individual shipping any more. Just the silver and trade fleets that sail every two or three years."

"So you raid towns?" Groot's eyes gleamed.

"Yes, but sometimes we trade instead. With so little shipping from Spain, some towns let us land, then buy what we're carrying."

The little boy pushed his lip out. "You trade? Like Uncle Han and Uncle Krun?"

Dirk had been introduced to those two earlier. They owned trading companies that dealt with the Netherlands.

"Sometimes."

The boy frowned. "But Uncle Han and Uncle Krun aren't exciting."

He ran off as the adults chuckled.

Groot said, "Doesn't make sense for Spain to restrict trade to their own goods and ports that way. Why, most of what they ship to the colonies is manufactured in the Low Lands or the Germanies anyway."

"Oh, yes." Michael nodded. "If the Spanish crown would open all their ports to foreign trade..."

"Meaning us Dutch," Marieke said with a smile.

"Might as well. We trade everywhere else in the world."

Dirk grinned. "Ahh, but then I would have no work."

Everyone laughed.

Pieter joined them. "Dirk, Jochem sent me over to see your tankard was full and you got something to eat."

Amidst good-natured protests, he led Dirk away to the trestle table set down the center of the room. At one end, near a stack of clean plates, four men were heartily discussing the value of liming their fields. A small girl squealed as an even smaller one chased her among the men's legs. The farmers greeted Dirk with friendly smiles, and one handed him a plate. Pieter took his tankard.

"I'll fill this for you." He strode off toward Jochem's casks and kegs.

The trestle table was sway-backed from all the food piled on it. Dirk's stomach growled. He forked sausages from a platter, then helped himself to shad, oysters, venison, and beef that simmered in thick sauces. As he reached for the dish of mashed pumpkin, his arm collided with Katrina's.

"Oh, there you are," he said. "I've been looking for you all evening."

She placed a pudding in the only empty spot on the table. "I'm working in the kitchen with Momma."

"Will you dance with me later?"

"Happily."

Something bumped his knee, and a little boy ducked under his arm to snatch a cookie off a tray. When Dirk looked up again, Katrina had started back to the kitchen. She didn't look so young tonight. Maybe it was her hair pinned on top of her head. Or the gown. It was no demure broadcloth, but a watered silk of delicate blue, the square neckline cut low across her bosom.

She returned from the kitchen with a plate of fried squash. Dirk shifted a stack of red apples to make room for it.

"You're lovely tonight," he said.

She blushed. "You look so handsome in your new clothes. They're wonderful. All the women say so."

Once more she floated off to the kitchen. Dirk watched her go, absently running a finger around the inside of his collar. It was tight. Or maybe it just felt that way because the whole costume felt strange. He adjusted the forest green frock coat and matching breeches.

When he'd asked the tailor for garments in the latest fashion, Dirk hadn't expected so much lace. Rows of it edged not only the collar ruffle, but also the white falling bands that covered his upper chest like two square dinner plates. There were rows of the billowy stuff around the hem of his knee-length breeches, and lace rosettes on his new shoes. The tailor had stitched on a lot of ribbons, too, even in places they weren't needed to hold anything together.

Mic walked by, a plate of meat and cheese in his hand and a smirk on his face. "Uncomfortable in those?"

"No," Dirk said, jerking at the yellow sash draped across his chest. "I'm adjusting it to lie better."

Mic ran a finger up Dirk's sleeve. "What did all this cost you?"

"Does it matter?"

"Not really." Mic grinned and shrugged inside his roomy buccaneer's tunic. "Just so it was worth the price."

Chuckling, he joined Dirk's uncles Kees and Everhart at a nearby table. Their discussion of the effects of English rule on Dutch trade and profits grew louder.

Pieter returned with a full tankard. Dirk thanked him and maneuvered through the laughing, chattering crowd toward a bench in a dark corner so he could eat. Across the room, Jan and two little boys played tug-of-war with Jan's belt. Baldric stood in a group of attentive folks, his face glowing with a liveliness Dirk had seldom seen. How kind of his relatives to include his friends, who had found none of their own people in New York.

Dirk straddled the bench and ate in the shadows, watching the generous people who filled the room. *How have I lived so many years without knowing them?* he wondered. The small empty place inside him grew and ached, then finally began to ease. Now he knew what could fill that emptiness, and he would never again live without it.

Later, when fiddlers played a lively tune, he danced with Katrina. Brightly dressed people swirled around them and smiled at him. *Oh, yes, Mic. The new clothes were worth the expense. If they helped these people accept me, I'd gladly pay the price ten times over.*

Edda brought empty trays into the kitchen and began filling them with little honey cakes. Behind her, Pieter's cousin Trudje and Aunt Louisa sliced beef with uncalled for energy.

"Exciting they may be," Louisa said, her second chin bobbling. "And I'll grant you their courage, but the bunch of them have disrupted this town and I for one will be glad to see them go."

Trudje sighed. "I can't make my boys go to school some days. They run off to tag after the pirates all day long." She pushed blond hair off her forehead with the back of her wrist. "And at night sometimes they're too excited to sleep."

"My Henk talks louder and gruffer whenever he's been around them." Louisa looked over at Edda. "And take care with that daughter of yours. I saw her go out to that ship of theirs the other day."

Edda smiled. "Katrina told me all about her adventure."

"Well, watch her. Those yellow-haired twins have had even wives on their backs already."

"I'm sure Dirk wouldn't let anything harm his cousin."

Edda's younger sister Juliana, satin skirts rustling, breezed into the kitchen. "Aren't they gorgeous," she said to the room at large as she stacked cookies onto a porcelain plate.

Edda looked up. "Who?"

"The sea rovers, of course. So strong and manly. I can feel their presence even away from them."

Trudje sniffed. "They're no more manly than our husbands."

"Oh, yes, they are." Juliana laughed. "Their lives are so exciting. And when they look at me, I shiver."

Edda glanced at Louisa. "They are but ordinary men with a dangerous profession."

"And you can feel the danger, just standing near them."

Louisa gasped. "Juliana! Think about your husband."

Juliana giggled. "I'd rather think about Pieter's cousin. And that dark one... so mysterious. He rarely smiles. Oh, confess, Edda, don't they excite you even a little? I wonder how Dirk got that scar down across his eye."

Louisa's knife slammed deep into the roast and stuck. She jerked it out. "What if Johan heard you speaking this way?"

"My darling husband wouldn't understand what I'm talking about." Juliana sighed. "I wonder what Dirk is like when he's angry."

"Quite frightening, no doubt," Trudje said.

Juliana gazed dreamily at the ceiling. "What a thrilling life they must lead down in the islands. And so romantic!" She clasped Edda's arm. "How can you be so calm? I am skittish being in the same room with Dirk. Then he smiles at me and I want to do all sorts of things with him."

"Certainly he's made no advances." Louisa fairly screeched, and she jabbed her knife on the roast so hard it slid off the platter.

"Oh, of course not, and I'd reject them if he did, but it's fun to imagine." Juliana winked at Edda and carried the plate of cookies into the other room. Edda heard her talking brightly, voice pitched higher than usual, laughter quicker and louder.

"That's exactly what I was talking about," Louisa said. "I tell you, if those pirates don't leave soon, there'll be trouble."

Edda shut out Louisa's voice and smiled to herself. She could understand her sister's daydreams. She'd never give up her secure life with Pieter for the transient, dangerous life of the Caribbean. Yet even now, as she added the last cake to the trays, she envisioned herself on a tropical beach on a warm, soft, moon-filled night. A fragrant breeze billowed her thin skirts. Gentle surf lapped at her ankles and she curled her bare toes to hold the sand as the waves retreated. A large, faceless presence—a man—came to her slowly, then carried her in strong arms toward the jungle where a delicious darkness awaited.

"Come dance with me," Pieter said in her ear, and she jumped.

"Yes, I'm finished now." Edda smiled up at him. "I'm glad I married you."

He gave her a quick kiss. "Good. Let me help with those." He picked up one of the full trays.

With Pieter right behind, Edda carried the other tray out into the main room, smiling at her silly fantasy. Then she stopped.

"What's wrong?" Pieter asked. "I almost tripped over you."

A flush warmed Edda's neck and her hands trembled. She hurried to set down the cakes before she spilled them. Then she put a hand on the edge of the table to steady herself.

Katrina was dancing with Dirk, her slender hand swallowed by his big one. The girl looked up with adoration plain on her face. The man smiled down, his eyes full of desire. She tugged at his mustache and he laughed.

Edda wanted to shout. *Not my baby! She is only fourteen. If you can give Juliana daydreams, what damage can you do to a little girl? And she is too fine for a man like you. Relative or not, you're a pirate. Oh, merciful God in heaven, a pirate!*

Dirk sat by an open window of the sparsely furnished room he shared with Mic, Baldric, and the twins. The taphuys below had quieted for the night and he could see the light from lanterns throughout the town was fading out. Behind the taphuys, shadows wavered in the tree-studded common. From beyond the trees, the noise of the wharf drifted to him over a chilly breeze.

A night watchman passed through the streets, calling for the curfew in Dutch.

"'I tijdt te bedde te gaen." A moment later, he repeated the call in English.

Dirk grunted. "It is not time to go to bed... at least not alone."

"Hmm?" Mic sat at a small table, squinting in candle-light at pamphlets that gave him news of the world.

The twins roused themselves off of their cots.

"The widow again?" Jan asked.

"Her sister's visiting, down from Fort Orange," Joost said.

Jan said, "Well, then, we should go pay our respects."

Laughing, they slipped out the door. Dirk did not expect to see them until morning.

Mic came to the window, cursing when he tripped over a low stool in the darkness.

"God almighty. Why must all the lanterns in this town be out by nine o'clock?"

Dirk shivered in the chilly air. He gazed down at the dead gardens and bare trees, and thought of warm island nights full of lively entertainment, and raids with bracing swordplay.

"It's time to go home," he said.

From his cot, Baldric said, "Past time. The men are fighting each other as well as the townspeople."

Mic added, "And we're almost out of money."

"We'll start provisioning tomorrow," Dirk said.

Mic headed for his own bed. "For a while I was afraid you'd marry that cousin of yours and settle here. I can't imagine you as a farmer."

"A farmer, no. Married...yes."

Mic plopped onto his cot in surprise.

Baldric sat up. "When did you decide this?"

Dirk shrugged. “Just now, I think.”

“You can’t settle here,” Baldric said. “Not with the rest of us going back to Port Royal.”

Puzzled by the frown on Baldric’s face, Dirk said, “I won’t settle here. I’m only twenty-four, much too young for all this peacefulness.”

“But what would you do with a wife?” Baldric asked.

“There are wives in Port Royal and decent homes to live in.”

“And what’s the *Serpent* supposed to do without its captain?” Baldric asked.

“I won’t leave the sweet trade. But there are things in this life, here in New York, that I want.”

Mic snorted. “And you’ll get them from marriage.”

“Marriage with Katrina.”

Dirk turned to gaze out the window. He’d solved his dilemma of wanting to stay and leave at the same time. Now that he’d made the decision, merely by saying it out loud, everything appeared simple. He could have the best of New York—Katrina—plus his life of adventure in the Caribbean. Following months at sea, his time in Port Royal would be full of the homey comfort he’d found here.

“The girl agreed to come with us?” Mic asked.

“I haven’t proposed, but she said she’d like to sail with me.”

“What will her parents say?”

“We shall see. I’m to dine with them again at the end of the week. I’ll talk to Pieter then.”

After two hours of mending clothes and listening to light-hearted gossip in Aunt Juliana’s kitchen, Katrina took a basket lunch out of town and to the bank of the North River. Dirk had already found a quiet place in a stand of willows out of the chill autumn breeze. He spread a length of canvas. Katrina laid out fresh bread, roasted venison, apples and sour cabbage, and plum wine. She’d also wheedled from Juliana two pumpkin dumplings fried just that morning.

For a while she and Dirk discussed the food, then preparations for the *Serpent’s* departure. Katrina had difficulty concentrating on the technical aspects of ship furbishing, however, for Dirk looked so handsome. He'd tied his dark wavy hair back with a leather cord. And despite the tongues clucking by certain matrons regarding short breeches and coatless tunics, Katrina liked them fine on Dirk. She ducked her head to hide what felt like a blush, but couldn't keep her eyes off him for long.

To her surprise, Dirk wanted to hear stories about her childhood and their mutual relatives in New York. She, on the other hand, wished to hear more about the Caribbean and his shipboard adventures. While he spoke, she envisioned those tall, skinny palm trees with a spray of fat leaves only at the top, the wide beaches and clear blue water that was warm enough to bathe in all year round.

"I would like to live there," she said with a sigh.

"If we married, I would take you there to live."

She laughed, then saw warmth but no twinkle in his eye. Her cheeks grew hot again.

"Dirk, I... You want to marry me?"

"I'll have to speak to your father."

"Oh. I... He'll agree, I know he will. He and Momma both like you."

"What do you want?"

"Why, I think... yes, I think I would... like to marry you."

He took a deep breath. "You must be certain. I'm leaving at the end of the week. You'll have to decide by then."

Dirk leaned close and kissed her on the cheek. She shivered.

"Are you cold?" His deep voice rumbled in her ear.

"Yes. No."

Dirk chuckled and put dishes into the hamper. "Of course you're cold, sitting still for so long. I am, too."

He stood and helped her to her feet. They were silent on the walk back to the town gate. Just outside, he handed her the hamper.

"I have to go aboard now. Think carefully. Give me your answer soon."

Katrina nodded, then stood in excited confusion as he strode alongside the wall toward the river. She wanted to go live with Dirk in the Caribbean, but there was so much to do for a wedding. They wouldn't need a celebration, just a clergyman and a ceremony. Still, banns might have to be posted and she'd have to make farewell visits to various relatives and friends.

She took the shortest path to Juliana's, along broad Gentleman's Street which led to the fort and the green. Usually she avoided the green because the English government had erected stocks there and she always felt sorry for the people locked in them.

Today a skinny, raggedy-dressed man hung in the stocks, teetering on tip-toes, a fat yellow squash opened upon his head. He must have been caught stealing one. The poor wretch had worn his neck and wrists raw against the rough wood, no doubt trying to avoid all the flies buzzing around his head.

She turned down the street to Aunt Juliana's house, and kicked a stone in the path. Her mother, aunts and grandmother didn't like everything about the new government either. More than once she'd heard them denounce those English laws forbidding married women to own property or write wills. No longer did daughters always inherit their parents' estates equally with sons, or keep their own surname upon marrying.

But she didn't have to stay in this place anymore. Dirk had just offered an escape to tropical islands, plus jewels and silks. And strong arms and kisses that made her tingle all over. The English also ruled Port Royal, but Dirk certainly didn't live a constricted life there. Surely, she wouldn't have to either.

Katrina ran the last few steps to Juliana's house, plopped the picnic hamper on the kitchen stoop, and raced back out the gate and to the East River.

Dirk still stood on the riverbank; a boat from the *Serpent* was only half-way to shore. She ran to him, caught his arm and stood panting for a moment. He smiled, but said nothing.

"Yes," she said between deep breaths. "I want to go to the islands with you."

Dirk swept her up, swung her in a circle and laughed in that splendid rich way that made her smile just to hear it. She was giggling when he set her down.

"Come to supper three days from now. Papa said this morning he had only two more days in the cornfield and he's always in a good mood when the harvest is done."

"I'll be there, but remember, I sail the next day."

"I don't have many dresses to pack and no chest of linens yet."

"You shall have the finest linens in the world. I shall win everything for you."

"*Vilkommen*," Edda's mother called without slowing her work at the spinning wheel.

Edda entered the long kitchen, settled in a chair and pulled knitting from an apron pocket.

"Was it so bad, your marriage to a sailing man?" she asked.

"Because I cried so much, you think it was bad?"

Edda nodded. "I was determined not to do the same."

"And so you married a farmer." A sweet, faraway smile flickered across her mother's face. "At the time, Daughter, I felt so lonely. I felt I was not receiving what my love for your father had earned me. Our days together were few and always broken by months of loneliness.

"Yet in those times together we were good to each other. Other women could go to bed angry and turn away from their husbands, knowing there was always a tomorrow. But for us, each night could easily be the last and we treasured them. Now when he's gone, I have no regrets over days of bickering or wasted nights."

"Then perhaps Katrina would be happy in that life also." Edda sighed. "I suppose I worry needlessly."

"She's found a young man to love?"

Edda nodded, remembering the thin layer of cornstarch on Katrina's face the day of her picnic with Dirk. And the secretive dreaminess afterward. "It's Pieter's cousin, Dirk."

"Not that pirate!"

"He's a privateer. Pieter says he has a commission."

"He may have a commission, but that man is none the less a pirate." Her mother's voice softened a little. "Not that it is so dishonorable a profession. Heaven knows what the Spanish empire stole from us in the Low Lands as well as from the Americas. I hold nothing against him for stealing some of it back from them, but he's not for Katrina. He would destroy her."

"He doesn't seem to be a cruel man."

"He isn't cruel. It's his strength, Edda. It would consume our girl."

They worked in silence a while. Finally her mother spoke. "Our Katrina, she has her heart set on Dirk?"

"I think so, yes."

"And how does he feel?"

"I don't know. Sometimes I think he'd never be content with a wife as... as ordinary as one of us. His life is so exotic."

"Perhaps he won't encourage her."

"Oh, Mama, he will be himself and he'll charm her the way he charms all women... as you well know."

"Yes, Daughter, I know." Young eyes in the wrinkled face glinted behind the spinning wheel. "That man doesn't use the pretty words some women love to hear. He charms with the life in his soul. It is primitive, uncultured, and therefore appeals strongly to the life in a woman. That is natural. Life reaches for itself.

"But strength also reaches for its equal. I don't think Dirk will find Katrina to be anything more than a sweet, pretty child. He won't want her."

"But he stays. The hurricane season is past. Kermis is past. And he's still here."

"His men grow restless. He'll leave soon."

"And maybe he'll want to take a part of us back with him." Edda's throat began to ache.

"To Port Royal? Our baby in that snake pit of whores and thieves?" Her mother shuddered. "You must not permit it."

"Can I prevent it? If I speak against him or threaten to send her to Fort Orange, she might even stow away on his ship."

"True. Youngsters who think themselves in love often times cease thinking altogether. This must be handled through Dirk."

"He's Pieter's family, Momma. I cannot simply tell him he's not good enough for Katrina. Nor can I refuse him our home. He's dining with us two days hence."

Her mother studied the yarn spinning off the wheel, then said, "Pieter must do it. Do you suppose you can drag him away from his beloved furrows long enough to come see me?"

"Yes, tomorrow evening," Edda said.

The ache in her throat had spread to her chest. There would be so much pain. Katrina's heart. Dirk's pride. Even Pieter would feel it, having to hurt his cousin.

Oh, Dirk, why couldn't you have wanted someone else's daughter?

Dirk leaned against a fence post, watching Pieter herd the last of his cattle into the barn for the night. They talked about Pieter's abundant corn harvest and Dirk's return to the Caribbean. The conversation was amiable, as always, but Dirk's mind wandered often to Katrina.

When Pieter finished, they headed toward the house. Katrina waved to them from the kitchen garden.

Dirk said, "Your daughter's lovely."

"I think so."

"So do a lot of the men in town. They turn to watch her walk by."

Pieter laughed. "Poor girl. She's like her mother in that."

"I suppose she'll be getting married soon."

A shadow crossed Pieter's face as if something had suddenly pained him, but he spoke brightly enough.

"Oh, not so soon. Her mother doesn't think it healthy for a girl to marry before she's eighteen or so."

Eighteen... almost four years from now. Katrina will not be sailing with me this year.

Dirk tried to keep his voice light. "Will she wait that long? If she chooses a mate before then, I mean?"

Pieter didn't look at him. "I don't think she's sweet on anyone yet, except maybe Simon, Zaal Ruyter's oldest boy. The Ruyters live just down the road, and we're hoping Katrina and Simon will marry someday. We'd like to keep her close by." He glanced at Dirk. "So we can play with the grandchildren, you see."

Dirk halted on the path. "It's not the lad Simon your daughter wants. She already agreed to marry me."

Pieter turned to face him. "She may not."

"I know she's young, but I'll be a good husband to her."

"She'll not marry anyone until she's eighteen. I will not reconsider that. Nor do I believe she's fit to be a sea rover's wife."

"I can provide all she needs."

"You are successful, true, but you are also at sea for many months at a time, and your work is dangerous. I don't want my daughter widowed young, especially if she's alone and so far away from us."

Dirk had no response to that. They started walking again.

"This is a good place for a family," Pieter said. "The air is healthy, the government stable. The soil is rich. It's a good place to live."

Dirk took a deep breath and blew it out through pursed lips. For three days he'd felt so confident of possessing Katrina, and now, in the space of a few minutes, she'd been snatched nearly out of his reach. *Perhaps I should kidnap the girl. No... my family would never again welcome me in New York, and I won't, can't, live with that loss.*

But the alternative—quit piracy and settle in the north—was just as bad. He belonged at sea, and in the Caribbean. He didn't want to farm. He might be satisfied with a trading enterprise, but that required money. And a lot more than he and Mic had buried under the floor in the storeroom of Willem's taphouse.

There was only one way for him to acquire enough wealth. He must go back on the account and take it from the Spanish. He'd have those four years to do it, as Katrina wouldn't be allowed to marry anyone else during that time. Every year he could sail north to renew their attachment. Beautiful as she was, other men would want her and she might fall in love with someone else while he was away. Nevertheless, he'd have to take that chance.

They reached the well beside the house. Pieter hauled up a bucket and poured clean water over their hands.

"I'll tell Katrina my decision tonight after you leave," he said.

Dirk nodded, with a smile that felt weak. They went in to supper.

Dirk mounted Uncle Jochem's gelding and, once on the road toward town, gave the horse its head. It plodded through the deepening gloom of twilight. At the southern edge of Pieter's farm, Katrina bounded out of the shadows. The horse shied, skittering into a split-rail fence. Dirk dismounted and tied the reins to a post.

Katrina ran to him. "What did Papa say? You talked to him before supper, but nobody said anything about it."

"We can't be married."

"Dirk, that can't be! Papa likes you!"

"We have to wait four years."

"That's almost for ever!" Her shoulders drooped for a moment, then her chin came up. "I shall hate it here without you."

She threw herself against him, wrapping her arms around his waist.

"Oh, Dirk, take me with you tomorrow."

"Your parents would never forgive me."

"You wouldn't be stealing me; I'd be leaving on my own, just on your ship, that's all. And they won't know until it's too late. I'll sneak away tomorrow before the tide goes out. Please, I won't be any trouble."

"We'd never be welcome here again."

"I don't care. I want to live free on the warm islands. I don't care if we ever come back."

She nestled her head against his chest. The scent of lilacs assailed him. With a ragged breath, he drew her arms from around his waist, held her away, and shook his head.

Katrina pulled out of his grasp. "But you're a pirate! You do this sort of thing all the time!"

"I don't kidnap women."

"You don't want me."

Dirk scooped her up with one arm around her waist and the other under her buttocks so that her face was even with his.

"Oh, yes, I want you. I want you to sail with me tonight. But your father is my cousin and I won't marry you without his permission. Also, there are things I need to do before I can care for you properly. They may take several years."

"But four years. That is such a long time."

"You might find someone else to marry by then."

"Never. Oh, Dirk, you will be back next year?"

"Every year that I can. Now, give me a kiss farewell?"

"Oh, yes."

Her arms were tight about his neck. He took another breath of lilacs.

"A kiss of farewell and promise," she said.

Katrina pressed her lips against his, and he ached to have her warm body, so sweet and fresh, next to his in the bunk aboard the *Serpent*, waves gently rocking them in their....

He eased her to the ground, out of his arms and stepped away. "I must leave."

She sniffed back tears. "I shall be here, waiting for you. I have nowhere else to go."

Dirk remounted, waved good-bye, and nudged the horse into a fast walk down the road. Four years. Hooves beat into the hard-packed dirt. Four years, and so much to do.

His disappointment gave way to an eagerness to return to the Caribbean, to wrest even more plunder from Spaniards. They had destroyed the home of his childhood, and now their treasure would build a new home for his future.

He urged the gelding into a canter.

Port Royal, 1668

The room above Willem's taphouse was stifling hot. Dirk stood by the open window trying to catch a breath of the trade winds that normally cooled Jamaica. He watched the street below, nearly empty now in the afternoon heat. Behind him, Mic struggled over the ledger for their expenses, while Baldric lounged on a bed. They planned to sling their hammocks in shade along the shore when Mic finished.

Dirk's thoughts were on the crispness of a New York autumn and Katrina's bright chatter. It had been almost a year since his last voyage to New York. Although she said she was still eager for their marriage, young men had begun spending time at Pieter's farm now. Dirk had observed others besides Simon Ruyter eye Katrina with a longing that matched his own. But he could not sail north to reinforce his position with her.

Down on the street, a burly man in tattered green coat and breeches hurried toward Willem's door. His hairy pot belly showed between the lapels of his coat.

"Dunstan's here," Dirk said.

"Is Whistle Breeches still wearing your old suit?" Baldric asked.

"Yes."

"Why does he wear clothes that are too small for him?"

"I don't think he knows how big he is," Mic said.

They all chuckled, and heavy footsteps pounded up the stairs. Dunstan burst panting into the room, a hammock slung over his shoulder. Dirk's fine suit from New York had lost most of its ribbons, and the lace hung grey and limp with dirt and grease. The shoulder and center back seams had ripped open several inches.

"Well," Dunstan said between pants. "Are you ready to go?"

"I'll be finished soon," Mic said.

"Oh, leave it," Dirk said. "You've studied those columns every day this week. The numbers never improve."

"We haven't taken a prize in over six months. If I can't find another way to finance the next voyage, we'll have to put everything we've saved into it."

Dunstan snorted. "If word gets around we don't win prizes, men won't sail with us anyway."

"I know that," Dirk said quietly.

"We should've joined Morgan's fleet last time he set sail." Dunstan settled his bulk on a bed. It creaked. He farted.

Dirk glared at him. "Morgan had a commission to raid Tortuga. You know very well the traders take what the pirates bring in there, and they send all their profits to France."

"Well then, what about Mansvelt's fleet?"

"He was raiding Curaçao." Dirk turned back to the window.

Curaçao was Dutch. He would never consider joining a raid on his countrymen. Yet Mansvelt hadn't raided that island after all. The excuse was bad winds, but the admiral had used his commission to raid the Spanish Main and sailed home rich.

"The Spaniards hold their treasure in big cities now," Baldric said. "Only a fleet can take a city."

"I realize that."

Each year there were fewer Spanish ships in the Caribbean. All the treasure galleons sailed to and from Spain in huge fleets, well-guarded by men-of-war. Only rarely did a storm or other trouble leave a straggler alone on the sea, ready prey for the *Serpent* lying in wait behind a mist-shrouded islet. But to join a fleet, to have the *Serpent* part of an armada commanded by someone else...

Duty to his crew demanded prizes. Dirk would have to find those prizes, and soon. Although as yet they had not, the other owners of the *Serpent* could out-vote his decisions at any time. Dirk's obligation to them increased with each failure.

He picked up his hammock and glanced at the three men. Baldric's face showed concern, but also acceptance. Dunstan frowned, his lower lip out. Mic looked half-angry, half-pained. No doubt he was still unable to accept the *Serpent's* latest failure and the severe blow to his purse.

"I'm tired," Dirk said, draping his hammock over his shoulder. "I'm headed for the shore."

Downstairs, he stopped at the center table to greet the twins, who held wenches on their laps. As they chatted, Willem's eight year old son Timmy burst into the taphouse, and shouted above the noise of afternoon customers.

"Morgan's back with millions and millions! He took Porto Bello!"

The taphouse grew silent. Mic's eyes glazed over. The twins ignored the women on their laps.

A seaport on the coast of Darien, Porto Bello served as the final collection point, after Panama, of all the silver from Peru, spices from the Philippines, and silk from China. Merchants held a great fair in Porto Bello during those springs when the fleet from Spain arrived. Between fairs, they stockpiled goods in numerous warehouses.

The brethren often talked longingly of that treasure, but four forts surrounded Porto Bello's long, narrow bay. The battle to take the city must have been fierce. Yet Henry Morgan had done it, and he'd returned with enough treasure to enliven Port Royal for months.

As quickly as the taphouse had quieted, the noise resumed. Amid excited shouts, tankards banged onto rough tables. Chairs, stools and benches scraped back, almost in unison, and everyone crowded out through the door. Willem swung his soup pot away from the cooking fire and flung off his apron. He hustled the last of his customers out, even giving Dirk a shove.

In the street, a river of people flowed toward the docks. It carried Dirk and his friends along until they reached Thames Street.

"My God," Baldric said. "The entire city must be here."

People lined Port Royal's main thoroughfare from the docks to the Royal Customs House. Every few seconds someone jostled Dirk as those behind tried to force their way to the front of the crowd. He planted his feet and waited.

At last Morgan appeared. A squat man with several chins and a long dark wig, he strutted up the street with a small bejeweled casket open upon his shoulder. Sunlight glinted off the gold and silver coins inside. Behind him marched nearly 500 men, each laden with more plunder.

The crowd cheered, the noise swelling as pirate after pirate filed past. Caps flew into the air. Doxies swooned. Merchants cheered while counting on their fingers.

Dirk's stomach tightened. What a mistake he'd made. Like Mansvelt, Morgan had raided the Spanish Main with a commission for another target. He'd taken Porto Bello, not Tortuga, and the *Serpent* should have been there. Dirk and his men should have been marching in this parade, sharing in this fabulous prize. It was his fault they were not.

Five pairs of eyes gazed at him.

"Next time," Mic said, "you make the decision to join a fleet, or it won't be yours to make."

A week later Dirk met with Morgan. Surprisingly clean and dressed in velvet and brocade, the plump little admiral welcomed Dirk with a broad smile and compliments for his reputation. Morgan, too, had been a slave in his youth, and Dirk thoroughly enjoyed the afternoon of brandy and story-telling he spent with the cocky Welshman. Dirk decided that if he must join a fleet, Morgan's would be best.

The *Serpent* was still in Port Royal's harbor when Jamaica's Governor Modyford issued another commission to Morgan to attack Spanish shipping and supplies stockpiled ashore. Dirk read one of the admiral's posted notices calling for privateers and ships, and immediately began furbishing the *Serpent* for the voyage. Day and night, hired criers strode the streets, calling men to the sea, and specifically to Isla Vaca, an island off Hispaniola, Morgan's chosen point of rendezvous.

The number of pirates in Port Royal swelled, by the hour, it appeared to Dirk. He and the other owners of the *Serpent* had their choice of men to fill out their crew. They chose tough fighters and men with other skills, such as carpentry, surgery or sailmaking, taking on so many men they had to sleep ashore in shifts while others worked aboard.

Then, before they could sail, the royal frigate *Oxford* arrived from England. The entire population of Port Royal waited and watched as the ship took on provisions. None of its crew came ashore, and within a week it sailed again. Dirk called a meeting of the *Serpent*'s crew. Men squeezed onto the deck, some straddling the guns, more draped along the rigging. There were cries of dismay as those at the edge of the mass of pirates slipped into the water-way alongside the rail.

Dirk stood on the ladder to the *Serpent*'s small poop deck.

"Men of the *Serpent*!" he shouted over the expectant rumble of voices. When all were quiet, he continued.

"That frigate from England came with orders to suppress piracy." Dirk raised his voice to carry over the grumbles and loud gasps. "Having done its duty here..." He waited for the chuckles to subside. "The *Oxford* now sails to Isla Vaca, where it will try to suppress Henry Morgan."

Hoots of derision and much laughter drowned out Dirk's voice. He waited only until it slowed, then cried, "Do we stay here in Port Royal and await the results of that meeting, or do we sail for Morgan's fleet on the evening tide?"

"Raise anchor!" a man shouted from the ship's waist. "I'm ready for a fight!"

The men roared their agreement. Dirk let the roar build, then waved his arms to quiet them. He pointed to a slow-moving cart being pulled by men along the rocky shore. It carried a precarious load of small casks.

"There's the last of our rum," Dirk said. "Bring it aboard, men, and we sail!"

Within minutes men had boats in the water and shortly thereafter had formed a brigade from cart to boats. Pirates hefted the rum casks with energy and laughter, then came aboard themselves. Mic took over. There were so many men aboard he had to divide them into shifts for sleeping. Some went below to stake out their territory, but all returned to the deck for setting sail.

When the tide turned, Farley had men already aloft for unfurling the sails. At Mic's signal, pirates lining the capstan bars leaned into their work. Cheered by their fellows, they trudged round and round, winding the anchor cable around the drumhead, slowly raising the anchor by its chain. As quickly as the anchor rose out of the water, men pulled it tight into the anchor bed on the larboard bow.

Dirk, standing beside the wheel, felt the tension of ship tugging against anchor ease. The *Serpent* floated free amidst the cheers of the crew. Farley shouted and half of the sails dropped into place along the yards. Crofton adjusted the wheel; the *Serpent* heeled to starboard and within an hour was at sea.

Five days later it lay at anchor again amidst other ships of Morgan's fleet at Isla Vaca. The *Oxford* lay there as well, docile and flying Morgan's personal banner. The admiral, Dirk quickly learned, had commandeered the vessel and made it his flagship almost immediately upon its arrival at the island.

The *Serpent* and its crew settled in to wait. So many men crowded together taxed the skill of all the officers to keep peace. Dunstan drilled everyone on the guns, demanding that everyone be able to load and fire them. Mic organized musket shooting contests, which Baldric always won until Dirk asked him to stop competing. There was gambling to occupy the men, and fights broke out. Dirk handled them, now and then grabbing combatants by the back of their shirt collars and crashing their foreheads together.

Thirteen ships and a thousand men had gathered at the island by the time Morgan called a war council of each ship's captain and second-in-command. On the afternoon of the council, Dirk, Mic, Dunstan, and Farley rowed one of the *Serpent's* boats to the *Oxford*.

"It's about time he called a meeting," Mic said as they climbed aboard the flagship. "We've been here two months. Every day it gets harder to provision the *Serpent*."

"And the men are fighting one with the other again." Farley grinned at Dirk. "As if ye did not know."

Dunstan farted, then spat over the side. "All that fighting spirit wasted. We should save it for the Spanish."

As Dunstan and Farley settled against a rail, Dirk and Mic entered the frigate's main cabin. Standing at the center of a long table, Morgan stroked tendrils of his wavy brown wig off his neck and greeted them by name. They took the only vacant seats, at the far end of the table, same side as Morgan.

A few minutes later, Morgan spoke slowly in English.

"Gentlemen, there are four treasure ports in the Caribbean worthy of a visit from a fleet such as ours." He paused for the chuckles. "Santiago de Cuba, Vera Cruz, Cartagena, and Panama."

Down the table, a grizzled fellow Dirk recognized as the captain of a cedar sloop from Bermuda cleared his throat. "I was to Santiago in sixty-two," he said. "We took the place, but it were difficult."

The man directly across from Morgan nodded. "I was there, too. 'Tis a powerful place. The entrance is but a slit in the cliffs and there's a strong fort to defend it."

"Maybe Santiago should be our fourth choice," Morgan said.

The men laughed.

"Make it our third choice," the fellow beside Dirk said. "Vera Cruz is empty except when the silver fleet is there. When it's not, there's nothin' but sand flies in that place."

"That's what they said about Porto Bello," Morgan said.

Chuckles rippled down the table again.

A little captain at the far end stood up. "I don't want to go to Panama. I'm a sailing man and I don't fancy marching seventy miles inland for a prize."

"It's a mighty rich city," someone called out.

"True," the little man said. "But after we take it, we have to carry everything back all those miles, with Spaniards and wild Indians all around."

The captains consulted one another.

Morgan raised his voice. "That leaves Cartagena. Who knows that city?"

"It's the richest on the Main," one man said.

"Also the strongest," another said. "More soldiers than we have brethren here."

"And they haven't been paid in almost three years."

Everyone turned to the man who'd made that statement.

"Are you certain?" Morgan asked.

The fellow grinned. His vigorous nod made the broken feather in his cap bob and sway. "I was trading there a few months ago. Things were bad. The governor can't pay the soldiers and they run off to farm to keep from starving. Spirits are low and even those who stay on duty have no heart for fighting."

A pleased murmur swept the table. Morgan let it swell. When it began to die, he said, “Cartagena appears to be the best prize for us. Shall we vote?”

With the target chosen, they thrashed out an agreement on the Articles. Most of the captains sounded as anxious as Dirk to preserve their autonomy. By majority vote, Morgan’s power was limited to battle situations when his orders must be obeyed instantly. Aboard each ship, the individual captains and quartermasters commanded. Ships could leave the fleet any time before the attack on Cartagena. A ship abandoning the fleet during the battle would forfeit all claims to any part of the prize.

They established compensation for privateers maimed in the fighting, set rewards for tearing down the Spanish flag on a fort, and for bringing in a prisoner when information was needed. Grenadiers would receive five pieces of eight for each grenade they threw into a fort, an extremely dangerous feat.

Then Morgan called for dinner. Serving boys served fresh roasted beef and rum, while men on the main deck fired salvos to celebrate.

Morgan stood, saying, “A toast.”

The men rose, tankards in hand.

“To Cartagena,” Morgan said.

“To Cartagena.” Dirk raised his tankard, then downed the contents.

The boys ran to keep tankards full for the round of toasts.

“To the King of England.”

“To his health.”

“To the Confederacy of the Brethren of the Coast.”

“To Cartagena.”

“To the Spanish. May they never pay their soldiers.”

Night fell and the celebration grew rowdy.

“What do you think?” Mic turned to Dirk, eyes glowing.

“A fleet might be a good thing.”

“Might be? Cartagena is a jewel of the Main. The brethren have never taken it.”

“Rich enough for you then?”

Mic snorted. “It will fill my coffers, and yours, too.”

Dirk laughed. "Remember, though–"

An explosion tore through the frigate, and half the ship disappeared. The laughing, drinking men on the other side of the table disappeared. Legs and hands and partial trunks flew into a red sky along with dishes, tankards, and planks. Smoke billowed from timbers still intact, and flames licked at the cabin furnishings. Beneath Dirk the remains of the *Oxford* listed. He slapped Mic's shoulder.

"Let's go!"

They scrambled through smoke and flames across the sloping deck to the gaping hole in the side. Fire caught Dirk's cotton tunic, seared his arm as he dove overboard. He struck cool water and Mic landed nearby. Dirk swam underwater away from the ship and falling wreckage. When his lungs began burning, he surfaced.

Yellow and orange flames lit a black sky. A glowing red spar whistled over Dirk's head and hissed into the water an arm's length away. The *Oxford's* mainmast crashed onto the waves. A great cloud of ash billowed in the air and with it came the stench of burnt powder and charred planking.

As the noise of the explosion died, shouts from surrounding vessels flew over the water, mingling with the survivors' cries for help. Mic broke the surface. They stroked toward the nearest vessel, the graceful sloop from Bermuda whose captain had been sitting near Dirk. He wondered whether the man had survived the explosion.

A few yards away, a man surfaced, coughed and sank again. Dirk thought of Farley, who could barely stay afloat. Dunstan could not swim at all.

Dirk and Mic swam to the sloop, where pirates lifted them over the side. They sat on the deck until they stopped panting, then joined those at the rail tossing thick ropes, knotted at the ends, to men in the water. Dirk threw a coil of rope time and again, until his arms and shoulders ached, and still men drowned before his eyes. One fellow screamed and thrashed about, never grabbing the rope Dirk kept tossing within easy reach.

With a great hiss, the *Oxford* sank, thrusting the small harbor into darkness relieved only by lanterns on the other ships. The great cloud of ash began to settle, further obscuring rescues.

Dirk squinted into the murky sky, throwing his rope yet again at what looked like a man in the water. Finally, the fellow caught the knot. Dirk and Mic tugged him through the waves, straining as he left the water and slid up the hull.

A great force jerked them forward, then released them. Dirk tumbled backward, struggled to maintain his footing on the slick, rolling deck. The end of the rope came flying over the side, landing in a wet heap beside him. He picked up the end, now missing its thick knot. Screams rose. He looked out over the churning black water. Triangular fins darted through the waves.

Sharks. Dirk swiftly tied another knot into the rope's end and threw it to the nearest man in the water. He came up over the side dripping water and seaweed, sobbing aloud his fear and gratitude.

The smaller boats tacked and rowed across the harbor all night long, dragging men aboard. The sloop was too large for such maneuvering among the other ships, so when they'd rescued all those within reach of their lines, the men aboard could only watch. Dirk stood in the stern, his ears full of men's screams and his heart full of anger. The shark attacks had no pattern, no more logic than the deaths that had come with the explosion. He shivered. Dunstan and Farley might be out there in the water, clinging to a floating spar, surrounded by sharks.

Dirk knew there was naught he could do but accept the fortunes of life. He'd seen big men, strong men, die from a tiny cut, and he'd seen weak, stupid men survive even the greatest battles. Tonight his ability to swim had saved him, but only after the initial explosion spared him. If he'd been sitting on the other side of the banquet table, he would be dead now. His strength and intelligence were no armor, and some day, without warning, luck would desert him.

He felt a prickle of bone-deep fear, which he obscured with growing anger.

In the morning, the pirates resumed their search for survivors, a grisly task amidst the feeding sharks. When Dirk and Mic finally reached the *Serpent*, they found Curtis, the ship's surgeon, bandaging Dunstan's left foot.

"I lost some toes in the blast." He gave them a pain-distorted grin.

"You're damn lucky it wasn't more," Curtis said.

The sunshine stung Dirk's fire-scorched arm and he moved into Mic's shadow.

"Where's Farley? Have you seen him?"

Dunstan grimaced and shook his head. "He was right beside me and then he was gone."

"He's probably on another ship," Mic said. "Or maybe he got to shore."

Dirk nodded, hoping the little sailmaker's meager swimming skills had saved him.

They never found Farley. Nor did they ever learn the cause of the explosion in the *Oxford's* magazine, although there were rumors a man had been smoking too close to the gunpowder stockpiled there. Word got around the harbor that Morgan and all those sitting on the same side of the banquet table had survived the explosion. All those on the opposite side had not.

The fleet dispersed. As the *Serpent* had not won a prize in a year, Dirk and his men could not wait for Morgan's fleet to recover and sail. Jamaica now was issuing commissions only to Morgan, and the Portuguese, finally at peace with Spain, had stopped issuing letters of marque. Without one of those dubious commissions that made sea roving somewhat legal, Dirk was forced to look for a fleet on Tortuga.

In Cayona, eight ships had already signed into a fleet led by a Frenchman named Francis L'Ollonais. Upon first meeting the man, Dirk eyed him with distaste. A powerful-looking fellow of average height, L'Ollonais wore ragged yellow breeches and a filthy scarlet coat. His short pointed beard carried a light coating of grime and he constantly ran his fingers through his greasy brown hair. Dirk reluctantly shook hands with him after signing the fleet's Articles. Only later did he think about the friends L'Ollonais kept close during the meeting. Two of them—the dark, broad-shouldered Baldessaire, and that fellow Melchior, with a face twisted by scars—Dirk was certain he'd met before, but he couldn't remember when or where.

The long strip of cowhide hissed, followed by a loud crack and a scream. The man tied to the *Serpent*'s mainmast jerked at the blow and slumped against his bonds. Blood flowed from his torn back. Mic, naked to the waist, raised the whip again and sent it flying.

"Six!" Grimbald called out.

Again the hiss, the crack, and the scream.

"Seven!"

Three more. Dirk tightened his jaw. *Three more stripes and it's over.*

Mic, his face like stone, stood inside the ring of men. He raised his arm for the next blow.

"Eight!"

After months of daily practice against a barrel, Mic could land a stripe within a quarter inch of where he aimed. He never placed one stripe on top of another, nor did the whip tear much flesh below the skin. The punished man always lived, though scarred.

"Nine!"

Still, the whip in Mic's hands bothered Dirk, and the rest of the crew eyed Mic warily whenever he carried it. If he cracked it into the middle of a dice game, all quarreling ceased immediately.

"Ten!"

It was done. Dirk relaxed his jaw. Curtis rushed to attend the wounds while Mic picked up his tunic and strode off, cleaning and coiling the whip.

"He's a cold bastard," a man nearby said.

"He don't have to be nice," another said. "Just honest and smart."

"Well, he's that."

Dirk joined Mic in the cabin they shared. Mic was standing at the table running a cloth across his chest. He raised an eyebrow. Dirk went to a small cabinet for a bottle of brandy. He took a long swallow straight, then filled two clay cups. Mic's hand shook as he took one. Brandy sloshed over the side.

"Was I wrong to want you as quartermaster?"

"No." Mic downed his brandy. "Except for the whippings, I like the position."

"The men aren't always easy around you."

"I don't need their friendship, only their respect."

Dirk refilled the cups. "You don't have much time for your charts any more."

"My charts?" Mic slammed his cup on the table, splashing brandy across the rough boards. "Are you feeling guilty for talking me into this?"

"You could have refused the job." Dirk gulped his brandy and filled the cup again.

"If the whippings upset you, my friend, prevent them."

"Me?"

"Old Michael there got his stripes for fighting. We tied Ian and Fairfax to the mast yesterday for the same thing."

"Men always fight on ships." Dirk finished off a third cup of brandy.

"Not on your ship... not this often anyway."

"It's my fault the men can't control themselves?"

Mic's voice grew harsh. "You control the mood of the ship. We've been at sea three weeks, and you've stayed shut up in this cabin most of the time. When you do leave it, you growl at the men. They expect better from you."

Dirk set the cup and bottle on the table and turned to stare out one of the tiny gallery windows. "I mourn Farley."

"So do a lot of us."

"Isn't it enough that I make most of the decisions and accept the blame for mistakes, the crew's as well as my own? Now I have to entertain them as well?"

Mic slipped his tunic over his head. "I keep my office because the men trust me never to cheat on a share-out. And because I'm quick-witted. But part of their loyalty to you comes from affection. Lose that and you lose the captaincy."

"Never mind that I lead them to rich prizes?"

"L'Ollonais leads us now."

Dirk swung around, his fists clenched. "Leave me."

Mic strode to the door, opened it, and listened for a moment. "Listen to the silence. Have the men on your ship ever been this quiet before? Before this voyage?"

He walked out, leaving the door ajar. Only the snap of sails and creak of spars broke the silence that crept in.

Dirk looked at the open door. Surely he had the right to mourn Farley. The old man had supported and defended him from the beginning of his captaincy. *And why did that explosion on the Oxford kill Farley, yet take only toes from Dunstan? Why Farley but not me? Why anybody?*

Somehow he'd lost control. The politics of Europe, the winds and storms of the sea, the very fates all had sent their grasping talons into his life, drawing him down paths of their choosing. They ate up his money supply and drew him farther away from his goal of a life with Katrina. And now, even worse, he was allowing another man—L'Ollonais, a man he didn't like and couldn't trust—to do the same thing.

He took Katrina's portrait out of his trunk. It had smudged some in the past two years, but whenever he looked at it, he once again saw her sitting on the tree stump, yellow gown flowing from her neat waist to the ground. He almost heard her laughter that sounded like sunrise, but it couldn't quite break the deathly quiet of the ship.

He rolled the portrait back into its waxed leather cover and replaced it in the trunk. He took a deep breath as he straightened. Putting half a smile on his face, he walked out into the silence.

On a bright morning near the end of their fourth week at sea, L'Ollonais's fleet of nine ships anchored off the Mosquito Coast not far south of New Spain. Once ashore, 280 pirates marched inland along a narrow road. L'Ollonais distributed brandy and rum. Stomping up and down the column of pirates, he shouted encouragement for the coming battle. He described in detail the treasure lying ahead. Dirk trudged along, silent amidst the pirates' growing bravado and drunken boasts. His right knee ached, a reminder of that long-ago beating from Gilbert.

Two leagues from the coast, they reached a lush valley split by a narrow river. Baldric thought he could see at least three warehouses in a city that lay at the near end of the valley. If goods from the interior had been stored there, the city would be worth taking.

Half the pirates charged off to raid out-lying plantations. The rest, including Dirk's crew, attacked the town. Soldiers there had defenses ready, and the fight was hard and bloody. Nevertheless, by early afternoon, the pirates were in control of the city and had begun the systematic looting. A pile of treasure grew beside the plaza's *quemadero*, a stone platform built for burning heretics. Chests of coins and jewels lay beside cotton bales and spice pouches. Golden statues, chalices, candlesticks and chunks of a silver-laden altar from a church were tossed onto the heap.

Wounded pirates gathered at the city's outskirts, where surgeons treated them. A small knot of *Serpent* crewmen sat on the ground to await Curtis with his salves and pastes. Dirk's chest bled from a long, horizontal cut, but when Curtis approached, Dirk waved him off to treat others first.

Mic joined them after inspecting the treasure at the *quemadero*. "We'll be rich after this voyage."

Out loud, he divided the booty into probable shares for men, taxes, and ship owners. The crew edged closer, eyes glinting and elbows nudging as they talked of how they'd spend their shares.

Dirk listened idly, wondering why he felt no elation. Instead, he was tired and merely satisfied that the raid had been successful. He counted his men, the wounded ones around him and the others as they gathered loot. All twenty-seven were alive.

Their arms full of booty, pirates who'd raided the countryside marched into the city amidst cheers from their mates. At the end of the procession stumbled a dozen richly dressed Spanish men with soft, pale hands. L'Ollonais came running from the plaza, rubbing his hands together. Right behind him trotted Melchior, Baldessaire and two others.

"Wretched cowards!" L'Ollonais said. "You run to the country and hide your wealth from us?"

With a laugh, he yanked at the hair of one and fingered the rich coat of another. He snatched a plumed hat, flung off his own tattered felt one and replaced it with the Spaniard's.

"Now we can begin," he said. "I'm sure these fools want to tell us where their treasure is hidden."

The pirates laughed while the Spaniards drew closer together, their faces growing pale. L'Ollonais kicked the last captive in line as they all filed down a street.

Dirk stood up to follow them. "There's no need for torture."

"You stay here," Curtis said. "Don't go walking around with a gash like that. You could bleed to death."

Mic caught Dirk's arm. "There's nothing we can do."

Dirk sat down to a game of dice with Mic, Dunstan and Crofton, but instead of concentrating, he listened for screams from tortured men. He quickly lost a lot of money.

Having tended the others, Curtis finally reached him. "Take off your tunic."

Dirk complied, then narrowed his eyes at the balding man. "Are you going to splash me with sea water?"

The surgeon tugged on his sparse beard and grinned.

"Not this time, but what matter? A big man like you can't be afraid of a little sting."

Curtis slapped a smelly green salve onto Dirk's chest and rubbed it into the wound. It burned on the raw flesh.

"What is this?" Dirk asked through gritted teeth.

"Oh, does it sting?" Curtis widened his eyes. "Perhaps I should have used the other. Here." He took a thin, flat stick from his chest of potions. "I'll scrape it off."

"Never mind. Just put the bandage on."

"Stop growling," Curtis said, then whistled as he tied a clean rag around Dirk's ribs. When finished he set aside his medicines and joined the dice game.

The noise in the city ceased. Dirk rose, pulling on his tunic. "I'm going to see what happened."

Mic, Baldric, and three others went along. When they reached the plaza, Dirk groaned. "That brain-sick pile of shite. He's killed them."

Only two Spaniards still lived to tell of hidden wealth. Ten half-naked corpses littered the ground, twisted into unnatural positions. Some lacked heads; others lay atop severed limbs. Some of the pirates had already donned the dead ones' fine clothes.

Dirk breathed fast and deep. His neck grew hot. He took a step toward L'Ollonais and the last two captives. Mic caught his arm. "What do you think you can do?"

Dirk shook him off. "I can't stand by and let him kill those men. Didn't we offer them quarter?"

"Yes, but... "

"Then I stop this. These two at least."

L'Ollonais ordered the last two Spaniards tied to trees. Dirk strode up behind him.

"Have they told you anything?"

"Of course." L'Ollonais grinned with yellow teeth, but his eyes showed no humor.

"Then free them. They've given us what we want."

L'Ollonais's face slackened for a moment, then he laughed and turned his back. Dirk clapped a hand on the smaller man's shoulder and spun him around, but his angry words died in his throat, for L'Ollonais's pistol was cocked and aimed at his heart.

He was going to die.

Dirk held his breath.

L'Ollonais stared at him, eyes growing wider and brighter with a queer light. Finally, he lowered the pistol and cocked his head.

"I kill all Spaniards. Every one. And the man who tries to stop me dies also."

Dirk exhaled. His own men stood with weapons ready, but they were so far away. The pirates nearby would give him no help, for they had all taken part in the tortures and he'd spoiled their fun. He raised his hands, palms up, and carefully backed away. L'Ollonais laughed, a high-pitched, humorless sound. His friends joined in.

Neck burning, Dirk retreated to his crew. Men closed in around him. L'Ollonais shoved the pistol under his belt and tugged a large knife free. He stomped over to the closer Spaniard, ripped the man's shirt open and plunged the knife up into his chest. The Spaniard screamed, then screamed again as L'Ollonais cut out his heart.

With a shout, Dirk lunged at L'Ollonais. Mic and Dunstan hauled him back. When the red cleared from his vision, he saw a musket aimed at him by the admiral's friend Melchior, whose scar-puckered face was twisted in a mirthless grin.

The last, white-faced captive moaned and swayed against his bonds as L'Ollonais approached, the still-beating heart in his hand. He grasped the Spaniard's nose with bloody fingers and pinched the nostrils shut. When the man opened his mouth to gasp for air, L'Ollonais shoved the heart in and pushed until the Spaniard choked.

The deed silenced every pirate. Dirk took deeper and deeper breaths that didn't settle his stomach. Around him, men vomited. One crumpled to the ground; another sank to his knees and put his head to the dirt.

Dirk turned on his heel and stomped out of the plaza, out of the town, and into the cool breezes of the countryside. He heard footsteps. Mic called, but Dirk marched on. Pain shot through his right knee at every step. He ignored it. Mic caught up with him. Dirk favored him with a glance and kept walking, staring at the path as it passed in a blur beneath his feet.

At last his heartbeat slowed and his stomach settled a bit, though his chest hurt as much as his knee. Fresh blood soaked his tunic. He halted and pressed on the wound. Mic stopped beside him, panting.

"Don't do anything foolish."

"I'm only walking."

"Angry walking. And bleeding while you walk. Don't let your temper cause more problems with L'Ollonais. Your death won't help those Spaniards."

Dirk took a deep breath of country air, but instead of fresh moist earth and the sweetness of growing crops, he smelled smoke. He looked about and saw a valley in ruins. Buildings roared with fires. Fields crackled and smoked. Just ahead, all the trees of an orchard had been chopped down. In a pasture, downed cattle and horses twitched and rocked, their hamstrings sliced.

"God damn them all. What have they done?"

He swung back to Mic, who looked haggard and miserable.

"This is like home," Dirk said. *Did a little girl, somewhere in this valley, die in terror, her play-dress a bloody shroud?* Suddenly exhausted, his shoulders slumped.

"First this, and then that...that spectacle in the plaza!"

"We didn't do this," Mic said. "And you tried to stop it."

"But I didn't stop it."

Dirk's throat tightened and he lifted his chin to stretch out the muscles. Fluffs of white drifted across a glorious blue sky in stark contrast to the devastation below. He looked at Mic.

"We have to leave the fleet."

During the long evening, while pirates loaded treasure onto the ships, three other captains approached Dirk with the same idea. Together they sought out Moses Van Vin, L'Ollonais's second in command. A large man, hard with muscles, Van Vin listened while tying his red hair back with a strip of leather. After hearing all their arguments, he shook his head.

"L'Ollonais gets bloody sometimes, but he's a tactical genius."

"Why can't we have a share-out now?" Irving, the tall, angular captain of an open launch stamped his foot. "Right here."

"L'Ollonais will never agree," Van Vin said. "He plans a raid on Darien. We'll need this many men. Besides, you are only four. What of the others? The rest of the men don't want to leave."

"We don't have to split the fleet," Dirk said. "We can just replace L'Ollonais as admiral."

Van Vin looked at him sharply. "This isn't a ship. You signed articles with a fleet and now you're talking mutiny. L'Ollonais will chase you to hell and back. So will we all if you leave the fleet with any booty before the share-out."

Dirk and the other three captains returned to their ships. In the morning, when the fleet sailed south for Darien, the *Serpent* sailed along.

They stopped for water in Caledonia Bay. Acla, a town less than a league inland, was reputed to be wealthy and an easy target. Each ship sent out a party to fill water casks while everyone else marched to Acla. So much walking in a few days had stiffened Dirk's right knee. It was soon throbbing. He was limping and in short temper by the time they reached the little town.

Weapons held high, the pirates raced into the village, then stopped, their battle cries fading. Murmurs of disappointment swept through the crowd. The houses stood open and empty, with walls bowed and parts of roofs fallen away. Cimaroons, descendants of runaway African slaves, stood in the doorways of a few palm-thatch huts.

Dirk shifted his weight to his good leg. All that walking for nothing, and now L'Ollonais was roaring curses and kicking at the pirates milling in the small plaza.

"I'll chop off some heads." L'Ollonais swung his cutlass in circles over his head. "Who promised me gold here? Who wants his blood to baptize this hell pit?"

He lit a torch at the communal fire pit and ran through the town setting all the huts ablaze. When an old woman tried to stop him from entering her hut, he chopped her down with his cutlass. Those villagers who couldn't slip away into the forest huddled together in the dusty street.

Dirk called L'Ollonais the foulest names he knew in Dutch. First murder, and now L'Ollonais was destroying the long-time relationship between pirates and cimaroons. For generations along the Main, according to Theo, cimaroons had hated Spaniards so much they gave their children Christian saint names to mock the Spanish deity. They helped raiding pirates, usually as guides and spies, but sometimes even joining in the fighting. In just a few minutes, L'Ollonais had turned these friends into enemies.

A straight-backed cimaroon in short leather breeches approached Irving, who waved Dirk over. They took the man to Van Vin.

"Gold in Careta," the man told Van Vin in Spanish. "Short walk from here. Spanish who live here before live there now. You leave this place, I show you much gold."

Van Vin ran after L'Ollonais. "Gold, Admiral! We found gold!"

L'Ollonais strutted up to the cimaroon. "Come here, you over-sized monkey. You have a name?"

"San Sebastian."

"A good Spanish name. Where's the gold, San Sebastian?"

The cimaroon motioned for the pirates to follow as he walked out of the town, L'Ollonais right behind. The rest of the pirates marched along the narrow trail slashing palm fronds and fern leaves out of their way. L'Ollonais talked of the easy victory and great treasure they'd soon win.

Dirk limped beside Van Vin. "Tactical genius?" he said in a low voice. "With this noise and smoke and no lookouts?"

Van Vin glared at him and hurried ahead.

Musket shots ripped through the band. The man in front of Dirk toppled, and beside him Mic caught a ball in the right shoulder. He shifted his cutlass to his left hand. Dirk and Jan closed in around him. Spaniards fired again from both sides of the trail. More pirates fell.

"Retreat!" L'Ollonais's voice screeched above the din of shouts and musket fire.

They fled, Spaniards swarming out of the jungle after them. At the edge of Acla, the pirates turned to fight.

All around him, Dirk's mates staggered or fell, bleeding heavily. His chest wound reopened; blood flowed down his stomach. He thrust and slashed with no plan other than to keep Spanish steel away from his friends and himself. His arms grew heavy and his shoulders ached and he thought the fighting would never end. But at last it did, and the musket fire and clash of blades gave way to cries of pain and moans of the dying.

A great weariness settled over Dirk. At least a third of the pirates lay dead. L'Ollonais stomped from one Spaniard to another, hacking at those still alive. He found San Sebastian sitting on the ground in a daze. Blood covered the left side of the man's black face.

"You did this!" L'Ollonais shouted. "You led us to this!"

With his cutlass hilt, he knocked the man unconscious. He ordered San Sebastian staked to the ground, arms and legs stretched wide. Then he returned to hacking Spanish corpses. Dirk's lip curled in disgust. As soon as his most serious wounds had been tended, he'd slip over and untie San Sebastian. By that time L'Ollonais might have lost interest or forgotten about him.

After he staunched the bleeding from his own chest wound, Dirk bandaged Mic's shoulder, then Baldric's upper arm. Curtis had deep gashes in his own thigh to attend, and there were so many other wounds. No one had escaped. And the dead... flies buzzed and vultures circled overhead.

Acla was quiet, but Dirk could feel people watching them from the jungle. *How many warriors lived in this village, or near it?* he wondered. *How soon will they, too, attack us*?

At the sound of L'Ollonais's cackling laughter, Dirk cursed himself for not untying San Sebastian sooner. The Frenchman stood over the cimaroon, his cutlass point slicing away the man's leather breeches. The blade bit into San Sebastian's groin and he moaned.

"Now wait." Moses Van Vin walked over to L'Ollonais. "The ambush... we made too much noise, gave them warning."

L'Ollonais punched Van Vin in the face and sent him sprawling. "Traitor!" He turned back to San Sebastian.

Fury surged through Dirk, washing away fatigue, pain and caution. He shook off Mic's restraining hand, stalked to L'Ollonais and thrust his cutlass against the Frenchman's throat.

"You're done! No more of this!"

Eyes narrowed, L'Ollonais stood motionless in the sudden silence. "You dare attack your admiral in combat? You die!" He raised his voice. "Kill him! I'm the admiral and that's an order!"

Swords whisked out of sheaths. At the edges of his vision, Dirk saw muskets pointed at him, but many more were aimed at L'Ollonais's friends.

"Drop the blade," Dirk said.

L'Ollonais's face hardened; his eyes grew cold and empty. He dropped the cutlass.

Dirk's voice boomed through the silence. "We split the fleet. Those who want to follow this madman, stay here. The rest of you, head for the ships. We leave now."

All but nine of the men moved toward the ships. Baldric and Dunstan trained muskets on those nine while Joost ran to cut San Sebastian loose. Dirk, his cutlass weaving in the air, backed away from L'Ollonais, who followed slowly. Melchior walked a step behind, his scarred, unblinking eye fixed on Dirk. The man's stubby hand twitched over the pistol in his belt.

It was a long walk back to the ships.

The men gave L'Ollonais the smallest vessel in the fleet, Irving's deckless launch, along with the small amount of booty already aboard it. The fleet set sail immediately, with San Sebastian aboard the *Serpent*. L'Ollonais stomped up and down the shore, waving his arms and screaming threats. Dirk watched the coast until it was lost from sight, and wondered what future trouble he had purchased with this mutiny.

They anchored at Curaçao for the share-out. Each man's portion equaled 1200 pieces of eight, plus a handful of jewels and a measure of silk and plate. As the pirates reloaded the ships and prepared to disperse, Dirk walked to the westernmost point of the island. He hardly recognized the place any more. Once Spanish, then Dutch, then Spanish, now Dutch again, the island still exported sugar, salt, dyewood, tobacco and copper. But lately it had been transformed into a depot for the sale of hundreds, if not thousands, of sick and starving West Africans.

Dirk strained his eyes to see Bentyn's Isle, but mist and distance prevented it. Baldric joined him, and after a moment he spoke softly.

"With all the towns we've raided and ships we've taken, I still don't feel avenged for that dawn." He shook his head. "Even when I kill a Spaniard, I'm not satisfied, for I doubt he was there. I hope each raid will be the one that stops the memories, but it never does. I'm always left with an ache not even gold and blood can ease." He was quiet for a few minutes, then asked, "Do you want to go back there? Now that it's Dutch again?"

"It's only a rock in the Caribbean," Dirk said. "Our people are gone. And I don't much care for Curaçao any more. My future is in the North." He hooked his thumbs in his belt. "Barbados."

"What?"

"Barbados. It's a haven for the Brethren I haven't seen yet. Let's go there now."

Since the rise of Tortuga, then Port Royal, as pirate havens, Barbados had become increasingly calmer and more law abiding. With less low-cost plunder at hand, the merchants there paid good prices for the *Serpent's* cargo. The crew, with pockets full of silver reales and pieces of eight, fanned out to enrich the taverns and doxies.

Although the crew agreed to stay a week, most of the men ran out of money in three days. Dirk and Grimbald the boatswain spent those days purchasing supplies for the remainder of their voyage. By the fourth day, Dirk was anxious to leave. As much as he'd wanted to come, Barbados was a long way from Port Royal and the safety of that city. He paced the deck all morning, counted and re-counted the crew members aboard. He stopped frequently to watch the last of the barrels of provisions roll up the gangplank.

Mic caught him on one circuit of the deck. With a grin, Mic pointed to the street that ran along the quay.

"I think everyone will be aboard in a few minutes."

Dirk glanced ashore. The twins were running toward the ship. A hundred feet behind them raged a middle-aged, balding man brandishing a fat knife. Silver buckles on his shoes flashed in the sunlight, and he shouted for bystanders to stop the twins. Most of the observers just laughed as Jan and Joost easily ducked away from the few who tried to catch them.

As the twins clambered up the gangway, Dirk grabbed the closest cutlass and stepped into the space. The pursuer reached the gangplank and shouted curses at the twins. But Dirk swished the cutlass in the bright sun and the man finally stopped shouting, and stood panting as he watched it. Then he stabbed his knife toward the twins who now flanked Dirk.

"If I ever see you two rogues again, I'll spit you on a pike and roast you for supper!"

He stomped off.

Dirk turned to the twins who merely grinned. "Wife or daughter?"

Jan laughed. "Both."

They trotted off to a small crowd of pirates already calling out for the details.

Dirk closed his eyes, and shook his head to suppress a smile.

Mic chuckled beside him. "I think we can leave now. Since everyone's aboard."

At sea again, Dirk felt safer, but still not at ease. Any day now he expected L'Ollonais, Melchior and their friends to appear on the horizon and cause trouble.

The high wind shifted again. Coming about to accommodate the new direction, the boom clipped Melchior on the head. He roared curses at the boom, the pelting rain, and the waves threatening to swamp them at any moment. Right now he should be safe and dry in the hold of one of the ships in L'Ollonais's fleet. But no, he was soaked to his bones on this deckless launch, and it was all the fault of that son of a Dutch whore, Dirk. Without that one, there would have been no mutiny, and the bastard Van Vin would never have abandoned them on the shore at Acla. Unprotected from the weather as they were now, they'd be lucky to reach Tortuga alive.

Tortuga. That's where Melchior had first encountered the wretched Dutchman years ago....

Though still a lad, Dirk had beaten Melchior's friend Baldessaire in a Cayona street fight. Afterwards, spectators crowded the winner and, en masse, walked off toward the taverns. Melchior stayed planted to the hard dirt, refusing to move even when bumped.

He was twenty-three years old that year, with straggly black hair hanging loose to his broad shoulders. Buccaneer garb, snatched off a corpse, covered the mass of ridges on his back, reminders of frequent lashings in his youth.

He scowled at Dirk, then went over to pick up his friend. Baldessaire winced.

"He's smart, Melchior. He got me with his head."

"No, he's lucky. That kind always got the luck with 'em."

"I knew what he was doing and I still did what he wanted me to." Baldessaire struggled to his feet, leaned heavily on Melchior and panted. "I should have taken him. He's smaller and younger."

"I suppose he was strong, like most of them buccaneers."

The two moved off slowly. Baldessaire, his arm over Melchior's shoulder, sucked in great ragged breaths. Melchior wasn't in the mood for talking.

The stamp of quality blood was all over that boy, despite his status as bond valet to a buccaneer. Clear-eyed, straight of limb, white teeth, and a hundred fools who wanted to be his friend. Every time one of that kind got in Melchior's life, his luck turned sour.

With his free hand he touched the puffy, oblong scar near his nose. He'd be handsome himself, without it. Damn the French village that branded him for thievery. He'd scratched at the wound for weeks to obliterate its meaning. Now the scar kept his right eye half-open all the time, but at least it didn't look like a brand.

Baldessaire's breath returned. "Did you lose much on me?"

"Didn't bet much."

Baldessaire stiffened at the insult and Melchior felt better.

"Cadfer's found a new boy," Baldessaire said. "He'll take the lad tonight in that room over Grane's punch house."

Melchior's foul mood retreated even further.

Cadfer was a slender, fair-haired man of twenty. His boy claimed to be seventeen, though he looked twelve, and he cooperated in the sex play. Melchior much preferred a struggle. The best part was the look on a boy's face when he first realized there would be no escape from Cadfer's assault, when that realization mingled with the first pain. But this was good enough.

Baldessaire slumped, eyelids drooping, on a bench beside Melchior. Silvanus, a fidgety little man, sat on the floor in front of them.

"I always enjoy this," Silvanus said. "And this boy is especially pretty." He elbowed Melchior's shin. "Look at him."

Melchior ignored Silvanus. He watched the play through narrowed eyes, hands clasped together between his knees. He shook until it was done, then grew calm. He stood up, kicking Silvanus over with the move, and went downstairs to the tavern. He snapped his fingers at Beryl, and the plain, ample-fleshed woman followed him out to the stable. There, among horses and mules, in soggy straw that stank of urine and manure, Melchior proved to himself that he had no interest in boys.

He was rough with Beryl, and when he finished said, "You're fat and old and too ugly to look at."

He pushed her face down into the filthy straw, then stood to tie his breeches. He itched to kick her, sprawled at his feet like she was. Instead, he threw some coins into the straw, returned her obscene gesture, and stomped out of the stable....

In the years since, Melchior had caught wind of Dirk now and again. There were tales among the brethren of him beating his buccaneer master and outwitting the Spanish on Cuba. But Melchior still harbored at Tortuga and so had never encountered the Dutchman again. 'Til now.

And here he was, causing a mutiny. Why did the cur have to interfere? What difference did it make whether that savage kept his balls or not? He was just a wild cimaroon, not anything valuable like a slave.

Melchior spat into the rain. He hadn't wanted to come with L'Ollonais, either, but he couldn't bring himself to sail with the likes of Dirk. L'Ollonais was a countryman, for what that was worth. He took rich prizes, too, and until the storm it looked like Melchior had made the right choice.

"Looky there," Silvanus called from the bow.

Melchior squinted ahead, but couldn't see anything.

"You little idiot, seeing things that ain't there."

Silvanus grinned, and Melchior suspected the wretched excuse for a pirate hadn't seen a thing.

Then somebody else cried, "Breakwater! Land!"

Melchior glanced at the stern, where L'Ollonais was working the tiller with one hand and drinking from a bottle of rum with the other.

Finally, L'Ollonais responded to the men's shouts and steered toward shore. A few minutes later the hull scraped sand.

Four men jumped over the side and tugged the boat ashore. When Melchior and L'Ollonais stepped onto the beach, everyone else helped tip the boat onto its side, hull toward the wind. Scrunched together and fighting for space inside, they waited for the storm to abate.

Just before nightfall, the rain slowed. L'Ollonais jammed an elbow into Melchior's ribs.

"Look at that. Wild Indians." L'Ollonais pointed to the tree line, where three Indios Bravos stood in the shadows of a thick forest. Their dark, almost naked bodies glistened in the drizzle.

"Watch this," Melchior said, loading his pistol. He fired.

The tallest Indian, in the middle, cried out, clutched his chest, then staggered against the others who dragged him into the forest.

L'Ollonais clapped Melchior on the shoulder. "Good shot. Did you see those brown devils run?"

The men laughed, and somebody said, "We shoulda kept one of them to dance for us."

"Go get one, Silvanus," Melchior said.

Silvanus laughed. "At first light tomorrow."

Soon after, the skies cleared entirely, and someone suggested a fire, but there was no dry firewood.

Melchior said, "At least now we don't all have to sleep under this damn boat."

L'Ollonais snorted and laughed, then helped him kick others out of the boat's shelter until they could stretch out themselves. Melchior drifted off to sleep, certain the storm would start again and everybody would want back under the hull.

In the morning, Melchior awoke facing the bottom of the boat. For a moment, he listened to the others grumble about stiff muscles and sand in their clothes. Cadfer and Silvanus were arguing over a piece of soggy bread Silvanus had squirreled away before the storm. Then suddenly, they quieted. Melchior rolled over and into the sharp point of an arrow.

Very carefully, he crawled out from under the boat. There were wild Indians everywhere, at least thirty, all armed with drawn bows. Fear ran up his spine and tingled his scalp. Cadfer, Baldessaire, and Silvanus were huddled together nearby, looking at him as if they expected him to do something.

"Don't look at me that way. I can't do anything. And what fool was supposed to be on guard?"

The nearest Indian whacked his jaw. Melchior flushed hot with fury, but dared not strike back. He leaned toward the boat. *L'Ollonais got us into this; he should think of something.* "Wake up," he said to the sleeping admiral. "Hey, L'Ollonais, git out here."

As L'Ollonais awoke with a curse and sat up, the Indians called his name to each other. A full dozen warriors surrounded him when he emerged from the shadow of the boat.

With ferocious gestures and prodding arrows, the Indians herded them off the beach. Melchior considered running into the jungle, but the one pirate who tried crashed only a few feet into the greenery before a flight of arrows caught him. He died in a tangle of ferns and creepers.

Melchior hunched in a squat, hands tied back and behind a slender palm tree, feet together and bound to the trunk. The seven other pirates had been tied the same way to nearby trees. L'Ollonais lay staked to the ground in the middle of a semi-circle of twelve thatch huts.

Upon entering the village that morning, the first warrior had shouted a few words, then, "L'Ollonais!" The villagers grew agitated, shouting the admiral's name, crowding the prisoners.

L'Ollonais chortled. "My fame reaches everywhere."

The Indians cut off his clothes, staked him out, and smeared his white skin with a thick syrup. Within minutes, the air around him was black with buzzing, biting, stinging insects. By mid-morning, insects had found Melchior, too. At first he cursed and thrashed about trying to escape them, then concentrated on untying his hands. L'Ollonais's screams, rising in volume throughout the day, drove Melchior beyond his own pain and fatigue.

All day, villagers roasted monkeys, iguanas, and a deer over a huge fire. At nightfall, they feasted. Melchior licked his lips. He hadn't eaten for two days. He was thirsty, too, and those devils were drinking and drinking. They drank so fast liquid poured out the corners of their mouths and dripped off their chins. It must be palm wine or some such liquor they had, because they were getting loud and clumsy. Even the children looked drunk as they skipped over to poke sticks at the pirates.

By that time, Melchior had freed his hands from the braided vine ropes. He longed to snatch the stick a little girl jabbed at his groin and break it across her sneering face. But if the Indians knew his hands were free, they'd retie him, probably better. So he waited, watching for a chance to untie his feet.

Women threw sand over L'Ollonais and chased away most of the insects with smudge sticks. His hoarse cries faded to loud, raspy breaths. Drumming started. Warriors danced in the firelight around L'Ollonais, their feet tapping a fancy pattern in the dirt. The drums grew louder, the beat faster. The rhythm filled Melchior's ears, made his heart pound, crept into his brain. His breath grew fast and shallow. The dancing collapsed into a frenzy of motion.

Steel flashed amidst the dancers. A man clad in a breechcloth swung a machete in circles over his headdress of bright parrot feathers and snake skins with the heads still attached. He danced close to the flames, then leaped over them. Snake fangs glinted in the firelight. The villagers roared their approval. The machete slashed through the flames. The cries grew louder.

Keeping one eye on the bodies weaving in the golden light, Melchior loosened the ropes around his feet. He returned his hands to the back of the tree. The others must have freed themselves, too. He could hear their rustling. But he kept his eyes on the Indians, waiting for the best moment to run.

The drums beat faster. The machete circled over the flames. It swirled over L'Ollonais's head three times. Then the blade sliced through L'Ollonais's left ankle, biting deep into the ground. The Indians cheered. L'Ollonais wailed feebly. Two men stooped under the flashing machete to retie his leg at knee and groin, then tossed the severed foot into the fire. The flames wavered and hissed.

Time to go.

Melchior slipped out of the ropes and around the tree. Cadfer quietly reached his side, then Baldessaire, then others. As they passed the tree where Silvanus was still frantically working at his bonds, Baldessaire hesitated. Melchior motioned for him to come along, but he bent to help Silvanus anyway.

The Indians cheered. The fire hissed. Melchior ran.

He found the trail to the beach and tripped along it in pale moonlight. The drums, the cheers, and the laughter grew fainter and fainter. He slowed to catch his breath. The others, strung out behind him, arrived one by one, gasping for breath.

The drums stopped. Then a loud, angry roar broke the silence. Melchior ran. Feet pounded on the trail behind him. His chest hurt. Blood throbbed in his ears. Each breath burned his throat. *I must have taken the wrong trail! I'm never going to reach the coast!*

But at last he stumbled onto the beach, the others right behind. The launch was still there. They righted the boat and shoved it into the water. Just as they scrambled aboard, Baldessaire and Silvanus burst out of the jungle.

"Run!" Cadfer yelled as the two raced across the sand.

Melchior raised the sail while others helped the two aboard. Wind slowly filled the canvas. Indians poured out of the jungle, into the surf. Arrows thudded into the hull and tore the sail. A young pirate Melchior never much cared for anyway slumped over the tiller, an arrow through his neck. As he clutched the arrow and begged for help, Melchior pushed him over the side.

Safe at sea, Melchior collapsed, exhausted. He needed food and something to drink. They'd have to land for provisions soon, risking capture by Indios Bravos again, this time and every time they landed. It was a long way to Tortuga and Cayona's nightlife. Melchior smiled, then frowned. He didn't have any booty to sell. Some of their meager share had been lost in the storm. The rest they'd left on the beach with the Indians.

So instead of anticipating the pleasures of Cayona, Melchior brooded over his most recent problems. Everything—their capture by the Indians, L'Ollonais's death, loss of their treasure—was due to the mutiny. And the mutiny had been caused by Dirk.

There were ways to destroy the Dutchman's tall, strong body, and see that handsome face contort in agony. Melchior touched the scar on his cheek. Maybe he would cut Dirk's face, give him another scar. Let him live with the ugliness for a while.

Until I kill him.

Port Royal, 1669

The card player lunged across the table. His knife slid between ribs and, with an upward twist, the buccaneer finished off the man from Paris.

The Parisian crashed to the floor. Two men carried the paunchy body to the tavern's back door and threw it into the alley. In the morning, soldiers would find a corpse and make inquiries, but nobody would know anything. The Parisian would join many others in unnamed graves on Los Palisados.

No one in the tavern knew the dead man's real name—he went by Jean—yet they all knew his business. He brought prostitutes from the streets, prisons, and workhouses of Paris to ply their trade in Port Royal. His wards, as he called them, were known to be young and pretty. Jean made a lot of money off these women, then he lost the money gambling. His newest ward watched him die, then fled the tavern. This was her first night in Port Royal, and although she was afraid of the streets, she preferred them to being questioned by authorities.

She'd been a prostitute three years, since the age of twelve. Her small, womanly body, combined with her pretty, child-like face and lustrous blond hair, assured her of plenty of business. She had successfully supported herself and various protectors. Simply the latest, Jean had been no better or worse than the others. Her release from prison, which he'd purchased, included the provision that she come to the New World.

So now she was in the colonies, alone, and witness to a murder. She was hungry, too, as she'd had nothing to eat all day. Lost and unable to find the room Jean had rented for them, she ran from shadow to shadow dodging the filthy, drunken men who roamed the streets. They towered over her, lurching, leering and grasping as she darted past. They screeched what might have been songs, or quarreled, shouting in languages she couldn't understand. Knife and fist fights erupted in her path. Now and then, someone fired a pistol into the air, or into the crowd.

She escaped the chaos by running into a narrow lane of closed shops and few people. As she stopped to catch her breath, a man four feet away drew his cutlass and knocked a clay bottle out of his companion's hand. The second man drew his own sword. Laughing, they waged a duel in the narrow lane, pausing once for a swallow each from the same bottle of wine. The girl pressed into a doorway, trying to make herself smaller as the blades rang and flashed in the glow of a street torch.

She hiccuped, the first warning that she was about to cry. She squeezed her eyes shut, but tears burned her eyelids, then slipped down her cheeks. She was so alone. No one to help her, no place to sleep. And she could be raped with no protector to stop it.

The sword fight slowed and moved along the street. She crawled from her hiding place and, crouching low, scurried in the opposite direction. Safely rounding a street corner, she straightened to run and plowed directly into the arms of a giant.

He lifted her, saying something to his companions in a strange guttural tongue. He laughed as she kicked and pounded her tiny fists against his bearded face. She opened her mouth to scream, but nothing came out. She was about to be raped. *Oh, sweet mother of God!*

Mic was strolling down Lime street with Dirk and Baldric, on their way to Willem's taphouse. With the sale of booty from the raids on the Mosquito Coast, Mic had enough money, even after saving most of his share, for a rousing dice game or two.

As Baldric finished relating what he'd heard about the death of L'Ollonais, a woman barreled around a corner and into Dirk. He scooped her up.

"Oh, ho! Here's a bit of fluff for my bed!"

Mic and Baldric laughed as the woman struggled.

"Such a fighter! Too feisty for me. Here, Mic." Dirk tossed the woman to him.

She was lighter than Mic expected. When she cursed in French, he shook her and in that language told her to be calm. He carried her to a nearby street lamp. She was lovely, and rather clean for a doxy. He wondered why such a woman was on the streets alone.

"What's your price?" he asked.

"Thirty... pieces of eight."

That was too low a price for one so young and pretty. Mic set her down.

"Are you poxed?"

Her eyes widened. "Certainly not, Monsieur. Are you?"

Dirk and Baldric hooted with laughter. The woman glared up at Mic.

"Then it's thirty pieces," he said. "Where's your bed?"

"I have no room."

"I'll not drop my breeches here in the street."

Baldric chuckled. "Oh, do it. She looks worth it."

"Bring her back to Willem's," Dirk said.

Mic hesitated. If the twins were not already using the rented room, they'd soon be pounding on the door, demanding to share it. An unwelcome disturbance at the very least. But the woman's price was so low he couldn't pass up such a bargain.

In Willem's doorway, the girl shied away from the light and noise. Mic caught her wrist.

"You do agree?" Dirk asked her.

She nodded, though woodenly. Mic tugged her inside and across the public room toward the stairs. Along the way he called greetings to the twins who were sitting in a cluster of women. He grabbed a small loaf of bread from the fireplace bench and led the girl upstairs to his room.

Mic bolted the door, lit a lantern and went to sit on his bed. Setting the bread down on a little table, he counted out thirty cobs from the pouch at his belt. The girl watched silently from the center of the room. Mic glanced up. She was unbelievably pretty and well-formed.

"The clothes," he said. "How much?"

She bit her bottom lip. "Five."

Marveling at his extravagance, Mic added five more coins to the pile. When he looked up, the girl had edged closer to the table. She reached out.

"Take it now," he said. "You'll earn it soon enough."

But instead of the coins, she snatched the bread and retreated a few paces to gobble it. While she swallowed the last bit, he took off his tunic and breeches. Throwing back the bedcovers, he sat again to watch her undress. She looked at him with huge grey eyes.

"Surely you aren't new to this," he said.

"Oh, no, Monsieur."

"Then why do you stand there? I paid you the extra."

She nodded, and with a trembling hand untied the drawstring of her skirt. As the waist loosened, the skirt billowed to the floor. Even more slowly, she tugged at the tie of her long blouse. The neckline fell open and she shrugged the simple garment off her shoulders. It too slid to the floor.

Her body was pale and smooth in the lantern light. Her skin looked like velvet stretched over high round breasts and gently swelling hips. Mic grew warm and his breathing deepened.

"Come here."

She came, but too slowly. He pulled her close between his knees. Holding her tight with his thighs, he ran his hands along her face, into her thick hair, down over her breasts.

"Beautiful," he whispered. Then he recognized the doxy's gaze shielding her eyes. The girl, the presence he'd felt while she ate the bread, was gone. Only the prostitute—the body and the experience—was left for him.

His hands roamed down to the soft fur at the top of her thighs, up to the peaks of her hipbones, then encircled her waist. She flinched. He looked up and saw a girl once more. His hands slipped around her back. She wriggled backward; Mic trapped her with his feet. Arms around her waist, he tugged her close again. She whimpered.

"What is wrong?"

When she merely shook her head, he pulled her face down across his knee to look.

"Oh, Lord."

Her back was a mass of welts. A lash had struck her many times only a few months ago. Some marks, red and inflamed, had to be more recent. A few still festered.

"Who did this?"

The girl buried her face in the mattress, muffling her reply. "The nuns."

Mic swung her up to perch on his other thigh. By God, she was little. And young.

"Why would they do such a thing?"

She hiccuped, and a few tears ran down her cheeks.

"For prostitution. I was—" Hiccup. "Arrested in Paris and they took me to the Convent of the Madelonettes."

"But your back... so many lines...."

She nodded, splashing a tear on his bare thigh. "One hundred lashes is usual."

"A hundred lashes!" he roared. "For prostitution?"

The girl started bawling. "It... it release me... damnation of my sin," she got out between sobs and hiccups. "But now I'm so ugly I'll never get married... nothing else for me to do but this."

Mic slid her, on her side, onto the bed. "Well, you're not doing this tonight. You can't lie on that back."

"I can. I need the money. Please."

Mic threw the bedcovers over her and she shrank against the pillow. How could anyone whip a girl for being a doxy? And with so many stripes? She'd always carry scars, but perhaps some of those welts could be helped. Striding to the door, he yanked it open and hollered for Willem's son Timmy.

The nine year old came running up the stairs.

"Is Curtis the surgeon downstairs?"

Timmy nodded, gaping at Mic's nakedness.

"Then go ask him to come up here. And bring me some wine and meat."

Timmy ran off and Mic walked back to the bed where the girl was still huddled between pillows. He pulled on his breeches. "What's your name?"

"Clarisse."

At Mic's shout for Timmy, Dirk looked up from his card game. When he saw the boy come down again, calling for Curtis, Dirk left the game. He pounded up the stairs. *If that little whore stabbed him....*

He flung open the door, ready to thrash somebody. Mic, half-dressed, was standing safe and sound by the bed. Dirk took a deep breath.

"What happened? Why'd you call for Curtis?"

His jaw clenched, Mic lifted the bedcovers and eased the girl onto her stomach.

Dirk frowned. "How? Who?" He spoke in French now, for the girl's sake.

Mic told him.

"But the recent ones. Who did that?"

From the pillow's depth the girl said, "Jean, on the ship. So I wouldn't run away when we landed."

Curtis finally arrived, out of breath and a little drunk. He set to work with his salves and lotions, at times clucking his tongue. It was the first time Dirk had ever seen him treat wounds gently. Even so, the girl moaned once and Mic leaned over the bed.

Curtis elbowed him away. "Stay out of my light, Lackwit."

The girl whimpered as Curtis rubbed his salves across the cuts. Mic glowered. Dirk winced.

She is so small, and that hair looks like Katrina's. She's thinner than Katrina, and not as pretty... nearly the same age, though, except around the eyes. Katrina looked fresh and innocent while this girl had old eyes.

Most of the women in Port Royal looked tired, beaten down, with sallow complexions. Only the flush of liquor gave them a healthy color equal to that of the women in New York. Maybe it was the heat here in the islands, or the insects, food, or poisonous night air. It might even be the repeated loss of homes to hurricanes, and babies to tropical fevers.

Pieter was right. Katrina doesn't belong in the Caribbean. He could support her, protect her from Spaniards and other pirates, but he could never protect her from whatever it was that sapped the energy and life from the women of Port Royal.

Curtis finished his work and left. The girl rolled onto her side, staring wide-eyed at the men towering over the bed.

"Where can I find this Jean?" Dirk asked.

"He... he's dead."

"He's lucky," Mic said, and at the heat in his voice the girl turned her face into the pillows.

Dirk returned to the card game downstairs, but sipped brandy rather than play. He gazed about the room. The taphouse looked and sounded as it always had. For eight years now the chatter, the music and gaming had been the same. The wenches had changed over the years, but only in shape and color of hair. They all had old eyes and hard lines around their mouths.

Dirk looked at his friends. Already the twins had lost a bit of their handsomeness to long nights and gallons of liquor. Baldric had appeared old, even as a youth, although lately he seemed more alive in port around Frieda than he did at sea, or even in battle.

Katrina would not die early from overwork, nor lose her youth to anything but time. But to keep her safe, he needed more money than he'd earned on this last voyage. And he had only a little over a year in which to do it.

Port Royal, Summer of 1670

Everyone in Willem's taphouse quieted for Dirk's toast.

"To Mariana, Queen Regent of Spain, who declared war on Jamaica."

People whooped with laughter and emptied their tankards.

With a grin, Dirk said, "To Governor Thomas Modyford, who declared war on Spain... without King Charles's permission."

There was more laughter, and serving wenches refilled cups and tankards for the crowd celebrating Henry Morgan's latest commission. He was to protect Jamaica from expected Spanish attacks, as well as destroy enemy vessels and war supplies being stockpiled ashore. For pirates, that meant Morgan's fleet would again sack the Main under the protection of the English flag.

Dirk sat back in his chair, pleased to be sailing with Morgan. Although the *Serpent* had captured a few prizes in the past year, there had been as many failures as victories. Most of his share of booty had gone to pay for daily expenses. Outfitting the yacht for this voyage had depleted his cache.

The *Serpent* would sail in the morning for Isla Vaca where, it was rumored, a thousand men had already gathered for the fleet. With Morgan to lead them, they'd sail home rich. And come next spring, Dirk would sail north to claim Katrina.

He called for more brandy and savored the fresh meat on his platter. It was the best he'd get for many months. While he ate, he appraised the serving wenches. The only female on this expedition would be a witch Morgan had commissioned to prophecy for the fleet.

Mic slipped away from the celebration and let himself into a small limestone house near the fruit market. He walked through a sparsely furnished sitting room-kitchen where a stew bubbled over the fire. Baldric's dog lay nearby, her tail twitching in a dream. Too old now to go on raids, she'd stay with Clarisse while Baldric sailed.

Surprised to find the seven-foot-square bedroom empty, Mic took off his boots and tunic and stretched out on the bed. Outside the single window, people strolled or staggered by in the moonlight. Arms behind his head, he watched their shadows play across the ceiling.

The sound of steps on the stone floor brought him out of a light slumber and he felt someone enter the bedroom. Clarisse's jasmine scent wafted to him.

"Where have you been?" His voice boomed in the small space, and he opened his eyes in time to see her jump. The flame on her candle wavered. "Out adding to the income I give you?"

"Oh, no, my love, I would not. I have not, since the night we met." She blew out the candle, then set it on the floor.

Mic pulled her to the bed and kissed her nose. "Take the frown off your face. Don't you know that I tease? Or do I still frighten you?"

"A little... sometimes."

"If I thought you could play me false, you wouldn't be here."

Clarisse sighed as she settled full-length on top of him. "I'm glad you're here."

"So am I." Mic wrapped his arms around her small body. Clean blond hair draped their faces and his lips found a certain spot on her neck. She moaned, and her hands began seeking, caressing, and setting his skin afire.

As he lost himself in her jasmine softness, Mic prayed he would live through the next raid, that he would come home to this woman and this joy.

Clarisse awoke in pre-dawn light as Mic rolled away.

"Must you go?" She yawned. "Can't you stay here just this once?"

"And how will we have the money for this house if I don't go earn it?"

"There's enough for us to live on for a long time. I haven't spent much."

Mic sat up, swinging his legs over the edge of the bed. "Buy a length of cloth and make a dress. Light green silk would be best, I think."

"I don't want a dress. I want you to stay home." Her voice sounded childish to her, but she couldn't help it. Life was so lonely and empty when he was away.

Mic leaned over her and smiled. "But I want you to have it. Make the collar go this way." He traced a finger along her chest. "And put the first lacing here." He caressed the well between her breasts.

She tried to smile. His face hardened and he stood.

"Do it for me."

"Of course."

He tugged on his breeches. "I am a sea rover and must sail. Why do you question it after all this time?"

"But the Spaniards attacked Montego Bay just last month. What if they come here to Port Royal? All you men will be at sea."

"When the Spaniards hear about Morgan's fleet, they will sail home to defend their own towns."

"But what of the peace?"

"You mean the Treaty of Madrid?"

"Didn't the English and the Spanish both sign that treaty? Isn't pirating illegal now? Won't the soldiers hang you?"

Mic pulled his tunic over his head. "Those fools in Europe signed it, but it won't be published here in the Caribbean for another nine months. That gives us just enough time to take a Spanish city before our raids become piracy again."

That was too complicated when she was so sleepy. "You'll come home with lots of treasure?"

"Naturally."

"But mostly you want to go adventuring with Dirk."

Mic sat and drew her naked body against his clothed one. "Yes, my love, I want to go adventuring with Dirk."

"I am jealous." She stuck out her lower lip.

"Of Dirk?"

Clarisse threw her arms around his neck. Tears stung her eyes. "I love you," she whispered. "Please come home to me."

"For me, you are home." He stroked her hair. "You are peace and strength and safety. I need those things, but I need other things, too. When Dirk goes on the account, I go with him. He is part of me."

Soon, too soon, Mic left. Clarisse smiled and waved from the bedroom window. As he walked out of sight, she hiccuped.

Nearly every adventurer in the Caribbean answered Morgan's call. Thirty-eight ships anchored around Isla Vaca. A few carried more than ten guns and over seventy-five men. The smallest boats had no deck and but a single sail. Pirates from as far away as Bermuda arrived in beautiful cedar sloops. Buccaneers left the hunt, filtering out of the Hispaniola highlands with bundles of boucan beef over their shoulders.

Even with the meat, provisioning over 2000 men was difficult. Morgan sent Edward Collier, one of his captains, to raid for food. Buccaneers returned to the highlands repeatedly to hunt. Dirk went along once, and wanted to kick himself for not remembering how much he loathed mosquitos, bloody tunics, smokey campsites, and the constant weariness of buccaneering, even without having to serve a brutal master.

After eleven weeks, Collier returned to Isla Vaca with maize and wheat, salted beef and rum. The privateers shook off their boredom, quit their squabbling, and squeezed onto the ships of the fleet. The *Serpent* signed on men until the deck could hold no more. Ship captains met with Morgan on the *Satisfaction*, his flagship. They worked out an agreement on the Articles and compensations for the maimed. Then they chose a target: Panama.

Dirk stood with the others to toast the voyage and the prize wallowing in treasure on the South Sea. A mere twenty-three leagues from the Caribbean, Panama had never been taken. Even the legendary Francis Drake had failed in his attempt. Yet Dirk knew in his bones that this time, with these men, Panama would fall.

Dirk's machete slashed at the endless greenery, hacking a narrow trail through the Darien jungle's dense undergrowth. Behind him, Jan and Baldric flailed away, further widening the path. Sweat ran down Dirk's back, soaking his shirt, and over his forehead into his eyes, blurring his vision. When he made a poor cut on a fern branch, it snapped back against his face. He cursed and, with great concentration, hacked the branch into little pieces. Jan pulled at his arm.

"Step back, Captain. Let a man work at it for a while."

Dirk handed Jan the machete and stepped aside. Jan handed the blade to Baldric.

"Here, Mate. Show us some power."

Joost smacked his brother on top of the head. Chuckling, Jan retrieved the machete and stepped to the front of the small band. Dirk dropped to the rear. Dunstan, in the remnants of an embroidered waistcoat and velvet breeches, shuffled just ahead of him, cursing steadily.

"An hour," Dunstan said. "Have we come a hundred feet even?"

"A little more than that," Mic said. "Thank God we have only half a league to go through this mess."

"Why do we have to go through the jungle anyway?"

"We couldn't attack the castle from the sea," Dirk said.

Yesterday, he'd stood on the deck of Joseph Bradley's ship as they made two passes off the coast of Darien and surveyed the castle of San Lorenzo for weak points. The castle loomed on steep cliffs, bristling with guns aimed to rake the Rio Chagres. A stairway cut into the cliffs led down to a riverside tower with eight guns and two batteries. Across the river mouth lay a reef obscured by a few feet of water. Incoming ships would be forced to sail north or south of it, under direct line of fire from the castle.

Bradley, charged by Morgan to capture that castle, chose to land on a beach more than a league up the coast. The next morning, 350 privateers marched toward San Lorenzo along the shore until forced inland where there was no path. Small bands of men cut trails through the jungle's dense undergrowth.

After a few more minutes of Dunstan's complaining, Dirk said, "We should have left you on Providence with the rest of the crew."

Dunstan snorted. "Stay on that God-forsaken rock of sand dunes and tents and more rats than men? With nothing to do but numb my arse while the rest of you take this castle? Feckit. Sitting and waiting is for women. I'm a fighting man."

Mic said, "Then fight the green enemy and give our ears some peace."

With another snort, Dunstan pushed to the head of the group and whacked Jan on the shoulder. Jan, already tired, handed over the machete.

"Here you go, Whistle Breeches."

"I do not fart," Dunstan said, then contradicted himself.

While the others laughed, Dunstan attacked the jungle. Jan dropped back.

Mic looked at Dirk. "I didn't want to wait on Providence either, but maybe one of us should have stayed with the ship."

"Crofton's aboard. He owns a share of her, too. We couldn't do anything that he can't."

So the Spaniards wouldn't know how many vessels and men he was leading, Morgan had allowed Bradley only three large ships. Those joining the attack would each earn an extra share of the plunder. Most of Dirk's men had volunteered. He left Crofton with a small crew to bring the *Serpent* to San Lorenzo once it had fallen. But despite his words to Mic, Dirk, too, had misgivings about leaving the ship at Providence with the rest of the fleet.

The only relief from trail blazing came from climbing over piles of boulders that littered the forest. Heaving himself over the third pile in half an hour, Dirk fell. His right foot slid into a narrow crevice while his body twisted downward. Pain stabbed through his right knee. He cursed himself for his clumsiness, then Gilbert for the beating that had first weakened the knee so long ago.

The rest of the journey was torture. Not even the tight bandage Curtis tied around Dirk's knee could ease the pain as he climbed up and down boulders, and limped over rough ground.

When at last he saw San Lorenzo, Dirk groaned. It looked as formidable from the jungle as it had from the sea. A deep ravine ran along the base of the outer palisade, a heavy log wall caulked with dirt and sand. Colonial soldiers and their Indian allies lined the tops of both inner and outer palisades. Muskets and bows ready, they stood under a shelter of palm and reed thatching. Between pirates and castle lay a broad, open plain, devoid of cover for the pirates during an assault.

Just as Dirk sank to the ground to rest his knee, Bradley ordered an attack. Dirk loaded his musket and brace of pistols, struggled to his feet, and limped along behind the others. Before he was half-way across the plain, the pirates retreated, leaving a few fallen men behind.

Almost immediately Bradley ordered another assault. Dirk again limped onto the field, this time working his way into musket range. Planting his feet, he fired, reloaded, and fired again until pirates swarmed past him in another retreat.

They rested in the shade during the hottest part of the afternoon. Across the plain, soldiers jeered and shouted insults. Dirk took stock of his crew. Baldric's thigh had caught an arrow. Efren, one of the men who had joined the *Serpent's* crew for this raid, was bleeding heavily from his right elbow. Curtis insisted the joint had shattered and the arm would have to be cut off above the wound.

His knee throbbing, Dirk lounged against a tree and tried to sleep. Nearby, grenadiers stuffed dried leaves, twigs and cloth into little clay pots they'd brought from Port Royal. They poured oil inside and closed the fire-balls with short cotton stoppers. While they worked, they chatted about spending their shares. For every fire-ball a man lobbed into the castle, he'd receive an extra five pieces of eight.

With sunset came another order to attack. This time, under covering fire, the grenadiers raced forward and dropped into the ravine. There, at the base of the palisades, they lit their fire-balls and tossed them inside.

The soldiers and Indians on the walls were easy targets against the sunset and as they fell, the pirates advanced. Dirk limped forward, men around him stumbling and falling. The wounded screamed; the dying sobbed.

He squinted through musket smoke. The fire-balls were doing some damage at last. The dry thatching over the defenders' heads caught fire, burned quickly, and collapsed onto the wooden palisades and stores of gunpowder stock-piled nearby. Logs caught fire. Explosions ripped along the walls. A huge bronze cannon burst, tearing out a section of wall. Pirates rushed for the breach as soldiers plugged it with musket fire.

The sun went down. Although the palisades were still burning, there was no longer enough light for fighting. Bradley ordered a retreat. As Dirk turned to go, an explosion filled the sky with noise and light. Flames licked at black smoke billowing up from the center of the castle. The soldiers were dark figures against the orange and red.

Dirk smiled wearily at Mic, who was standing beside him.

"I hope that was the powder magazine."

Mic nodded. "Sounded like it."

The castle burned all night. Around midnight, soldiers visible against the blaze crept down the stone stairs to the tower and batteries where boats were tied.

Baldric lay stretched out on the grass beside Dirk. "I wonder if there'll be any soldiers left in the castle come morning."

Joost yawned. "Let's hope not."

"Isn't there an easier way to Panama?" Jan asked.

"There's only one road over the mountains," Mic said. "We can sail up the Rio Chagres and meet the road at Las Cruces, or take the road from Porto Bello."

"And since Morgan took Porto Bello, I'm sure fortifications there have been strengthened." Dirk rubbed his aching knee. "We could never take it now."

"Maybe we won't take this place either." Mic sighed.

At dawn they charged the castle. This time, Bradley declared, they would go over the walls or die.

With pirates racing by him, Dirk limped toward the charred palisades, a hoarse cry in his throat. Little musket fire came from the castle. Perhaps the last of the Spaniards were escaping down the cliff stairway.

Then, as the pirates neared the walls, all the Spanish guns fired at once. Musket balls, fired from cannon at point-blank range, tore through the privateer army. A ball whistled past Dirk, burning a bloody trough in his neck. Fifteen feet in front of him, Bradley writhed on the ground, both feet shot away. Grimbald, the *Serpent's* boatswain, lay dead. And Joost was down, moaning and holding his left hip.

The army pressed forward, leaving the wounded behind, until at last they entered the castle. Inside, fighting with his cutlass, Dirk felt safer. There was no defense against musket balls, neither strength nor skill nor wit. But with a blade, a man had a chance.

The Spaniards retreated to a small, half-burned keep. Bradley, carried inside the charred walls, offered them quarter. The Spanish commander refused and so, fighting to the last man, all the Spaniards died.

The victors cheered as an English flag rose over the castle's smoking timbers.

In the second week of January, a pirate on watch in San Lorenzo cried, "Sail, ho! A sail!"

Everyone capable of walking crowded the rebuilt walls to see. Dirk and Mic, both tall enough to see over the heads of others, stood back.

"There's the fleet," Mic said.

Dirk grinned. "At last."

The past days had been full of hard, onerous work. Immediately after the battle, they buried the dead, Spanish and pirate alike, between the remains of the two palisades. Thirty pirates had died in the fighting, and every day there were more to bury. So far, seventy-five men, including Bradley, had died of wounds that festered in the sticky, bug-filled heat.

The *Serpent* lost four men: Grimbald, Curtis, Efren, and Radford, barely fifteen and on his first voyage. Without Curtis and his healing salves, Dirk fretted about his wounded men. Each day he carried Baldric out past the sandy surf and doused his torn thigh in the water. Afterwards Dirk bound the wound with strips of cotton rinsed frequently in the sea.

He and Jan did the same to Joost, who howled and kicked each time the salty water washed over his raw flesh. Dirk was not convinced it helped, but Curtis and Ogden, the crew's surgeon before him, both had sworn by the healing power of sea water, and the daily dousings were the best he could do. Now, two weeks later, Baldric, Joost and the few others who used sea water were healing well.

Small bands of pirates ranged through the forest every day to hunt. A raiding party assaulted the nearby village of Chagres, but found it deserted. Everyone else had spent the hot days rebuilding the palisades and fort.

Now, with the fleet in sight, the vigil at San Lorenzo had ended. Thirty-five ships, their sails full, raced for the river. The *Satisfaction* fired a salvo in greeting. A castle gun answered.

Dirk squinted at the fleet, trying to locate the *Serpent*.

"There she is." Mic pointed. "Astern the *Satisfaction*."

Pride crept into Dirk's voice. "I see her now." The elegant yacht skipped across the waves.

"I wonder if they will sail north or south of the reef," Mic said.

Dirk glanced at the froth of water covering the reef that lay across the river mouth. "I don't think they can get through on the north side. I wager they go to the south."

"No wager," Mic said. "South is my choice, too."

On came the fleet, driven by a strong wind. The flagship, with the *Serpent* in its wake, drew near. It made no move to sail either north or south of the reef.

"What is she doing?" Dirk frowned at the speed of the flagship. Soon it would be too late to avoid wrecking.

"Hard over to larboard," he said. "Go about, heave to! Furl the sails! Anything!"

But the *Satisfaction* closed in faster and faster, the *Serpent* right behind. Dirk caught his breath as the flagship sailed onto the reef with a loud crunch. Worse, the yacht seemed about to do the same.

"Crofton!" he shouted. "What's the matter with you?"

His beloved yacht followed the *Satisfaction* onto the coral. The *Serpent's* hull crumpled like dried bread crusts. The masts and yards slammed into the water.

Mic groaned. "That's all we own! My sea charts, land maps... everything!"

The watching pirates roared their dismay as three more ships crashed on the reef before the fleet turned aside.

Dirk pushed his way through the crowd and ran down to the beach. Crofton could swim a little. If he made it to shore alive, Dirk would strangle him.

Dirk dove into the surf and dragged men out of the churning water until he found Crofton. He carried the navigator onto the sand and propped him against a piece of driftwood. Crofton sputtered and coughed as Dirk shook him.

"Did you go blind, old man? Why did you sail onto the reef?"

Crofton blinked. "Reef?" His eyes were vague. There was a deep bruise on his forehead, several days old.

"Sorry," he mumbled. "I...don't... riggin'... fell... follow *Satisfaction*."

Frustrated, Dirk rushed off to find the rest of his crew. He spent most of an hour dragging men from the sea, dumping his own in a little circle on the beach. When he thought he had them all, he stood in their midst and demanded an explanation for the *Serpent's* destruction. None spoke. He interrogated them in English, French, and Spanish. They cowered in the sand, not one willing to stand and tell him anything.

Shaking his fist, he stomped back and forth, calling the men every vile name he could think of. When he ran out of French and English curses they could understand, he switched to Dutch. He cursed them for their stupidity and cowardice and, in the end, cursed himself for having left his yacht in their care.

With corpses and remnants of ships still washing ashore, Dirk prowled the beach until he found Morgan. The admiral was sitting on a boulder just below the castle, busily wringing water out of his yellow velvet coat. Men were sprawled around him, exhausted from their swim in the roiling surf. When Dirk marched up, they ceased moaning and coughing.

"What in God's name happened?" Dirk asked through gritted teeth. "You sat on Providence Island for three weeks while we risked our lives to take this place." He snapped a wrist at the castle. "We trusted you to bring our ships here safely!"

Morgan's face darkened, but Dirk ranted on.

"I lost good men in that battle and now I don't even have a ship. How could you sail over the reef?"

Morgan's voice was low and threatening. "We didn't know it was there."

Dirk's voice boomed over the beach. *"Didn't know it was there?"*

The spectators edged closer.

"How could you not know it was there? Bradley knew it was there! What about your navigator? I can't believe he didn't know it was there!"

"When I find him, I'll ask him."

"And your witch!" Dirk bellowed. "Surely that old crow could have predicted the lay of that reef!"

"She's dead, van Cortlandt."

Dirk's hands curled into fists. "You didn't even know where your own ship was sailing!" he said. His voice rose again. "Two thousand men follow you! How could you be so..."

He stepped back and swallowed the rest of his tirade, but it was too late. Morgan, mouth hard and eyes glittering with resentment, clasped the hilt of his sword. Dirk's stomach tightened. He had made the admiral's ignorance public, and knew that one day Morgan would make him pay for it.

Dirk burned with anger for the next week. Only Mic and Baldric were willing to be near him. When Morgan asked for men to stay in San Lorenzo during the attack on Panama, Dirk ordered the survivors of Crofton's crew to volunteer. They acted grateful to be away from him, which made him angrier still.

In the smaller remaining ships, the army of privateers set sail up the Rio Chagres. Still in a foul temper, Dirk settled in a long canoe with six of his eleven men. They were quiet while he brooded. Even before starting the march across the isthmus, he'd lost a ship and with it all the money he'd spent outfitting for this voyage. Katrina's portrait, locked in a small trunk, had been lost as well. Without her likeness to look at every day, she seemed remote and unattainable.

More importantly, he'd lost friends: Curtis, Grimbald and others. More of his crew would stay at San Lorenzo to either heal or die of their wounds. Crofton still suffered dizziness and a frequent loss of the priceless memory that had made him a true sea artist.

The canoe glided among thirty-six other little boats and piraguas, most of which had been found along the coast. Up ahead sailed seven of the fleet's smallest ships. Paddling eased the tension in Dirk's shoulders, and though his knee grew stiff in the canoe, it felt good to have his weight off it for a time.

When they rounded the first bend in the river, sounds of the ocean faded. Mangrove trees with tangled roots grew to the very edge of the water. Palm, bamboo and mahogany fought for space and sunlight among huge cedar trees that rose a hundred feet before the first branch appeared. Their crowns, at times 150 feet in diameter, formed a dense canopy.

Near the riverbanks, herons dove for fish. Once in a while an alligator slid into the water to rest in the shallows with just its eyes showing. Ashore, hummingbirds darted among the scarlet passion-flowers now in full bloom. Multi-hued parrots lounged in low branches, while somewhere, out of sight, troops of monkeys chattered.

Dirk's thoughts drifted back more than a year to his last visit in New York. Katrina had matured, grown taller, lovelier, and even more like her mother. He strained his memory for the sound of her laughter, and he ached to hold her.

Although she had reaffirmed her desire for their marriage, she acted more restrained than usual and did not, as was her custom, beg him to take her along when he sailed. Dirk had risked much by not visiting her this past fall. At the time, he believed it more important to be part of Morgan's fleet, to spend the autumn preparing for this raid on Panama.

Now, however, life with Katrina lay beyond his reach, as did his plan for becoming a trader. There was no money left for investment, not even enough to outfit another ship for more raiding. To acquire a ship, he and his men would have to steal one, make a few small raids, and build up another cache. He must start over, as if he were eighteen years old again.

For two days they paddled upriver. Inside that cool, green world, Dirk relaxed and his mood lifted. He considered the raid ahead, for therein lay his future wealth.

By the end of their third day on the Rio Chagres, the privateers had eaten the last of their food. Declaring the jungles full of game, Morgan had made no provisions for other supplies. Everyone assumed there would be stockades to raid as well.

On the following day, they found one of those stockades. Dirk crept with 200 others through the jungle to the stronghold. At Morgan's signal, they raised a cheer and rushed the chest-high walls. No shots were fired as they swarmed over the enclosure. It had been abandoned. There were no weapons or food to steal.

Another day passed without food. As Dirk weakened, he worried about Baldric and Joost, not fully recovered from their wounds. He'd not been able to convince either one to remain at San Lorenzo.

They pushed upstream. Rainstorms had washed giant trees into the riverbed. Now in the dry season the trees lay in mud, creating snags and sandbars. The river grew so shallow, the seven ships had to stop. Weapons were shifted to the canoes and most of the men were forced to walk.

Again, there were no trails. For eight leagues the men hacked through brambles, cane brakes, and dense webs of creepers. Wood ticks, centipedes, and huge red and black ants attacked them as they struggled. There were snakes, too, and scorpions and tarantulas. Men who left the winding riverbank to find a short-cut were quickly lost. Walking through the rough terrain made Dirk's knee throb.

Still there was no food. Surely the jungle was teeming with hogs, deer, and wild turkey, but the noise of 1500 men must have frightened the game away, Dirk thought. Not even San Sebastian could catch anything. They passed three more Spanish stockades, all burned. Leather provision bags, boiled a long time, served as a meal. Dirk cursed Morgan and the Spaniards with every painful step.

On their sixth day out from San Lorenzo, they reached Venta de Las Cruces, where the Royal Road met the Rio Chagres. An ambush awaited them, and soldiers meant food. After the last shot was fired, the pirates raced into the village, but found it burning. That night, stray dogs became supper, and when the men discovered sixteen jars of Peruvian wine they fought bitterly for a swallow. Dirk and his men arrived too late for even a sip. At first angry, they were grateful a few hours later. All the men who drank the wine became ill, and rumors spread that the wine had been poisoned.

The next day Dirk sweated easily and tired quickly, but the pangs in his gut had disappeared. For the first time in days, he thought perhaps they might actually reach Panama. From Venta de Las Cruces, they would march on the Royal Road.

In use for over a century, it was known throughout the Caribbean as the Gold Road for all the treasure that had passed over it. There'd be no more slashing at greenery for an hour just to advance a few yards. To cross the mountains and for the final push into Panama, Morgan's army would march upon the Spanish kings' own highway.

In actuality, it was a bumpy, rutted mule track barely wide enough for four men to walk abreast. Strung out so far along the road, the 1500 privateers were vulnerable to attack. Ordered to march in the rear guard, Dirk and his men were especially so. Although Morgan sent out patrols to deal with ambushes, three of Dirk's men were killed and three more wounded. The heat of the jungle weighted them, slowed them. His knee ached every moment, and his limp slowed him further.

On their fourth day without food, they broke out of the still shadows of Darien. A fresh breeze swept across the broad savannah before them. Dirk took deep breaths and stretched in the sunshine. Around him, men laughed and talked of the great prize that lay just ahead. They acted as if they'd won a victory. Dirk smiled. Perhaps they had. Francis Drake, wondrous pirate that he was, had never completed his march across Darien. Already these men had done better.

They marched on. Dirk limped along, his pain fading. They crested a small hill and suddenly stopped. The entire army spread out over the hilltop, staring in silence.

A league away, sparkling in the hot sun, lay the South Sea, Balboa's Pacific. A galleon and small coasting craft rode lazily at anchor in a wide bay. Farther out, the outlines of islands stood dark against the bright sky.

Closer, almost close enough to touch it seemed to Dirk, sat Panama, beckoning them with its towers and spires. A sea of white roofs undulated over houses of pink or blue or yellow. Around them lay a dark mass of shacks and palm huts that extended into the edge of a mangrove swamp. The city had no wall and its three guns were trained on the harbor. The Royal Road, now a dusty trail, led straight to the city over an unguarded bridge.

Closer still, a large herd of bulls grazed on the plain at the base of the hill.

"I wonder why they didn't drive off the cattle?" Joost leaned on his musket.

Jan grinned. "Maybe it's part of their defense."

Baldric snorted. "What can cattle do but stampede?"

"On buccaneers?" Dirk laughed. "That's no stampede. That's supper."

As dawn streaked the eastern sky, Dirk and the remaining eight men of his crew inched to a position on a wooded hill overlooking the Mata Asnillos savannah. Although unable to make out faces, he could see the padded doublets and silver helmets of the Spanish cavalry centered over the Royal Road. Panama's infantry, dressed in ragged cotton shirts and breeches, formed a long line across the plain.

Mic crouched at Dirk's side to point at a man in a silver-chased doublet riding back and forth in front of the army, waving a sword.

"Wonder if that's the governor," Mic said under his breath. "Can you understand what he's saying?"

Though a stiff breeze carried snatches of the man's shouts to Dirk's sensitive ear, he shook his head. "None of it."

He waved a hand toward the north. One by one his men turned to look, and grew still. Morgan and a thousand privateers marched in four orderly squadrons under red and green flags and banners. Behind the pirate army ranged two large herds of bulls. Dirk smiled. Fresh beef for supper last night had certainly renewed his strength. The clear eyes and buoyant strides of his men told him they felt the same.

Then he frowned, frustrated not to be part of the battle. Morgan, no doubt remembering Dirk's outburst at San Lorenzo, had ordered him and his men to patrol the hillsides west of the savannah. After the battle they were to scour the countryside for wealthy Spaniards who had fled the city. Ransoms would make a hefty addition to the booty taken from Panama itself.

Dirk gripped his musket and tapped the sharpened cutlass hanging at his belt. His future wealth, as well as his life with Katrina, lay in the hands of the men on the savannah. He resented depending on others for something so important.

Baldric scooted closer and pointed toward the rear of Morgan's army. Dirk cursed softly as horsemen appeared behind the bulls grazing on the hillside. With shouts and pistol shots, the caballeros urged the herd into a lumbering stampede. To escape the herd, the pirates would have to run straight into the lances and arrows of the Spanish infantry.

A dozen or so men in Morgan's army—buccaneers by their dress—broke from the ranks, jerked off their long tunics, and ran flapping the garments at the bulls. The animals stopped, milled about, then turned and charged into the caballeros.

From all around Dirk came snickers and low jeers. Nearly laughing himself, he motioned for quiet. The men ignored his order until Morgan's signal flag, far out on the plain, dipped once, twice, then after a pause, a third time.

"Here they come," Baldric said.

Over the hill on the savannah's eastern edge came a small contingent of privateers, clanking weapons and flashing blades in the sunlight. Two squadrons of Spanish cavalry sprang into a charge, riding straight toward the main body of privateers instead of those on the hillside. Fire from Morgan's men felled those caballeros in front.

The remaining cavalry fired their pistols, wheeled out of danger, circled west and galloped back to the city.

At last a few of the infantry nearest Dirk shouted and flung arms toward the pirates on the far hill. With shouts of "¡*Viva el rey*!" a hundred or more soldiers raced across the front of the Panama army toward the hill. The pirates there retreated.

The man in the silvery doublet cantered his horse to the front of the charge, waved his sword back and forth, and shouted. The infantry surged past him. He flipped a hand at a flagman. Red and gold banners rose twice, and the whole army charged the pirates on the hillside. Just as the Spanish army reached the bottom of the hill and seemed about to overrun the few privateers there, 300 more pirates marched over the hilltop.

The privateers held the advantage of height, wind, and the sun to their backs. They met the Spanish charge at the base of the hill with accurate musket fire, followed by deadly handystrokes. Then Morgan's thousand men attacked the Spaniards' flank.

The Spanish infantry fired their weapons once, hurled them at the onrush of pirates, and fled. A commander tried to halt the retreat by shooting some of his own men. Soldiers, horses and bulls scattered for Panama or the mountains. Dirk's men stood and cheered.

"Catch some horses," he said. "If we have to chase Spaniards, we may as well ride."

He led the eight down to the edge of the plain and halted, his men gathering around him.

"No wonder we routed them so quickly," Mic said.

Most of the infantry were Indians, mestizos, or Africans armed with lances and bows. Some wielded arquebuses, weapons a century old, and nearly worthless against the modern muskets and experienced swordsmen of Morgan's army.

"With all their wealth, this is the best they could do?" Dirk snorted. "Everybody meet back here with a horse."

The men scattered into the smoke of musket fire and the screams of battle. Dirk caught and mounted a large, sturdy-looking dun mare. She bucked under the strange weight, and he dismounted to lengthen the stirrups. When he'd finally calmed her and remounted, he looked up to see a young mestizo aiming an arquebus at him. Dirk raised his musket, then hesitated.

His face scrunched, the youth tried to balance the weapon on its forked prop and load it at the same time. He fumbled, spilling as much powder on his shoulder as in the arquebus. Finally, after letting the weapon fall to the ground while he secured a twig match, the boy raised the gun, aimed, and lit the fuse. He jumped as a loud poof of smoke knocked the weapon to the ground and blackened his coppery face. Dirk propped the butt of his musket on his boot and laughed out loud. The mestizo grinned sheepishly.

A buccaneer on horseback rode by and cut the boy down with a cutlass. The man waved his blade in salute before chasing down a slender Indian armed with only a short lance. Sucking a breath in through his teeth, Dirk wheeled his horse away.

When all his men had secured mounts, he led them toward the mountains west of the savannah. Four more small bands of pirates galloped off in other directions while the main body of Morgan's army chased the Spaniards across the savannah toward Panama, taking no prisoners.

From behind Dirk came an explosion. The mare reared. He settled her, then reined around just as another explosion rent the air. A third followed. A fourth. All through the city explosions spewed smoke and flames. As the cedar and mahogany homes of Panama caught fire, flames roared from one end of the city to the other.

Mic rode up. "Damn it all, there goes half our prize!"

Dirk scowled. Without the city itself to ransom, their prize would be smaller. Much smaller.

"Let's go!" he shouted, kicking his horse toward the mountains. If they couldn't ransom the city, they would need a lot of captives.

Twelve days after the battle Dirk finished his third foray into the countryside. His men bound their eleven prisoners and began the arduous trek back to what was left of Panama. The explosions on the day of the battle had set off a blaze that consumed the city. He'd heard that pirates and Spaniards together fought the fires for a day and a half, but in the end only a few buildings remained: three royal warehouses, the cathedral, the governor's home and the occasional house built of stone.

The pirates had settled in to wrest every last coin from the ruined city and it inhabitants. Morgan chose the cathedral as his headquarters, and he ordered wealthy captives held in the warehouses until they could be interrogated and their ransoms were paid. Dirk and his men spent their days riding from village to lonely hacienda, hunting people worth a ransom. The Spaniards must have felt safe in the hills. They took few precautions and were easily captured.

Now Dirk rode at the head of the little train, closing his ears to the prisoners' wails. Within a week, all would be released to their families unharmed, though much poorer. They could travel only as fast as the slowest prisoner, a stout, pale woman who stumbled every third step and collapsed in the trail twice an hour.

By early afternoon, Dirk had grown tired of it. He reined the big mare in among the captives and thrust his cutlass tip under the woman's wobbling chin.

"I know your plot, Woman," he said in Spanish. "You hope to slow us enough for soldiers to catch us."

Her teeth chattered. "N-not true. I... I swear."

"We'll hang you, after the men have enjoyed you."

The woman's eyes rolled back and her face drained white. She slumped. Dirk shifted the blade to avoid cutting her.

"Oh, for Christ's sake, don't faint."

"I... I won't," she whispered, tears forming next to her nose. "P-please don't."

"You'll walk faster? Not give me any more trouble?"

At her weak nod, he eased the cutlass away. She staggered backward and fainted into the bound arms of her countrymen who muttered and cooed and patted her arms. Dirk's men laughed. He growled, and urged his horse to the head of the train. It was going to be a slow trip to Panama.

But at least once there, he'd be comfortable. Dunstan was holding a house for them. Jan and Mic had found the deserted place after their first return with prisoners. The two-story stone house and walled gardens stood beyond the reach of flames and explosions that had destroyed the city, yet lay too close to the fighting for the owners to remain. Even better, few pirates ventured so far from the activities of Panama. Thus the stone house was somewhat private, quiet and secure.

Dirk rode on, ignoring his prisoners' sobs and moans. A cool fragrant garden and a real bed to sleep on awaited him.

They entered Panama's ravaged plaza, past blackened tree trunks and stone-lined ash piles that once might have been flowerbeds. At the row of warehouses, Dirk heard men grumbling in one, the higher voices of women complaining in another. The stench of dirty, sweating people and their wastes drifted out of the small high windows. Six pirates were herding a group of women toward the warehouses. Eyes dull and lips cracked, the captives stumbled as pirates kicked and prodded them along.

Dirk left his men to deposit their prisoners while he reported to Morgan. At the cathedral on the other side of the plaza, Dirk dismounted, tied the horse to an iron post and climbed twelve steps to the massive carved doors. He paused just inside 'til his eyes adjusted to the dim light, then headed toward the altar, where Morgan stood at the base of a short stairway.

At his feet, two smirking pirates had wrestled a woman to the floor. As she thrashed about, the farthingale that held her skirts out flew into the men's faces. A section of the whalebone frame caught on one pirate's ear. The woman wailed, the two pirates cursed, and the spectators roared with laughter.

Finally Morgan said, "Break the damn thing."

One of the men pinned the lady to the floor by her shoulders while the other stomped on her skirts. The screams and laughter grew louder as whalebone cracked and the skirts collapsed.

Dirk chuckled. Jan should have been here to see this. He claimed a lady's farthingale once saved his life when her fat grandee of a husband almost caught Jan tumbling her. Jan hid under her skirts, within the great boxy frame, and tickled the lady's nether parts while her husband ranted his suspicions.

Morgan's helpers finally subdued the woman long enough to remove her shoes and squeeze fat, twisted-grass matches between her toes. At a wave of Morgan's hand, one man lit a match from a burning candle. The woman screamed and fainted.

Morgan spat. "Douse it."

The other pirate yanked the match out from between the woman's toes and dipped it in a small bucket sitting nearby. The flame hissed, and the prisoners huddling beside the altar steps let out a collective sigh.

Dirk pushed his way through the eager audience of pirates. As far as he knew, old Harry Morgan didn't enjoy torture. Most of the Spaniards were frightened enough that threats worked as well as violence, so the sport the pirates had gathered to watch might never occur. Dirk stopped at the edge of the crowd. Morgan waved him closer.

"Ah, there you are, van Cortlandt. How many this trip?"

"Only eleven."

Morgan's eyebrows arched.

Dirk shrugged. "The rest must have gone to sea."

"Everything went to sea." Morgan's second chin quivered. "Well, ride out again tomorrow. No, don't go out again. We can't stay here much longer."

Morgan turned back to the revived woman, bent over her, and spoke in Spanish. "Where did you hide your treasure?"

The woman gazed wide-eyed at him and shook her head. Morgan motioned for his man to light another match between her toes. This time she fainted before the match caught fire.

Morgan slapped his thigh. "Get that woman out of here. Bring me someone else."

The pirates dragged her over to the group of captives.

"God curse them all. The richest city in the Spanish empire," Morgan said, "and we've yet to collect enough for a decent share-out."

Dirk pressed his lips together. Winning enough on this raid to replace the *Serpent* and sail north appeared more remote every day. He turned to leave. A loud cry stopped him.

Morgan's helpers had grabbed another woman. Her cry sounded angry, not fearful, however, as she kicked one of the pirates across the kneecap. When he dropped her arm to clutch his knee, she punched the other man's face. He jumped away, eyes watering, a hand clapped over his nose.

The lady glided toward the altar. She wore no farthingale, and her skirts dragged on either side. Though her black dress hung loose about her waist, the heavy silk swayed gracefully, with its soft sheen still visible under a layer of dust. Her reddish hair, mark of a Castilian, had been awkwardly pinned away from her face. Yet the woman walked as if she were on her way to a ball.

Her chin high, her brown eyes snapping with fire, she halted in front of Morgan. Dirk stepped to the side of the altar for a better view and leaned against a wall, his arms folded over his chest.

An imperious smile crossed the woman's face before she said loudly, "Speak your piece, little man. I have no patience for this nonsense."

Dirk bit the inside of his cheek. He dared not laugh. Morgan was sensitive about his height and the woman towered over him by several inches.

When he spoke, Morgan's voice was tight. "What's your name?"

The woman's voice rang out calm and full with a prominent Castilian lisp. "Natalia de Vizzarón y Montoya."

"Where is your family?"

"My father is with Governor Guzman in Los Santos."

"And the others?"

"I have only an uncle in Spain."

"Where did your father hide your treasure?"

"He sent it to sea on a ship."

Morgan frowned. "The galleon with the nuns?"

"Perhaps." She shrugged. "He did not tell me."

Morgan's face grew red and he glared at the cowering prisoners. He brushed past the woman to pace in front of them.

"I know how big your galleons are. All the ships of Spain together could not hold the wealth of this city. You have hidden it ashore and I will find it."

Strutting back to Natalia de Vizzarón y Montoya, Morgan leaned close and breathed into her face. "Understand?"

She did not flinch.

"I will find your treasure, *Señorita*. If you won't tell us the location willingly, I shall learn it by torture. If you do not give me gold or jewels, I shall take your personal treasure."

He reached out, hand curved to cup one of her breasts. She slapped it away. Her fellow prisoners gasped; the pirates laughed.

Morgan backed up three steps. His face hardened.

"Your ransom is set at twenty thousand pieces of eight. Arrange to have it paid soon or we will take it out in service." His gaze raked her body.

"How dare you speak to a noblewoman of Spain in such a manner." She threw back her head. "I will kill myself before I become your whore. But it matters little what happens to me. My countrymen will avenge what you and your animals have done to this city. You will hang on a gibbet in the tide. We will draw and quarter you, and your bones will bleach white in the sand."

She drew a deep breath and stomped up the steps to tower over Morgan again. "If you drag me to your heathen bed, watch your back, for I shall thrust a knife into it. In your sleep or at your meals. You will have to kill me, or I shall kill you."

Morgan glared up at her. "Kill you? No, I won't kill you after. When I'm through with you, I'll throw you to my men." He looked her up and down. "As many of them as will have you."

The woman's cheeks paled and she clasped her hands behind her back. They quivered, but she held herself upright and still.

"Two days, *Señorita*. Your ransom in two days, or you shall be given to my worthy mates. Now stand aside and take note of how I extract information from stubborn people."

The woman glided back toward the other prisoners, standing apart from them and taking deep breaths. Dirk grinned at Morgan. It was one of his more frightening bluffs. He didn't dare rape the woman, for then the unusually high ransom would never be paid.

When Morgan ordered a thumbscrew applied to a merchant a few minutes later, Dirk left the cathedral. His business was done, and he had no wish to hear delicate bones crack under the screw.

Outside, as he mounted the mare, a great crowd of pirates charged into the plaza. A youth raced ahead of them.

"A ship!" he cried. "A ship from Payta!"

The pirates surged toward the cathedral, calling for Morgan. When he appeared in the doorway, the men all shouted at once.

"A ship, Harry! A ship!"

"From Payta!"

"King's ransom!"

"They didn't know we was here!"

"Into the harbor, full of cargo from the Orient!"

"Silks, gold, emeralds!"

"Spices an'—"

Morgan called for a horse and joined the crowd as it rushed back to the harbor, a league away. Dirk nudged his mare into a trot, arriving as the first boatloads of cargo came ashore. He halted at a good vantage point and shifted in the saddle. His nostrils contracted. The flood tide had not yet covered the foul-smelling mud exposed by low water.

The first boat from the galleon carried three chests of gems, the captain of the ship, another officer, and a beautiful woman. Morgan helped her out of the boat and allowed her to sit on one of the chests. He called for a litter to take her to the governor's house.

Dirk rode slowly back to Panama along the harbor, gazing at the sea. Many Spaniards had sailed before the pirates' attack and anchored at the nearby pearl islands. Perhaps they'd believed themselves beyond the reach of land-bound pirates. But several fishing boats remained on shore, so pirates used them to attack the treasure-laden vessels at the islands. Now, less than two weeks after capturing Panama, the pirates had a fleet of ships prowling the coast in search of other prizes.

Dirk thought of the *Serpent*, splintered and dead on the reef at San Lorenzo, pieces of her drifting to shore for days afterward. A measure of sadness lessened the familiar surge of anger. He longed for the sea and wished Morgan had sent him with the pirates' makeshift fleet.

He left the harbor's stink behind, only to reenter the city and its odors. Morgan at least had the sense to order corpses identified and buried as quickly as possible. Yet there was nothing to be done with the stench of burnt homes.

The mare ambled through a poorer section of the city. Here the fire's destruction was complete, for the houses had been built entirely of cedar or thatch. Charred timbers lay against mounds of ashes and piles of rubble five feet high.

Dirk circled the plaza and the great crowd of people who were milling about. Near the governor's house a little knot of men were torturing a well-dressed Spanish gentleman. The fellow was staked to the ground, wet cordeles around his forehead. Blood ran from many wounds. Dirk stopped his horse and thought of intervening, but counted the number of pirates he'd have to thrash. Nine-to-one were not good odds.

A hulking pirate knelt beside the Spaniard's head. His victim screamed and the crowd laughed. The pirate, dangling an ear on the tip of his knife, rose to display his trophy. *Melchior... So easy to recognize with that puckered face and mirthless smile. And right beside him that thick-shouldered brute Baldessaire.* Cursing, Dirk moved on. Alone he could do nothing, and the Spaniard would survive without his ear. But why couldn't Melchior have died with L'Ollonais?

Beyond the cathedral, Dirk rode between huge piles of grey and black timbers. A few still smoldered and, when disturbed, released smoke and sparks into the air. Now and then he came across pirates breaking apart a stone wall or fountain, looking for treasure that might have been secreted beneath the tiles.

The mare walked over a pile of ash, kicking up clouds of soot. Dirk reined her down a cleaner path through the rubble. A short distance away, a cream-colored gelding with delicate legs walked toward a small stand of trees at the edge of the city. He nudged his mare in that direction. No use letting a good horse wander off.

Black skirts swished beside the gelding's legs. When the horse stopped in front of a low, crumbling wall, the skirts disappeared as a woman's face appeared over the top of the saddle. Red hair glinted in the sun. It was that woman who had defied Morgan in the cathedral, the Lady Natalia. For a moment she and Dirk stared at each other. Then she pulled herself onto the saddle and galloped for the trees.

"Damn you, Morgan," Dirk growled. "I spend two weeks collecting prisoners and you let them escape. There go twenty thousand pieces of eight."

The mare flicked her ears. The woman disappeared into the woods.

Dirk kicked his horse into a gallop after her.

The lady had ridden deep into the woods before the mare drew alongside the smaller gelding. Natalia glanced at Dirk, then kicked the gelding for more speed. When Dirk reached for her reins, she jerked them away. Responding, the gelding side-stepped into a tree, then stumbled.

Leaning heavily into his stirrup, Dirk caught the woman round the waist. As her horse went down, he hauled Natalia up onto his own. He eased the mare to a halt amidst a flurry of hands scratching his face and elbows beating on his ribs. Hard-soled shoes clipped his left shin. The mare skittered under the extra weight and the skirts swirling about her ears. Then a fist landed in that tender spot under Dirk's nose.

Eyes watering, he tucked the reins beneath the saddle and pinned Natalia tight against his chest with both arms. When she grew still, he eased his grip. She snatched the knife from his belt and stabbed. He ducked aside, but the blade still caught his shoulder. The wound wasn't deep, but it so surprised him that, without thinking, he cocked a fist and clipped her on the chin.

She swayed; her light brown eyes crossed. Dirk grabbed the knife and shoved it into his belt behind him. He settled the mare, then turned Natalia so she straddled the horse in front of him. She slumped against his chest, her head bumping the wound in his shoulder. He winced.

The gelding had wandered off a short distance and Dirk considered leading it back to Panama. Then Natalia stirred. Controlling her plus two horses would be impossible. He reined the mare toward the city.

Natalia straightened, shook her head, then squirmed as if to throw herself off the horse. Tightening his arm around her waist,

Dirk growled, in Spanish, in her ear, "Calm yourself. I'm only taking you to the warehouse."

"Where there is little water and even less food, and never a chance to sleep. Someone is always crying, or screaming in a nightmare."

"You won't be there long. Only 'til your father brings the ransom."

She let out a torrent of Spanish so fast he couldn't understand anything but the curses. He chuckled, and got an elbow into his ribs for it. Stifling another chuckle, he nudged the mare into an easy trot.

By the time they left the woods, Natalia had slackened against his chest. There was still a tense alertness in her, however, so he did not relax his hold. He was tempted to tell her that Morgan was bluffing, that he made threats merely to frighten captives into gathering ransoms more quickly. But then, she would inform all the others in the warehouse and they'd produce no treasure at all.

"So, my fiery lady," Dirk said in Dutch. "You will have to endure the warehouse a few more days."

To reach the plaza Dirk could not avoid riding past Melchior and his mates. Their victim lay quiet on the ground, blood coating the side of his head. Melchior swaggered around him, demanding loot. When there was no response, Melchior kicked the man, then snapped his fingers at one of his companions.

"Check him, Silvanus."

Pushing a lock of oil- and dirt-stiffened hair behind his ear, the scrawny little fellow bent over the Spaniard.

In a voice full of whiny disappointment Silvanus said, "The bastard died."

Baldessaire knelt, placed a hand over the man's nose and looked in his eyes. "Dead, all right."

Melchior cursed and kicked his victim again. The crowd grumbled.

"Stupid ones," Natalia said. "He had no treasure."

"You knew him?" Dirk asked.

"He was a servant. Merely a half-wit who worked in the house of Señor Gabriel de Sylva."

"He's not dressed like a servant."

She gave a short, bitter laugh. "It is a simple matter to don the clothes of your master when everyone has left the house."

Dirk clamped his jaws shut. He should have interfered earlier. Of course a half-witted servant would not understand that pirates chose their ransom victims by the richness of their clothes. And what wealthy Spaniard, in the agony of torture, wouldn't claim to be merely a servant ignorant of hidden wealth? He cursed Morgan for allowing the doubly wasteful death.

They rode on across the plaza toward the warehouses. Natalia stiffened and leaned forward as the mare halted. A large crowd of pirates were milling about in front of the women's warehouse, laughing, chattering, and gesturing toward the large, stone building. Pirates dragged five wailing prisoners out and lined them up on the broad steps. Morgan's clerk, Gregory, raised his arms to quiet the crowd.

"These wenches refused to pay their ransom," he cried, "and now they are available to any worthy man who has the coin for their purchase."

A cheer went up as the crowd surged closer. Natalia quivered in Dirk's arms and he felt as if Morgan had plunged a fist into his gut. He'd trusted the admiral to protect these captives, to hold them for ransom only. Now, to sell them for rape? Morgan was no better than Melchior or L'Ollonais. He only dressed and spoke better.

The first auction ended and Gregory handed the woman to her buyer. She screamed and collapsed at the pirate's feet, waving her arms feebly and pleading for mercy. The pirate dragged her around a corner of the warehouse, and everything was silent until a high, thin wail pierced the air. It quickly dwindled to silence, and the crowd laughed.

"Damn you to hell, Morgan," Dirk muttered. How many of the women he'd captured in the countryside would be sold for rape? He looked at the snickering, leering men intent on the next auction. They disgusted him. He did not want to be counted as one of them.

Natalia shifted, and he looked down at the woman who had given him such a tremendous fight. She would die defending herself from rape. He tightened his hold on her. Although he could not prevent the sale of the other women, he could ensure that no one, not even Morgan, raped this one.

She'd be in great danger if he released her, but if he took her to the house where his crew, perhaps the only men in Panama he trusted, were waiting, they could hold Natalia for ransom there and his word alone would protect her. It would be a flagrant disobedience of Morgan's orders, however, and Dirk considered the consequences.

The auction of the second woman ended, and she faced her buyer with a blank face and empty eyes. Dirk yanked on the reins so sharply that the mare reared, throwing Natalia's head against his wounded shoulder. The stab of pain fed his anger. He kicked the mare into a gallop away from the auction.

At the house, Mic was waiting by the door. Dirk swung out of the saddle and hit the ground with relief. His knee ached, and his bloody shoulder felt stiff and heavy. He tossed the reins to Mic before reaching up for Natalia.

She kicked him in the chest and he stumbled backward. The horse sprang forward in response to the wild kick in the ribs Natalia gave it. Mic lost one of the reins, but jerked on the other. The horse twisted and fell on its side. Natalia flew off, landing with a loud grunt. As Dirk ran over, she came up off the ground swinging her fists.

With a sigh, Dirk resigned himself to more pain and bruises, bothering to protect only his face and groin. He half-dragged, half-carried Natalia through the open door and released her into the wide entry hall where Baldric, the twins, and Dunstan were playing cards on the floor. She stumbled, caught herself, and lunged for the door. Dunstan closed it in time.

Baldric rose, and the twins scrambled to their feet, grinning. Natalia retreated from Joost's outstretched hand, bumped into Dirk, and jumped away as if burned.

"This is the lady Natalia," Dirk said in Spanish. "She's worth twenty thousand pieces of eight in ransom, so guard her carefully. I've given my word that no one here will hurt her." He looked at them one by one. "No one will do anything to her but keep her in the house."

"Agreed." Jan spoke in Spanish, too. "But do you think she might want to play with us?"

Dirk tugged aside his bloody tunic to expose the knife wound. "This is how she played with me."

Baldric whistled and gave Natalia a quick glance. "She carries a knife?"

"She used mine."

The men laughed. Natalia's shoulders dropped away from her ears, and her fists loosened.

Mic stomped in, slamming the door shut behind him. "The mare isn't hurt," he said in Dutch. "I stabled her in the barn out back. Now tell me what you're doing with that woman and was that blood I saw on your shirt?"

"She stabbed him." Dunstan chuckled between farts. "With his own knife."

Mic looked at Dirk, then glared at Natalia, who lifted her chin. He looked at Dirk again.

"She tried to kill you?"

Dirk told him of the capture.

Mic snorted. "You can't keep her here. What if Morgan finds out she's here instead of the warehouse? He could take away your shares of the plunder, have you flogged, or worse."

"Morgan let her escape from the cathedral. If I hadn't caught her again we'd be out the whole ransom."

"Take her back."

"I can't." He described the auction at the warehouse.

Mic shook his head. "If she's worth such a big ransom, Morgan won't let anything happen to her. Dirk, she's just a Spaniard. Why be responsible for her safety?"

Dirk watched Natalia's quick, furtive glances at the front door and the passage leading to a small library.

"Why? Probably to spite Morgan, as much as to protect her."

"And now what do we do? Spend all our time guarding her?"

"We're leaving Panama within a week. If the nine of us can't hold one woman for that long, we don't deserve a share of the prize."

Mic put his fists on his hips, tapped his foot, looked at the ceiling, sighed, and finally said, "Let me look at that shoulder. We'd better douse it with salt water."

Dirk grimaced, but sat by the dining table in the *sala* to let Mic wash and bandage the wound. Afterwards Dirk inspected the house for ways Natalia might possibly escape.

The library and *sala* each had a row of windows facing the road, but they were all covered with wrought iron grillwork. The garden wall stood seven feet high, and the lone tree in the yard between *sala* and kitchen was too small to climb. The kitchen had no exterior windows, only a large one open to the enclosed patio. A tiny chapel built into the opposite wall also had but a single interior window. The gate to the barnyard behind the garden was closed. The iron bolt and catch had rusted together. Dirk tried the gate. It held.

He walked up a curving iron staircase to the balcony overlooking the patio. The four bedrooms above the main part of the house also had barred windows facing the road. He paused in the room he shared with Mic. There were two narrow beds. Mic's could easily be moved to another room, leaving Dirk's for Natalia. He could sleep—

He didn't know where he would sleep and, gazing at the beds, grew very tired. He lay down for a short rest, and slept until the sun set and Baldric woke him for supper.

Baldric set out a plate of roasted chicken and flat bread for Natalia, but she did not join the men at the table. She remained standing in a corner of the *sala* until they left to resume their dice games on the floor of the entry hall. Dirk played with one eye on her through the archway. Finally, she approached the plate of food and, still standing, gobbled everything. She retreated to a window, gazed at the road a while, then wandered out to the patio. Confident she couldn't escape the garden, Dirk paid more attention to the game.

There was a knock at the door. Without rising, Joost stretched out to open it. Mic chided him for not looking first to see who was there, and when the door opened fully, Dirk added a few curses of his own. He stood, gauging the distance to where his cutlass leaned against the wall.

Six pirates, all of whom Dirk recognized from the torture killing of the half-wit servant, crowded the doorway. With drunken laughter and curses in English and French, they stumbled over each other pushing their way inside. One plopped down to join the dice game while three others ran across the room and on through the house. Two entered warily, and the last one hesitated when he spotted Dirk. Then, with a contorted smile, Melchior stepped inside.

Baldessaire said, "We heard you captured a house. You find anything in it to share with your brethren?"

"Wine?" The stranger on the floor grinned up at Dirk, raising his brows.

Dirk shrugged. "A little food. You're welcome to it."

A loud, feminine screech, followed by a howl of pain, came from the garden. Dirk groaned and rushed outside. All the men came after him.

By the staircase, a little man clung to Natalia's arm, ducking punches and hopping as she kicked him.

"Hang on, Silvanus," one of Melchior's men called, then said to the others, "I'll wager ten cobs the little scut never swives her."

The others laughed. Silvanus's face flushed.

Dirk's voice, as deep and deadly as he could make it, boomed across the garden. "Release her!"

Everyone quieted. Natalia jerked her arm out of Silvanus's suddenly shaky grasp. He pouted and glanced at Melchior.

Uncertain whether he'd just rescued Natalia or Silvanus, Dirk said, "Stand away."

Silvanus jumped, causing a few snickers. Melchior stepped forward, a hand resting on the hilt of his saber. He looked Natalia over.

"That woman is for sharing."

"No."

"But you're not busy with her," Silvanus said.

Dirk wanted to smack him for the whine in his voice.

"For sale," Melchior said.

"I'm not finished with her."

"Another night then."

"Not any night."

Melchior shrugged. "Someday."

Glaring at the man, Dirk strode across the patio to Natalia. Despite the eager-to-kill look in her eyes, he caught one wrist, ducked under a punch, and picked her up over his shoulder. Ignoring kicks against his thighs, thumps on his back, Spanish curses, and the men's laughter, Dirk trudged up the stairs and along the balcony to the room he'd been sharing with Mic.

As soon as he set her down inside, Natalia snatched a wooden religious statue from a niche and raced across the room. With the wild eyes of a cornered cat, she stood on the far side of a bed, hefting the statue.

"You promised you would not do this!"

Dirk held up a hand. "Think, Lady. If you throw that thing at me you'll have no weapon at all."

Natalia hesitated, lowered the statue, and bounced it against the palm of her other hand. Dirk bolted the door. When he turned back, she'd raised the statue again.

"I won't touch you."

"That is not what you told your friend down there."

"I brought you here to protect you."

"To a bedroom? Do you think I am a fool? I understand the French tongue, you filthy pirate. I understood every word you and those other animals said."

"Then you heard that I wouldn't sell you."

"Because you were not finished with me. And why not let him have me? Do you fear that he might release me?"

Dirk snorted. "I wouldn't let Melchior have you even to punish you."

"What difference would it make to me? He is a pirate. You are a pirate. You steal and burn and kill. You loot our churches and take even what belongs to God." She shook the statue. "And you rape, not to satisfy your lust, for there are prostitutes willing to lie with you swine."

She paused for a breath and her eyes glistened. "Those women today, they will all die. Maybe of injuries, maybe of sorrow. Or perhaps by their own hands, and for the sin of suicide they will burn in hell. To run a blade across their throats would have been kinder."

"My men won't harm you. But Melchior, the one with the scarred face, he killed that half-wit servant this afternoon."

She caught a breath. Her eyes widened.

"If you leave this house, he'll find you. You're safer here."

"With the likes of you? Bah! One pirate is as bad as another! I give to you the same promise I gave to Morgan. Force me to lie with you and I shall kill you. You will not live to spend a single reale of what you have stolen."

Heat rose on the back of Dirk's neck. Why couldn't this woman see the difference between him and Melchior, between him and Morgan?

Natalia tossed her head. "You pirates are all animals. I will never be safe with any of you."

His hands twitched, eager to shake her, to slap that imperious, contemptuous look off her face. But he took three deep breaths instead. She must be terrified, and her only weapons against his size and strength were fierce words and a small statue. He slid to the floor and rested against the door. *What does it matter if she understands the difference between me and Melchior or not? In a few days her ransom will be paid and she'll be gone from my life.*

He knew what kind of man he was, and he knew what his friends were. That was all that mattered.

After three days of tense vigilance, Dirk saddled the dun mare and rode into Panama. Natalia's ransom might have arrived, and he needed time alone, away from the house. She had relaxed enough for the others to safely guard her.

The cathedral still rang with the shouts and screams of interrogations, and the warehouses still emitted foul odors and prisoners' wails. Dirk rode on to the harbor, where pirates were spiking the cannon along the sea wall. They forced metal spikes into touch holes and broke them off flush with the barrel. The big guns would have to be melted down and recast before they could be fired again.

Captured ships crowded the harbor. Between them and the shore a steady stream of boats rode low with treasure. Piles of booty lined the beach. On three ships, men chopped down masts. Dirk winced as a mizzenmast creaked aft, slammed through the ship's elaborate taffrail and tumbled into the sea. It was a shameful waste of good ships, even if necessary for the army's safe return to the Caribbean.

There had been talk among the men of sailing captured vessels up and down the western coast of South America. Dirk had heard many pirates speak eagerly about sacking Lima and Santiago, with or without Morgan's permission. But if they sailed, the remaining pirates would be more vulnerable to the counterattack they expected from the governor of Panama. So Morgan had ordered the masts chopped off all the ships.

Dirk headed back toward the city. He was ready to leave Panama. He'd had enough of Spaniards, a city of rubble, and the likes of Morgan and Melchior.

Natalia paced the garden, around and around near the walls, seeking a place that might give her a toehold, a handhold, anything to help her climb over the walls. On each pass she tried the gate, and each time the rusted bolt held. She didn't know how long that big Dutchman would be gone, but this was her best chance to escape. The drunkards he'd left to guard her were preoccupied with their silly games.

The early afternoon sun grew warm on her black dress. Resting on a stone bench under the scrawny grape arbor, she viewed the garden with distaste. The whole place had withered from lack of attention. Only weeds thrived, and in one corner flies buzzed over the pirates' midden heap. The fountain was dry, though its pool still held perhaps two feet of water.

This neglected garden was so unlike that of her husband Rafael's home in Lima. She thought wistfully of the large running fountains, mirror pools, and the narrow paths winding among fruit trees and flowers. Then she realized with a start that she had not thought of the house, or the man, in nearly a month.

An only son, Rafael had possessed great wealth and many prospects, but he drank or gambled away his income from the family's shipping business. Natalia suspected his parents had contracted for the marriage with her as much for her strong bloodlines as for her dowry. Perhaps they hoped she would infuse Rafael with ambitions and a desire to work. If not, she would at least give them strong grandsons.

Initially generous and complimentary of her vigor and spirit, they were kind and sympathetic when she miscarried her first pregnancy. As the months, then a year, passed with no sign of another, their manners grew more distant. They engaged her less in conversations, entertained without including her, and reduced her personal staff to a single maid. More than once they hinted that she was lacking, as Rafael certainly enjoyed women and produced enough bastards to embarrass them.

Then two years ago, a situation in the Philippines required the presence of a family member. Rafael had never been to sea for any length of time and claimed to hate it, but his father was ill, so he had to go. Natalia could still see his petulant face as he stood waving farewell on the ship's foredeck.

Handsome, charming, fun-loving and lazy, Rafael was about to do the only work of his life, and it was just like him to weaken and die aboard ship. A year passed before word of his death from a fever reached Lima. The news made her a childless widow, an unwanted extra mouth in her in-laws' home.

She mourned Rafael, for a short time anyway, until she learned that he'd gambled away her entire dowry. Even now, after all these many months, her neck grew hot with fury just thinking about it. By squandering her dowry, he had squandered her future. She had little chance of remarriage without it.

When she proposed returning to Spain, Rafael's parents acted relieved. Another year passed while she sent a letter to her Uncle Fernando and awaited a reply. He gave his reluctant permission for her return, and mentioned a position as *dueña* to his own infant daughter. Natalia had no desire to live in her uncle's home, and at twenty-three, she was not ready to play widowed chaperone. Still, she had no other choice. Without a dowry, she could not even join a convent where she might advance her education.

She shifted on the stone bench. Uncle Fernando's castle in northern Spain was small and damp. She had never gotten on well with Fernando's second wife. *Even so, living with that woman is preferable to staying captive to these pirates.* Natalia crossed her arms over her stomach to hold in growing anger. *How could we have lost Panama?* Her heart ached, even while her mind knew the answer.

Henry Morgan had announced his intention to capture Panama by sending a pistol to Governor Guzman. When the castle at San Lorenzo fell, many in Panama, including Natalia's hosts, fled with their valuables to the countryside. Soldiers, too, left the city, ostensibly to guard important citizens on their trek to the hills. Retreat was a common defense against pirates in the New World, and possibly the best course of action, though Natalia's Castilian blood cried out for a bolder stance. A hundred and fifty years after the noble conquistadors had won this land, she watched their descendants run instead of fight.

From a tower of the cathedral, she followed the battle, embarrassed that a wealthy Spanish city would send poorly armed slaves and mestizos out to defend it. When the caballeros made their one pass at the pirates before galloping back to Panama, she burned with shame.

Now Natalia rocked back and forth, fighting down anger as she considered how to escape this New World, with its weakling Spanish *criollos* and loot-hungry pirates who destroyed cities and families as easily as they guzzled liquor. She must return to Spain, where she could live among the strong, brave people of Castilla.

But in Castilla waited Uncle Fernando and an empty life under the thumb of his sour wife. Natalia's hands balled into fists and she ached to....

There was nothing she could do. She had no weapon. The walls were too high to climb, the gate didn't budge, and eight pirates were lounging between her and the front door. A lump rose in her throat. She swallowed it back down. Tears were as useless as anger.

The yellow-haired twins burst out the door, bearing sabers and wearing ridiculous grins as if they expected her to be happy to see them. She turned away. They began a playful sword fight that gradually quickened and drew closer. Having grown up in a family of soldiers, Natalia was not impressed by the twins' abilities, and after a while they quit.

Joost, the homely one, sank to the ground near her feet, propping his saber against the bench. He smelled of rum and Natalia longed to cuff him. On her other side, Jan bent close, making a comment in that ugly Dutch tongue, to which his brother laughed. Jan stroked her hair. She slapped his hand away. He stepped back with a mock howl of pain, then caught her hair on his saber tip. She sat very still, cheeks growing hot. He loosened a hairpin, and a tendril fell, brushing her face.

Natalia ducked away, snatched up Joost's saber, and sprang from the bench. With the saber's hilt in both hands, she beat the sword against Jan's. He made a few short thrusts which she parried.

"Ah, swordplay with a woman," he said in Spanish. "My favorite sport!"

Joost chuckled. Jan made a little bow. Natalia slashed his sword arm above the elbow. He yelped and jumped back, clamping a hand over the gash. While he blinked, she pressed forward, her blade flashing in the sunlight as it slammed against his. Jan's saber flew into the air, landing twenty feet away. Before he recovered, Natalia leaped between Jan and the sword. She waved the saber under his nose. He retreated.

Joost remained on the ground beside the bench, chortling, as Natalia backed Jan all the way to the wall. When she pinned him there, saber tip pressing into his stomach, a flash of fear crossed Jan's eyes.

"My Lady...?" All the laughter had gone from Joost's voice now.

"How does it feel to be helpless?" Natalia asked. "With no place to run and to know that within moments you will die?"

She took a deep breath and drew back her arm to push the saber through him to the wall.

A cutlass point dug through silk to her breast. She looked up the curving blade at Dirk, his face hard, eyes cold.

His voice was a deep growl. “If you kill him, you die soon after.”

“You would lose the ransom.”

“His life is worth more than any ransom to me. What is his death worth to you?”

Natalia hesitated, so tempted to kill this pirate who stood breathless beneath her sword. His death might indeed be worth dying for. And her own death would release her from this terrible captivity.

The cutlass bit into her skin, forcing an answer. She turned slowly to Dirk, who kept the blade point against her.

“He is not worth dying for,” she said. “Not before I kill you.”

She jumped away. The blade tore her dress and scratched her right breast. Ignoring the sting, she beat the cutlass aside with her saber. Then after a moment’s pause, she attacked.

Natalia realized immediately that despite all the fencing lessons of her youth, she didn’t have a chance against Dirk. While she struggled to remember specific maneuvers, he merely tapped away every thrust. Unused to sword work, she soon tired. Using both hands together did not help. Her fingers grew numb and her arms felt so heavy she could barely raise the saber. Then Dirk caught it in a swing that snatched the hilt out of her hands.

Natalia looked at the sword lying in a bed of half-dead flowers, then up at Dirk.

“Next time,” she said, “I shall kill you.” She stomped out of the garden.

Dirk watched her march up the stairs to her room. When the door slammed shut, he caught Jan by the front of his tunic.

“What in the name of God happened here? I leave eight able-bodied men to guard a single unarmed woman and what do I find?” He shook his cutlass in the air. “Not only does she have a weapon, but she’s about to kill you. What did you do to her?”

Jan squirmed as fabric tightened around his wounded arm. “Nothing, nothing.”

"I gave my word she'd be safe here and I damn near had to kill her to save you." Dirk gave Jan another shake. "I thought I could trust you."

Jan jerked his tunic out of Dirk's grasp.

"We didn't do anything to her. We came out for exercise and when we stopped and tried to talk to her, she grabbed the sword and… " He shrugged.

"You threatened her?"

"Dirk." Joost sauntered over with both sabers. "Do we ever have to threaten a woman?'

Dirk glared at him. The twins never attacked or coerced women. But then, he couldn't remember any woman refusing them either. Perhaps Natalia had, and they simply didn't believe her. But they should have considered her fears before they teased her. He took a deep breath.

"For a stupid game you would have died and cost us twenty thousand pieces of eight."

"You'd have killed her?" Joost grinned. "Just to avenge this worthless bag of bones?" He hopped away from Jan's swinging fist, then headed toward the house. "I need some brandy."

"Me, too." Jan followed him. "Wonder how she learned to use a sword that way."

They disappeared into the hall.

Dirk walked slowly back to the house. The twins were still laughing about the sword fight. His anger lessened, only to be replaced by sadness that they had, in a way, betrayed him. They weren't cruel, only foolish, but he'd never again trust them completely.

He glanced up at the door to Natalia's room. *Would I have killed her?* No amount of ransom was worth the life of one of his childhood friends. When he brought the woman to the house he thought he'd have to protect her from other pirates, not protect his friends from her. Dirk was glad she had backed off and not forced him to carry out his threat.

"What manner of woman are you?" he asked softly.

If he meant to keep her in the house he would have to learn more about her. There could be no more surprises like this one.

Natalia flung the door of her room shut. It rattled against its jamb and the noise infuriated her. She kicked it, pretending it was Dirk.

"I hate you, Dutchman! And I hate the men of this city who let you take Panama and put me in this cage!"

He had honored his word and protected her from others, but that made her even angrier. It was humiliating that her survival depended upon the inclinations of a heathen. And his mere presence carried a sexual threat.

Natalia snatched a bronze candlestick from the tiny bedside table and threw it across the room, then heaved the table after it. On her way to pick them up, she gave the bed a good kick, then yanked the straw mattress to the floor. As she kicked it across the room, she cursed her husband for not leaving her any money, cursed the soldiers for losing Panama. She picked up a pillow that had fallen to the floor and swung it against the nearest bedpost.

"I *hate* this prison! I hated that prison Rafael called a house in Lima, and I shall hate living in that castle prison in Spain!"

She swung the pillow harder. She detested being female and so helpless that she must go from one cage to another, from one male keeper to another, and the only escape from either was death. The pillow seams tore. A few feathers floated out. She beat the pillow harder against the bedpost. *I should have killed that worm. Then at least the big one would have released me from this cage and all others for eternity.*

The pillow seams gave way, scattering feathers everywhere. Thrown off balance, Natalia fell into the wooden bedpost, cracking her head. She sank to the floor and tears came.

"Oh, God," she whispered, "I do not really want to die, but I cannot live this way anymore. And I do not believe my life will ever be any better."

As feathers settled around her, great racking sobs welled up in her chest. She gave in to them at last.

Immediately after supper, Natalia retreated to her room to avoid Dirk. For two days now he had been trapping her in corners, demanding she talk to him. He would ask a question and sit until she said something, anything. Then he would ask another question and sit staring at her until she answered.

And the questions! Already she'd told him that she had come from Spain to marry a stranger, that the union had been short, unhappy and childless, and that she had learned to use a sword as a child, as did many girls of her class in the rugged hills of northern Castilla. She did not want to tell him more.

Worse than the interrogations were the power and suppressed temper of the man. When her barbs and insults cut, his face darkened or his jaw tightened, yet he never retaliated. His voice always remained calm. She longed to say something, do something, to shatter that complacency. Not that she wanted to witness the explosion, or be the recipient of his violence, but when he acted so controlled and even kind, she found it difficult to hate him.

Natalia paced the small room, nearly overcome with boredom. She might retrieve a book from the tiny library downstairs, but only if she were willing to walk past the pirates. They would stare as she passed, maybe even stop their games to leer at her. No, tonight boredom would not drive her from the sanctuary of this room.

In the end, it was the stifling heat that sent Natalia outside into the light breeze on the balcony. She leaned against the wooden rail. The sun had left a pink glow on the horizon and deepening gloom filled the garden below. Laughter and raucous chatter, in English and French as well as Dutch, filtered up from the entrance hall.

Downstairs, a door opened, spilling light onto the patio and a shadow appeared. Natalia backed away from the rail. A single lantern bobbed out to the center of the garden and clanked onto a stone bench near the pool. She eased closer again to the rail, leaning over to see who had invaded her solitude. Dirk. She stepped behind a post.

He glanced around, cocking his head to one side as if listening for something, then propped the ever-present cutlass against the bench. He unbuckled his belt, dropped it beside the lantern and pulled off his tunic. After rolling his shoulders and stretching, he rubbed the place where Natalia had stabbed him. She felt a pang of guilt, conflicting with pride, that she had given him the wound.

He untied the drawstring of his breeches. They slid to his ankles and he stepped out of them. Perhaps she should return to her room. But no, the heat there was unbearable. She slipped around the post.

Natalia had never seen any man but her husband naked. Dirk's body did not have the excellent proportions and sheer beauty of Rafael's. Even at thirty her husband had been as slim as a youth, and his limbs had moved with lithe grace. Dirk possessed instead a strength visible in the dim light, and power she could feel even from the balcony. Heavy muscles covered his deep chest, and his thigh muscles rippled as he walked to the pool.

Rafael had been more handsome. The scar running down across Dirk's eye marred his features. *How was he injured there?* she wondered. *How many other scars does he carry? How many battles has he fought?*

Dirk slid into the pool and a little groan escaped as he settled on the tiled bottom. The past week had been full of trying days. Morgan had allowed his men such a free rein that atrocities against the Spaniards were increasing daily. Restless pirates were ranging through the ruined city and more of them had shown up at the door here looking for excitement, liquor, and someone new to torture.

He scrubbed himself with a scrap of linen. It felt good to be clean again. Hoping to ease the tension that plagued his body, he soaked a while longer. He massaged the tightened muscles of his chest and recognized a familiar ache—not fatigue, but desire.

He'd not had a woman since that last night in Port Royal. Here, the few available doxies had to be shared, with a line forming and encouraging shouts from the men awaiting their turn. Those men probably couldn't finish the act without their friends cheering them on. They'd surely wither if they were ever shut in a room alone with a woman like Natalia. He glanced up toward the balcony as one of the shadows darkened. His lust stirred, but not for that Spaniard.

Still, with enough to eat in the past week or so, she'd lost her boniness, and even filled out her dress again. Some of the wildness had left her eyes, and she was almost pretty. He'd learned that she was married at seventeen and widowed at twenty-two. She rode a horse well, could handle a sword, and had been reared to manage a large household. So many details, yet he knew her little better now than he had the day he captured her.

Dirk sighed. *It shouldn't be so complicated for nine men to guard a single woman.* But it was. She tried to escape nearly every minute, and the twins still preened and flirted, trying to entice her into their bed. Every day Mic insisted Dirk return her to the warehouse. And given half an excuse, San Sebastian would gladly kill her. Just thinking about it tightened the muscles in Dirk's neck.

He glanced up at the balcony again, this time catching a glimpse of skirts. *If she smiled, would her eyes dance? Crinkle at the corners? Would her lips part, or just curve in a smooth line? If I kissed her, would she slap me or return the kiss?Slap me, surely.* He sank under the water to rinse the dust out of his hair.

Natalia stood at the rail again, watching and imagining herself in a man's arms. She had not experienced it much since the first days of her marriage, when she and Rafael were friends. Before he used her pregnancy as an excuse to take a mistress. Before the miscarriage and recriminations. Before Rafael stopped coming to her bed.

She fought growing desire, angry at Dirk for rousing such feelings in her. If he'd been cruel, she could hate him. If he had trembled before her temper, she could despise him for his cowardice. Either way she would not be in such turmoil now.

The lantern light caught a movement in the grass. A gleam eased toward the stone bench, and Natalia held her breath as a snake slid into the circle of light. There were so many snakes in the jungles of the New World. Perhaps this one was venomous. It slid up the pedestal of the bench, then toward the lantern.

It might be harmless. If not, the Dutchman might die this night. Quickly or in agony, it didn't matter. She would be free of him and the contrary emotions he caused. Natalia gripped the rail and bent forward to watch. The snake hesitated at Dirk's belt, then slithered on toward the light. Dirk did not act as if he saw it.

If he died, she would be killed, or taken back to that miserable warehouse to wait until her ransom failed to appear. How much could she resent that heathen when she was well-fed and safe in her bed at night?

As the snake crossed Dirk's tunic, it stopped, raised its triangular head to look around, then coiled into the folds of cotton. Dirk climbed out of the pool, rubbing himself briskly.

His skin will dry quickly in the warm night air. How soon will he don his tunic? I should warn him. He has kept his word.

He stepped into his breeches, pulled them up to his waist.

Let him die and put an end to his pirating forever! Save other Spanish cities from the fate of Panama. So many died protecting the city. Could what lies ahead for me be worse than what they suffered?

Dirk removed his breeches, returned to the pool and began to wash them.

Natalia gripped the rail, her breath coming in tiny, soundless gasps. *Let him die. Put an end to the feelings I have for him.*

Dirk wrung out the breeches, shook them, and donned them once more. He walked toward the bench.

Natalia held her breath. She imagined the snake inside the white garment, poised to strike, the big hand reaching into the folds, the snake rearing its head, lashing at the intruder, fangs sinking into soft flesh.

Let him die! the proud Spaniard in her said. *The cost will be small.*

Warn him! admonished the frightened, practical woman.

Dirk bent over his tunic. She would soon be free of him. He reached out. Natalia shut her eyes and held her breath, waiting for his startled cry of pain.

"¡Cuidado!"

Natalia opened her eyes. Dirk straightened to stare at the balcony. She was hanging over the railing, mouth still open. She swallowed.

"A serpent... in your tunic."

With the tip of his cutlass, Dirk tossed the tunic into the air. The snake dropped out. In one movement he flicked the tunic away and sliced off the snake's head. Body and head landed on the stone bench with soft thuds. The body whipped back and forth.

Trembling, Natalia retreated into her room to stare out the front window.

Faint footsteps sounded on the stairs, then on the balcony. She had left the door open. She started across the room to close it, then stopped as lantern light cast shadows about the small room. Natalia held her breath. Dirk filled the doorway.

He set the lantern on a low stand near the door, glanced at Natalia's hands to check for a weapon, then tried to read her face.

"Thank you."

She nodded.

The blood rush from killing the snake receded, and the familiar ache returned. Now that Natalia's lips weren't curled in a snarl, Dirk wanted to kiss her. In the lantern light, her skin looked like satin. He took a step forward.

She swayed, as if she might bolt.

He took another step, caught her gaze. Her eyes were soft and vulnerable. A third step brought him close enough to hear her breathing, close enough to feel the warmth of her body. His hand rose, brushed her cheek. "Why?"

She jerked, blinked, then turned away to stand at the window. "I want to kill you myself."

Dirk took a deep breath and let it out slowly. "A short while ago you didn't want me to die. Now you do. Because I touched you?"

Natalia shrugged a square shoulder.

"Was your marriage so bad that you want to kill a man for touching you? Did you want to kill your husband, too?"

"Rafael was not worth the effort. And he rarely touched me."

"Maybe you chased him off with your temper."

She swung back to him, her eyes flashing. "My husband wished me to be meek and obedient and... weaker than he."

"I've heard that strong women often feign meekness for the sake of their marriage."

"I did so, for a while. Then I could no longer bear the betrayal of myself." She turned away, and shrugged again. "After a time it was not important. I do not care for cowards."

He stepped closer, touched the red-brown hair fallen about her shoulders. "Not all men are cowards."

"Ha! You are cowards! Or bullies who will force a woman!"

He spun her by the shoulders and pushed her against the wall. Her eyes filled with contemptuous victory.

"Which are you?" she asked. "Will you force me now, or do I frighten you too much?"

Dirk was torn. Torn between leaving to prove himself not a bully and staying to prove himself a brave man. And torn most of all because he wanted to slake his passion with her, to conquer the spirit of this woman who defied and confused him.

Slowly, he placed a hand on her neck. Her rapid pulse throbbed beneath his fingers. He stroked her jaw with his thumb and then brushed her lips with his own.

"Am I coward or bully? You tell me."

He walked out.

Before he could duck, the clay goblet whistled past Dirk's ear and crashed against the *sala* wall.

"You gave me your word." Natalia reached for another cup.

"I have no choice. Morgan knows you're here and he's ordered me to take you back to the warehouse."

"You lying heathen!"

The second cup flew across the dining table. He jumped away and it, too, crashed against the wall.

"You promised I would remain here until my ransom arrived!"

Mic, sitting calmly at the end of the table, set down his wine goblet. "Where is that ransom? Why haven't we seen it yet?"

Natalia glared at him then back at Dirk. "It is because of last night!"

"No. We're leaving Panama tomorrow."

"Then why do you not release me now?"

When Dirk hesitated, Mic said, "You are going with us."

"Mic—" Dirk shook his head.

She whirled on Mic. "With you? Why?"

"We're taking a few hundred prisoners with us. Pay your ransom in three days, or you'll be sold as a slave in Jamaica."

Natalia paled and turned back to Dirk. "A slave? Jamaica?"

He looked at her, unable to tell her the threat of slavery was another of Morgan's bluffs. Everyone was to be released at the end of three days, ransom paid or not.

"But surely your father will come with the ransom," he said. "Morgan's posting the announcement everywhere."

Her eyes widened. She swallowed hard and stalked out of the room.

Dirk stared after her. "Damn you, Mic."

Mic laughed.

Half an hour later, Dirk lifted a sullen Natalia sideways onto his horse and mounted behind her. As he took the reins from Mic, she stiffened. Arms crossed, left shoulder brushing his chest, she stared at the scattered trees as they rode toward Panama. Trees gave way to flowing grasses of the Mata Asnillos savannah, and Natalia's jaw clenched tighter with every ragged breath she drew. Dirk sighed. He finally held the woman in his arms and felt cold enough to shiver.

Natalia shifted on the pommel. "Never should I have trusted you. You are a pirate, like the others. In Maracaibo, this beast you call Morgan put the wife of the alcalde, an old woman, naked into a barrel of gunpowder. She was too frightened to speak and so they set a match to..."

Dirk let her talk on. What she said was true.

"And three years ago Morgan destroyed Porto Bello. He used Holy Fathers and Sisters as shields for his men during an attack on one of the forts, and the holy ones all died."

"Spanish soldiers fired on them."

"They had no choice."

"They could have accepted Morgan's offer of quarter."

"Quarter, bah. He would not have kept his word either."

Dirk was tempted to tell her of Halsey, a member of his first crew, who offered quarter to a Yucatan village and died for it.

"And everyone has heard what that despicable French pirate did on the Mosquito Coast, hamstringing all the animals, torturing and killing everyone he..."

Dirk shut out the memory of L'Ollonais and saw in his mind's eye the ravaged buccaneer camp he'd found as a youth on Hispaniola. He thought of the slaughtered dogs, the Spanish lance pinning a little boy to a tree.

"All for a bit of gold. You are greedy, vile creatures!"

Greedy? Yes, but not for gold alone. And Dirk remembered with still-sharp pain that dawn so long ago when Spaniards raided his home.

He looked down at Natalia, watched her mouth jerking in angry words, but he heard nothing. *How dare she compare me to L'Ollonais and Morgan? In the week she's been with me, hasn't she seen the difference? And doesn't she realize that even Morgan is no worse than her own countrymen on a raid?*

The hot rush of temper flooded through Dirk. They were in the plaza now. He urged the mare into a faster walk.

"When I first sailed from Spain, ladies told me that pirates were half-beast, with the head of a monster. I assumed they told the stories to frighten each other. But now I know they were telling me the truth, only we cannot see the animal part. Your body is human, but your soul is not. If you have a soul at all."

Dirk halted the horse and jerked Natalia around to face him. She slipped half-way off the saddle, dangled over the warehouse steps.

He said, "If I am an animal, I will tell you who taught me to be one."

Natalia struggled, her legs straining to reach the steps below, hands flailing at the saddle for support as Dirk told of atrocities he'd seen Spaniards commit. When she protested, he shook her into silence. His voice rose as he told of his mother's screams, then grew soft and deadly as he spoke of Anneke.

"No," Natalia whispered, quiet at last and looking bewildered. "They would not have done such a thing to a child!"

"Oh, but they did." Dirk took a deep breath. "You don't want to be a slave? Neither did I. But I was one, for seven long years. Your pious countrymen did all that and you dare call me a soulless beast who looks like a man? Lady, count yourself lucky I am not Spanish."

He dropped her. Natalia tumbled onto the steps, scrambling for a footing amidst her long skirts. Two pirates rushed up to hustle her inside the warehouse. She looked back at Dirk once, her face full of confusion, as if believing him but not wanting to.

Dirk kicked the horse into a gallop back across the plaza, scattering pirates and scavengers as he passed.

Long before he reached the house, Dirk slowed the mare to a walk. He cursed himself for the show of temper. He'd wanted to silence Natalia, to shatter her lovely vision of valiant and pious Spaniards. He had told her the truth to hurt as well as make her understand.

For ten years he had sought revenge for his family's death, believing himself justified in becoming a pirate. But somewhere in those years he'd stopped thinking about vengeance, and piracy had become a way of life for him, an exciting way to survive. It was no longer a driving need for revenge, but simply a habit.

He had caused a lot of Spaniards pain, but Natalia was the first to know why. Now he was sorry, for she hadn't done him any harm. He rubbed the healing wound in his shoulder. Even that she had done out of fear, and she had good cause to be afraid of pirates.

Just after dawn the next morning, Dirk and his men sat on their horses watching Morgan lead 175 mules loaded with large chests out of the ruins of Panama and onto the Royal Road. Three hundred and fifty dark-skinned slaves followed, carrying more treasure. Then came 600 hostages, prodded along by pirates who cursed and kicked them into a shuffling march that raised a low cloud of dust. Women wailed and cried for mercy. A few fainted. Some of the braver men tried to run, but pirates knocked them back into the crowd.

Dunstan whistled, from both ends. "Look at all that booty. I hear there's seven hundred fifty thousand pieces of eight in them chests. That'll buy me a tankard or two in Port Royal."

Jan sighed. "And the women. They're waiting for me."

"And me," Joost said.

"All of them with their palms out to be crossed," Mic said.

Dirk smiled. It was almost over. In two weeks they'd be on a ship once more, in the calm of the sea. Within two months he'd be home in Port Royal, and in four he'd sail to New York. Katrina would be eighteen by then, and his at last.

He thought of the little portrait lost in the wreck of the *Serpent* and wondered whether Katrina had changed much. She couldn't have grown prettier. And that structured life in the northern colonies probably hadn't become freer. But he'd build a life somehow, perhaps with frequent voyages to the Caribbean. Katrina would make his life in the North good.

Turning to Mic, Dirk said, "Do you think there's enough treasure for us to outfit a small cargo ship with our shares?"

"Thinking of becoming a trader?"

Dirk grinned. "Maybe even an honest one."

Mic rubbed the side of his jaw for a few moments, then nodded. "Folks in the North are hungry for luxury goods. You could easily sell spices, silks, gems. Plus sugar and mahogany."

"You? Don't you mean we?"

"This is the last raid for me. I won't go to sea again."

"But why not?"

Mic shrugged. "I think that by the time we land in Port Royal I'll be a father."

"Pirates don't have children, that they know of anyway."

Mic chuckled. "Clarisse didn't tell me, but I suspected. I thought it would be safe to leave her for a few months, but we've been gone five already."

"I'm sure she's well. A child doesn't mean you have to quit the sweet trade."

"Men die too easily at sea," Mic said. "I hate what Clarisse, with or without a child, will have to do if I die."

"You are not going to die."

Mic smiled. "Of course not."

Dirk, his men, and Gregory, the clerk who kept a list of prisoners and their ransom amounts, were part of the rear guard that rode out

of Panama at noon. Every now and then a Spaniard raced up to the train, his purse bulging. Gregory carefully counted the money before sending a pirate forward through the train to find the ransomed hostage.

When the train halted for the night, Morgan allowed the captives a bit of water, but refused to feed them. He said that when the people of Panama learned their loved ones were starving, they'd pay ransoms more quickly. As far as Dirk could tell, though, the flow of ransom money didn't increase nearly as much as did the volume of wailing and praying.

The next morning he found Natalia. Her face was stony, and her gaze flickered over him without emotion. He kept her in sight as they plodded along the trail, and when they settled for the second night, Dirk rode by to drop some bread into her lap. She glared up at him, then silently passed the bread to a woman nearby who had two young children.

With a nod and a grin, Dirk rode toward the rear of the train.

The late afternoon sun burned and the air was thick with moisture. Inside her black dress, Natalia was sweltering. On the first night, under cover of darkness, a woman had helped her unlace the dress and loosen her stays, yet not even that extra space helped. Sweat slid down her forehead and stung her eyes. Her hair fell from its pins and stuck against her neck. She pinned it up again, but without a mirror or help from another woman, Natalia suspected she looked like the crazy hag who used to live outside her father's gates.

Thousands of marching feet churned the dirt road into a knee-high cloud of dust. It coated Natalia's dress with a fine film and her teeth gritted on the stuff. Her swollen feet burned with every step. Dirk rode by with Baldric, their horses kicking up more dust. She snarled after them.

She understood Dirk's motives for becoming a pirate. The heat in his voice and the pain in his eyes had been real. He hadn't lied to her. That her countrymen were capable of the deeds he described made her heartsick. So she forgave the boy who yearned for revenge, but not the man who had given his word, then betrayed her. And at the moment she hated him for being on horseback while she and her people had to walk.

The slow train was a severe hardship on most of the people, even healthy men. Some walked numbly, eyes down, a murmured prayer on their lips. Just ahead, an elderly lady walked stiff and proud. A young mother led a toddling boy by the hand. Beside Natalia stumbled a big, hearty-looking man who told frightful tales of Spanish gentlefolk sold as slaves. Hour after hour he recounted their backbreaking labors in English fields, their agonized deaths from frequent beatings.

Natalia's ransom would never come and unless she did something she would be lost. In spite of what her countrymen had done, had become, in the New World, she was a true daughter of Spain. She would not go meekly into slavery, would not go at all if any way out presented itself.

The old woman collapsed without a sound at Natalia's feet. She and the wheezing story-teller carried the lady to the side of the trail. As the train passed by, Natalia stroked the woman's forehead and fanned her with a leaf.

All around lay the dense forest of Castillo del Oro. It was dark and full of enough unseen, though oft spoken of, dangers to keep everyone on the trail with little guarding. Still, Natalia wanted her fellow countrymen to do something, anything beyond praying to God for deliverance. A few glanced at her in passing, with no expression on their faces.

The old woman struggled to sit up.

"Rest easy, *Doña*," Natalia said.

The lady shook her white head. "I am more comfortable when I sit."

Natalia nodded and proffered her hand. They sat in silence, watching the train pass.

The storyteller, his face fearful, lumbered to his feet and stumbled back onto the trail. The old woman stiffened, and Natalia glanced up. Dirk sat on the dun mare a short distance away, watching them.

"Would you help me rise, child?" the woman asked.

"No, we shall stay here." Natalia patted her arm. "You need more rest," she said while looking at Dirk.

His mouth twitched. Then he rode on, weaving among people on the trail. A few minutes later a pirate marched through, crying, "Halt for the night!"

Natalia settled for sleep, finding a bump in the road for a pillow. She took off her shoes, grimacing at the torn and stained stockings, then retrieved from her bodice the scrap of petticoat that served as mosquito netting for her face.

All around, people coughed, clearing their lungs of dust. A young woman crooned a lullaby to her baby. Shadows deepened. Jungle noises grew louder. Natalia heard the hoot of a giant owl, a jaguar's cry, and the buzzing of thousands of insects. She slapped at mosquitos and fretted over her ransom, due tomorrow, until exhaustion dragged her into sleep.

At the earliest hint of grey dawn, Natalia woke, her thoughts still on the ransom she'd promised and promised. She stretched to ease the aches of lying too long in one position, and entered the still-dark jungle to relieve herself. She needed to go only a few feet for privacy. The thick foliage closed behind her, cutting off sight of the trail. She sighed. If only the jungle were not so dangerous.

As the sky brightened, pirates roused hostages with kicks and curses.

"Get moving, you miserable beasts!" one shouted. "Today starts your slavery!"

The hostages groaned, murmured complaints, and then began to move. The smell of raised dust drifted in the foliage. Natalia dreaded rejoining the train, but it was her only alternative to death in the jungle.

A pirate on horseback crashed through the edge of the greenery within a few feet of her. She ducked behind a bush, holding her breath. She thought surely he would see her and drag her back onto the road, but he passed as if she were invisible. She glanced down. It was difficult to see her black dress in the early morning shadows.

The train shuffled on, with the clop of horses, the jingle of tack and weapons, the hostages' complaints and pirates' curses. Natalia thought of the proud, kind *doña*, and the terrified man who had cried out in his nightmares but talked incessantly to hide that fear in the daytime. *How can they accept bondage without a fight? I can not.*

Nor could she escape into the jungle. Torn between two fates, unable to choose, she did nothing.

The train moved past her. Her stomach tightened and her breath grew short. The hostage train or the jungle? Slavery or death? If she didn't decide soon, the train would pass her completely and the jungle would be her only option. The train would pass by, leaving an empty road.

Natalia bit her lip to keep from laughing. ¡*Dios mío*! She need only stay here until the road was empty, then walk back to Panama.

She sat on a fallen tree to wait.

At dawn, Dirk rode past awakening hostages on his way to report to Morgan. It had been an uneventful night, with only three ransoms paid. Dirk's relationship with the admiral remained civil, but not friendly, so he spoke tersely and headed back to the rear guard. As he passed Natalia's resting place of the night before, he realized he hadn't seen her that morning. Although she might have changed her position in the train, he'd just ridden the length of it. Uneasy, he found her white-haired companion of the day before, and asked where Natalia might be.

The old woman shook her head. Dirk hesitated, looking about for Natalia's dark red hair. He peered into the jungle. *She wouldn't be so foolish as to run in there. She'd soon lose her way and, once lost, could live no more than a few days. Still, she might prefer possible death to what appeared to be certain slavery.*

He dismounted, tied his horse to a tree and walked a little way into the brush. He saw only deep shadows and layer upon layer of shades of green. *Her dress was black; I'll never see her amidst the foliage.* Trying to shrug off his growing uneasiness, Dirk returned to the road.

Natalia heard Dirk's voice and caught a glimpse of his cotton tunic in the greenery. *Damn that pirate. Will I never be rid of him?* Here he was, certain to ruin her one chance for escape. She rose and backed away in a twisting path to keep dense growth between them. When he finally left, she blew out the breath she'd been holding and collapsed onto an exposed root of a huge cedar tree. She would stay there until the train passed.

Moisture seeped from the foliage as the temperature rose. Natalia sweated and daydreamed of a cold morning in Spain. After a while, she heard only the chirping of birds and smiled. The train must have passed. She walked toward the road and freedom.

But the road was not where she thought it should be. And she had come such a short distance. Perhaps ducking around trees and bushes to avoid Dirk had confused her. She tried to go back to the cedar tree and start again, but she couldn't find the tree. The road ran north and south, and she had left it on the western side. Surely, by going east, she was bound to reach the road. Natalia looked up. Sunlight filtered weakly through the green canopy. As best she could, skirting huge trees and bushes taller than herself, she walked toward that soft light.

Shortly after midday, Dirk watched the last captives hurry toward Panama. Morgan had released them all, ransom paid or not. Many glanced over their shoulders as if afraid he would change his mind. The pirates closed ranks to march to the northern coast and their ships.

Dirk searched the fleeing crowd for Natalia, his uneasiness growing into concern. When all the train had passed, he knew she had gone into the jungle. He cursed her foolishness. Giving Mic a short explanation and ignoring his matelot's frown, Dirk left his men with the rear guard and, with San Sebastian beside him, hurried forward along the trail.

At the place where Natalia had been sitting with the old woman, San Sebastian searched the edge of the jungle while Dirk paced beside the road. Finally the cimaroon nodded. "She went here."

"Did she come out?"

"Not here."

Dirk looked into the jungle. *I shouldn't have taken her back to the warehouse. I should have known she would not accept the prospect of slavery without a struggle.*

The army's rear guard passed by. Mic stopped, working to keep his horse from prancing down the road after the others.

"You didn't find that woman?"

"No."

"You're coming with us now?"

Dirk glanced at the jungle. He muttered, "If she's still in there she'll die." *His responsibility or not, she shouldn't die now because of Morgan's bluff. She should be safely with her father.*

"You go on. We'll catch up with you."

With a snort of disgust, Mic rode off. Dirk unsaddled and released his mare. At his nod, San Sebastian moved into the jungle, slowly following a trail Dirk couldn't even see.

After three days on the road without food, Natalia tired quickly. She regretted not having taken a bite or two of the bread Dirk had dropped in her lap. She glanced around. *Are any of these plants edible?* She sat on the trunk of a fallen mahogany tree to loosen her clothing and take off her shoes. Her skin felt thick and heavy with sweat. Somewhere, unseen, water dripped. Natalia licked her lips.

Insects chirped, clicked, and whined. They buzzed around her eyes, got caught in her hair. Ants crawled up her legs. She swatted and brushed away tiny creatures, scratched at their bites until her hands, feet and face reddened with welts. She frantically tried to remove the first three things that crawled down back of her neck and into her dress. Thereafter, she settled for killing them inside the dress. Finally she forced her shoes back onto her swollen feet and set off into the jungle again.

With the sun directly overhead and no shadows to guide her, Natalia tried to climb a tree to see where she was headed. Clumsy in the dragging skirts, she climbed no higher than four feet before slipping on moss and sliding back down. As she fell, her left sleeve ripped almost away, hanging to the yoke of her dress by only a narrow strip of cloth. Now even more skin lay exposed to insects.

Everywhere Natalia looked, one wavering mass of green melted into another. She swallowed her growing panic and moved on, keeping a hand up to push aside foliage. Within minutes, her hand brushed something that left painful red welts on her palm. A short while later, she stumbled against sharp-edged leaves that tore her dress, cutting deep enough to scratch her legs.

In late afternoon she sank, exhausted, onto a fallen tree, and almost cried. She was back on the mahogany log where she had rested that morning.

Cicadas sang to each other, and somewhere monkeys squealed. In the still air, moss hung motionless from the trees. Bushes thrust broad leaves toward her and, underfoot, smaller plants and vines lapped against her ankles. Roots of trees and the larger branches of ferns were covered with more vegetation, green or grey parasites. Dead plants decomposed into the floor of the jungle, filling the air with the scent of decay. In no time at all, once living things would be part of the soft, hot, moist carpet.

The temperature dropped and shadows lengthened. Natalia limped once more through the brush. She didn't know where to go, but if she did not move, the jungle would creep over her body and absorb her into itself.

In the growing darkness she tripped. She clawed at a drape of heavy creepers, but they gave way under her weight, and she went down amid a tangle of vines. Lying there, sniffing back tears, she thought how easy it would be to submit to the jungle.

Her death would make no difference to anyone. Uncle Fernando might receive the news of her disappearance with regret, but more likely with relief that she would not burden his household. Rafael's parents in Lima did not expect any news of her. If no one ever saw her again, they might wonder what happened, but their lives would continue unchanged.

Only Natalia herself cared, and until now that had been enough. But now she was so tired of fighting the jungle, so tired of fighting the people who lived outside it. If she survived the jungle, she would be as miserable as before, and as lonely.

Lying in the creepers, she cried for herself, and for her parents who had died in a plague when she was thirteen. She cried because her husband had not loved her, and her relatives did not want her. She cried because there was no one to pay her ransom and she'd had to run and now she would die.

The lengthening shadows worried Dirk. It was unlikely Natalia would survive the night. There was plenty to eat in the jungle, and water was available simply by breaking off a section of a water vine, but she wouldn't know such things. She could starve in the midst of plenty, or die from eating something poisonous. Soon the light would be too faint for even San Sebastian to track her. Worse, the trail they were following might not be hers.

Out of tears, Natalia struggled to her feet and trudged on, not knowing where. When it grew too dark to see more than a few feet in front of her, she sat on a rotting log and waited. She prayed for a quick death, but expected a slow one of starvation and thirst. The piercing mating-call of thousands of cicadas would soon drive her mad. Perhaps in madness death would be easier.

A big cat snarled close by. Startled, Natalia looked around for this new danger. She might, after all, be spared the slow, creeping death of the greenery. She shivered as stoic acceptance disappeared and terror grew in her belly.

San Sebastian stopped suddenly, staring straight ahead into a tiny clearing. Dirk peered over his shoulder. Natalia sat on a log, elbows on her knees, staring at a spot on the ground between her feet. Dirk glanced at the treetops. Only a bit of light filtered down to them now.

"We stay here," San Sebastian said. "I will find meat." He slipped past Dirk and disappeared into the jungle.

At the sound of a twig breaking under Dirk's boot, Natalia raised her head.

"Oh." She blinked, swallowed hard, and gave him a crooked smile. "God has abandoned me. I prayed for death and He sent you."

Dirk sat beside her on the log. "Why did you leave the road?"

"I will not be a slave."

"But if you had waited—"

"There is no ransom." Tears filled her eyes. "It is ten years since my father died. There is no one to pay a single reale for me."

He leaned back. "You lied to Morgan? All those weeks you promised a ransom, you were lying?"

She nodded, teeth clamped on her lower lip.

"Not lying," he said. "Bluffing. All those days I used your ransom as an excuse to protect you."

Natalia raised her chin, as if daring him to retaliate.

He took a deep breath. "Oh, lady, how brave you are." Then he chuckled. "But you have outwitted yourself. Morgan released all the captives this morning."

"I am free? If I had stayed with the others?" She slapped at her torn dress, shuffled her feet. "This was all for nothing?"

When he nodded, she laughed, then burst into tears. After a moment, Dirk lifted her onto his lap.

"You're safe now."

He held her against his chest and let her cry.

It was only later, lying beside the fire, nestled in the curve of Dirk's arm that Natalia remembered. Even while knowing there would be no ransom, he had come for her. She rolled over to ask why, but her throat was too tight for speech.

Smiling, with warm eyes crinkling at the corners, he stroked her cheek with a knuckle. Natalia ducked her head to hide quick tears, and slept very well that night.

It was past midday when Dirk stepped onto the trail, glad to be out of the oppressive foliage. San Sebastian took a few steps north toward the Caribbean and waited.

Natalia cocked her head. "I shall remember you, Dutchman, perhaps in my prayers." She headed south, and waved without turning back. "*Adiós.*"

Dirk strode after her, caught her by the arm. "You're coming with us."

She jerked her arm away. "You told me I was free." She continued walking, backward. "I am grateful for what you have done, but I shall not go with you."

Dirk kept stride with her. "You'll never catch the others. You'll be alone for at least two nights. I didn't save you from the jungle only to let you die on the road."

Natalia stopped, put her hands on her hips, and tapped a foot.

"There's a village on the northern coast where you'll be safe," he said. "I'll take you there."

While Natalia considered it, Dirk glanced back at San Sebastian. The cimaroon stood rigidly, nostrils flared, jaws hard. The man might not tolerate Natalia's presence for long, if at all. Still, Dirk could not leave her alone on the trail.

Finally, Natalia sighed, tossed her head and marched north without looking at either man.

That night they camped near the Rio Chagres. While Dirk turned a monkey carcass over the fire, Natalia brooded. San Sebastian sat just outside the firelight, watching them both with unreadable eyes.

Five days later, they reached the rebuilt castle of San Lorenzo. Dirk halted at the edge of the forest, alert to something wrong. Instead of crews bustling to ready ships for a sea voyage, a great crowd of pirates roamed the beach, breaking into loud arguments and fistfights. The large ships of Morgan's fleet had disappeared, and men were fighting over the smaller vessels remaining. They chased boats out into the surf, piling aboard two and three deep, overloading one boat 'til it swamped. A few of the pirates swam to shore; the others drowned.

Dirk gave Natalia his hunting knife. "Stay here, out of sight."

She retreated into the cover of the trees. Dirk and San Sebastian stepped out onto the beach, and within minutes were surrounded by the remnants of the *Serpent*'s crew, all talking at once.

"Morgan's gone!"

"Stole the treasure, he did!"

"We was cheated!"

"Ships, too."

"He ran off with everything!"

"How close is the Spanish army?"

"Cap'n, how we gettin' home?"

"Quiet," Dirk said, looking around for Mic or Baldric. He waved Dunstan closer. "What happened? Where's Morgan? The ships?"

Dunstan cursed. "Morgan's gone. That spawn of the devil sailed off last night with most of the ships."

"And most of the treasure!" came a shout from the back of the crowd.

A heaviness settled in Dirk's gut. "Before the share-out?"

"We had the share-out." Dunstan shook his head like an angry bull.

"Then why are so many still here?"

"That hell-bound little pile of dung took the treasure back to Port Royal with him in the middle of the night."

"Tell me from the beginning."

"We had the share-out yesterday afternoon." Dunstan's voice grew loud and angry. "By the time the clerks finished counting and dividing, all we got was two hundred pieces of eight."

"Two hundred? With all that treasure? How can that be?"

"That's right, lad." Harlan hawked and spat, then stepped closer. "That's what we asked old Harry last night." The man stuck out his lower lip and picked twigs out of his beard.

"We accused Morgan of not putting all the treasure in the share-out," Dunstan said. "That weasel stripped down to his bare feet to show he wasn't hiding anything. But you saw how much treasure there was. How could our shares be only two hundred?"

Dirk closed his eyes, took a deep breath and let it out with a sigh. Two hundred pieces of eight wouldn't last a week in Port Royal, especially after the main treasure arrived and drove up prices. And in the currency of New York it amounted to only ten English pounds. With the shares of all his friends combined, there wouldn't be enough to outfit a ship for trade.

His shoulders slumped. It would take months, even years to collect the money for his trading venture. Years of danger in which every battle risked his life. A year and a half had passed since he'd last seen Katrina. Already she might have grown tired of waiting and married another. And piracy with a small crew in a single ship would be difficult, if it could be done at all. The Treaty of Madrid had been signed months ago. Now, after the destruction of Panama, even the government of Jamaica would enforce it.

He asked Dunstan, "Why did Morgan run off?"

After a string of curses, Dunstan said, "There was talk last night about a mutiny and another counting. That thieving coward snuck off in the middle of the night. Damn him to hell! I'll cut him to pieces if I ever see him again."

"Where's Mic? Baldric?"

Dunstan jerked his head to the west. "They went hunting. There's not much to eat around here anymore."

Harlan tugged at Dirk's sleeve. "How we getting home?"

A lot of faces gazed at Dirk. The few boats Morgan had left behind would hold perhaps a fourth of the pirates on the beach. Somehow Dirk must find boats, and gather food and water casks... all without letting other pirates know what he was doing. And all before the soldiers in Porto Bello learned how vulnerable they were and attacked.

Pushing down his bitter disappointment in the share-out, Dirk started to work.

Natalia watched the angry men on the beach, backing farther in among the trees whenever the crowd surged her way. The rebuilt fort appeared deserted, so she walked up the path toward it, saying a short prayer by the mass grave between the palisades before moving inside.

The sun beat down on the castle's dried timbers and brittle thatch. A faint sea breeze wafted through the confines, and flies buzzed over the seeds and rotted skins of fruit tossed into corners. She peered into all the rooms and felt the presence of ghosts, Spanish and pirate alike, in the empty, silent spaces built upon ashes. *What fighting and bleeding and dying there must have been in defense of this place!*

Rounding a corner, she tripped over the rotting corpse of a dog or monkey. Cursing under her breath, she scraped carrion off her shoe with Dirk's knife, then wiped the blade on the ground and went out to the parapet for fresher air.

Down on the beach, the horde of what looked like a thousand pirates undulated on the sand. Voices rose in a low roar. Natalia looked for Dirk, and found him on the western edge of the beach. He stood in a small group of men, and with strong gestures sent them off in various directions.

Soon, finally and forever, she would be free of the man. It was strange then, that the prospect did not make her happier. She did want to go home to Spain, to the safety of cool arid hills and her birthplace, even if it was now ruled by her shrewish aunt. There would be neither pirates and nor husband to bother her. Perhaps she would fill her days by riding horses and reading books.

Even a lover might be possible. Widows often took lovers, and as long as they were discreet, no one persecuted them. But Natalia sighed to think of the men available to her: older men bored with their wives, or younger ones so undesirable no high-born woman would have them. They would be arrogant and confident of her gratitude that any man would want her in her circumstances. And they would be right, for the family castle was a long way from cities and society.

How would it be for a man to really want me? Smoothing straggly hair away from her face, she looked down at her dress. It was ragged and stained and dusty. She tugged the yoke a little higher on her shoulders. What a mess she was, and for the first time in many weeks, she cared.

Her curiosity about the castle satisfied, she walked toward the courtyard and palisade gates. Rounding the last corner near the inner gate, she heard a shuffling. She gripped the knife. Heavy footsteps came from somewhere between her and the outer gate. She looked around for another weapon and found only a short, thick piece of wood. She picked it up and backed into a dark corner.

When the steps died away she edged cautiously out into the courtyard, seeing no one, but feeling as though someone were watching her. She hurried toward the gate. At the inner palisade she breathed easier. There remained a mere twenty feet to the outer gate and the trail to the beach. She stepped into the open space between the log walls.

A leering, scar-puckered face popped around the outer palisade's open gate. A cry of surprise stuck in her throat, Natalia jumped backward. The man stepped into the gateway and cocked his head. He grinned, then spoke in French.

"So the Dutchman no longer guards the chicken. That means the fox can take a bite."

Natalia took another quick step back, gripping the knife in the folds of her skirt. When she hefted the chunk of wood, he laughed.

She remembered him now. *This is the pirate who tortured that servant in Panama. Melchior, it is. The pirate who offered to buy me from Dirk.* She retreated, hoping to keep enough distance between them while she circled through the fort, until he no longer blocked the way to the gate. In her skirts she probably couldn't outrun him, but there must be places to hide in the forest.

Melchior rushed at her, arms outstretched. Natalia held her ground, fighting down the urge to flee. At the last possible moment she flung the wood at his head. It missed, but he ducked and threw up an arm. In that instant she scooted past him in a dead run for the gate. With the knife in one hand, she snatched at her skirts with the other. His labored breathing closed in behind her.

Natalia tripped on her skirts and fell onto her side. As she landed, she rolled. Melchior stooped to grab her, but tripped over her kicking feet and dropped hard, his right hand reaching for her. She stabbed it. Melchior grunted as the blade crunched through tendons. Natalia scrambled to her feet and ran, this time lifting her skirts high with both hands.

She darted out of the castle and down the trail, not even looking for a hiding place among the trees. She raced with all the speed her legs possessed for the only safe place she knew: Dirk's shadow.

Mic returned by mid-morning. He'd found no food, but he'd left Baldric a league up the coast with two single-masted, rough, yet seaworthy, fishing boats.

"We should sail this afternoon," Dirk said. "Tomorrow morning at the latest."

Mic nodded. "You heard about the share-out?"

"Dunstan told me. You're keeping my share?"

Mic frowned.

"You didn't let the twins have it! They'll have found a woman to spend it on by now."

"Since you weren't here, Morgan wouldn't give me your share. Nor San Sebastian's either. For all they knew, you were dead and I was trying to take extra."

Dirk's voice rose. "Our vessel shares?"

"We have no ship."

Dirk's neck burned. He took deep breaths, clenching his jaw until his teeth ached. His hands curled into fists. Men scurried away from him.

"Nothing!" Dirk stomped out a tight circle in the sand. "Not a God damned thing after all the months of work! All the fighting and risking my life. After losing our ship and all we invested in this voyage!" He stomped to the water's edge and kicked a piece of driftwood back into the surf. "Not one blessed, chewed off hunk of a cob! Not even a crushed pearl!"

Then Natalia came scrambling across the sand and he almost laughed at the irony of it. He'd spent six months of his life and every coin he possessed to come and raid the Spanish Main. Then he lost even his paltry share because he'd spent a day in the jungle rescuing a Spaniard. And what a Spaniard! A stubborn, imperious, temperamental wench in a ragged dress, with filthy hair and sunburned cheeks, who had, apparently, already lost his best knife.

Yet the glorious smile she wore as she skidded to a stop in front of him was worth at least 200 pieces of eight.

Dirk found nine more men to join the remaining fourteen of his original crew. He picked experienced fighters and those skilled as carpenters, surgeons or sailmakers. For an hour, as he wended through the crowd, a brown-haired youth followed a dozen feet behind. Three times the lad hurried ahead to cross Dirk's path and gaze at him with frightened eyes. The third time Dirk passed him over for older, stronger-looking men, the lad's narrow shoulders drooped.

Dirk said, "What's your name, boy?"

The hazel eyes filled with hope. "Gibbie."

Dirk forced a little smile and jerked his thumb over his shoulder in the direction of the fishing village. "Go west. And keep quiet about it."

The boy grinned, clapped a hand over his mouth, and ran across the beach. The other crew members slipped off from the crowd in groups of three or four. Dirk followed with Natalia, strolling the league to a narrow beach where Baldric and Dunstan were stowing supplies aboard the deckless boats.

"We found the boats in a village farther west along the shore," Dirk said to Natalia. "You can reach it before dark."

Natalia looked ahead along the empty coast, then back toward the abandoned pirates, out of sight around a curve. As she hesitated, Dirk nodded toward the boats.

"Or come with us. We'll find a safer place for you."

She began to shake her head, then stopped.

"Decide quickly." Dirk smiled and caressed her cheek with a knuckle. "We have to sail now."

As Dirk helped load gathered foodstuff into the boats, San Sebastian approached with five dead birds. He tossed them aboard, then glanced at Natalia. He studied Dirk for a moment.

"You take that Spanish woman with you?"

"I think so, yes."

San Sebastian nodded, then stepped aside as Dirk handed a water barrel up to Mic in the bow of the smaller boat. Dirk turned back for the last barrel and saw San Sebastian striding toward the forest. At the edge of the beach, the cimaroon turned, raised his musket, and disappeared into the trees.

Natalia imagined living in the fishing village, and considered the danger from the mass of pirates left at San Lorenzo. It might be a year before she could secure passage to Spain and the limited, boring life awaiting her there.

The smaller boat, full of men, bobbed toward the open sea. What adventures would the pirates have before they arrived at their island home? She envied them their voyage, free as the wind pushing them across the water. What strange and wondrous things they might see and do. Things she would never see, things she would never experience.

"Natalia?" Dirk stood knee-deep in the surf, wet clothes outlining broad shoulders and muscular limbs.

A few more days, that's all I want. A few more days of his company. A single grand adventure on the high seas, a voyage I can talk about in the coming years. When I've had that, I will be ready to face my future in Spain.

Excited and frightened, Natalia ran across the sand. Dirk lifted her into the boat.

Around a bend in the river, a three-masted ship listed against a short dock, the wooden hull scraping gently on the pilings. The village beyond, though colorful with flowers in bloom, appeared devoid of people, animals and even birds. A church, door ajar, stood at the far end of the plaza, beckoning the pirates ashore.

Mic took four men with him on a quick inspection of the area. He soon returned, shaking his head. "It's abandoned. The villagers must have heard of Morgan's fleet being near and left the place to us."

Dirk grinned. "How generous of them."

The other pirates scrambled out of the boats and up the riverbank. Dirk lifted Natalia to the dock, and they walked toward the village behind the men.

"Will we stay here long?" she asked.

"I don't know." Dirk's gaze drifted back to the river. "If we can make that ship seaworthy again, the repairs will take at least a week. If Thacher says it can't be fixed, we'll leave tomorrow or the day after."

"We will sleep inside tonight?"

He glanced at the mud-brick buildings. It would be good to sleep on something softer than planks and more stable than a cresting wave. He pointed to a two-story house that fronted on both the plaza and the river.

"We can stay there. Will you be content alone for a while?"

She nodded. He returned to the damaged ship.

Natalia stood in the center of the plaza as pirates swarmed over the village, racing in and out of mud-and-straw brick shops and homes, the little church and even smaller warehouse with a royal crest carved on the door. The men carried supplies for the ship, but little else, down to the river. She smiled at their grumbles about the lack of coins and gems.

She no longer feared them, and she knew most of their names. In the past days Dirk had often ridden in the smaller boat to maintain discipline or raise spirits. Left in the larger boat under the protection of a somber Baldric, Natalia learned that a well-placed jab of her elbow kept all but the twins away. Eventually, even they grew too hungry and tired to bother her. Now she ignored them all as she studied the town built up around a sunny plaza in the Spanish pattern.

Abundant South American foliage overran the edges of the plaza, climbed the walls of houses and even bloomed in cracks in the tile roofs. Frequent rains had weathered the mud bricks and warped the wooden beams, making the buildings appear ancient. Although begun as a copy of something Spanish, the village had been altered by the persistent realities of the New World, as had the people of Lima and Panama. As even Natalia herself was changing.

Aboard the pirates' boat, she had lived in a hostile world governed by basic needs and fears. After the first evening, when they slipped past Porto Bello in the dark, there was little to eat and Dirk closely rationed the water. They dared not land often to hunt for food, according to Dirk, because Indios Bravos frequently loosed arrows at boats that drifted too close to shore. The men were equally afraid of drifting far from land where a sudden squall could swamp the boats.

For eleven days, Natalia sat squeezed tight among the big, smelly pirates, her only bit of privacy found behind Dirk's broad back. Her skirts were always wet from the boat's leaks that kept the men constantly bailing water. Hair dripping with salt spray, she was cold at night and she burned all day in the sunshine. Even a year in a fishing village awaiting rescue would not have made her half so miserable.

Now, on solid ground again, Natalia felt exhilarated, exhausted, and grateful to be alive. Nothing mattered but living to see the sun rise tomorrow morning. Comforts were to be enjoyed whenever and wherever found. Safe, for a while at least, she longed for rest in a soft bed. She entered the house Dirk had chosen, feeling like an intruder. The ground floor was a large shop, half-full of housewares and coarse fabrics. Four tables stood empty except for a film of dust. Perhaps the owners had removed their most valuable stock before leaving. Since someone had also covered crude items, Natalia believed they planned to return when the danger of pirates had passed.

The stairway at the back of the shop led to living quarters above. A corner bedroom had a good view of the river to both the west and south, no doubt the reason Dirk had chosen this house. She walked through a connecting door into a second, smaller room.

It was a woman's room with canopied featherbed, a large open chest, now empty, and a dressing table with a mirror. Natalia approached the rare item gingerly, hardly recognizing her reflection. Her face had browned in the sun and there were red patches on her nose and cheeks. Her hair, now brighter red than she had ever seen it, lay in brine-covered tangles about her shoulders. The few remaining hairpins stuck out at odd angles.

Her silk dress was in tatters, the fabric stiff with encrusted salt and dirt. One puffed sleeve dangled near her elbow; the embroidered yoke held up the bodice by a few threads. She would need no help from a maid to remove this dress.

Still staring at herself, Natalia picked up a plain wooden comb from the table, removed the last pins from her hair and began to work through the tangles. When one of the comb's teeth broke off in a snarl, she didn't know whether to laugh or cry.

Natalia walked through the rest of the house, finding in an alcove something more precious than the mirror: a large copper bathtub. She searched all the rooms again for something to wear after bathing. There were only a few articles of clothing tucked away in otherwise empty chests, but she finally found a thin cotton nightshift. It was so new the sleeves' embroidery had not been finished. Yellow stitches outlined a delicate bird in mid-flight.

Hearing Dirk's booming laughter, Natalia walked outside onto a balcony that ran across the back of the house. It overlooked a small courtyard with a well and kitchen, plus a gate that opened to the riverside. Beyond the wall, Dirk and Thacher climbed over the ship, the carpenter gesturing at different parts.

Natalia rested her elbows on the balcony rail, her chin in her hands. What little rest she'd gotten at sea had been under Dirk's arm, his chest as her pillow. It had not occurred to her at the time that he was resting his own head against the hard planks of that leaky boat. Yet no matter how little he slept, or how many problems the others heaped upon his shoulders, he always managed to do his work. Then he took on the chores of others too tired or weak to continue. And still, whenever he looked at her, he smiled, deepening the fan lines at the corners of his eyes.

Over the days the scar across his eye had become endearing instead of menacing. *How could I once have believed Rafael more handsome?*

Natalia sighed. *Rafael is dead. Why can't my memories of him stay buried, too?* She pushed them to the back of her mind.

The bed called and sleep tempted more than a bath. Natalia sank onto the thick feather mattress. It curled up around her, like Dirk's arms. How comforting his arms were. How unlike Rafael's, whose embrace had always meant lust, a demand for sex.

Rafael again... She was too tired to fight off her memories. As her body grew heavy and still, five year old memories grew strong and vivid. And in that twilight before sleep, they trapped her....

Lima's streets were dry, and nineteen year old Natalia collected dust on the hem of her emerald silk gown as she strolled through the markets. Though carrying a basket for purchases, she'd bought only a single green ribbon in three hours of wandering among the booths.

Merchants called to her from tents as she passed. Dark-skinned women from the eastern highlands sat on blankets and held up brightly striped alpaca shawls. Occasionally a beggar child tugged at her gown, but Natalia's few coins had long since been given to the first child who asked, so now she ignored the pleas and the promise of bargains, and walked on, trying to muster the courage to go home.

Yesterday, Rafael had returned from a long hunting trip with fresh meat from the mountains and wild stories. Drunk from liquor, excitement and self-adulation, he threw the entire household into an uproar. At nightfall, he left to spend the evening gambling with friends at the home of his latest mistress. Come morning, he still had not returned.

Hurt by Rafael's pointed neglect and facing another empty day, Natalia had left the house immediately after breaking her fast. Now, at midday, she was hungry and weary. She left the markets and trudged home.

She entered the gate and, as always, was struck by the serene beauty of the residence Rafael's parents had built. It was a small-scale palace of arches, *loggias*, balconies and tile mosaics in the architectural style of southern Spain and Morocco. A fountain dominated the central courtyard where flowers and orange and lemon trees scented the air. Natalia loved the villa, so opulent and sensual compared to the dank, stone castle of her own family. Yet she never lost the sense of irony that she could be so miserable in such a lovely place.

Her Indian maid ran to greet her. *"¡Señora! La doña* calls for you."

Natalia nodded, then grasped the girl's chin, the better to see a darkening lump on the creamy gold cheek. "Who did this, and why?"

"It is nothing, *Señora.*" The girl knelt to brush dust off Natalia's skirts. "Merely your mother-in-law angry I did not accompany you to the market."

"Where is *la doña*?"

"In her sitting room. She awaits you there."

"Go to my suite. Stay out of her sight for the rest of the day."

"Yes, my lady."

The girl scampered off. Natalia took a deep breath to hold down that all-too-familiar combination of anger and trepidation, then went to find her mother-in-law.

The older woman's salon was the sunniest room in the house, but Natalia dreaded visiting her. Not yet fifty, with few white streaks in her dark hair, Rafael's mother, Pilar, was intelligent and robustly healthy, and she had an extensive education for a colonial woman. She and Natalia should have been friends.

Natalia knocked on the salon door and was given permission to enter. Pilar was sitting near a big window overlooking the courtyard. As Natalia finished a short curtsy, the older woman set aside her ever-present needlework and motioned toward a low stool.

Natalia sat, but did not wait for the usual sad gaze and pained sigh that preceded a lecture.

"You struck my maid."

Pilar shrugged. "She neglected her duty to accompany you whenever you appear in public."

"I insisted she remain at home. I need no escort."

"There is little danger to your person, of course, in walking alone in the markets, but your solitary wanderings reflect badly upon the reputation of this house. I will tolerate them no longer."

"There was no need to strike the child."

"You were not here to receive it."

Natalia flushed. Pilar raised an eyebrow, then continued. "The next time there will not be a mere tap on the cheek."

Natalia breathed heavily. "I will send the girl away."

"Do not be foolish. Who would dress you, and arrange your hair? You require someone to serve you."

And any maid would be equally vulnerable to the woman's wrath. Natalia nodded in submission.

"There is no need for you to go to the markets at all, Daughter. Anything you desire can be fetched here."

"I go for the exercise and to relieve my boredom."

"You must have children. Then there would be no boredom."

Natalia swallowed. "I have certainly tried."

"You have lost only one. Every woman loses at least one. It has been more than two years. Surely you have finished grieving for a child that was barely started."

"Perhaps I would not have suffered so if Rafael had not—"

Pilar cut her off with a sharp wave of a slender white hand. "Men take mistresses. It is their nature. Did you expect him to be, shall we say, attentive while you were carrying? I did not rear my son to be so sinful or barbaric."

Natalia bit her tongue on what she thought of Rafael's sinfulness, and suppressed the memory of her pain and bewilderment at his betrayal.

"Your body is healed and still there is no child. You are nearly twenty. I should have at least two grandsons by now."

"Rafael will not, shall we say, attend me."

"Do not be flippant, Girl. I know the state of your marriage as well as your womb and can only conclude that you have been remiss."

"I?"

"My son is a healthy man with the appetites of youth. Only your rejection would keep him from your bed."

"I have never forbade him!" Natalia said. Once she had welcomed Rafael's touch, and they had spent long hours into the night whispering and giggling under the blankets.

"Perhaps you have not rejected him directly, but your past behavior is no longer of any concern. From today, Daughter, you must find a way to breed. Why else do you think we brought you all the way from Spain?"

"I suppose... I hoped that your husband and you, and Rafael, would be the family I lost when my parents died."

"You were already seventeen when you came to us. Surely you knew that a bride does not marry a family, but rather makes one with her body. Not even a dowry like yours can compensate for such a lack."

Pilar continued with a lecture on how to entice a wayward husband to the marital bed. Natalia heard little of it. When Pilar finally dismissed her, she stumbled from the room, her head aching with unshed tears.

Ashamed that she could not protect her maid, Natalia avoided the shelter of her suite and went directly to the stables. She ordered her favorite gelding saddled and, within minutes, was galloping the horse down a lane toward the open Peruvian countryside.

But she could not run away from Pilar's words, from the hurt of being told once again that she had no value beyond the childbearing capacity of her womb. She sobbed aloud as she rode across fields, and pastures full of sheep, through little villages. On and on she went, for more than an hour, passing a rock quarry and a played-out silver mine, and still she had not left her in-laws' holdings.

Bent low, half-blinded by tears, she nearly collided with a peasant leading a llama. The gelding reared, throwing her. She landed on her backside in the dirt. The well-trained horse stood nearby, while black impassive eyes in a deeply-lined copper face watched her rearrange skirts and her dignity. The llama snorted its opinion of the matter, and spat toward the horse.

Within Spanish areas of influence, llamas had been displaced by horses and sheep. Regarded by herders as pests and competition for pasturage, few llamas were seen in cultivated regions. She was a long way from home.

Natalia led the horse to a rock and re-mounted. With a nod to the peasant, she nudged the gelding into a canter. She wasn't sure where she was, but the horse knew in which direction his stable lay. He needed only a light rein and no urging at all to stay at a good pace.

The fall eased Natalia's sorrow, allowing her anger to build unimpeded. By the time she reached the stables, she had no more capacity for tears. She slid to the ground with a determined thump and tossed the reins to a groom. When Rafael accosted her on the path back to the house, she was in no mood to placate anybody.

The bleary-eyed man grabbed her arm. "Wife, I will not allow you to take complaints of me to my lady mother."

Natalia jerked her arm free. "So she has spoken with you as well."

"And tells me you feel the need of more attention."

"She desires grandchildren. Have you no wish for sons?"

"As does every man, but I cannot sire anything upon a woman who is ever astride a horse instead of her husband."

"At least the horses are available."

Rafael's narrow face reddened. "You have ridden for the last time!"

"What did you say?" She might lose her sanity without a daily ride in the fresh air and sunshine.

"I have forbidden the grooms to ever saddle a horse for you again. You will ride in a litter as befits a proper lady."

"But why?"

His finger stabbed toward her face. "All this riding caused you to miscarry my son and no doubt it prevents you from conceiving again."

Natalia gasped. "That cannot be true. The Book of Kings tells of the Most Catholic Queen Isabela conceiving and bearing while riding almost into battle against the Moors."

"Never mind a queen dead nearly two hundred years." Rafael's voice rose. "If you had stayed in the house, if you had been more womanly, you would not have lost the child!"

Natalia shouted back, "If you were more of a man you would have gotten a stronger babe on me and it would not have died!"

Rafael's palm cracked against her cheek. The blow turned her head aside, and for an instant she was stunned. Then she slammed the back of her hand across his soft, pale face.

He stepped back in shock, the trace of fear in his eyes quickly shadowed by outrage. In the few moments he stood speechless, Natalia fled into the house.

That night Rafael came to her bedchamber, dismissing her maid with a jerk of his head. The girl hesitated. Rafael kicked her thigh. "Go!"

She ran. Natalia rose from the dressing table where she had been braiding her hair for sleep. "I am in no mood tonight for your attempts at fatherhood."

Rafael gave her a sloppy smile. "It matters not what you are in the mood for. I am your husband." He stood over her, his long-fingered, white hands balled into fists. "I possess all rights to your body." He leaned close, breathing wine fumes into her face. "And you have your duty."

Natalia had no argument against his claims. He could beat her for disobedience, kill her for adultery, and most certainly could demand carnal relations at any time. There was no escape from this man, at least not tonight. So she submitted, and hated herself for not resisting, even while knowing she dared not.

After that night, whenever Rafael came to her bed, he pretended they were friends again. Yet each time, Natalia retreated to a place outside her body from where she could watch and understand, but not feel. Although her husband owned her body, she would not grant him access to her soul. She withheld it to spite him, for the great disappointment he was to her, and because she could not trust him with it....

In the depths of a stranger's featherbed, surrounded by pirates in the jungles of the Main, Natalia curled into a tight ball to ward off the hurt and loneliness. At last she drifted into an exhausted sleep too deep even for dreams.

The ship listing in the river possessed the stern castle and deep waist of a galleon, but lacked the multiple decks. Mic insisted the ship was a flute by virtue of its rounded stern and wide hold. Thacher argued that the bent stern and mix of square and triangular sails, especially the smack-style mainsail, made the ship a cromster. Dirk didn't care what the oddly styled vessel was. He was more concerned that once repaired it might not float. Perhaps it had been abandoned for reasons other than the hole in the starboard side.

By late afternoon Thacher had inspected every inch of the ship. He'd nodded reassuringly at the broken spars, waved a casual hand at the torn sails, the missing guy lines. The keel was sound, he declared, and everything else reparable. Furthermore, he was confident the surrounding forest held all the materials needed for repairs.

Dirk smiled at the news. A ship would make the voyage home much safer and faster. The hold would shelter the men during bad weather, and with luck they might fill it with treasure.

When Thacher finally climbed off the sloping deck and lumbered up the riverbank, Dirk went to check on Natalia again. At mid-day he'd taken her some food only to find her sleeping, in chemise and a single underskirt, sprawled face up on the bed.

A fly had found its way inside the bed's mosquito netting. Dirk lifted the net and chased it out. Natalia frowned and whimpered, but her face smoothed out again. Still asleep, she rolled away from him, and her underskirt rose, leaving him a glimpse of pale thigh and buttock. After a moment, he reached over, caught the edge of the underskirt and tugged it down past her knees. He had closed the netting and left.

Now, halfway to the house, Dirk saw Natalia climbing the back stairs to the balcony, a dripping water bucket in each hand. He'd seen the tub; no doubt she planned a bath. His fatigue vanished and he changed course. After checking on the guards posted around the village, he walked upriver and, in a clear backwater, washed off three weeks of jungle and ocean travel.

Evening shadows had deepened by the time he entered the house. He bolted the front door, climbed the stairs to the living quarters and pushed open the door of Natalia's room. The hinges creaked and she stopped combing her wet hair at the dressing table. A thin, damp shift clung to her arms, shoulders and breasts. Through the mirror's reflection, Dirk watched the surprise in her eyes change to wariness.

He stepped into the room, closing the door. She stiffened. He took the comb from her hand and ran it down the length of hair gleaming red in the glow of sunset. Dirk had not imagined her hair would hang past her waist, nor be so heavy in his hands. Her neck was moist and warm where his hand brushed it. As he ran the comb through her hair again and again, Natalia closed her eyes, swaying with the tugs on her scalp.

The drying hair floated in Dirk's hands. He gathered it, lifted it aside to kiss the hollow beneath her ear. She trembled. When he straightened and caught her gaze in the mirror again, he saw passion as well as wariness.

He walked through the connecting doorway into the other bedroom, leaving the door ajar.

Natalia watched Dirk's reflection until he left. In the other room a boot fell, then another. Fabric rustled so faintly that she might only have imagined his tunic dropping to the floor. In her mind she saw him shirtless in the fading light, and she longed to push her naked breasts against the soft curls on that broad chest. The touch of his lips remained on her neck, and she swayed with the imagined feel of large hands roaming down her ribs, past her waist, down to cup her buttocks with warm pressure.

Natalia rose and gazed at the half-open door. Beyond it, Dirk opened window shutters. Although she yearned for his embrace, she feared it also, for his strength and controlled passion had tinged his invitation with danger. Yet he had shown no desire to prove his manhood or mastery over her. He simply wanted her. As she wanted him.

She walked toward the door.

Dirk stood by the open window fighting the urge to march into the other room, pick up Natalia and take her to his bed. But as much as he would gain by such a move, he would also lose. He must wait.

All his life he'd gone after whatever he wanted, even women. Especially women. But every other woman he'd brought to bed had been a doxy, and the sex between them a simple exchange of favors. She took his coins; he took whatever pleasures he'd paid for. He owned all those women, for a time at least, as he could never own the Spaniard in the next room.

A brilliant orange and burgundy sunset faded into darkness. Dirk lit a lamp, carried it to a small table near the bed, then glanced through the doorway to the other room. Unable to see Natalia, he parted the mosquito netting and climbed into the wide bed.

Patience, he told himself. *And if she comes to you, be careful.*

The bed creaked. At the door, Natalia hardly breathed, knowing that if she crossed the threshold of this room, there would be no retreat. If she went to him, he would demand more, and he had the power to take more, than she might be willing to give. If she opened her heart, gave him entrance... When they parted, she would suffer a loneliness sharper and deeper than any she had known.

The faint lamplight spilling into her room faded, leaving her in darkness. With a sob of fearful desire caught in her throat, she slipped through the doorway.

Dirk sat up as Natalia glided into the room. The outline of her body was barely visible through the plain, shapeless shift. He wanted that garment off her, but he hesitated to suggest it. Doxies undressed for sex only with a great deal of coaxing and many extra coins. Perhaps ladies never did. But it was enough that she was here. He parted the netting. After a moment, she came to the bed and climbed in. The netting closed behind her.

They knelt, facing each other, and he kissed her. Through the shift, his fingers raced over the places he knew women liked to be touched. Her breaths deepened; her nipples grew hard under his thumbs. He half lifted her, ready to ease them both down onto the bed.

Then he stopped, and sat on his heels.

Natalia's eyes opened as she too sat back. "Something is wrong?"

Dirk brushed a wisp of hair off her face. "No." He moved closer, placing a knee on either side of hers. "Nothing is wrong."

He leaned down for a kiss and her eyelids drifted shut again.

"Look at me," he said, his voice gruffer than he intended.

The brown eyes opened. Holding her puzzled gaze with his own, Dirk's fingers traced the smooth planes of her face. One hand caressed the nape of her neck while the other tugged at the drawstring of her shift. He eased the gathers to the ends of the string, widening the neckline, then slid the gown off her shoulders. It fell into folds around her hips, her hands underneath. He kissed her lips, her neck, her breast. She moved as if to push him away, but her hands, now free, stroked his cheeks and she slipped her arms around his neck.

Every ache disappeared, leaving Natalia with the feel of Dirk's kisses, the feathery caresses up the inside of her thigh, along the curves of her breasts. She nuzzled him, discovering the smell of a clean, healthy man. Not the heady, erotic scent of perfume, but rather a scent she could feel deep in her belly. He sank to the bed, drawing her down on top of him. One of her knees slipped between his thighs.

His scars were white ridges in the moonlight. She touched the one she had given him, then traced a bumpy furrow that crossed his chest. *How close this wound had come to his heart... How close he must have been to death...* She lay her head on that scar, remembering the deep wounds his heart had suffered. Yet it beat on, in defiance of those wounds. Surely it was this stubborn life within that had drawn her to him. It validated her own survival, fed her exhilaration at being alive.

Dirk's arms encircled her, supporting her as they rolled over. His body blocked out the moonlight and even the netting draped around them. His scent filled her. There was nothing in her world but this man, this body, this life, all drawing her down and around, as if into swirling waters, warm and strong and dark, and she began to drown in them.

Dirk entered her and within the cocoon of his embrace Natalia felt exposed and vulnerable. She panicked.

She stiffened, ever so slightly. He'd expected it. Women withdrew a part of themselves from the act. Some sooner than others, but every one by the time of penetration. Always intent on the sensations running through his own body, he rarely thought about it. He let his body settle into a compelling rhythm, then stopped.

As he rested motionless within her, Natalia's eyes opened. He smiled and stroked her cheek with a knuckle. All of her was with him again, but only for a moment. When she left once more, he tried to follow, to capture, retrieve, thrusting harder, seeking something he could not name. His body grew hot and full and demanded he cease all coherent thought. He surrendered, and there was only his blood beating in great thumps, flooding through him, out of him.

Propped on his elbows, he rested his head beside hers, then rolled off and lay exhausted, satiated. And still hungry.

There were hours and hours left in the night.

"To arms! To arms!"

The shout crashed through Dirk's sleep. He reached under the bed for his cutlass, then hesitated in the following silence, unsure whether he'd heard or dreamed the warning. Late morning sunlight, already hot, streamed in through the windows. Natalia lay on her side, curled away from him, bedding draped over her naked hip. Smiling, he nudged her awake.

"Boats coming up-river! To arms!"

Dirk rolled out of bed, yanked on his clothes, and to Natalia's sleepy inquiry, said, "Get dressed. If there's trouble, find a place to hide."

By the time he raced down the stairs and out the front door, his men had filled the plaza.

He caught Baldric. "Take some men with muskets onto the roofs."

Then he ordered half the men into ambuscades around the plaza and led the rest to the pier. With muskets primed, they hid behind the shacks, empty crates and barrels lining the river. Everyone quieted. Dirk held his breath, and soon heard the sound of oars, along with muted voices.

The sun grew hot. His bad knee stiffened from squatting behind a wooden crate. Just as he shifted to a different but no more comfortable position, two boats rounded the bend into view. He took a deep breath of relief. At that distance he couldn't recognize any of the men in the boats, but their clothes and the rough, mixed English and French speech marked them as pirates.

He stood and shouted, "Whence do you come?"

"From the seas!"

Dirk's men rose from their hiding places with a cheer. They crowded into the water to help dock the boats. The newcomers piled out. Mic, standing beside Dirk, counted them as they came ashore.

"Nineteen."

"Good," Dirk said. With nineteen additional men they'd have a decent crew for the little cromster on the voyage home. They'd be strong enough to raid along the way, thereby salvaging some part of this Panama expedition.

Then Melchior, face as pale as his scars, walked by with fever-bright eyes. He carried his right arm close to his chest, cupping the elbow in his left hand. The cradled arm was swollen and streaked with red. He shuffled into the shade of a tree in the plaza.

"My God," Dirk murmured. "I wonder what happened to him."

Mic said, "I don't think he'll give us any trouble now."

In early afternoon, when all the pirates were settled in, James the surgeon took one look at Melchior's arm and declared that it had to come off at the shoulder. Melchior protested, but James insisted he'd die without the amputation.

Melchior's friends plied him with brandy and all the rum they could find for several hours. When he passed out, they carried him into the sunshine in the plaza and laid him on a wooden bench brought from the church, then lit a small fire. A few curious men stayed close to watch, but most left the plaza, leaving three of Melchior's friends to hold him down.

Dirk returned to the house where he and Natalia had slept. He found a bottle of rum in a storage closet, then headed up to his room.

Natalia greeted him from the top of the stairway. "That man, he came to the house in Panama."

Dirk climbed the steps. "He's nothing to worry about now, though." He shuddered. "James is about to cut off his arm."

Her eyes widened. "Why?"

"A wound festered. Such a little wound, too, in his hand."

Natalia paled, then swayed. He rushed up the last few steps to catch her. She shook off his hands and ran into her room, slamming the door. He stared at the door for a moment, then entered the other bedroom and sat by the west window. With his foot, he dragged a little table close, plunked the bottle of rum down on it, and watched the sun slip west toward the tree-lined riverbank.

There were screams. Dirk took a long swallow of rum and held out his right arm. To lose it, his sword arm, his livelihood. He flexed his hand. Everything he had, everything he hoped to have, depended on this arm. It might be easier to lose a leg or an eye.

He was a lucky man just to be whole and healthy and to have his friends likewise. No matter what had happened with the share-out in Panama, at least he'd lost nothing more precious than money. Even that he might regain, now that they'd found the ship and had enough men to sail it.

The screams died away. The surgery must be finished. A moment later, there came another long scream, higher and sharper than the others. The searing was done. Soon after, the stench of burnt flesh wafted to him on the light breeze.

Dirk took a long, ragged breath. *Such pain now and such misery in the recovery... if there is one.* The surgery could kill Melchior as easily as would the festering wound. Survival itself would be painful for many months.

At nightfall, Natalia came to him, silent and quivering. Her mouth tasted like wine, and she clung to him. Dirk gladly lost himself in her passion.

At dawn, the little ship, renamed *Vengeance*, lurched slowly out of its night anchorage. As patched sails unfurled and caught the wind, the ship steadied. It heeled to starboard and skipped over a chopping sea.

With a firm nod, Crofton passed the helm to Dirk and trotted off to oversee trimming the sails. Dirk grinned into the sunshine as the last sails billowed into smooth arcs. How good it was to be at sea, breathing crisp, salty air. He was captain of a pirate crew again. Mic was quartermaster, Dunstan, the gunner. Life was just the way it should be.

Melchior's men had grumbled when Dirk was elected captain instead of their candidate, Baldessaire. But Dirk's men outnumbered them, and as long as he controlled his own men, he controlled the ship. Now, at sea just a short week and a half, the entire crew had settled into a calm routine.

The ship picked up speed. He'd been fond of both the *Avenger* and the *Serpent*, but this vessel was special. He and the others had rebuilt her during the past weeks, and he knew every plank, every inch of keel, every line, and yard of sail. This ship was his in a way the others never had been. When Mic financed the purchase of all the ownership shares, the two of them would truly own it.

Now they were sailing home with a full crew and plenty of brandy, wine, coffee and flour, all scrounged from the abandoned village. Large barrels lined the rails, fresh water seeping between swollen slats. Pork and beef, preserved over a boucan, were stored in the hold along with a few trinkets, clothes, including several priests' robes, and fabrics taken from the village. Two nights before, they'd slipped past Cartagena, the strongest city on the Spanish Main. With any luck, they would sail past the rest of the northern coast of South America without incident.

An hour later Mic came to relieve Dirk at the wheel. He jerked a thumb over his shoulder.

"Natalia's out on deck again."

"She needs the fresh air."

"She's tossing knucklebones with the twins, and they're teaching her how to cheat."

Dirk laughed. "Thanks. I won't toss bones with her anymore."

"Are you taking her all the way to Port Royal with us?"

"Still worried about riots among the men?"

Mic scowled. "Things are calm for now, but I doubt they'll stay that way."

"I told the men we're holding her for ransom. And since the captain's in charge of all prisoners, there won't be any trouble."

"Probably not from our men."

"Nor from Melchior's either. They're lost without him at full strength."

Mic frowned, but Dirk's mind was not on problems of discipline. He gazed down into the ship's waist. Dressed in a simple cotton blouse and a full brown skirt she'd sewn while in the village, Natalia sat cross-legged on the deck. Pig knuckles bounced in front of her. She laughed and held her hands out to Jan and Joost. They each gave her a coin.

"What of your plans for Katrina?"

"None of that has changed," Dirk said. But he hadn't thought of Katrina in weeks. He tried to envision the pretty blond girl as he'd last seen her. The warmth and peace of her parents' home came back to him with a rush of nostalgia, but the girl's face was elusive.

"And the Spaniard?"

How lovely she looked in the sunlight, the breeze lifting her glossy red hair away from her face. Dirk shrugged. "Natalia will sail to Spain from Port Royal. This will be a pleasant voyage home, nothing more."

"I see."

Dirk climbed down to the waist and headed for his cabin. "Natalia, come here."

"Later."

"Now. I want to talk to you."

She didn't look up. "I can listen while I play."

Dirk walked over, hauled her up with an arm around her waist and carried her tight against his side to the cabin. She struggled, laughing and spewing some of the more interesting curses the twins had taught her in several languages.

In the cabin, he kicked the door shut and bolted it.

Natalia stood, hands on hips, by the table. "I am not a trained dog to come when you call."

"Untrained dogs are more obedient than you, but you will learn." Dirk sat on the bunk they shared at night and patted the thin straw mattress. "Come here."

Natalia crossed her arms. "No."

"I am the captain. You must obey me."

She shook her head, biting off a grin.

With a growl, he stalked her. Natalia retreated behind the table. He lunged across, missed her, and rolled over the table. She darted past him toward the door, giggling like a girl. He cut her off, then chased her around the cabin, nearly pinning her on Mic's bunk. She slid away at the last moment. Passing the table once more, Natalia picked up a loose stool and, just as Dirk closed in, turned to hold the stool between them. He backed her into a corner. She stood pinned by the stool's legs while the seat held him an arm's length away.

"Do you submit, Woman?"

"In a stalemate? Are you mad?"

With another growl, Dirk yanked the stool out of her grasp, pinned her hands behind her back and untied the drawstring of her blouse with his teeth. He nuzzled her bosom, then heaved her over his shoulder. Halfway to his bunk, he changed his mind, bent her over the end of the table and pushed up her skirts. She protested, laughing deep in her throat. Tight between her thighs, he pushed hard, reached around for her breasts. She arched her back, wriggled, and he was quickly done.

A few deep breaths later, he picked her up, took her to his bunk, tugged off all their clothes and started over, face to face.

Natalia woke late to the sound of two blades clashing. It was a common sound aboard, as the men liked to practice their handystrokes. She climbed out of the bunk and splashed her face and throat with water from a covered bucket. After running a comb through the worst tangles in her hair, she wandered out into the sunlight.

The sky was a brilliant blue, with only a few puffy clouds high overhead. Natalia shook her head at Jan's invitation to join the ever-present gambling in the waist. In the stern she greeted Dirk at the wheel, then wandered to the bow, where the clash of steel was ringing.

She climbed the foreward ladder, then halted. Melchior was sparring with one of his men. The one-armed pirate struggled, panting, with a saber in his left hand. His strokes were awkward, his face hard with concentration and beaded with sweat. When he caught sight of Natalia, he lowered the blade. A crooked grin puckered the skin around his scarred eye. He stepped closer.

"The woman," he said. "I heard you were aboard." He waved the saber in the air. "Yes, I practice, and someday I shall use this sword against the man." He pointed it toward Dirk in the stern. "And then..." he tilted his pelvis forward, "I shall use *this* sword on the woman."

Natalia flushed and retreated, bumping into Baldric, who was coming up the ladder.

"Go below," Baldric said, then stepped between her and Melchior.

Natalia went below.

Baldric marched aft and told Dirk about the threats.

"Melchior can't harm either of us," Dirk said. "He was teasing her."

"I don't think so. Natalia's frightened."

Dirk raised an eyebrow, but went to his cabin where he found Natalia huddled on his bunk. He sat beside her. "So Melchior frightens you. He can't hurt you now."

"He hates me."

"He only enjoys scaring you."

"I... it is my fault he lost his arm."

"He lost it to a wound."

She described Melchior's assault at San Lorenzo, and Dirk's sympathy for the man disappeared. Natalia had real cause to be afraid. Melchior's hatred would make him strong and eventually he'd seek revenge against both Dirk and Natalia.

Dirk sighed. His life aboard the *Vengeance* was not so splendid after all.

When Dirk asked, Crofton said he knew of an island where they could revictual the ship and perhaps hire a few women for the rest of the voyage home. It took a day for the navigator to remember its location, but within a week of Melchior's threats, the *Vengeance* landed at an isle in the Windward Islands.

The native island dwellers welcomed the crew ashore with a three-day celebration. The pirates feasted, consorted with women, and restocked the ship with food, water, and earthen jugs of palm wine. By the time the pirates left, three women had agreed to sail along in exchange for a few trinkets and passage to an island east of Puerto Rico.

Within a few days, the ship settled into a routine of quarrels and sporadic fighting. Mic, in charge of keeping the peace, soon declared that three women available to all the men were more trouble than one woman out of everyone's reach. Ultimately, he rationed time spent with the women as well as the food and wine.

Every day, somewhere on the ship, Melchior practiced handystrokes. Dirk winced at the man's clumsiness, but he could not pity him. Not while Dirk remembered the attack on Natalia. Even through childlike movements, malevolence emanated from the man.

Despite Mic's calculations, they ran out of water. By good fortune, Dominica, an island of plentiful, sweet water, lay close. Crofton, however, insisted that Caribes, who savored the taste of long pig, lived beside an excellent bay on the leeward side of the island. So after dusk the *Vengeance* eased to an anchorage on the windward side. They lit no lamps and muffled the rigging. With a spy glass Mic examined the shoreline for signs of the cannibals. Finding none, he ordered a boat lowered.

The soft bumps of boat against ship's hull crashed in Dirk's ears. When the boat splashed onto the water, he held his breath, listening for sounds of Caribes on the shore. Minutes passed. He heard nothing. The four-man landing party donned priests' robes taken from the little village church west of Cartagena and descended by ropes to the boat.

Mic was the last to go over. Dirk punched him on the shoulder, and watched him descend the rope ladder.

At a sharp, angry cry behind him, Dirk whirled. Natalia strode across the deck, a hand up. He leapt for her and clamped a hand over her mouth.

She broke away. "What?"

He smothered her voice again and dragged her across the deck. She squirmed, kicked, and snarled beneath his hand. Heart pounding in fear she'd be heard, Dirk maneuvered her down the ladder to his cabin. As he eased the door shut with an elbow, she fought out of his grasp.

"How *dare* you! I am not one of your me—"

He clapped one hand over her mouth, jerked her close with the other. "You will be quiet," he said in her ear. "Or I'll thrash you."

Natalia's fingernails dug into his wrist. He shook her.

"If you make any more noise and those men die, I will truly beat you. Understand?" He held her tight against him until she nodded.

Once released, Natalia stepped back, her hands balled into fists. Her harsh whisper came through the moonlit darkness. "If you beat me I shall cause more trouble aboard this ship than you can imagine!"

She could indeed cause a great deal of trouble. Her presence alone had been trouble enough. He suspected, as well, that striking her would end their friendship. But he'd thrash her anyway if Mic and the others were hurt because of her noise.

"Be quiet!" he whispered.

Perhaps Natalia would take a beating to rid the world of four pirates. No matter how fine their time together had been, she was still, and always would be, a Spaniard. The time they'd spent on the ship and in that colonial village had been time out of place. Upon returning to the larger world of Port Royal and of empires at war, they would revert to their old positions as enemies. But he wasn't ready for that.

"Please."

She finally nodded. Then her whisper came from between clenched teeth. "Why do they wear the sacred robes?"

He stepped closer to speak. "We need water. There are cannibals living on that island and they don't eat priests."

"Perhaps it is God's favor that protects them, not the robes."

"Legends tell of an entire tribe that became ill after eating a priest. Now anyone in a robe is considered a future bellyache, so we use the robes as protection." Dirk took a deep breath. "I'm going back up on deck now. I think it best you stay here."

He left Natalia in the cabin and returned to the rail. He watched the dark island, willing the men to find sweet water, even a small barrel of it, and come back safely. He stood guard there until Mic climbed up over the rail with a grin on his face.

The extra water eased tensions aboard the ship for two days. Then the rum and palm wine gave out, and the women began quarreling with each other as well as the men. Mic stayed busy settling fights. He finally banned drinking except at mealtimes, and banned gambling altogether. That left the men with little to do but sharpen their blades and shorten their tempers.

Melchior continued his daily saber work. His strokes grew smoother, his thrusts more deadly, even without his right arm for balance. Although he still had not attained the expertise of most pirates, it was obvious that in time he'd be a tolerably good fighter again. As he gained strength, his men complained more and fought on any provocation.

One cloudy morning as Dirk finished his turn at the wheel, a heated argument broke out in the waist.

"Not again," he said to Thacher, who'd come to replace him. The carpenter rolled his eyes.

Dirk climbed down to the waist. Baldric was punching and kicking and rolling about the deck with Cadfer, a friend of Melchior. Gibbie, the youth from London, was hopping around them, shouting.

Now and again he dove in for a punch at Cadfer. Dutch, French and English curses filled the air.

Men dashed from all over the ship to watch. Some climbed the rigging for a better view. They cheered the fighters on, wagering on the outcome. Mic ran to the cabin for his whip, while Dirk and Dunstan jumped into the fray. The two big men tried to pry the combatants apart, while Gibbie tried to land kicks and punches. Dirk caught the tail of his shirt, yanked the boy out of the brawl and threw him against a stack of torn canvas.

"Stay there!" he roared when Gibbie bounced back toward the fight.

Gibbie's eyes rounded. He jumped up and down just out of Dirk's reach, shouting encouragement to Baldric, who didn't need it. He was fighting the much larger Cadfer with a ferocity Dirk had never seen in Baldric. His promises, in Dutch, to kill Cadfer were loud and clear.

Dirk reached for Baldric's left foot and was kicked with the right. Dunstan grunted and cursed, then ducked one flying fist, only to have his nose bloodied by another. Cadfer and Baldric rolled over and over, Dirk and Dunstan scrambling after them. Baldric ended up on top, his hands around Cadfer's throat. As Cadfer's face turned purple, Dirk grabbed Baldric's arms and tried to pry him off, but the little man's grip was too strong.

"Stop this!" Dirk growled, then recoiled as Baldric turned on him. The man's eyes were full of hatred and a lust for killing that made him seem a stranger. Not even in battle had Dirk seen such a look in his friend's eyes.

In that moment of staring at Dirk, Baldric's grip on Cadfer's neck must have eased. Dunstan managed to break Baldric's hold, and Cadfer and Baldric rolled over the deck again. Their audience cheered.

Above the noise came a loud whistle and a crack. Dirk swung around and saw Mic rearing back for another blow of his whip. Dirk dodged out of the way as the second warning landed within inches of the fighters. Dunstan, too, backed off. Baldric and Cadfer remained intent on each other.

Mic's third blow landed squarely on them. They paused a moment, then resumed the fight. Mic laid the whip on twice more. The men fell apart at last, panting and bleeding. Their clothes hung in tatters from the fight and cuts of the whip. Still, Cadfer flashed a mocking smile. Baldric's eyes glittered with hatred.

Dirk hauled a bucket of seawater up over the side and doused Baldric with it. He flinched as saltwater soaked his wounds, but he didn't take his eyes off Cadfer, who now was standing among his friends in the bow.

"My cabin!" Dirk said. When Baldric hesitated, Dirk shoved him that way. "*Now*!"

Baldric squared his shoulders and walked down into Dirk's cabin. Their sport finished for the time being, the crowd dispersed to their games and their quarrels. Mic remained in the waist coiling his whip, then tapping it against his thigh while he glared at the men.

Dirk joined Baldric in the cabin, slamming the door behind him. "What monster from hell has possessed you? You know the law about fighting aboard."

Baldric's jaws clamped shut.

"What if Mic has to flog you for this?"

"It will be worth it."

Dirk closed his eyes to contain his temper and at the same time shut out the sight of Baldric tied shirtless to the mainmast, striped and bleeding.

"What happened?"

When Baldric remained silent, Dirk repeated the question in a roar that demanded an answer.

"It doesn't matter now."

"It *does* matter! You don't fight over nothing!"

Baldric hesitated, then words came tumbling out.

"For days now that bilge rat has been fondling Gibbie, so today I stopped him."

Dirk sighed. "There are always men like that aboard. You simply leave them alone."

"I can tolerate it between men, but Cadfer likes boys. Gibbie doesn't want Cadfer's petting. That whoreson threatened to have his friends hold the boy down."

"He wasn't serious."

"This has been going on since we set sail, and it is serious."

"I didn't know."

"Of course you didn't know, any more than you saw what a danger Melchior is to Natalia."

Dirk took a deep breath. How much had he missed by spending so much time with Natalia? How many other problems were smoldering on the ship, ready to burst into flames at the slightest provocation?

"If it was so obvious, why didn't anyone tell me earlier?" He took another deep breath. "And why was it only you that took up for the boy?"

Baldric gazed steadily at Dirk, then finally said, "When we were sold... separated...my master..."

Mic stomped in, slamming the door and throwing the whip onto his bunk.

"God Almighty! We run out of food and rum and there's trouble! We have a lone woman aboard and there's trouble! So we get more food and more liquor and more women, and there's more trouble!" He glared at Baldric.

Baldric shrugged. "Next time I'll kill him. Then he won't give you any more trouble."

"And then we'll have to hang you!" Mic turned to Dirk.

"Yes, I'll do something. I'll find us a prize."

That afternoon Dirk huddled with Crofton over a makeshift chart, and they chose several possible targets on islands in the Lesser Antilles. Dirk announced their plans to the crew, hoping that news of an impending raid would ease tensions between the two factions. For a day or two, the ship sailed with little trouble, but then, impatient for action, the men began swordplay.

As blades clashed, so did tempers. A slight mishap with a sword, a nicked shoulder, or a jest made with serious eyes were enough to start a fight. All day Mic stalked the deck, a deep frown on his face, and every night he fell into his bunk exhausted.

When they drew close to the first target, they anchored and sent spies ashore. The ship was quiet, the men subdued, while they waited for a report. Dirk watched the jungle for an hour, then left the rail to go below. After their argument over the priests' robes, it had taken him a week to entice Natalia back into his embrace. She'd probably like the upcoming raid even less. This time, though, he would explain everything beforehand.

Ten minutes later Dirk left the cabin feeling satisfied. Natalia had listened quietly, nodded when he finished and gave him no argument.

Soon after, the spies returned bearing good news. With a tired smile, Mic announced that a poorly guarded merchant's schooner lay anchored in the harbor. Apparently this village was an early stop along the schooner's route, for it rode low in the water and its decks were piled high with crates and barrels. Best of all, the village had no soldiers.

The excitement of leading a raid returned to Dirk full force. Once ashore, with the others gathered behind him awaiting his signal to attack, the combined energy of so many men filled him with strength and power. Dirk hefted his cutlass. How good it felt.

He ordered the charge.

Natalia watched preparations for the raid in a silent, black mood. After the men had gone off, she paced the deck until she could no longer bear the sound of musket fire, the distant cries of fear and pain. She retreated to the cabin and sat on a bench, her elbows on the table, her head in her hands.

She had forgotten how Dirk lived. *He is a pirate after all... a leader of pirates. The hands that so often caressed me now grip a sword that will kill my countrymen. Maybe those hands will be bloody when he returns to me.*

Natalia remembered Dirk's hands hard on her when he threatened to beat her for making noise. In Panama, when he'd threatened to kill her, she had not believed him. She had depended upon his greed for her ransom to restrain him. Now she knew the threat had been real. He was fully capable of carrying it out.

She shivered with a bone-deep fear worse than any she'd felt in Panama. At least then anger had tempered the fear. Yet worse than her dread of Dirk's true nature was the dismay over her forgetfulness. She had let time with him blind her to his livelihood. It scared her to think she could care for a man like that, could lie in his arms night after night. *I hope he does not survive this raid.*

Yet if Dirk perished, she would die also. Or at least she would want to, for he was her only protection from a ship full of pirates.

Natalia was a prisoner again, dependent upon a heathen for her safety. So she sat in the dark, and she waited.

The men came aboard laughing and jabbering about the raid. When Natalia heard Dirk's booming voice, she collapsed onto a bunk. Relief washed over her, for her own safety and, possibly, his.

Dirk burst into the cabin, eyes glinting with liquor and excitement. She did not see any wounds. He slapped a glass bottle on the table, then lit the lantern swaying from a beam overhead. He sat on a bench, drank without a cup, and grinned.

"It was a good raid. We took the schooner. It had only five guards. The church didn't yield much, but we found rum." He waggled the bottle at her. "And some coins in a shop."

Now that they both were safe, Natalia's anger flashed. She stalked over to the table. "How many people did you kill?"

"Not one. We offered quarter and they took it."

"Quarter? You offer quarter and that makes the raid good?" Natalia leaned over the table. "Your offer of quarter was nothing. With it you demand that those people allow you to enter their homes and steal everything they have."

Dirk frowned. "But with quarter, nobody died. It was quick. We didn't burn the town or the church."

"But you *raided* the church."

His face darkened. "I told you this raid was necessary. Why are you so angry?"

"Because you are a sea robber."

"Of course I'm a sea robber."

"You do not fight for survival, for your faith, or even in duty to your country." Natalia slapped the table with her palm. "You fight for pleasure, out of greed! There is nothing honorable in what you do! It is thievery! Simple thievery!"

He banged the bottle on the table. "It is not so simple!" He stood, towering over her, his face dark and angry. "This was for you as well as the treasure." He leaned close. "The men won't keep me as captain if I don't find prizes, and if I'm not captain I can't protect you."

"I understand that."

"Then why are you ranting this way?"

"Because you are a pirate!" Anger checked her growing confusion.

Dirk crashed both fists onto the table. She jumped, grateful for the table between them.

"I am a *pirate*!" he roared. "You have *always* known that! Why does it bother you so much after all this time?"

Natalia stared at him, unable to answer, knowing only that she was terrified of this man, of something in him that she couldn't name or define.

Dirk straightened. "The men will be drunk. Don't leave the cabin." He stomped out, slamming the door behind him.

Natalia made her way to the bunk. She curled into a ball, quivering with anger and fear.

In the morning, the crew held the share-out on an isolated beach. Melchior's men, still nominally under the leadership of Baldessaire, wanted the schooner. It was best for piracy. That pleased Dirk, as he wanted the cromster for trade. It would hold more cargo.

Trouble came with division of the prize. Melchior declared that each crew should have half, plus a forty-share for the owners. His men, outnumbered by those remaining with Dirk, would then receive larger individual shares. It would have been an unusual split, though not unheard of. Mic argued against it, and in the end a vote was taken. Dirk's crew, bigger by five, voted for equal shares to each man.

Melchior's men boarded the schooner, grumbling and glaring. Melchior, however, wore a little smirk. When they raised sail and disappeared, Dirk breathed easily again.

A week later, amidst the Leeward Islands, the *Vengeance* entered a hidden cove on an unnamed islet for careening. Mic, anxious for news of Clarisse and the child she was carrying, protested any delay in the voyage. Crofton, however, insisted that barnacles encrusting the hull were creating too much drag and made the ship unwieldy. A mild squall could sink her.

They anchored as close to shore as the keel allowed and carried the cargo ashore, piling powder and balls on the beach. Men rolled starboard guns to the larboard side and lashed them to the rail. The ship listed toward shore. They tied thick ropes to the masts, ran the ropes around palm trees that lined the narrow beach, and slowly pulled the ship onto her side.

Dirk stood with a dozen others on the sloping deck as the ropes strained and the masts creaked in their steps. When the deck was almost vertical, they climbed over the rail and onto the hull. Dirk crawled down to the water line, braced himself against slimy wood, and attacked the hard barnacles with a dull-bladed hand axe. The others spread out around him, each chopping at the seaweed-draped shells. They all knew what to do. Ships sailing warm waters had to be careened and scraped at least twice a year.

As he worked, Dirk watched for the tell-tale holes of the toredo worm. They bored into wooden hulls, creating passages, often riddling a vessel before anyone knew of their existence. Such riddled ships were so structurally weakened that a hard bump against a rock or a single blow from a cannon might collapse the entire vessel.

Men cursed as their hands slipped and grazed sharp barnacles. Within an hour Dirk's hands and forearms were covered with cuts. Sweat ran into his eyes and his shirt clung to his back. In another hour his knees were stiff and bruised, and his back ached.

Still, he pounded and pried at the shells as quickly as possible, for the *Vengeance* on her side was extremely vulnerable. A cannon ball striking below the water line might sink her. If a shot landed in the keel, they'd have to scuttle her. The crew was in danger, too, for mobility was their best defense. If the island proved to be inhabited by unfriendly Indians, or worse, Spaniards, the pirates' escape would be delayed, perhaps fatally.

The day before, Mic had rowed ashore with men to hunt for food and signs of other people. He'd also ordered the most agile men up the palm trees to keep watch out over the water. Although the cove wasn't visible from the sea, Crofton had known about it and others might, too.

So Dirk fretted as he worked until, after three hours, Gibbie came to take his place on the ship's hull. The youth took a deep breath, set his jaw, and attacked the barnacles. Dirk climbed down the castle and dropped into the water. He gasped at the chill and salt sting in his cuts, but stayed long enough for a short swim. Then he waded ashore. There were other tasks to complete before nightfall.

Huts must be built, for the careening might take weeks. Trees that would yield a good quality tar must be found, felled and distilled. Then the tar itself must be distilled even further into pitch for coating the hull. They also needed to find a source of fresh water and food.

Dirk trudged across the beach, wringing water out of his tunic. There was so much to do, and every day they remained on the island they were in danger.

On the third day of placid watching, Natalia announced she was going for a walk.

"Don't go far," Dirk said, although he now knew the island to be uninhabited and relatively safe.

She nodded, pulled a saber from a nearby pile of weapons and walked off down an animal path through the woods.

Dirk watched her go. Since the raid Natalia had shared his bunk, there being no other place for her to sleep. But she had lain stiffly with her back to him. He'd grown accustomed to her silence. It saddened him, though, that soon they'd be in Port Royal where he'd put her aboard a ship bound for Spain, most likely without settling this coldness between them.

At mid-day Dirk finished his turn at hull scraping and went in search of Natalia. When the path she'd taken crossed a creek, he turned up it. Although the water was barely ankle-deep and covered only half the bed, he might find a pool deep enough to bathe in. Keeping to dry rocks at the edge, he followed the creek as it curved away from the ship, toward hills at the center of the island.

He heard the splash of a waterfall and hurried around a bend, eager to scrub himself clean in sweet water. He found water spilling over a ledge three feet above him, but with a flow so slight it could only make him wet, not clean. He returned to the animal trail.

A short distance farther down the path he came to a sheltered cove. Massive driftwood littered the black sand beach. Natalia stood in the surf, holding her skirts knee-high while waves foamed about her ankles. She gazed at him a moment, then walked farther down the beach.

Dirk pulled off his boots, threw his tunic across a piece of driftwood and waded into the water a few yards before diving under a wave. He swam along the shore, and between the waves caught glimpses of Natalia still walking. His pace through the water quickened. She'd been a troublesome burden from the start. Because of her he'd lost his share of the Panama prize. Meager as it was, he'd certainly earned it.

His arms crashed into the water. Since then he'd endured countless arguments with Mic and many days of keeping peace among his men. Now she wouldn't let him touch her because he tried to regain a little of what he'd lost. *Well, in a few weeks I'll be rid of that Spaniard.*

His strokes slowed. He'd made those sacrifices willingly, and protecting Natalia had not felt like a hardship. He had been happy with her company, more content and more alive than he'd felt in a long time.

When he exited the water, Natalia was sitting just beyond the surf, braiding her hair. He spread his tunic on the sand and sat down close enough to touch her. Yet she seemed so far away, almost as if in her mind she had already returned to Spain. He would miss her. In truth already did miss her laugh that made him smile, their arguments, her courage and curiosity. And the way she fit in his arms, her soft burnished hair nestled under his chin.

Finally he said, "You're still angry?"

"Not anymore. Disappointed a little, that you are not as I wanted to see you." She gave him a wry smile. "But I forgive you for that."

"Good."

He watched the waves curl and foam, then looked at the empty blue sky. He dug his toes into dark, moist sand and glanced around at the tall palms towering over thick green brush. It was a beautiful place, so quiet and private. If only they could stay here and ignore the outside world.

Again he broke the silence. "You're afraid?"

"Yes."

"Of me?"

"I do not know. It is... something that feels like a part of myself."

A tear glistened on her cheek. He reached out to brush it off, but Natalia quickly wiped it away.

"I was not supposed to care," she said. "And that is what I forgot. I was not to care about you or what you do. I wanted this voyage to be beautiful and endless, and it is neither. I never imagined the loss of that *chimera* would hurt so much."

Small waves shushed onto the beach and slid away. Another tear spilled from her eye. Dirk cupped her cheek with his hand and thumbed away the tear. Closing her eyes, Natalia leaned into his hand. He caught the ends of the unfinished braid, now hanging down her back, and combed it out with his fingers. He tasted salt and sunshine on her lips, untied her clothes and slipped them off, his mouth following his hands. She did the same to him and they lay naked on a tangle of clothes.

They came together, then parted for a moment, and a sweet-scented inland breeze dried the moisture that had built up on his skin. They moved into the familiar dance, but this time there was no laughter, no play, nothing new that might not please.

The morning sun was hot on his face, then on his back. He moved slowly within her, biding his time between thrusts. With a hand on either side of her face, his thumbs traced her eyebrows, cheekbones, jaw line. She was silent, and he whispered no endearments, no promises, for they had no future together.

The relentless tide undulated closer with every broken wave foaming over the sand. Water licked at Dirk's feet, and his body moved faster, responding to life as old and deep as the sea. He moaned aloud as wave after wave of pulsing blood dragged him from her and back into his own body.

Afterwards, they bathed in the sea and settled on their clothes to dry in the sun. Almost asleep, Dirk heard a soft clash. He sat up, listening intently.

"What is it?" Natalia asked.

"Something at the ship."

"I heard nothing."

"Quiet. Let me listen."

Natalia yawned and stretched, then sat up as he strained to hear something more. *A musket... faint, but a musket.* He scrambled to his feet.

"Stay here, out of sight." He pulled on breeches and tunic.

"What is it?" Natalia rose to her knees.

"I don't know, only that there's trouble." Dragging his cutlass by the leather wrist strap, he tugged on his boots as he crossed the sand.

By the time Natalia finished dressing, Dirk had disappeared. With a frown, she followed.

Dirk raced down the path to the careening cove. Angry shouts grew louder. A cannon boomed. He broke out of the forest and into a mass of pirates running to and fro, shouting and waving their swords in the air. Two muskets fired, followed by screams. The women tripped pirates in their haste to escape a still-unseen danger. Mic and Dunstan were chopping at the lines holding *Vengeance* onto her side. A cannon fired and the ball splashed near the cromster's hull. On the sea a low ship with a Spanish flag sailed straight for the cove, a single forward gun still smoking.

"Spaniards!" Cursing, Dirk ran to help Mic and Dunstan. Standing between two lines, Dirk sawed his cutlass through one, then the other. He ran for the last rope as *Vengeance* groaned and righted herself. With lines, men on shore brought her around so that her bow was facing the enemy, leaving the Spaniards the smallest possible target.

Dirk called to Baldric. "Take men into the trees! Make sure they all have at least a musket and a pistol! And plenty of balls and powder!"

Baldric nodded and grabbed the four closest men. Dirk hailed the twins and pointed to the pile of ammunition on the beach

"Get that into the woods!"

They scooped up bags of powder and balls, and scurried off the beach. A woman ran by, hollering. Dirk caught her by the arm, shook her, then pushed her toward the woods.

The approaching ship fired two more guns. They had been loaded with weighted chains that scissored through the *Vengeance*'s rigging and sliced James the surgeon to pieces. Although this time the pirates fired back, they could not hold off the other vessel. At the last possible moment before ramming, the Spanish schooner came about and crashed sideways against the *Vengeance*. Grappling hooks flew onto the cromster, tying the ships together. Men swarmed over the boarding nets.

Dirk stared. *These men are pirates. But pirates never attack each other! If they came to steal, how could they know the* Vengeance *is carrying any cargo?*

As more of the schooner's crew tumbled into shallow water to wade ashore, Dirk growled and hefted his cutlass. Right behind that little worm Silvanus came Melchior, brandishing a saber in his left hand. Dirk's men also recognized the attackers and their angry roar filled the cove.

Dirk raised his cutlass and, shouting a battle cry that his men took up, he plunged into the fiercest battle of his life. Neither side fought to subdue the other with treasure as the prize. Instead, they fought to kill, with each musket shot aimed at the heart, each crippling sword blow prelude to a fatal one. Through it all, Dirk's anger grew because he was forced to be in such a fight against men he'd sailed with just a week ago.

Beside him, Thacher went down, a last cry gurgling out of his torn throat, blood flowing over a blue velvet waistcoat he'd captured in Panama. Dirk turned on his killer. He'd beaten this man Baldessaire before. Dirk's cutlass strokes grew bolder, till Baldessaire gave him a glancing blow to the head, slicing his ear. Dirk shook his head to clear his vision. Blood trickled down his neck, reminding him to concentrate on the fight, not his memories.

A musket fired nearby, and Baldessaire stumbled as a ball pierced his thigh. With both hands on the hilt of his cutlass, Dirk slashed the blade into the man's neck.

Baldessaire fell without a cry.

From the woods, Baldric waved to Dirk, poured powder into the pan of his musket, then powder and ball down the barrel. A thump of the butt on the ground tamped the musket as Baldric faded back among the trees.

Natalia hid in dense brush, horrified by the raging battle. The noise of swords and smoking muskets over screams of pain and shouts of anger and triumph was so great she covered her ears. And there was Melchior, looking her way. Surely it was impossible for him to see her, but he came closer and closer, in a direct path, pausing only to slash men out of his way. *Dios mío, has he come for me?* Her breath caught in her throat. If he came any closer he would find her.

She edged onto the animal trail, then fled toward the cove and the saber she'd forgotten to bring.

Blades clanged right behind Dirk. He whirled, cutlass ready, but Dunstan had the fight well in hand. Catching a glimpse of Melchior near the row of palms, Dirk stepped that way. Then two pirates attacked. After a few minutes of fierce struggle, Mic came to his aid.

"Thanks."

Mic grunted in reply. For a while the four men swayed in fierce handystrokes. Silvanus, with a shortsword in his hand, crept up behind Mic. Before Dirk could shout a warning, Silvanus arched the sword across the back of Mic's right thigh. Mic crumpled, and Silvanus scrambled away.

"Mic!" Dirk leapt to protect him from the other two pirates.

With a foot on either side of Mic, Dirk fought on. The other men's blades flashed more quickly and closer. Then a shot rang out and one of them fell, bumping Mic. Dirk winced at Mic's cry, but it was proof he was still alive. Dirk finished off the other pirate, then knelt to check Mic's wound.

Baldric shouted.

Dirk looked up.

Baldric was charging across the beach, musket primed and aimed toward Dirk.

"Behind you!" Baldric screamed in Dutch.

Dirk spun around.

Cadfer, just twenty feet away, was aiming a pistol at him.

Baldric fired, missing Cadfer while running so fast. Baldric, still running, poured powder and shot into his musket barrel.

Cadfer swung toward Baldric and leveled his pistol.

"Stay back!" Dirk shouted at Baldric while trying to reach Cadfer before he fired.

Cadfer switched targets again as Dirk raised his cutlass.

Then Baldric fired, catching Cadfer's shoulder with the shot.

Cadfer turned and fired his pistol. The ball tore a hole in Baldric's gut. He twisted and fell onto his side, blood gushing out onto the sand.

Dirk crossed the few feet to Cadfer in great leaps. His cutlass sliced through the man's shoulder. With a scream, Cadfer fell to his knees.

"You killed them! You killed them both!" *To live without Mic and Baldric?* Dirk swung his cutlass down with both hands. "You miserable creature!" The cutlass slashed down again, then again, and again until the body at Dirk's feet no longer resembled anything human, until hatred and rage had become a fever that burned through his body.

He turned, faced up the beach and raised his cutlass again.

"Melchior!" he shouted, "I come for you!"

The cutlass was light in his hands. Theo the freebooter called from Dirk's memory.

"Easy now. Let the blade do the work."

He was enthralled as the blade whirled through the air, polished steel glistening with blood in the bright sun. The redness filled his vision. He plunged once more into the fight.

The sounds of battle dimmed as the roar of fury grew in his ears. And over the roar came a sweet and pungent tune. The cutlass sang to him as it sliced through soft bellies, chimed against other blades, glided across throats. The song filled him with glorious strength, and he danced from fight to fight, killing swiftly and with a ferocity that forced his own men to step aside. He saw so clearly the faces of his enemies, and would not stop until each of them lay dead in the sand.

When no more enemies stood fighting, Dirk sought those who lay writhing in pain from their wounds. And those who stared listlessly up at him as his cutlass slashed downward. He paused only to watch the hatred or fear or resignation in their eyes dissolve into blackness.

At last there remained no enemies to kill, but fury still coursed through Dirk's body and he looked about, seeking another foe. He flexed the blade in the air and its very lightness called for more blood. Across the battlefield, a pirate in a dirty tunic moved. With an exultant cry, Dirk bounded toward him, leaping over bodies to get at that last, still-living enemy.

The pirate rolled over. Dirk, thirty feet away, raised his cutlass in both hands for the killing blow. The man saw him coming. Fear wiped out the pain in his pale blue eyes. A moment later, the fear disappeared, replaced by relief. Mic smiled weakly and shut his eyes.

Ten feet away, Dirk skidded to a stop. For an instant he froze. Then his arm went slack and the sudden weight of his blade dragged him to his knees. His heart began to beat once more and his scalp prickled with returning blood. From the pit of his belly, horror spread throughout his body, tightening his chest so that it took all his strength to breathe.

"Oh, Mic... If you hadn't turned over, if you hadn't smiled... Oh, God in heaven, I would have killed you. My matelot, my brother, forgive me. How I could I have come so close?"

Dirk turned to look at the scene behind him and had to close his eyes on the broken men, the pools of blood, and the sight of his crew mates crouched still as statues in fear of him.

I did this. Like the Spaniards... like Morgan and Melchior... like L'Ollonais....

Although he closed his eyes, Dirk could not shut out the sight of his carnage, nor the memory of other times his mind had retreated before his fury. He saw again his hands around Gilbert's neck. And a girl, her mouth open in a soundless scream while the destruction of her village flamed against her face.

Like L'Ollonais, the worst of them.

"Yes," Dirk said. "Like the worst of them. I am the worst of them."

As faith in his own goodness died, an icy blackness filled Dirk's head. He took a great, rasping breath and roared as the ice swept down to sear his heart.

His cry faded away on the light tropical breeze. The weak moans of his wounded men, the broken cries of the dying, came to him. The air stank of blood and urine and voided bowels. Black flies swarmed over wounds, settling on any man not strong enough to fight them off.

Dirk stood. His body ached everywhere and his skin burned in a hundred places where blades had slashed it open. He was tired, so tired, and his cutlass was too heavy to lift. He stepped off toward Mic, then saw that Jan was tending Mic's leg. Dirk went in search of Baldric.

He found the little man curled around his beloved musket. Dirk cut off a section of his own tunic, knelt, and flapped the cotton at flies buzzing over Baldric's face.

"What a hard life you had, my friend." He thought of that long ago dawn when he dragged a nine year old Baldric through a burning cornfield. He thought of Baldric's stricken face and blank eyes the day they were sold. Even now the memory tightened Dirk's throat.

He gazed down at his friend, now at peace and younger looking than he had appeared since their slavery. What happened during those seven years of bondage that changed timid little Baldric into a hard, old-looking man afraid of nothing by the time he was sixteen?

What had driven him to fight Cadfer over the assault on Gibbie? To fight even though, had Cadfer died, Baldric would have been hanged. And had Baldric loved Frieda? Dirk had seen him with her often but had never questioned the relationship. Had Baldric wanted to stay in Port Royal with her instead of coming along to Panama? Would he have left piracy after this voyage as Mic planned to do?

No, Baldric always would have followed Dirk anywhere, with the same devotion he'd shown as a child, trusting Dirk to lead and protect him. It was a trust Dirk had ultimately betrayed, leading Baldric to this fight, this horrible end.

All around, men continued to bleed. Others lay grotesquely in death, their bodies hacked apart by his own cutlass. The twins stumbled by, carrying Mic toward a hut.

Mic, oh Mic... From their earliest meeting as boys when they'd fought to a draw, Mic had been so much a part of his life. That wholehearted friendship had led Mic to a crippling injury that might yet kill him. Dirk moaned, for life without Mic was unimaginable.

Guilt stabbed him deeply for having brought his friends to this. Two decades earlier, when he first led his little gang out into the night for pranks, Dirk had never imagined this end. *What has become of us all, we sons of peaceful farmers?*

He had changed so gradually over the years that he'd been unaware of it. During all that time his life hadn't seemed so different, for he still led others off into the night for adventures. Yet now, with the fragments of his life lying about him in the bodies of shipmates turned enemy, Dirk hardly recognized himself.

He thought of that day, fifteen years ago, when he and Mic had discovered a sacred cave on Hispaniola. He decided then he'd fallen from God's grace and his soul was lost, and thus gave himself permission to follow the course of piracy. How naive he'd been, for now he truly was damned. Not by fate or the whims of a capricious god, but by his blindness to the total and final consequences of his own actions.

"No more of this," he promised Mic and Baldric and himself. "No more sea roving."

Turning to Baldric, Dirk closed the dark, fatigue-encircled eyes and covered the face with the piece of tunic.

"My friend, always at my back, dying to protect me. Did you know that a part of me would die with you?"

Dirk's youth, with its hope and moral certainty, receded from his conscious memory. It drifted slowly, painfully away, out of his reach, leaving an aching void. He tried to imagine his future, but could not. He tried to envision Katrina. Sweet, blond and oh-so-pretty Katrina. Her image was elusive, dancing close then darting away, taking along the life he had dreamed of making with her, a life so much like the one her mother and his own had made, a life he desperately wanted, but could not live. He'd lost his past, and with it, his future with her.

Dirk tired of looking inside himself, for he saw nothing there. Near the huts, he found a shovel with a half-broken handle. He trudged to the edge of the beach, where the earth was firm, and began to dig a grave.

From somewhere, Dirk heard the clash of steel, an echo of the battle. He heard it again and looked around. No one else appeared aware of it. Shaking his head to clear the echo, Dirk resumed shoveling. But the sound came again from the direction of the cove where he and—

"Natalia!"

He dropped the shovel and ran across the battlefield, slowing only to snatch his cutlass from the sand. He plunged into the woods, raced along the path toward the cove. The clash of steel grew louder.

He groaned. *Who got past me? How did he find her? And who defends her now?*

Dirk broke out of the forest at a dead run, but stopped short at the edge of the black sand. Beyond the jumble of driftwood was Melchior, red and wheezing from exertion, fighting Natalia. Face hard with concentration, she was holding her own in the deadly battle.

Then she tripped on her skirts. A shout caught in his throat, Dirk rushed toward them, leaping over driftwood, his boots slipping on the sand, certain he would be too late. Melchior jumped at Natalia, saber raised for the fatal cut. He laughed, and Dirk's heart twisted. But Melchior's jubilation died quickly as Natalia stumbled sideways and thrust her saber up through his belly. The tip flashed briefly in sunlight as it broke out through the back of his shirt.

Twenty-five feet away, Dirk stopped his charge and forced himself to breathe again. Natalia gave a short cry of victory and with a foot pushed Melchior off her saber. The man gaped at her, his mouth working as he made feeble thrusts that she easily parried. She slammed the sword into him, over and over. He yelped at each slice until he fell sideways and lay still in the sand. She continued to hack crimson stripes on his body.

"No!" Dirk filled with dread for her. He sprang forward. "Stop!"

Natalia swung toward him, still hacking the saber on empty air. Dirk jumped out of the blade's reach. At his retreat, she shouted in triumph, threw back her head and raised the reddened blade high into the sunlight. Her face shone with exhilaration and blood lust. Her eyes glittered and her lips parted in a slight smile.

It was the most beautiful face Dirk had ever seen. And the ugliest.

Natalia took a great breath, shuddered, and lowered the saber. Her shoulders drooped. The blade fell from limp fingers to embed itself in the sand. She turned away from Dirk. The sight of Melchior's body struck her and she crumpled to the sand beside it. She touched it, then pushed at it, and drew away hands covered with blood.

Dirk backed into a driftwood log and dropped onto it. In Natalia he'd believed that he had captured an exotic prize, to enjoy and someday release when his pleasure ended. But he'd caught instead a looking-glass, a mirror with an image he could never escape.

Natalia rose, wiping her hands at her skirt. She looked around the cove, then at Dirk. Bewilderment and fear swept across her face as she walked stiffly to stand before him. Perhaps she came to him for comfort, but he had none to give her.

"You must go home," he said. "I will find you passage home."

Her voice sounded dull. "Home?"

"To your family... to Spain."

"Spain?" She blinked. "What is there for me in Spain but empty years of remembering?"

"You cannot stay here." He meant in the Caribbean, but gestured toward the sea and Melchior's corpse.

Natalia's gaze followed the sweep of his arm. Long moments later when she looked again at Dirk, her eyes were brimming with tears. She lifted her hands to him. "But I love you."

Dirk flinched before the words reached him. Her bloody hands were condemnation of his mindless carnage, his betrayal of her. He had promised to keep her safe. If he had not brought her along on this voyage, if he'd not kept her prisoner in Panama. If only he had protected her from Melchior.

"There is no place for me." Natalia sobbed, and stumbled away from him, across the beach. She vanished between the palm trees.

Dirk looked at his own blood-spattered hands.

"I have no home either," he said to the empty cove.

He longed to disappear also, to lose himself deep in the forested hills. Natalia would soon be lost there among the greenery and the scent of flowers and a silence broken only by birdsong.

A high, cut-off scream came from the forest. *She'll be lost among deadly snakes, alligators, and plants that cut and poisoned!*

"No!" He ran after her. "Wait! Come back!"

He crashed into the forest, chasing her along the jagged path she'd broken through the underbrush, down a steep slope where she might have fallen and did leave behind part of her skirt. Exhaustion and fear made it hard for him to breathe, but he pushed on.

Near a bend in the creek he finally caught her. Leaves and twigs had snagged in her hair, and blood was dripping from a gash on her jaw. She fought to escape him.

"Release me!"

"You'll die in the forest alone."

"I *want* to die!"

"No!" Dirk held her more tightly against him.

"It is me!" Natalia beat on his chest and arms. "What I feared and hated so much in you is in *me*! I beg of you, let me go!"

Dirk used the last of his strength to keep her in his arms.

"No," he said in a low voice. "That evil is in me, not you. The guilt is mine, not yours. My greed and lust and my cutlass are to blame. The responsibility for what we did is all mine."

As he continued to speak, Natalia collapsed against him and shook with great sobs.

Dirk could well imagine the deadened emptiness she felt. Even so, she was warm, living flesh in his arms, a body and soul more precious than his own. For this woman had touched him in a raw and fiery and tender place, a place deeper than memories, a place not even Mic could reach.

When her sobs quieted, he said, "You saw it in me and forgave me. You must forgive it in yourself."

"I cannot," she mumbled into his chest. "I am so tired."

"Then I shall do it for you."

Dirk picked her up and struggled through dense foliage with his burden that was at once both heavy and light. At the creek, he waded up the shallow bed to the low out-cropping and set her down.

They stood together under the waterfall, Natalia's forehead against his heart, his chin on her wet hair, his arms draped about her shoulders. The paltry flow of water was enough to begin loosening the caked sand and dried blood on them both.

"We'll find a place away from the Caribbean," he said. "A land that is neither Spanish nor Dutch."

"Where?"

"I don't know, but we'll find it and build our lives there."

"You would do that for me?"

"Yes. Oh, yes!"

Dirk spoke with a strong lilt in his voice, for he felt himself coming alive again, and knew in his bones he was already home.

Acknowledgments

Many thanks to

my parents, Inga and Harold Strait, for teaching me that creativity has value;

my sister, Kathy Bergman, for her early enthusiasm for the story;

my brother, Dave Strait, for giving me my first thesaurus;

Willard Simms, for teaching me so much about story structure;

David Poyer, for his strong encouragement;

Truus and Hermann Hassig, for the Dutch;

and members of all my writing critique groups, for your invaluable contributions to my skills.

About the Author

Debrah Strait began her storytelling career during a rural Ohio childhood, making up tales to put herself to sleep at night, to keep herself awake at school, and to make cleaning horse stalls go faster. After graduating from college with a teaching certificate she went to work in a bank, then spent several years writing real estate advertising copy. Later, she drove off to Hollywood where she won cash and prizes on the game show *Tic Tac Dough* and collected many fine anecdotes to repeat at cocktail parties. She also learned another form of storytelling by typing movie and television scripts for five years.

From Los Angeles, Debrah moved to Jacksonville, Florida, where she tried to sell cemetery plots, but didn't, despite the huge pool of potential customers. She did, however, finish her first novel, *The Sweet Trade*, as well as publish interviews and real estate articles in local papers. Then a vehicle ran her down in a crosswalk. Figuring it would be safer to recover from the injuries in a small, quiet town, she moved to Bisbee, Arizona, where killer bees attacked her. Still, she managed to finish a middle-grade novel, *The Dragon's Gold.* She continues to write short stories, flash fiction, and haiku. Debrah is also working on a sequel to *The Sweet Trade*. Visit her website at DebrahStrait.com.

Printed in Great Britain
by Amazon